Contending Forces

THE SCHOMBURG LIBRARY OF
NINETEENTH-CENTURY BLACK WOMEN WRITERS

General Editor, Henry Louis Gates, Jr.

Titles are listed chronologically; collections that include works published over a span of years are listed according to the publication date of their initial work.

Contending Forces

A Romance Illustrative
of Negro Life North and South

PAULINE E. HOPKINS

With an Introduction by
RICHARD YARBOROUGH

OXFORD UNIVERSITY PRESS
New York   Oxford

Oxford University Press

Oxford   New York   Toronto
Delhi   Bombay   Calcutta   Madras   Karachi
Petaling Jaya   Singapore   Hong Kong   Tokyo
Nairobi   Dar es Salaam   Cape Town
Melbourne   Auckland

and associated companies in
Berlin   Ibadan

Library of Congress Cataloging-in-Publication Data

Hopkins, Pauline E. (Pauline Elizabeth)
Contending forces.
(The Schomburg library of nineteenth-century black
women writers)
I. Title. II. Series.
PS1999.H4226C66   1988   813'.4   87-24744
ISBN 0-19-505258-7
ISBN 0-19-505267-6 (set)
ISBN 0-19-506785-1 (PBK.)

10 9 8 7 6 5

Printed in the United States of America
on acid-free paper

The
Schomburg Library
of
Nineteenth-Century
Black Women Writers
is
Dedicated
in Memory
of
PAULINE AUGUSTA COLEMAN GATES

1916–1987

PUBLISHER'S NOTE

FOREWORD
In Her Own Write

Henry Louis Gates, Jr.

One muffled strain in the Silent South, a jarring chord and a vague and uncomprehended cadenza has been and still is the Negro. And of that muffled chord, the one mute and voiceless note has been the sadly expectant Black Woman, ...

The "other side" has not been represented by one who "lives there." And not many can more sensibly realize and more accurately tell the weight and the fret of the "long dull pain" than the open-eyed but hitherto voiceless Black Woman of America.

. . . as our Caucasian barristers are not to blame if they cannot *quite* put themselves in the dark man's place, neither should the dark man be wholly expected fully and adequately to reproduce the exact Voice of the Black Woman.

—ANNA JULIA COOPER, *A Voice From the South* (1892)

The birth of the Afro-American literary tradition occurred in 1773, when Phillis Wheatley published a book of poetry. Despite the fact that her book garnered for her a remarkable amount of attention, Wheatley's journey to the printer had been a most arduous one. Sometime in 1772, a young African girl walked demurely into a room in Boston to undergo an oral examination, the results of which would determine the direction of her life and work. Perhaps she was shocked upon entering the appointed room. For there, perhaps gathered in a semicircle, sat eighteen of Boston's most notable citizens. Among them were John Erving, a prominent Boston merchant; the Reverend Charles Chauncy, pastor of the Tenth Congregational Church; and John Hancock, who would later gain fame for his signature on the Declaration of Independence. At the center of this group was His Excellency, Thomas Hutchinson, governor of Massachusetts, with Andrew Oliver, his lieutenant governor, close by his side.

Why had this august group been assembled? Why had it seen fit to summon this young African girl, scarcely eighteen years old, before it? This group of "the most respectable Characters in *Boston,*" as it would later define itself, had assembled to question closely the African adolescent on the slender sheaf of poems that she claimed to have "written by herself." We can only speculate on the nature of the questions posed to the fledgling poet. Perhaps they asked her to identify and explain—for all to hear—exactly who were the Greek and Latin gods and poets alluded to so frequently in her work. Perhaps they asked her to conjugate a verb in Latin or even to translate randomly selected passages from the Latin, which she and her master, John Wheatley, claimed that she "had made some Progress in." Or perhaps they asked her to recite from memory key passages from the texts of John Milton and Alexander Pope, the two poets by whom the African claimed to be most directly influenced. We do not know.

We do know, however, that the African poet's responses were more than sufficient to prompt the eighteen august gentlemen to compose, sign, and publish a two-paragraph "Attestation," an open letter "To the Publick" that prefaces Phillis Wheatley's book and that reads in part:

We whose Names are under-written, do assure the World, that the Poems specified in the following Page, were (as we

verily believe) written by Phillis, a young Negro Girl, who
was but a few Years since, brought an uncultivated Barbarian
from *Africa*, and has ever since been, and now is, under the
Disadvantage of serving as a Slave in a Family in this Town.
She has been examined by some of the best Judges, and is
thought qualified to write them.

So important was this document in securing a publisher for
Wheatley's poems that it forms the signal element in the
prefatory matter preceding her *Poems on Various Subjects, Religious and Moral*, published in London in 1773.

Without the published "Attestation," Wheatley's publisher
claimed, few would believe that an African could possibly
have written poetry all by herself. As the eighteen put the
matter clearly in their letter, "Numbers would be ready to
suspect they were not really the Writings of Phillis." Wheatley and her master, John Wheatley, had attempted to publish
a similar volume in 1772 in Boston, but Boston publishers
had been incredulous. One year later, "Attestation" in hand,
Phillis Wheatley and her master's son, Nathaniel Wheatley,
sailed for England, where they completed arrangements for
the publication of a volume of her poems with the aid of the
Countess of Huntington and the Earl of Dartmouth.

This curious anecdote, surely one of the oddest oral ex-
aminations on record, is only a tiny part of a larger, and
even more curious, episode in the Enlightenment. Since the
beginning of the sixteenth century, Europeans had wondered aloud whether or not the African "species of men," as
they were most commonly called, *could* ever create formal
literature, could ever master "the arts and sciences." If they
could, the argument ran, then the African variety of humanity was fundamentally related to the European variety. If not,
then it seemed clear that the African was destined by nature

to be a slave. This was the burden shouldered by Phillis Wheatley when she successfully defended herself and the authorship of her book against counterclaims and doubts.

Indeed, with her successful defense, Wheatley launched two traditions at once—the black American literary tradition *and* the black woman's literary tradition. If it is extraordinary that not just one but both of these traditions were founded simultaneously by a black woman—certainly an event unique in the history of literature—it is also ironic that this important fact of common, coterminous literary origins seems to have escaped most scholars.

That the progenitor of the black literary tradition was a woman means, in the most strictly literal sense, that all subsequent black writers have evolved in a matrilinear line of descent, and that each, consciously or unconsciously, has extended and revised a canon whose foundation was the poetry of a black woman. Early black writers seem to have been keenly aware of Wheatley's founding role, even if most of her white reviewers were more concerned with the implications of her race than her gender. Jupiter Hammon, for example, whose 1760 broadside "An Evening Thought. Salvation by Christ, With Penitential Cries" was the first individual poem published by a black American, acknowledged Wheatley's influence by selecting her as the subject of his second broadside, "An Address to Miss Phillis Wheatly [*sic*], Ethiopian Poetess, in Boston," which was published at Hartford in 1778. And George Moses Horton, the second Afro-American to publish a book of poetry in English (1829), brought out in 1838 an edition of his *Poems By A Slave* bound together with Wheatley's work. Indeed, for fifty-six years, between 1773 and 1829, when Horton published *The Hope of Liberty*, Wheatley was the *only* black person to have published a book of imaginative literature in English. So central was this black woman's role in the shaping of the Afro-American literary tradition that, as one historian has maintained, the history of the reception of Phillis Wheatley's poetry *is* the history of Afro-American literary criticism. Well into the nineteenth century, Wheatley and the black literary tradition were the same entity.

But Wheatley is not the only black woman writer who stands as a pioneering figure in Afro-American literature. Just as Wheatley gave birth to the genre of black poetry, Ann Plato was the first Afro-American to publish a book of essays (1841) and Harriet E. Wilson was the first black person to publish a novel in the United States (1859).

Despite this pioneering role of black women in the tradition, however, many of their contributions before this century have been all but lost or unrecognized. As Hortense Spillers observed as recently as 1983,

> With the exception of a handful of autobiographical narratives from the nineteenth century, the black woman's realities are virtually suppressed until the period of the Harlem Renaissance and later. Essentially the black woman as artist, as intellectual spokesperson for her own cultural apprenticeship, has not existed before, for anyone. At the source of [their] own symbol-making task, [the community of black women writers] confronts, therefore, a tradition of work that is quite recent, its continuities, broken and sporadic.

Until now, it has been extraordinarily difficult to establish the formal connections between early black women's writing and that of the present, precisely because our knowledge of their work has been broken and sporadic. Phillis Wheatley, for example, while certainly the most reprinted and discussed poet in the tradition, is also one of the least understood. Ann Plato's seminal work, *Essays* (which includes biographies and poems), has not been reprinted since it was published a century and a half ago. And Harriet Wilson's *Our Nig,* her compelling novel of a black woman's expanding consciousness in a racist Northern antebellum environment, never received even *one* review or comment at a time when virtually *all* works written by black people were heralded by abolitionists as salient arguments against the existence of human slavery. Many of the books reprinted in this set experienced a similar fate, the most dreadful fate for an author: that of being ignored then relegated to the obscurity of the rare book section of a university library. We can only wonder how many other texts in the black woman's tradition have been lost to this generation of readers or remain unclassified or uncatalogued and, hence, unread.

This was not always so, however. Black women writers dominated the final decade of the nineteenth century, perhaps spurred to publish by an 1886 essay entitled "The Coming American Novelist," which was published in *Lippincott's Monthly Magazine* and written by "A Lady From Philadelphia." This pseudonymous essay argued that the "Great American Novel" would be written by a black person. Her argument is so curious that it deserves to be repeated:

> When we come to formulate our demands of the Coming American Novelist, we will agree that he must be native-born. His ancestors may come from where they will, but we must give him a birthplace and have the raising of him. Still, the longer his family has been here the better he will represent us. Suppose he should have no country but ours, no traditions but those he has learned here, no longings apart from us, no future except in our future—the orphan of the world, he finds with us his home. And with all this, suppose he refuses to be fused into that grand conglomerate we call the "American type." With us, he is not of us. He is original, he has humor, he is tender, he is passive and fiery, he has been

taught what we call justice, and he has his own opinion about it. He has suffered everything a poet, a dramatist, a novelist need suffer before he comes to have his lips anointed. And with it all he is in one sense a spectator, a little out of the race. How would these conditions go towards forming an original development? In a word, suppose the coming novelist is of African origin? When one comes to consider the subject, there is no improbability in it. One thing is certain,—our great novel will not be written by the typical American.

An atypical American, indeed. Not only would the great American novel be written by an African-American, it would be written by an African-American *woman:*

Yet farther: I have used the generic masculine pronoun because it is convenient; but Fate keeps revenge in store. It was a woman who, taking the wrongs of the African as her theme, wrote the novel that awakened the world to their reality, and why should not the coming novelist be a woman as well as an African? She—the woman of that race—has some claims on Fate which are not yet paid up.

It is these claims on fate that we seek to pay by publishing The Schomburg Library of Nineteenth-Century Black Women Writers.

This theme would be repeated by several black women authors, most notably by Anna Julia Cooper, a prototypical black feminist whose 1892 *A Voice From the South* can be considered to be one of the original texts of the black feminist movement. It was Cooper who first analyzed the fallacy of referring to "the Black man" when speaking of black people and who argued that just as white men cannot speak through the consciousness of black men, neither can black *men* "fully and adequately . . . reproduce the exact Voice of the Black Woman." Gender and race, she argues, cannot be conflated, except in the instance of a black woman's voice, and it is this voice which must be uttered and to which we must listen. As Cooper puts the matter so compellingly:

> It is not the intelligent woman vs. the ignorant woman; nor the white woman vs. the black, the brown, and the red,—it is not even the cause of woman vs. man. Nay, 'tis woman's strongest vindication for speaking that *the world needs to hear her voice*. It would be subversive of every human interest that the cry of one-half the human family be stifled. Woman in stepping from the pedestal of statue-like inactivity in the domestic shrine, and daring to think and move and speak,—to undertake to help shape, mold, and direct the thought of her age, is merely completing the circle of the world's vision. Hers is every interest that has lacked an interpreter and a defender. Her cause is linked with that of every agony that has been dumb—every wrong that needs a voice.
>
> It is no fault of man's that he has not been able to see truth from her standpoint. It does credit both to his head and heart that no greater mistakes have been committed or even wrongs perpetrated while she sat making tatting and snipping paper flowers. Man's own innate chivalry and the mutual interdependence of their interests have insured his treating her cause, in the main at least, as his own. And he is pardonably surprised and even a little chagrined, perhaps, to find his legislation not considered "perfectly lovely" in every respect. But in any case his work is only impoverished by her remaining dumb. The world has had to limp along with the wobbling gait and one-sided hesitancy of a man with one eye. Suddenly the bandage is removed from the other eye and the whole body is filled with light. It sees a circle where before it saw a segment. The darkened eye restored, every member rejoices with it.

The myopic sight of the darkened eye can only be restored when the full range of the black woman's voice, with its own special timbres and shadings, remains mute no longer.

Similarly, Victoria Earle Matthews, an author of short stories and essays, and a cofounder in 1896 of the National Association of Colored Women, wrote in her stunning essay, "The Value of Race Literature" (1895), that "when the literature of our race is developed, it will of necessity be different in all essential points of greatness, true heroism and real Christianity from what we may at the present time, for convenience, call American literature." Matthews argued that this great tradition of Afro-American literature would be the textual outlet "for the unnaturally suppressed inner lives which our people have been compelled to lead." Once these "unnaturally suppressed inner lives" of black people are unveiled, no "grander diffusion of mental light" will shine more brightly, she concludes, than that of the articulate Afro-American woman:

And now comes the question, What part shall we women play in the Race Literature of the future? . . . within the compass of one small journal ["Woman's Era"] we have struck out a new line of departure—a journal, a record of Race interests gathered from all parts of the United States, carefully selected, moistened, winnowed and garnered by the ablest intellects of educated colored women, shrinking at no lofty theme, shirking no serious duty, aiming at every possible excellence, and determined to do their part in the future uplifting of the race.

If twenty women, by their concentrated efforts in one literary movement, can meet with such success as has engendered, planned out, and so successfully consummated this convention, what much more glorious results, what wider spread success, what grander diffusion of mental light will not come forth at the bidding of the enlarged hosts of women writers, already called into being by the stimulus of your efforts?

And here let me speak one word for my journalistic sisters

who have already entered the broad arena of journalism. Before the "Woman's Era" had come into existence, no one except themselves can appreciate the bitter experience and sore disappointments under which they have at all times been compelled to pursue their chosen vocations.

If their brothers of the press have had their difficulties to contend with, I am here as a sister journalist to state, from the fullness of knowledge, that their task has been an easy one compared with that of the colored woman in journalism.

Woman's part in Race Literature, as in Race building, is the most important part and has been so in all ages. . . . All through the most remote epochs she has done her share in literature. . . .

One of the most important aspects of this set is the republication of the salient texts from 1890 to 1910, which literary historians could well call "The Black Woman's Era." In addition to Mary Helen Washington's definitive edition of Cooper's *A Voice From the South*, we have reprinted two novels by Amelia Johnson, Frances Harper's *Iola Leroy*, two novels by Emma Dunham Kelley, Alice Dunbar-Nelson's two impressive collections of short stories, and Pauline Hopkins's three serialized novels as well as her monumental novel, *Contending Forces*—all published between 1890 and 1910. Indeed, black women published more works of fiction in these two decades than black men had published in the previous half century. Nevertheless, this great achievement has been ignored.

Moreover, the writings of nineteenth-century Afro-American women in general have remained buried in obscurity, accessible only in research libraries or in overpriced and poorly edited reprints. Many of these books have never been reprinted at all; in some instances only one or two copies are extant. In these works of fiction, poetry, autobiography, biography, essays, and journalism resides the mind of the nineteenth-century Afro-American woman. Until these works are made readily available to teachers and their students, a significant segment of the black tradition will remain silent.

Oxford University Press, in collaboration with the Schomburg Center for Research in Black Culture, is publishing thirty volumes of these compelling works, each of which contains an introduction by an expert in the field. The set includes such rare texts as Johnson's *The Hazeley Family* and *Clarence and Corinne*, Plato's *Essays*, the most complete edition of Phillis Wheatley's poems and letters, Emma Dunham Kelley's pioneering novel *Megda*, several previously unpublished stories and a novel by Alice Dunbar-Nelson, and the first collected volumes of Pauline Hopkins's three serialized novels and Frances Harper's poetry. We also present four volumes of poetry by such women as Mary Eliza Tucker Lambert, Adah Menken, Josephine Heard, and Maggie Johnson. Numerous slave and spiritual narratives, a newly discovered novel—*Four Girls at Cottage City*—by Emma Dunham Kelley (-Hawkins), and the first American edition of *Wonderful Adventures of Mrs. Seacole in Many Lands* are also among the texts included.

In addition to resurrecting the works of black women authors, it is our hope that this set will facilitate the resurrection of the Afro-American woman's literary tradition itself by unearthing its nineteenth-century roots. In the works of Nella Larsen and Jessie Fauset, Zora Neale Hurston and Ann Petry, Lorraine Hansberry and Gwendolyn Brooks, Paule Marshall and Toni Cade Bambara, Audre Lorde and Rita Dove, Toni Morrison and Alice Walker, Gloria Naylor and Jamaica Kincaid, these roots have branched luxuriantly. The eighteenth- and nineteenth-century authors whose works are presented in this set founded and nurtured the black women's literary tradition, which must be revived, explicated, analyzed, and debated before we can understand more completely the formal shaping of this tradition within a tradition, a coded literary universe through which, regrettably, we are only just beginning to navigate our way. As Anna Cooper said nearly one hundred years ago, we have been blinded by the loss of sight in one eye and have therefore been unable to detect the full *shape* of the Afro-American literary tradition.

Literary works configure into a tradition not because of some mystical collective unconscious determined by the biology of race or gender, but because writers read other writers and *ground* their representations of experience in models of language provided largely by other writers to whom they feel akin. It is through this mode of literary revision, amply evident in the *texts* themselves—in formal echoes, recast metaphors, even in parody—that a "tradition" emerges and defines itself.

This is formal bonding, and it is only through formal bonding that we can know a literary tradition. The collective publication of these works by black women now, for the first time, makes it possible for scholars and critics, male and female, black and white, to *demonstrate* that black women writers read, and revised, other black women writers. To demonstrate this set of formal literary relations is to demonstrate that sexuality, race, and gender are both the condition and the basis of *tradition*—but tradition as found in discrete acts of language use.

A word is in order about the history of this set. For the past decade, I have taught a course, first at Yale and then at Cornell, entitled "Black Women and Their Fictions," a course that I inherited from Toni Morrison, who developed it in the mid-1970s for Yale's Program in Afro-American Studies. Although the course was inspired by the remarkable accomplishments of black women novelists since 1970, I gradually extended its beginning date to the late nineteenth century, studying Frances Harper's *Iola Leroy* and Anna Julia Cooper's *A Voice From the South*, both published in 1892. With the discovery of Harriet E. Wilson's seminal novel, *Our Nig* (1859), and Jean Yellin's authentication of Harriet Jacobs's brilliant slave narrative, *Incidents in the Life of a Slave Girl* (1861), a survey course spanning over a century and a quarter emerged.

But the discovery of *Our Nig*, as well as the interest in nineteenth-century black women's writing that this discovery generated, convinced me that even the most curious and diligent scholars knew very little of the extensive history of the creative writings of Afro-American women before 1900. Indeed, most scholars of Afro-American literature had never even read most of the books published by black women, simply because these books—of poetry, novels, short stories, essays, and autobiography—were mostly accessible only in rare book sections of university libraries. For reasons unclear to me even today, few of these marvelous renderings of the Afro-American woman's consciousness were reprinted in the late 1960s and early 1970s, when so many other texts of the Afro-American literary tradition were resurrected from the dark and silent graveyard of the out-of-print and were reissued in facsimile editions aimed at the hungry readership for canonical texts in the nascent field of black studies.

So, with the help of several superb research assistants—including David Curtis, Nicola Shilliam, Wendy Jones, Sam Otter, Janadas Devan, Suvir Kaul, Cynthia Bond, Elizabeth Alexander, and Adele Alexander—and with the expert advice of scholars such as William Robinson, William Andrews, Mary Helen Washington, Maryemma Graham, Jean Yellin, Houston A. Baker, Jr., Richard Yarborough, Hazel Carby, Joan R. Sherman, Frances Foster, and William French, dozens of bibliographies were used to compile a list of books written or narrated by black women mostly before 1910. Without the assistance provided through this shared experience of scholarship, the scholar's true legacy, this project could not have been conceived. As the list grew, I was struck by how very many of these titles that I, for example, had never even heard of, let alone read, such as Ann Plato's *Essays*, Louisa Picquet's slave narrative, or Amelia Johnson's two novels, *Clarence and Corinne* and *The Hazeley Family*. Through our research with the Black Periodical Fiction and Poetry Project (funded by NEH and the Ford Foundation), I also realized that several novels by black women, including three works of fiction by Pauline Hopkins, had been serialized in black periodicals, but had never been collected and published as books. Nor had the several books of poetry published by black women, such as the prolific Frances E. W. Harper, been collected and edited. When I discovered still another "lost" novel by an Afro-American woman (*Four Girls at Cottage City*, published in 1898 by Emma Dunham Kelley-Hawkins), I decided to attempt to edit a collection of reprints of these works and to publish them as a "library" of black women's writings, in part so that I could read them myself.

Convincing university and trade publishers to undertake this project proved to be a difficult task. Despite the commercial success of *Our Nig* and of the several reprint series of women's works (such as Virago, the Beacon Black Women Writers Series, and Rutgers' American Women Writers Series), several presses rejected the project as "too large," "too limited," or as "commercially unviable." Only two publishers recognized the viability and the import of the project and, of these, Oxford's commitment to publish the titles simultaneously as a set made the press's offer irresistible.

While attempting to locate original copies of these exceedingly rare books, I discovered that most of the texts were housed at the Schomburg Center for Research in Black Culture, a branch of The New York Public Library, under the direction of Howard Dodson. Dodson's infectious enthusiasm for the project and his generous collaboration, as well as that of his stellar staff (especially Diana Lachatanere, Sharon Howard, Ellis Haizip, Richard Newman, and Betty Gubert), led to a joint publishing initiative that produced this set as part of the Schomburg's major fund-raising campaign. Without Dodson's foresight and generosity of spirit, the set would not have materialized. Without William P. Sisler's masterful editorship at Oxford and his staff's careful attention to detail, the set would have remained just another grand idea that tends to languish in a scholar's file cabinet.

I would also like to thank Dr. Michael Winston and Dr. Thomas C. Battle, Vice-President of Academic Affairs and the Director of the Moorland-Spingarn Research Center (respectively) at Howard University, for their unending encouragement, support, and collaboration in this project, and Esme E. Bhan at Howard for her meticulous research and bibliographical skills. In addition, I would like to acknowledge the aid of the staff at the libraries of Duke University, Cornell University (especially Tom Weissinger and Donald Eddy), the Boston Public Library, the Western Reserve Historical Society, the Library of Congress, and Yale University. Linda Robbins, Marion Osmun, Sarah Flanagan, and Gerard Case, all members of the staff at Oxford, were

extraordinarily effective at coordinating, editing, and producing the various segments of each text in the set. Candy
Ruck, Nina de Tar, and Phillis Molock expertly typed reams
of correspondence and manuscripts connected to the project.

I would also like to express my gratitude to my colleagues
who edited and introduced the individual titles in the set.
Without their attention to detail, their willingness to meet
strict deadlines, and their sheer enthusiasm for this project,
the set could not have been published. But finally and ultimately, I would hope that the publication of the set would
help to generate even more scholarly interest in the black
women authors whose work is presented here. Struggling
against the seemingly insurmountable barriers of racism *and*
sexism, while often raising families and fulfilling full-time
professional obligations, these women managed nevertheless
to record their thoughts and feelings and to *testify* to all who
dare read them that the will to harness the power of collective
endurance and survival is the will to write.

The Schomburg Library of Nineteenth-Century Black
Women Writers is dedicated in memory of Pauline Augusta
Coleman Gates, who died in the spring of 1987. It was she
who inspired in me the love of learning and the love of literature. I have encountered in the books of this set no will
more determined, no courage more noble, no mind more
sublime, no self more celebratory of the achievements of all
Afro-American women, and indeed of life itself, than her
own.

A NOTE FROM
THE SCHOMBURG CENTER

Howard Dodson

The Schomburg Center for Research in Black Culture, The New York Public Library, is pleased to join with Dr. Henry Louis Gates and Oxford University Press in presenting The Schomburg Library of Nineteenth-Century Black Women Writers. This thirty-volume set includes the work of a generation of black women whose writing has only been available previously in rare book collections. The materials reprinted in twenty-four of the thirty volumes are drawn from the unique holdings of the Schomburg Center.

A research unit of The New York Public Library, the Schomburg Center has been in the forefront of those institutions dedicated to collecting, preserving, and providing access to the records of the black past. In the course of its two generations of acquisition and conservation activity, the Center has amassed collections totaling more than 5 million items. They include over 100,000 bound volumes, 85,000 reels and sets of microforms, 300 manuscript collections containing some 3.5 million items, 300,000 photographs and extensive holdings of prints, sound recordings, film and videotape, newspapers, artworks, artifacts, and other book and nonbook materials. Together they vividly document the history and cultural heritages of people of African descent worldwide.

Though established some sixty-two years ago, the Center's book collections date from the sixteenth century. Its oldest item, an Ethiopian Coptic Tunic, dates from the eighth or ninth century. Rare materials, however, are most available for the nineteenth-century African-American experience. It is from these holdings that the majority of the titles selected for inclusion in this set are drawn.

The nineteenth century was a formative period in African-American literary and cultural history. Prior to the Civil War, the majority of black Americans living in the United States were held in bondage. Law and practice forbade teaching them to read or write. Even after the war, many of the impediments to learning and literary productivity remained. Nevertheless, black men and women of the nineteenth century persevered in both areas. Moreover, more African-Americans than we yet realize turned their observations, feelings, social viewpoints, and creative impulses into published works. In time, this nineteenth-century printed record included poetry, short stories, histories, novels, autobiographies, social criticism, and theology, as well as economic and philosophical treatises. Unfortunately, much of this body of literature remained, until very recently, relatively inaccessible to twentieth-century scholars, teachers, creative artists, and others interested in black life. Prior to the late 1960s, most Americans (black as well as white) had never heard of these nineteenth-century authors, much less read their works.

The civil rights and black power movements created unprecedented interest in the thought, behavior, and achievements of black people. Publishers responded by revising traditional texts, introducing the American public to a new generation of African-American writers, publishing a variety of thematic anthologies, and reprinting a plethora of "classic texts" in African-American history, literature, and art. The reprints usually appeared as individual titles or in a series of bound volumes or microform formats.

The Schomburg Center, which has a long history of supporting publishing that deals with the history and culture of Africans in diaspora, became an active participant in many of the reprint revivals of the 1960s. Since hard copies of original printed works are the preferred formats for producing facsimile reproductions, publishers frequently turned to the Schomburg Center for copies of these original titles. In addition to providing such material, Schomburg Center staff members offered advice and consultation, wrote introductions, and occasionally entered into formal copublishing arrangements in some projects.

Most of the nineteenth-century titles reprinted during the 1960s, however, were by and about black men. A few black women were included in the longer series, but works by lesser known black women were generally overlooked. The Schomburg Library of Nineteenth-Century Black Women Writers is both a corrective to these previous omissions and an important contribution to Afro-American literary history in its own right. Through this collection of volumes, the thoughts, perspectives, and creative abilities of nineteenth-century African-American women, as captured in books and pamphlets published in large part before 1910, are again being made available to the general public. The Schomburg Center is pleased to be a part of this historic endeavor.

I would like to thank Professor Gates for initiating this project. Thanks are due both to him and Mr. William P. Sisler of Oxford University Press for giving the Schomburg Center an opportunity to play such a prominent role in the set. Thanks are also due to my colleagues at The New York Public Library and the Schomburg Center, especially Dr. Vartan Gregorian, Richard De Gennaro, Paul Fasana, Betsy

Pinover, Richard Newman, Diana Lachatanere, Glenderlyn Johnson, and Harold Anderson for their assistance and support. I can think of no better way of demonstrating than in this set the role the Schomburg Center plays in assuring that the black heritage will be available for future generations.

INTRODUCTION

Richard Yarborough

Widely considered the period of the first real efflorescence of black writing talent in the United States, the Harlem Renaissance saw the initial appearance of works by such authors as Langston Hughes, Jessie Fauset, Jean Toomer, Sterling Brown, Zora Neale Hurston, Arna Bontemps, Countee Cullen, and Nella Larsen. Even this partial roster conveys how remarkably fecund the 1920s and 1930s were for Afro-American literature. Perhaps Alain Locke provides the best characterization of that era in his landmark essay "The New Negro." The term "New Negro," however, dates neither from Locke's use of it in 1925 nor from its appearance several years earlier in the radical journal *The Messenger,* edited by A. Philip Randolph and Chandler Owen.[1] Rather, we initially encounter the phrase in the late nineteenth century—with Booker T. Washington's *A New Negro for a New Century* (1900), just one of its more noteworthy manifestations.[2]

It is similarly misleading to view the Afro-American literary landscape after the Reconstruction and before the 1920s as a virtual wasteland, only intermittently relieved by the appearance of the odd black writer here and there. Just as the first significant use of the term "New Negro" occurred around the turn of the century, these years also saw the rise of a new group of gifted and ambitious black authors, including Charles W. Chesnutt, Paul Laurence Dunbar, Anna Julia Cooper, Sutton E. Griggs, Alice (Moore) Dunbar-Nelson, and James D. Corrothers. Offspring of the Reconstruction period, these writers found more outlets for publication open to them than had been afforded to blacks at any time since the height of the abolition movement. Not only were their works appearing in such white periodicals as *Harper's Magazine, Bookman, Century Magazine, Literary Digest, Lippincott's Monthly Magazine, Atlantic Monthly*, and *Critic*, but the rise of Afro-American journals provided them with alternative, often less restrictive forums for expression. The dominant creative force behind one especially important such publication, the *Colored American Magazine*, was Pauline E. Hopkins, the single most productive black woman writer at the turn of the century.

Unfortunately, Hopkins's extraordinary record of publication has gone largely unrecognized. In contrast, scholars have noted the impressive output of several turn-of-the-century black male writers. For example, between 1893 and his death in 1906, Paul Laurence Dunbar published four novels, four collections of short stories, and six volumes of poetry; Charles W. Chesnutt, three novels and two collections of short stories between 1899 and 1905; and Sutton E. Griggs, five novels between 1899 and 1908. Yet Hopkins was just as prolific. Between mid-1900 and 1905, she published four novels (three of them serially), at least seven short stories, one historical booklet, over twenty biographical sketches, and many other essays and feature articles. Furthermore, the quality of her work is as striking as the quantity.

Born in Portland, Maine, in 1859, Pauline Elizabeth Hopkins was raised in Massachusetts and educated in the Boston public school system.[3] A member of a talented family (her granduncle was the poet James M. Whitfield), she encountered her first literary success at the age of fifteen, when her essay on "Evils of Intemperance and Their Remedy" won the ten-dollar prize in a contest sponsored by the well-known black writer William Wells Brown and the Congregational Publishing Society of Boston. Early in her life, Hopkins showed promise as both a playwright and an actress in musical drama as well. Although information regarding these years is scant, we do find record of an 1880 production of one of her plays, *Slaves' Escape; or the Underground Railroad,* performed by "Hopkins'[s] Colored Troubadours."[4] Constituted in part by members of her family, the Troubadours also gave concerts in the Boston area, with Pauline, the soprano of the group, winning special praise. Her interest in both the stage and black history continued into the 1890s, when she began presenting special lectures on Toussaint L'Ouverture and other topics. Like many aspiring Afro-American authors of the day, however, she soon discovered that she would have to earn her living in order to write and not vice versa. Accordingly, she studied stenography, and after passing the civil service exam, she received a position with the Bureau of Statistics, where she worked for four years.

A new phase of Hopkins's literary career began in 1900, when her short story "The Mystery Within Us" appeared in the inaugural issue of the Boston-based *Colored American Magazine,* founded by four transplanted black Virginians: Walter Wallace, Jesse W. Watkins, Harper S. Fortune, and Walter Alexander Johnson. Committed to the success of the periodical, Hopkins quickly became one of its chief contributors, and even published some of her work under her mother's maiden name, Sarah A. Allen—quite possibly to prevent her own name from appearing too frequently. Hopkins also played an active role in the administration of the magazine itself, serving as literary editor from mid-1903 through mid-1904.

When they started the *Colored American,* Walter Wallace

and his associates also founded the Colored Co-operative Publishing Company, one of several such black ventures toward the end of the nineteenth century.[5] In addition to producing the journal, their press issued *Contending Forces: A Romance Illustrative of Negro Life North and South* (1900), Pauline Hopkins's best known novel and her only fiction published in book form during her lifetime. Described in a prospectus as "pre-eminently a race-work dedicated to the best interest of the Negro everywhere," *Contending Forces* was specifically designed to effect social change.[6] In her preface, Hopkins explains, "I am not actuated by a desire for notoriety or for profit, but to do all that I can in an humble way to raise the stigma of degradation from my race."[7] Particularly aware of the potential power of fiction to shape attitudes toward blacks in the United States, Hopkins argues that the responsibility for rendering accurate depictions of their experiences lay with Afro-Americans themselves: *"No one will do this for us; we must ourselves develop the men and women who will faithfully portray the inmost thoughts and feelings of the Negro with all the fire and romance which lie dormant in our history"* (p. 14). In *Contending Forces*, she took up her own challenge.

   Like other black writers of her day, Hopkins strove to use her fiction to facilitate the uplift of her race by presenting Afro-American readers with moral guidance and instruction through exemplary characters. However, she also knew that accomplishing this uplift would entail the removal from blacks of what she called "the stigma of degradation." The full achievement of this latter goal depended in turn upon the writer's depiction of Afro-American characters who would be acknowledged by the white reader not only as human beings but also as embodiments of white bourgeois values, manners, and tastes. In her preface, Hopkins describes her motivation for reaching out to this white audience: "I have presented both sides of the dark picture—lynching and concubinage—truthfully and without vituperation, pleading for that justice of heart and mind for my people which the Anglo-Saxon in America never withholds from suffering humanity" (p. 15).

In their desire to appeal to the minds and especially the hearts of white readers, many nineteenth-century Afro-American novelists adopted the sentimental romance as the most effective literary vehicle for conveying their urgent message. Thus it comes as no surprise that *Contending Forces* is filled with the trappings of this fictive form: We have noble heroes and virtuous heroines, melodramatic situations, unsavory villains, exotic locations, highly emotional scenes, amazing coincidences, an alternately light-hearted and star-crossed love affair, and even touches of the supernatural.[8] One particular trait of this genre—the theme of lost and recovered familial connections—appealed with special force to black writers like Hopkins. And how could it be otherwise? Relatively few Afro-Americans of any background at the time could say with certainty that their family trees were free of unexplained gaps and missing branches. Accordingly, several black figures in *Contending Forces* have complicated and often mystery-ridden histories. As the character Mrs. Smith says, "[T]here are strangely tangled threads in the lives of many colored families" (p. 373). In Hopkins's fictive world, we never really know someone until we know his or her past. As bloodlines are traced, hidden connections discovered, and inherited traits revealed, her novel dramatizes the conflicts and reconciliations that inevitably ensue upon such often troubling knowledge and reflect the black community's search for social order in the wake of the chaotic disruption of slavery. In *Contending Forces,* this search is successful, for all loose ends are tied up by the book's conclusion, and the moral balance restored. Furthermore, in the sanguine light of Hopkins's romantic and yet deeply political perspective, this restoration of order entails the breaking down of the color line that, in dividing the races, often separates members of the same family.

   The sentimental novel's common theme of female virtue under siege struck responsive chords in the imaginations of nineteenth-century Afro-American writers as well. In fact, the focus on the sexual exploitation of black women goes back to the first extant Afro-American novel, William Wells Brown's *Clotel* (1853; later editions under the title *Clotelle* appeared in 1864 and 1867). In 1900, this issue was especially pressing because of the degree to which the more virulently racist commentators of the day were obsessed with the sexuality of Afro-Americans. In particular, the white popular media often described the behavior of blacks as governed by their allegedly uncontrollable passions. This contention led directly to the widespread stereotype of the black male as rapist. Black women, in turn, were presented as generally incapable of comprehending, much less embodying, the high moral propriety and sexual restraint that typified the white bourgeois feminine ideal. In response to what Hopkins called "a most malicious slander, an outrage against a worthy class of citizens," contemporary Afro-American women mobilized to their own defense.[9] For example, the creation in 1895 of the National Federation of Afro-American Women in Boston resulted primarily from the publication of a scurrilous open letter by a white Missouri journalist who contended that black women were unchaste.[10] Such attacks on contemporary black women were marked by references to the apparent inability of female slaves to meet the rigorous standards of true womanhood that so dominated the Victorian sensibility—a clear case of damning the victim for being victimized. Turn-of-the-century Afro-American women were thereby held accountable not only for their own moral condition but also for the sexual degradation associated with their collective slave past. As historian Paula Giddings puts it, they had "to defend their moral integrity as women" by "defending this history of all Black women and redefining the criteria of true womanhood."[11]

Hopkins's depiction of her major female characters in *Contending Forces* must be viewed in the context of this extremely heated and complex struggle. The first such figure is Grace Montfort, the wife of a British slaveholder from Bermuda named Charles Montfort. On the one hand, she easily fits the conventional mold of the high-minded, beautiful heroine who dies after falling prey to an immoral villain—in this case, Anson Pollock. On the other hand, the uncertainty regarding her racial identity limits her usefulness as an exemplar of cruelly assaulted black womanhood. A more accurate representation of the plight of turn-of-the-century Afro-American women is Sappho Clark, who, while exceeding every criterion for chastity and self-control, remains guilt-ridden because of some unspeakable secret in her background. Finally shown to be in no way culpable for her "sin," she transcends her personal history and thereby postulates a similar victory on the part of Afro-American women who could argue that they, like Sappho, had passed through the cleansing fire of pain and exploitation and emerged the purer for it. Granted, Sappho's intense suffering and unrelenting spirituality may, at times, strain the credulity of today's reader. When she is onstage, one often shares Will Smith's sense that he is "in the presence of a saint" (p. 309), and her formal diction ("nay" versus "no") reinforces this impression. We must remember, however, the political implications of Sappho's sentimentalization, for Hopkins ultimately offers her heroine as a living counterargument in the fierce debate in which the reputation (and therefore the status and treatment) of Afro-American women was at risk—high stakes indeed.

The depiction of Sappho Clark raises another important topic as well: Hopkins's endorsement of contemporary ideas regarding the role of race and ancestry as determinants of physical and psychological development. Not only the most virtuous character in the novel, Sappho is also the most beautiful, and her appeal resides for the author primarily in her near-white appearance: "Tall and fair, with hair of a golden cast, aquiline nose, rosebud mouth, soft brown eyes veiled by long, dark lashes which swept her cheek, just now covered with a delicate rose flush, she burst upon them—a combination of 'queen rose and lily in one' " (p. 107). Hopkins further attributes some of Sappho's finer character traits to her white ancestors, a monied French family.

Hopkins's presentation of the Smiths, the black bourgeois family about whom the plot revolves, manifests even more dramatically the often frustrating complexity of her treatment of racial heredity. On the one hand, the mere depiction of well-adjusted, healthy mixed-blood characters like Mrs. Smith and her children, Will and Dora, calls into question contemporary antiblack claims that the mulatto constituted some sort of racial mongrel, fated to a marginalized existence of anxiety, frustration, depression, hypersensitivity, and even madness. Dora's declaration—"I am not unhappy, and I am a mulatto" (p. 152)—therefore serves as a significant rebuttal of one key contention of late-nineteenth-century racist ideology.

On the other hand, in an effort to undermine the stereo-
typical image of the mixed-blood black, Hopkins yields
ground on a more fundamental issue; her portrayal of Mrs.
Smith and her children—the direct descendants of Charles
and Grace Montfort—best exemplifies this tendency. Although Hopkins vaguely hints that "there might even have
been a strain of African blood polluting the fair stream of
Montfort's vitality, or even his wife's" (p. 23), the couple's
cultivation and dignified manner—what one might call "good
breeding"—are never traced to any possible African fore-
bears. When these qualities appear in the Smiths, Hopkins
implies that they result from the mixed-blood family's white
ancestry:

> Man has said that from lack of means and social caste the
> Negro shall remain in a position of serfdom all his days, but
> the mighty working of cause and effect, the mighty unex-
> pected results of the law of evolution, seem to point to a
> different solution of the Negro question than any worked out
> by the most fertile brain of the highly cultured Caucasian.
> Then again, we do not allow for the infusion of white blood,
> which became pretty generally distributed in the *inferior* black
> race during the existence of slavery. Some of this blood, too,
> was the best in the country. Combinations of plants, or trees,
> or of any productive living thing, sometimes generate rare
> specimens of the plant or tree; why not, then, of the genus
> homo? Surely the Negro race must be productive of some
> valuable specimens, if only from the infusion which amal-
> gamation with a *superior* race must eventually bring.
> (p. 87; emphasis added)

Given the negative portrayal of most white Americans in
Contending Forces, we can safely read the phrase "the most
fertile brain of the highly cultured Caucasian" as sarcastic.

However, we cannot so readily dismiss the subsequent references to "white blood" and "a superior race." Rather, we must reluctantly conclude that in striving to convince the skeptical white reader that "valuable specimens" like Will and Dora do exist, Hopkins never challenges the basic assumption that races can be ranked qualitatively.

Ultimately, the depictions of Sappho and the Smiths suggest not only that physical and, most importantly, psychological characteristics are racially determined and can be inherited, but also that the dominant traits in mixed-blood blacks derive from the white side of their family tree. Even more confusing is the inconsistency with which Hopkins handles this issue. For example, in her portrayal of another mixed-blood figure, John Langley, she attributes his moral failings alternately to the "bad mixture" (p. 91) of his ancestry, to "the phrenological development of his head" (p. 226), and to the wretched environment in which he was raised. Finally, if some of her characterizations in *Contending Forces* reveal an endorsement of potentially racist views of personality and behavior, her positive treatment of two dark-skinned blacks— Madame Frances, a mysterious fortune-teller, and the heroic Luke Sawyer—demonstrates that occasionally she could also break free of such restrictive racial conceptions.

Although *Contending Forces* springs primarily from the tradition of the sentimental romance, we find in it traits of "political fiction" as well. As one might expect, Hopkins's use of such diverse generic modes causes marked inconsistencies in tone. Such discordances characterize a great deal of early Afro-American fiction before World War I, as black writers struggled to discover a vehicle that would satisfy their urge toward realism without undermining their adoption of popular literary forms. In the particular case of *Contending*

Forces, these moments result from Hopkins's attempt to incorporate political commentary and debate into her otherwise relatively conventional sentimental novel. Thus her "fairy tale of love and chivalry" (p. 398) is periodically interrupted by sections of text dedicated to barely dramatized discussions of what was then called the "race question." For instance, a meeting of the American Colored League, an organization "made up of leading colored men [from] all over New England" (p. 224), affords Hopkins the opportunity to present a broad sampling of black opinion regarding the best response to violent racial oppression.[12]

Although these speeches and arguments rarely bear directly on the romantic plot, they do offer a fascinating view of the ideological struggles taking place in turn-of-the-century black America. Accordingly, one is not surprised to find that many of the debates in *Contending Forces* echo the battle between W. E. B. Du Bois and Booker T. Washington over educational policy and the advisability of black political activism. Hopkins goes even further, in fact, and actually models two of her characters after Du Bois and Washington. The first is Will Smith, the young romantic hero of the novel. Working as a hotel bellboy in order to help support his family, Will assiduously prepares himself to attend Harvard and then pursue "a course in philosophy at some good German university" (p. 167). The resemblance between Will and Du Bois—who did, in fact, study at Harvard and in Germany—extends to their positions on education as well. Will laughs "at the idea of Latin and Greek being above the caliber of the Negro and likely to unfit him for the business of bread-getting" (p. 167); he even contends that "no Negro college . . . ought to bestow a diploma upon man or woman who had not been thoroughly grounded in the rudiments of moral

and natural philosophy, physiology, and political economy"
(p. 168). On other topics he is equally outspoken. In a direct
attack on lynching, he notes with bitter irony that the lynchers
are *"men who created the mulatto race . . . by the very means
which they invoked lynch law to suppress"* (p. 271). Like Du
Bois and other activists at the time, Will maintains an un-
flappable confidence in the power of logical argument to
counteract racism, and he sees black self-assertion as the key
to racial progress. Moreover, the rallying cry of this new,
aggressive stance—"We must *agitate*" (p. 272)—foreshadows
one of the crucial tenets of the Niagara Movement's Declaration of Principles, issued by Du Bois five years after the
publication of *Contending Forces*.

The president of a black industrial school in Louisiana,
Dr. Arthur Lewis stands at the opposite end of the ideological
spectrum from Smith and obviously represents the Washing-
tonian position. Convinced that "industrial education and the
exclusion of politics will cure all our race troubles" (p. 124),
he has the following motto: "If you want honey, you must
have money" (p. 126). In contrast to more militant blacks,
Lewis counsels,

> If we are patient, docile, harmless, we may expect to see that
> prosperity for which we long, in the years to come, if not
> for ourselves then for our children. I am an optimist in
> regard to the future. . . . We should strive to obtain the
> education of the industrial school, seeking there our level,
> content to abide there, leaving to the white man the superiority
> of brain and intellect which hundreds of years have developed.
> (pp. 250–51)

Although she clearly disagrees with many of his ideas, Hopkins remains sympathetic with Lewis. For instance, in an
especially perceptive and fair interpretation of Lewis's (and,

therefore, Booker T. Washington's) political posture, she writes, "Such ideas as Doctor Lewis set forth in his many brilliant speeches in behalf of his people were logical, and showed a mind capable of grasping the needs of the moment— an infinity of powerful thought under a tyrannous self-suppression" (p. 288). Then, when Lewis begins to court Dora, Hopkins's sympathy becomes enthusiastic approbation: "He was willing to work, to wait, to serve, if only he might claim her love at last. Oh, the nobleness of a good man's love!" (p. 304). Ironically, if Lewis's decision "to work, to wait, [and] to serve" precludes Hopkins's unqualified endorsement of his strategy for racial progress, it nonetheless makes him an admirable suitor. Hopkins's convincing depiction of Lewis reflects the extraordinary degree to which she empathizes with most of her black characters. Refusing to imply any direct correspondence between a figure's political stance and his or her moral condition, Hopkins possesses the imagination and insight to see that the connections between personality and ideology are quite complex.

In contrast to many of her fellow novelists, Hopkins also continually stresses in *Contending Forces* that Afro-American women are just as politically conscious and active as men like Smith and Lewis. Thus the section on the American Colored League is balanced by an earlier chapter called "The Sewing-Circle," in which we see black women meet to review "events of interest to the Negro race which had transpired during the week throughout the country" (p. 143). As one critic perceptively puts it, "Hopkins infuses the cult of domesticity with political messages, so that seemingly innocuous gatherings of women proclaim the significance of the black women's club movement." [13]

The portrayal of a figure named Mrs. Willis offers an

especially fascinating look at the political life of bourgeois
Afro-American women. The "brilliant widow of a bright
Negro politician" (p. 143), Willis was, we learn, the primary
force behind her husband's success. Accustomed to manipu-
lating power, she stands at the social and intellectual center
of her community, a position she holds by "sheer force of
will-power and indomitable pluck" (p. 148). A perceptive
judge of character and "shrewd in business matters," she can
be particularly ruthless when her male peers are fooled by
what Hopkins calls "her apparent womanly weakness and
charming simplicity" (p. 144).

Obviously attracted to this woman's strength of mind and
forthright feminism, Hopkins seems somewhat unsettled,
however, by the extraordinary extent of Willis's driving
ambition. At one point, for example, Sappho is tempted to
confide in Willis, but she cannot overcome "a wave of
repulsion toward this woman and her effusiveness, so forced
and insincere" (p. 155). Nonetheless, Willis's advice to
Sappho impresses the younger woman "in spite of herself"
(p. 157). Similarly, although she points out Willis's selfishness in attempting to profit financially from her skill as a
lecturer on the "woman question," Hopkins acknowledges
that her efforts lead to "the formation of clubs of colored
women banded together for charity, for study, for every
reason under God's glorious heavens that can better the
condition of mankind" (p. 147). Moreover, Willis unstint-
ingly strives to prevent the younger black women from
absorbing self-destructive racist ideas—especially those casting doubt upon the chastity of the Afro-American female.
Like Sappho, Hopkins never resolves her feelings toward
Willis, a powerful figure who captures the author's imagination to a greater extent than her small role in the novel
might indicate.[14]

Hopkins's concentration on the political behavior of Afro-American women also causes her to relax the stifling restraints of the sentimental literary conventions to which she is otherwise committed. This tendency has its greatest impact on the portrayal of Sappho, who comes most alive during the sewing group's discussions and in her conversations about men, work, and politics with the down-to-earth Dora. For example, disturbed by Dr. Lewis's conservatism, Sappho protests to her friend, "But you can see, can't you, that if our men are deprived of the franchise, we become aliens in the very land of our birth? . . . Temporizing will not benefit us; rather, it will leave us branded as cowards, not worthy a freeman's respect" (p. 125). And when she learns of Lewis's chauvinism, she bluntly terms him an "insufferable prig" (p. 126). Such scenes suggest that Sappho is designed to do more than carry the bulk of the sentimental weight of the novel. Hopkins uses her heroine as an important political mouthpiece as well. That Sappho, like her creator, works as a stenographer both strengthens this link between character and author and undermines a bit further the melodramatic excess of her depiction elsewhere.

Like most nineteenth-century Afro-American novels, *Contending Forces* is far from an unproblematic text. At the very least, it should remind us of how difficult it was for black writers to reject widely accepted concepts of race and culture that were frequently employed to denigrate blacks and to justify racial oppression. Furthermore, Hopkins's own elitist views mar her treatment of lower-class black characters like Sarah Ann White and Ophelia Davis, and the neat resolution of the intricate plot may not sit well with modern readers weaned on psychological realism.

These flaws pale, however, when viewed next to the book's virtues, many of which devolve from Hopkins's commitment to rendering in both political and consistently human terms a complex Afro-American community where ex-slaves, menial laborers, and middle-class blacks mingle. Indeed, *Contending Forces* provides us with a more detailed examination of Northern bourgeois black life than any Afro-American novel since Frank J. Webb's *The Garies and Their Friends* (1857). The depth of Hopkins's look at Boston's black society results largely from her decision to present few important white characters and to relegate instances of white racism to the first four chapters of the novel, which are set several decades before the main action. This approach permits her to de-emphasize interracial contact and to highlight the workings of the self-sufficient Afro-American community. Finally, one cannot overemphasize the centrality and fullness of her depictions of black women. Only Frances E. W. Harper's *Iola Leroy* (1892) presents as serious a contemporary fictional treatment of the experiences of Afro-American women. In general, *Contending Forces* proves to be a richly textured and engrossing novel, certainly one of the most important produced by an Afro-American before World War I.

After the publication of *Contending Forces*, Hopkins spent several years writing for the *Colored American*. In the spring of 1904, however, the black businessman Fred R. Moore bought the magazine and its press and moved the offices to New York City. Moore's takeover signaled not just a change in fiscal management but also a dramatic shift in editorial policy, for his primary source of support was Booker T. Washington, who was not above attempting to stifle periodicals critical of his programs.[15] It is hardly coincidental that Hopkins's name no longer appears as literary editor after the April 1904 issue, and that in November we find the following notice in the *Colored American*:

On account of ill-health Miss Pauline Hopkins has found it necessary to sever her relations with this Magazine and has returned to her home in Boston. Miss Hopkins was a faithful and conscientious worker, and did much toward the building up [of] the Magazine. We take this means of expressing our appreciation of her services, and wish for her a speedy return to complete health.[16]

A few years later, Du Bois recalled a different reason for her departure: "It was suggested to the editor, who was then Miss Pauline Hopkins, that her attitude was not conciliatory enough."[17] One indication that Hopkins in fact found her own political views in conflict with those of the new regime at the *Colored American* was the appearance of her first article in the *Voice of the Negro* only one month after the announcement of her "illness." Explaining how the magazine had sent Hopkins to New York City to report on the opening of the new subway system, the *Voice*'s editor, J. Max Barber, touts her presence as a "special" contributor as something of a coup for his periodical.[18] On Hopkins's part, the relatively radical stance of Barber's *Voice* must have made for more comfortable ideological quarters.

In addition to continuing her journalistic work, Hopkins displayed other literary ambitions as well. Especially noteworthy was the formation, in 1905, of her own publishing company, through which she issued a small history text entitled *A Primer of Facts Pertaining to the Early Greatness of the African Race and the Possibility of Restoration by Its Descendants—with Epilogue.* After this, however, we do not pick up the trail of Hopkins's literary production again until 1916, when she and Walter Wallace founded a magazine entitled *New Era.* Unfortunately, it lasted for only two issues and then ceased publication.

As did her contemporary, Charles W. Chesnutt, Hopkins

survived to witness the early flush years of the Harlem Renaissance. However, in contrast to Chesnutt, who was awarded the NAACP Spingarn Medal in 1928, she received no belated recognition for her accomplishments, and she faded from public view soon after the failure of *New Era*. She was working as a stenographer at the Massachusetts Institute of Technology when she died of burns suffered in a tragic accident in her home in August 1930.

Unlike some literary works which appear briefly in the limelight before eventually falling into neglect, *Contending Forces* has never been given the attention it merits. Largely as a result of the size of its press, Hopkins's novel was released with little fanfare and apparently no comment from the white mainstream literary community. That the rest of her considerable corpus was published primarily in Afro-American magazines with small circulations contributed further to Hopkins's relative anonymity. One would hope that this reissue of *Contending Forces* will be but the first step toward a true appreciation of this ambitious, productive, and underread author.

NOTES

1. For example, see "The New Negro—What Is He," *The Messenger* 2 (August 1920), cited in *Voices from the Harlem Renaissance*, ed. Nathan Irvin Huggins (New York: Oxford University Press, 1976), pp. 23–25. Locke's essay can be found in *The New Negro* (1925; rpt. New York: Atheneum, 1975), pp. 3–16.

2. Booker T. Washington, N. B. Wood, and Fannie Barrier Williams, *A New Negro for a New Century* (1900; rpt. Miami, Fla.: Mnemosyne, 1969). See also Wilson J. Moses, "The Lost World of the Negro, 1895–1919: Black Literary and Intellectual

Life before the 'Renaissance,' " *Black American Literature Forum* 21 (Spring–Summer 1987):61–84.

3. Following Ann Schockley's lead, most scholars cite 1859 as the year of Hopkins's birth. However, in her entry on Hopkins in the *Dictionary of American Negro Biography*, Dorothy Porter presents 1856 as the date.

4. In addition, scholars have found reference to other plays, including *One Scene from the Drama of Early Days*, but apparently nothing more than the title has survived.

5. A fine study of the history of black publishing houses is Donald F. Joyce's *Gatekeepers of Black Culture: Black-Owned Book Publishing in the United States, 1817–1981* (Westport, Conn.: Greenwood Press, 1983).

6. *Colored American Magazine* 1 (September 1900): n.p.

7. Pauline E. Hopkins, *Contending Forces: A Romance Illustrative of Negro Life North and South* (Boston: Colored Co-operative Publishing Co., 1900), p. 13. All subsequent references will be indicated parenthetically in the text.

8. Many of Hopkins's writings manifest her fascination with mysticism.

9. [Pauline E. Hopkins], "In the Editor's Sanctum," *Colored American Magazine* 7 (April 1904):297.

10. Also see the July 1904 issue of *Voice of the Negro*, which contains articles on the topic by such leading Afro-American women as Nannie H. Burroughs, Josephine Silone-Yates, Mary Church Terrell, and Fannie Barrier Williams (*Voice of the Negro* 1 [July 1904]).

11. Paula Giddings, *When and Where I Enter: The Impact of Black Women on Race and Sex in America* (New York: William Morrow, 1984), p. 85.

12. Hopkins's use of the word "men" here belies the role of black women in such groups. In fact, along with ten other women and nine men, Hopkins herself was a charter member of the Colored American League, an organization started in 1904 primarily to provide support for the struggling *Colored American Magazine*. A possible prototype for the American Colored League in *Contending*

Forces was the National Afro-American League, founded by T. Thomas Fortune in 1890 and resuscitated by Fortune and Bishop Alexander Walters as the Afro-American Council in 1899.

13. Jane Campbell, "Pauline Elizabeth Hopkins," in *Afro-American Writers before the Harlem Renaissance*, vol. 50 of *Dictionary of Literary Biography*, ed. Trudier Harris and Thadious M. Davis (Detroit, Mich.: Bruccoli Clark, 1986), p. 185. See also Pauline E. Hopkins, "Club Life among Colored Women," *Colored American Magazine* 5 (August 1902):273–77.

14. Mrs. Willis may be modeled after Josephine St. Pierre Ruffin, a leader in the women's club movement and one of the most influential black women in the Boston community of the late nineteenth century.

15. See August Meier, "Booker T. Washington and the Negro Press: With Special Reference to the *Colored American Magazine*," *Journal of Negro History* 38 (January 1953):67–90.

16. "Publishers' Announcements," *Colored American Magazine* 7 (November 1904):700.

17. [W. E. B. Du Bois], "The Colored Magazine in America," *Crisis* 5 (November 1912):33. For a revealing, first-hand look at Hopkins and the struggle for control of the *Colored American*, see William Stanley Braithwaite, "Negro America's First Magazine," *Negro Digest* 6 (December 1947):21–26. The aforementioned *Crisis* article is usually attributed to Du Bois; however, Braithwaite's name appears on the *Crisis* masthead as a source of help in the production of the journal, and he may have contributed to this essay.

18. *Voice of the Negro* 1 (December 1904):587; see also p. 580.

SELECTED BIBLIOGRAPHY

Berzon, Judith R. *Neither White Nor Black: The Mulatto Character in American Fiction*. New York: New York University Press, 1978.

Bone, Robert A. *The Negro Novel in America*. Rev. ed. New Haven, Conn.: Yale University Press, 1965.

Braithwaite, William Stanley. "Negro America's First Magazine." *Negro Digest* 6 (December 1947):21–26.

Brooks, Gwendolyn. Afterword to *Contending Forces: A Romance Illustrative of Negro Life North and South*, by Pauline E. Hopkins. 1900; rpt. Carbondale, Ill.: Southern Illinois University Press, 1978.

Campbell, Jane. *Mythic Black Fiction: The Transformation of History*. Knoxville, Tenn.: University of Tennessee Press, 1986.

———. "Pauline Elizabeth Hopkins." In *Afro-American Writers before the Harlem Renaissance*. Vol. 50 of *Dictionary of Literary Biography*, ed. Trudier Harris and Thadious M. Davis, pp. 182–89. Detroit, Mich.: Bruccoli Clark, 1986.

Carby, Hazel. " 'On the Threshold of Woman's Era': Lynching, Empire, and Sexuality in Black Feminist Theory." In *"Race," Writing, and Difference*, ed. Henry Louis Gates, Jr., pp. 301–16. Chicago: University of Chicago Press, 1986.

[Du Bois, W. E. B.]. "The Colored Magazine in America." *Crisis* 5 (November 1912):33–35.

Giddings, Paula. *When and Where I Enter: The Impact of Black Women on Race and Sex in America*. New York: William Morrow, 1984.

Gloster, Hugh M. *Negro Voices in American Fiction*. Chapel Hill, N.C.: University of North Carolina Press, 1948.

Johnson, Abby Arthur, and Ronald M. Johnson. "Away from Accommodation: Radical Editors and Protest Journalism, 1900–1910." *Journal of Negro History* 62 (October 1977):325–38.

———. *Propaganda and Aesthetics: The Literary Politics of Afro-American Magazines in the Twentieth Century*. Amherst, Mass.: University of Massachusetts Press, 1979.

Johnson, Charles S. "The Rise of the Negro Magazine." *Journal of Negro History* 13 (January 1928):7–21.

Joyce, Donald Franklin. *Gatekeepers of Black Culture: Black-Owned*

Book Publishing in the United States, 1817–1981. Westport, Conn.: Greenwood Press, 1983.

————. "Magazines of Afro-American Thought on the Mass Market: Can They Survive?" *American Libraries* 7 (December 1976):678–83.

Lamping, Marilyn. "Pauline Elizabeth Hopkins." In *American Women Writers: A Critical Reference Guide from Colonial Times to the Present*, ed. Lina Mainiero, vol. 2, pp. 325–27. New York: Frederick Unger, 1980.

Loggins, Vernon. *The Negro Author: His Development in America to 1900*. New York: Columbia University Press, 1931.

Meier, August. "Booker T. Washington and the Negro Press: With Special Reference to the *Colored American Magazine*." *Journal of Negro History* 38 (January 1953):67–90.

"Pauline E. Hopkins." *Colored American Magazine*. 2 (January 1901):218–19.

Porter, Dorothy B. "Pauline Elizabeth Hopkins." In *Dictionary of American Negro Biography*, ed. Rayford W. Logan and Michael R. Winston, pp. 325–26. New York: W. W. Norton, 1982.

Shockley, Ann Allen. "Pauline Elizabeth Hopkins: A Biographical Excursion into Obscurity." *Phylon* 33 (Spring 1972):22–26.

Tate, Claudia. "Pauline Hopkins: Our Literary Foremother." In *Conjuring: Black Women, Fiction, and Literary Tradition*, ed. Marjorie Pryse and Hortense J. Spillers, pp. 53–66. Bloomington, Ind.: Indiana University Press, 1985.

Washington, Mary Helen, ed. *Invented Lives: Narratives of Black Women, 1860–1960*. Garden City, N.Y.: Doubleday, Anchor Press, 1987.

yours for humanity,

Pauline E. Hopkins.

HE CUT THE ROPES THAT BOUND HER, AND SHE SANK UPON
THE GROUND AGAIN. (See page 69.)

Contending Forces

A ROMANCE ILLUSTRATIVE OF NEGRO LIFE NORTH AND SOUTH

BY

PAULINE E. HOPKINS

WITH ILLUSTRATIONS AND COVER DESIGN BY

R. EMMETT OWEN

*" The civility of no race can be perfect
whilst another race is degraded."*
— EMERSON.

BOSTON, MASS.
The Colored Co-operative Publishing Co.
5 Park Square
1900

COMPOSITION AND PRESSWORK BY
FISH PRINTING COMPANY.

Dedication.

———

To the
Friends of Humanity Everywhere
I offer this humble tribute
written by
one of a proscribed race.

CONTENTS.

LIST OF ILLUSTRATIONS.

PREFACE.

In giving this little romance expression in print, I am not actuated by a desire for notoriety or for profit, but to do all that I can in an humble way to raise the stigma of degradation from my race.

While I make no apology for my somewhat abrupt and daring venture within the wide field of romantic literature, I ask the kind indulgence of the generous public for the many crudities which I know appear in the work, and their approval of whatever may impress them as being of value to the Negro race and to the world at large.

The colored race has historians, lecturers, ministers, poets, judges and lawyers,— men of brilliant intellects who have arrested the favorable attention of this busy, energetic nation. But, after all, it is the simple, homely tale, unassumingly told, which cements the bond of brotherhood among all classes and all complexions.

Fiction is of great value to any people as a preserver of manners and customs — religious, political and social. It is a record of growth

and development from generation to generation. *No one will do this for us; we must
ourselves develop the men and women who will
faithfully portray the inmost thoughts and
feelings of the Negro with all the fire and
romance which lie dormant in our history,*
and, as yet, unrecognized by writers of the
Anglo-Saxon race.

The incidents portrayed in the early chapters of the book actually occurred. Ample
proof of this may be found in the archives
of the courthouse at Newberne, N. C., and
at the national seat of government, Washington, D. C.

In these days of mob violence, when lynch-
law is raising its head like a venomous monster, more particularly in the southern portion
of the great American republic, the retrospec-
tive mind will dwell upon the history of the
past, seeking there a solution of these monstrous outbreaks under a government founded
upon the greatest and brightest of principles
for the elevation of mankind. While we
ponder the philosophy of cause and effect, the
world is horrified by a fresh outbreak, and
the shocked mind wonders that in this — the
brightest epoch of the Christian era — *such
things are.*

Mob-law is nothing new. Southern sentiment has not been changed; the old ideas close in analogy to the spirit of the buccaneers, who formed in many instances the first settlers of the Southland, still prevail, and break forth clothed in new forms to force the whole republic to an acceptance of its principles.

"Rule or ruin" is the motto which is committing the most beautiful portion of our glorious country to a cruel revival of piratical methods; and, finally, to the introduction of *Anarchy*. Is this not so? Let us compare the happenings of one hundred — two hundred years ago, with those of today. The difference between then and now, if any there be, is so slight as to be scarcely worth mentioning. The atrocity of the acts committed one hundred years ago are duplicated today, when slavery is supposed no longer to exist.

I have tried to tell an impartial story, leaving it to the reader to draw conclusions. I have tried to portray our hard struggles here in the North to obtain a respectable living and a partial education. I have presented both sides of the dark picture — lynching and concubinage — truthfully and without vituperation, pleading for that justice of heart and mind for my people which the Anglo-Saxon in America never withholds from suffering humanity.

In Chapter XIII. I have used for the address of the Hon. Herbert Clapp the statements and accusations made against the Negro by ex-Governor Northen of Georgia, in his memorable address before the Congregational Club at Tremont Temple, Boston, Mass., May 22, 1899. In Chapter XV. I have made Will Smith's argument in answer to the Hon. Herbert Clapp a combination of the best points made by well-known public speakers in the United States — white and black — in defense of the Negro. I feel my own deficiencies too strongly to attempt original composition on this subject at this crisis in the history of the Negro in the United States. I have introduced enough of the exquisitely droll humor peculiar to the Negro (a work like this would not be complete without it) to give a bright touch to an otherwise gruesome subject.

THE AUTHOR.

CONTENDING FORCES.

CHAPTER I.

A RETROSPECT OF THE PAST.

WE wait beneath the furnace-blast
The pangs of transformation;
Not painlessly doth God recast
And mould anew the nation.
Hot burns the fire
Where wrongs expire;
Nor spares the hand
That from the land
Uproots the ancient evil.
— J. G. WHITTIER.

In the early part of the year 1800 the agitation of the inhabitants of Great Britain over the increasing horrors of the slave trade carried on in the West Indian possessions of the Empire was about reaching a climax. Every day the terrible things done to slaves were becoming public talk, until the best English humanitarians, searching for light upon the subject, became sick at heart over the discoveries that they made and were led to declare the principle: "The air of England is too pure for any slave to breathe."

To go back a little way in the romantic history of the emancipation of the slaves in the islands will not take much time, and will, I hope, be as instructive as interesting. Tales of the abuses of the slaves, with all the sickening details, had reached the Quaker community as early as 1783, and that tender-hearted people looked about themselves to see what steps they could take to ameliorate the condition of the Negroes in the West Indies, and to discourage the continuation of the trade along the African coast

Thomas Clarkson, a student at Cambridge, was drawn into writing a prize essay on the subject, and became so interested that he allied himself with the Quakers and investigated the subject for himself, thereby confirming his own belief, "that Providence had never made that to be wise that was immoral; and that the slave trade was as impolitic as it was unjust."

After strenuous efforts by Mr. Pitt and Mr. Fox, Parliament became interested and instituted an inquiry into the abuses of the slave trade. Finally, Mr. Wilberforce was drawn into the controversy, and for sixteen years waged an incessant warfare against the planters, meeting with defeat in his plans for ten consecutive years; but finally, in 1807, he was successful, and the slave trade was abolished.

These assailants of the slave trade had promised not to try to abolish slavery; but in a short time they learned that the trade was still carried on in ships sailing under the protection of false flags. Tales of the cruelties practiced upon the helpless chattels were continually reaching the ears of the British public, some of them such as to sicken the most cold-hearted and indifferent. For instance: causing a child to whip his mother until the blood ran; if a slave looked his master in the face, his limbs were broken; women in the first stages of their accouchement, upon refusing to work, were placed in the treadmill, where terrible things happened, too dreadful to relate.

Through the efforts of Granville Sharpe, the chairman of the London committee, Lord Stanley, minister of the colonies, introduced into the House of Commons his bill for emancipation.

Lord Stanley's bill proposed *gradual* emancipation, and was the best thing those men of wisdom could devise. Earnestly devoted to their task, they sought to wipe from the fair escutcheon of the Empire the awful blot which was upon it. By the adoption of the bill Great Britain not only liberated a people from the cruelties of their masters, but at the same time took an important step forward in the onward

march of progress, which the most enlightened
nations are unconsciously forced to make by
the great law of advancement; " for the civility
of no race can be perfect whilst another race is
degraded."

In this bill of gradual emancipation certain
conditions were proposed. All slaves were
entitled to be known as apprenticed laborers,
and to acquire thereby all the rights and privileges of freemen. " These conditions were
that prædials should owe three-fourths of the
profits of their labors to their masters for six
years, and the non-prædials for four years. The
other fourth of the apprentice's time was to be
his own, which he might sell to his master or
to other persons; and at the end of the term
of years fixed, he should be free."

In the winter of 1790, when these important
changes in the life of the Negro in the West
Indies were pending, many planters were following the course of events with great anxiety.
Many feared that in the end their slaves would
be taken from them without recompense,
and thereby render them and their families
destitute. Among these planters was the
family of Charles Montfort, of the island of
Bermuda.

Bermuda's fifteen square miles of area lays
six hundred miles from the nearest American

coast. Delightful is this land, formed from coral reefs, flat and fertile, which to the eye appears as but a pin point upon the ocean's broad bosom, one of "a thousand islands in a tropic sea."

Once Bermuda was second only to Virginia in its importance as a British colony; once it held the carrying trade of the New World; once was known as the "Gibraltar of the Atlantic," although its history has been that of a simple and peaceful people. Its importance to the mother country as a military and naval station has drawn the paternal bonds of interest closer as the years have flown by. Indeed, Great Britain has been kind to the colonists of this favored island from its infancy, sheltering and shielding them so carefully that the iron hand of the master has never shown beneath the velvet glove. So Bermuda has always been intensely British, — intensely loyal. Today, at the beginning of the new century, Bermuda presents itself, outside of its importance as a military station for a great power, as a vast sanatorium for the benefit of invalids. A temperate climate, limpid rivers, the balmy fragrance and freshness of the air, no winter, — nature changing only in the tints of its foliage, — have contributed to its renown as a health-giving region; and thus Shakespeare's magic island of Prospero and Miranda has become, indeed, to the traveler

> The spot of earth uncurst,
> To show how all things were created first.

Mr. Montfort was the owner of about seven hundred slaves. He was well known as an exporter of tobacco, sugar, coffee, onions and other products so easily grown in that salubrious climate, from which he received large returns. He was neither a cruel man, nor an avaricious one; but like all men in commercial life, or traders doing business in their own productions, he lost sight of the individual right or wrong of the matter, or we might say with more truth, that he perverted right to be what was conducive to his own interests, and felt that by owning slaves he did no man a wrong, since it was the common practice of those all about him, and he had been accustomed to this peculiar institution all his life.

Indeed, slavery never reached its lowest depths in this beautiful island; but a desire for England's honor and greatness had become a passion with the inhabitants, and restrained the planters from committing the ferocious acts of brutality so commonly practiced by the Spaniards. In many cases African blood had become diluted from amalgamation with the higher race, and many of these "colored" people became rich planters or business men (themselves owning slaves) through the favors heaped upon them by their white parents. This being the case, there might even have been a strain of African blood polluting the fair stream of Montfort's vitality, or even his wife's, which fact would not have caused him one instant's uneasiness. Moreover, he was a good master, and felt that while he housed his slaves well, fed them with the best of food suited to their occupations and the climate, and did not cruelly beat them, they fared better with him than they would have with another, perhaps, or even if they held property themselves.

The speeches of Mr. Pitt, Mr. Burke and others, together with the general trend of public sentiment as expressed through the medium of the British press, had now begun to make an impression upon some of the more humane of the planters on this island, and among them was Mr. Montfort. Uneasiness now took the place of his former security; thought would obtrude itself upon him, and in the quiet hours of the night this man fought out the battle which conscience waged within him, and right prevailed to the extent of his deciding that he would free his slaves, but in his own way. He determined to leave Bermuda, and after settling in some other land, he would gradually free his slaves without impoverishing himself; bestow on each one a piece of land, and finally, with easy conscience, he would retire to England, and there lead the happy life of an English gentleman of fortune.

With this end in view, being a man of affairs and well acquainted with the whole of the American continent, he naturally turned his eyes towards the United States, where the institution flourished, and the people had not yet actually awakened to the folly and wickedness exemplified in the enslavement of their fellow-beings. For reasons which were never known, he finally made choice of Newbern, N. C., for a home.

Sunday was and is the high holiday in all tropical climes. On that day the slave forgot his bonds. It was noon; the early service of the Church of England was ended. The clergyman of the parish had accompanied Charles Montfort home. Mrs. Montfort was visiting friends, so the two gentlemen dined alone. The clergyman was rather glad that he had the opportunity of seeing Mr. Montfort alone, and had used all his powers of persuasion to turn him from his proposed exodus. It was of no avail, as the good man soon found;

and with a sigh, he finally took his hat and prepared to leave. Both stood outside the house upon the broad walk beneath the shade of the fragrant cedars and the fruitful tamarind trees. The silence of deep feeling was between these two men. The clergyman could only remember the reverence he had always received, and the loving service given him by this family. Montfort thought with pain of the holy ministrations of this silver-haired man, who had pronounced the solemn words that bound him to his gentle wife, had baptized his children, and (tenderest act of all) had buried the little daughter whose grave was yonder, beneath the flowering trees in the churchyard. Yes, it was sad to part and leave all these tender ties of friendship behind.

"The bishop will come himself, Charles, to persuade you that this is a dangerous step you are about to take," finally the good man said, breaking the silence.

"Why dangerous? Is it any more so for me than for those who left England to build a home here in the wilderness?"

"Different, very different. The mother hand was still over them, even in these wilds. Out there," and he pointed in the direction of the bay, "they tell me that for all their boasted freedom, the liberty of England is not found, and human life is held cheaply in the eyes of men who are mere outlaws. Ah! but the bishop," he continued with a sigh, "he can tell you; he has seen; he is not a weak old man like me. He will talk you out of this plan of separation from all your friends."

Again silence fell upon them. In the direction of the square a crowd of slaves were enjoying the time of idleness. Men were dancing with men, and women with women, to the strange monotonous music of drums without tune, relics of the tom-tom in the wild African life which haunted them in dreamland. Still, there was pleasure for even a cultivated musical ear in the peculiar variation of the rhythm. The scanty raiment of gay-colored cotton stuffs set off the varied complexions, — yellow, bronze, white, — the flashing eyes, the gleaming teeth, and gave infinite variety to the scene. Over there, waterfalls fell in the sunlight in silvery waves; parti-colored butterflies of vivid coloring, and humming-birds flashed through the air with electrical radiance; gay parrakeets swung and chattered from the branches of the trees.

"Where, my son," said the clergyman, indicating the landscape with a wave of his hand, "will you find a scene more beautiful than this? How can you leave it and those who love you and yours?"

"Beautiful, indeed; and I will confess that it grows dearer as the time for my departure draws near," answered Montfort. " I will walk with you," he continued, as the clergyman turned in the direction of the road. As they passed through the wide entrance gates a Negro woman was weeding her little garden; her pickaninny was astride her back, spurring his mother as a rider his horse. The woman and the child looked up and smiled at the master and his guest, and the woman put the child on the ground and stood upright to bob a queer little courtesy. They walked along in silence until they reached the plaza.

" My son, will you not be persuaded?"

" Father, I have made up my mind firmly, after due consideration. I believe it is for the best."

They paused a moment at the square; then the holy man said solemnly, as he raised his hand in benediction: " If it then be for the best, which God grant it may be, I pray the good Father of us all to keep you in safety and in perfect peace." He turned and disappeared in the crowd.

Charles Montfort was immediately surrounded by his friends, who greeted him joyously, for he was a genial man and had endeared himself greatly to his neighbors.

"Still determined to leave us, Charles?" inquired one.

"Yes, for the good of myself and family. How can we submit tamely to the loss of our patrimonies without an effort to reimburse ourselves when a friendly land invites us to share its hospitality?"

"There is truth in your argument for all who, like you, Charles, have a large venture in slaves. Thank heaven I am so poor that a change of laws will not affect me," said one.

"Where a man's treasure is, there also is his heart. It is nature. Almost you persuade me, Charles, to do likewise," remarked another.

"As I have told you, I will retain my patrimony and free my slaves, too, by this venture in the United States under a more liberal government than ours."

"Ah! Charles," remarked another listener, "you forget the real difference between our government and that of the United States. And then the social laws are so different. You will never be able to accustom yourself to the habits of a republic. Do you not remember the planters from Georgia and Carolina who fought for good King George, and were stanch Royalists? They retired to the Bahamas when our cause was lost in the American colonies. My brother has just returned from a trip there. He tells strange tales of their surprise at many things we do here. I fear it is but a cold welcome you will receive from men of their class."

"Certainly," replied Montfort, "I shall try to be a good subject or citizen of whatever country I may be compelled to reside in for a long or short time."

"But surely you will not expose your wife to the inconveniencies of life in that country," said another.

"She has had her choice, but prefers hardships with me to life without me," proudly returned Montfort.

"A willful man must have his way," murmured one who had not yet spoken, "and I will give you three months to stay in the land of savages before you will be returning to us bag and baggage."

"Well," laughed Montford, "we shall see."

Twilight had fallen now, and Montfort bared his head to the refreshing sea breeze which fluttered every leaf. When he bade his friends good night, finally, and started on his homeward walk, the arguments of the good clergyman and of his friends were present in his harassed mind, and he wondered if he were doing wrong not to be prevailed upon to yield to the opinions of others. Once he almost determined that he would give it all up and remain in this land of love and beauty. To collect his scattered thoughts and calm his mind he turned toward the bay, and stood upon the beach, still allowing the breeze to play about his heated temples. Never before had he appreciated his home so much as now, when he contrasted it with the comparative barrenness of the new spot he had chosen. The water was alive with marine creatures; the sea aflame. The air was full of light-giving insects, incessantly moving, which illumined the darkness and gave life to every inanimate object. Over all the moon and stars were set in the cloudless deep-blue sky of coming night. Alas! his good angel fled with the darkness, and morning found him more determined than ever to go on with his project.

When it became generally known in Bermuda that Charles Montfort had decided to leave the place of his birth and establish himself in a foreign land, many friends gathered about him and advised him to reconsider his determination. Montfort laughingly invited them to join him in his new venture, and then earnestly pointed out to them the dangers which threatened their fortunes. He painted his plans in glowing colors, and ended by promising them that in less than twenty-five years he would land in England, a retired planter, his former slaves free and happy, and he himself rich and honored.

Having an immense amount of property to transport, it happened that Mr. Montfort was compelled to make two trips to Newbern before he removed his family to their new home; but after much energetic work and many difficulties, the little family looked through blinding tears at the receding shores of what had been a happy home. A week later a noble ship stood off the shores of North Carolina. On the deck was Charles Montfort; his wife hung upon his arm; beside the devoted couple were Charles, Jr., named for his father, and Jesse, the young darling of his mother's heart. Silently they gazed upon the fair scene before them, each longing for the land so recently left behind them, though no word of regret was spoken.

CHAPTER II.

THE DAYS "BEFORE THE WAR."

O FREEDOM! thou art not as poets dream,
A fair young girl with light and delicate limbs,
　　．　　．　　．　　．　　．　　．
Thy birthright was not given by human hands:
Thou wert twinborn with man.

THE shores of Pamlico Sound presented a
motley crowd of slaves, overseers, owners of
vessels, and a phantasmagoric landscape very
charming to eyes unaccustomed to such scenes.
It was near the noon siesta. In the harbor lay
three or four vessels ready to be loaded with
their freight of rice, tobacco or cotton. The
sun poured its level rays straight down upon
the heads of all. A band of slaves sang in a
musical monotone, and kept time to the music
of their song as they unloaded a barge that had
just arrived:

> Turn dat han' spike roun' an' roun',
> 　Hol' hard, honey; hol' hard, honey.
> Brack man tote de buckra's load,
> 　Hol' hard, honey; hol' hard, honey
>
> Neber 'fo' seed a nigger like you,
> 　Hol' hard, honey; hol' hard, honey.
> Allers tinkin' 'bout yer ol' brack Sue,
> 　Hol' hard, honey; hol' hard, honey.

Ef I was an alligater what'd I do ?
   Hol' hard, honey ; hol' hard, honey.
Run 'way wid ol' brack Sue,
   Hol' hard, honey ; hol' hard, honey.

Massa ketch yer, what'd he do ?
   Hi, hi, honey ; hi, hi, honey.
Cut yer back an' ol' brack Sue's,
   He, he, honey ; he, he, honey.

I cuss massa 'hin' de fence,
   Hol' hard, honey ; hol' hard, honey.
Massa don' hyar make no differyence,
   Hol' hard, honey ; hol' hard, honey.

Turn dat han' spike roun' an' roun',
   Hol' hard, honey ; hol' hard, honey.
Brack man tote de buckra's load,
   Hol' hard, honey ; hol' hard, honey.

As the refrain died away the bell for the noon rest sounded faintly in the distance, gradually drawing nearer, and again their rich and plaintive voices blended together in sweet cadences as they finished placing the heavy load to the satisfaction of their drivers:

Hark, dat merry, purty bell go
   Jing-a-lingle, jing-a-lingle, jingle bell,
Jing-a-lingle, jing-a-lingle, jing-a-lingle bell,
   Jingle bell, jingle bell.

Even so sang the children of Israel in their captivity, as they sat by the rivers of Babylon awaiting deliverance.

Just now a ship, which had some time since appeared as a dark spot on the horizon, turned her majestic prow and steered for the entrance to the sound. Immediately the pilot boat in the harbor put out to her. Everyone on the shore became eagerly intent upon the strange ship, and they watched the pilot climb aboard with all the interest which usually attends the slightest cause for excitement in a small community.

The ship came on very slowly, for there was little wind, under topsail, jib and foresail, the British flag at the peak and the American flag at the fore. The people on shore could see the captain standing by the pilot, the anchor ready to be dropped, and the bowsprit shrouds loose. But now their interest was divided with a new arrival. A man on horseback rode down to the shaky wooden platform which served as a landing place for passengers; behind him, at a respectful distance, rode a white-haired Mulatto. The man leaped from his horse and threw his reins to the slave, signaled a couple of Negroes in a boat, jumped into it as they, obedient to his sign, pulled alongside the wharf, and was rowed swiftly out to the advancing ship, which was now making considerable headway toward the shore.

Among the idlers on the wharf was one whom everyone addressed as Bill. He was large, or rather burly, carried a rawhide in his hand, and from his air of authority toward them, was evidently the overseer of the gang of slaves who were loading the tobacco barge. From out the crowd a man who had been sitting idly on a bale of cotton moved toward him.

"Holloa, Bill," he said, addressing the owner of the rawhide.

"Howdy, Hank"; returned Bill, surveying the other curiously, "whar in time did you drap from?"

Hank did not reply directly. He shifted the tobacco quid in his mouth from one cheek to the other, then with a nod of the head toward the approaching vessel, asked: "Whar's she from?"

"Hain't been in town lately, I reckon, or you'd know all about the 'Island Queen' from Bermudy. Planter named Montfort on her. He's movin' his niggers here to Caroliny; gittin' too hot fer him back thar," replied Bill, with a backward jerk of his thumb in the supposed direction of Bermuda. "How's things up yer way?"

"Fair, fair to middlin', Bill; thar's been some talk 'bout a risin' among the niggers, and so we

jes tuk a few o' them an' strun 'em up fer a eggsample to the res'. I tell you, Bill, we jes don't
spec' to hav' no foolin' 'bout this yer question
of who's on top as regards a gentleman's owning his niggers, an' whomsoeveder goes ter
foolin' with that ar pertickler pint o' discus-
shun is gwine ter be made a eggsample of,
even ef it's a white man. Didn' hyar nuthin'
'bout a circus up our way, did yer?"

Bill scratched his chin and shook his head in
the negative.

"Wall, 'twas this here way: Jed Powers,
you 'member Dan Powers' Jed, don' yer? Dan
thet was tarred an' feathered fer selling good
likely whiskey ter niggers?" Bill nodded in
the affirmative. "Jed Powers wuz seed walkin'
with Jimison's wench Violy. Be blowed ef he
wasn't gittin' ready ter cut an' run ter Canidy
with her!"

"Don' b'lieve yer, durned ef I do," said Bill.

"Fact! Be durned ef it ain't jes so."

"Wall! of all the onnat'rall cusses!"

"But his wurst offense, in gineral, wuz thet
he wuz meanin' fer to marry her!" Hank
paused in his narrative to allow a full appreciation of his statement to be impressed upon
Bill's mind.

"Wus an' wus!" groaned the latter. "What
is we comin' to, by thunder! I allays took Jed

to be a decen' sort o' cuss, too. What's the committee doin' 'bout it ? "

" Wall, we sot out to stop thet fun, anyhow. We got him after a hot chase, an' we put him in jail; an' las' week we guv him his trial. Jedge sentenced him to fifty lashes an' hangin' by the neck untell he wuz dead. But some-how or nuther folks is gittin' squeamish. Jedge don' durst to hang him; he'll jes guv him the fifty lashes an' a talkin' to on the immoralty o' his acts an' ways. Jedge tol' him he wuz young an' had a chance to 'pent from the desolute ways o' his youth, of which his wurst failin' wuz a-wantin' to marry niggers, leastwise he'd end in hell, shure. Jedge tol' him everythin' 'cordin' ter law an' jestice. We wuz calkerlatin' ter have a celebrashun to which all the leading citizens o' this county would 'a' been bid, but, o' course, not havin' the hangin' sort o' took the ginger out o' the whole business."

" I hain't a doubt o' yer horsepertality in case o' the event, Hank; we's allays got along mighty comf'table tergether," replied Bill, nod-ding an emphatic approval of all that Hank had said. The whole speech had been liberally punctuated with copious floods of tobacco juice, which formed a small river between the two men.

" Best thing I know of down our way," said

Bill, after they had taken another good look at the ship, "the best thing I know of was a raffle over ter Jellison's auction-rooms. A raffle's a great thing fer pickin up bargains in niggers an' horses. This pertickler one was fer a bay horse, a new light buggy an' harness, an' a Mulatto gal Sal. The whole thing wuz wurth fifteen hundred dollars, an' we had fifteen hundred chances at a dollar a head. Highest throw took first choice; lowest, the remainder. Winners to pay twenty dollars each fer refreshments."

"Leetle bit selfish o' you, Bill, ter keep all thet to yerself," said Hank, giving Bill a reproachful glance.

"Mabby so, mabby so. But you won't lose nuthin', Hank, ef I can help yer in the footur. 'Pears like some one wuz a-tellin' me," he continued reflectively, "thet yer wuz a-wurkin' fer the county 'bout thet time fer board an' clo's."

"Be durned ef I wuzn't," replied Hank with great candor. "Shot at a free nigger an' killed Brady's dog Pete. Ef it'd been the nigger I'd happened ter kill, hit would 'a' been all right; but bein' 'twas a bluded hound thet had tred hundreds o' runaways, it wuz anuther question; an' not havin' the muney ter pay a fine, an' Brady bein' purty mad, why in I went fer a munth."

"Wall, as I was a-sayin', ter perceed, by a lucky chance it wuz my fust choice, an' I choose the gal. I knowed she wuz a fust-class breeder an' my muney wuz shure fer a hundred per cent on her."

"I swear ter gosh, but yer right, Bill; mate her with the right sort an' you's got yer own muney."

Both men now turned their attention to the advancing ship.

"I see ol' Pollock's got 'em in tow," remarked Hank reflectively, after a moment's silence. "Ans Pollock's as crafty as can be. No 'fense meant, yer know; seems he's yer boss still; mean cuss ef he's rich's a jedge"; he continued, "s'pose they've got a heap o' money, too."

"Can't say as to thet," replied Bill, "but they bought Pollock's ol' place, an' it looks as though money might be plenty the way everything has been fixed up fer the missis."

The noon hours were now over, and a great deal of confusion reigned, caused by the arrival of a ship in port with so rich a man as Mr. Montfort aboard. The two friends became separated in the ensuing bustle which attended the landing of the party. During the preceding conversation a carriage and teams for transporting the baggage and slaves had drawn up alongside the shore; and as Mr. Montfort stepped on the rickety wharf and assisted his wife to do the same, a murmur of involuntary admiration ran through the motley crowd of rough white men and ignorant slaves.

Grace Montfort was a dream of beauty even among beautiful women. Tall and slender; her form was willowy, although perfectly molded. Her complexion was creamy in its whiteness, of the tint of the camellia; her hair, a rich golden brown, fell in rippling masses far below the waist line; brown eyes, large and soft as those seen in the fawn; heavy black eyebrows marking a high white forehead, and features as clearly cut as a cameo, completed a most lovely type of Southern beauty.

The two children followed their mother closely. They were sturdy boys, who resembled her in the beauty of their features; and in Jesse, the baby, a still greater resemblance could be traced, because the hair had been allowed to remain in long, soft curls. So they came ashore to their new home, obsequiously waited upon by Mr. Pollock, and lovingly attended by their numerous slaves. In an instant the family was seated in the waiting vehicle; and before the spectators could fully realize the beauty and elegance of the newcomers, they were whirled away, and the carriage was lost in a cloud of dust.

Hank Davis and Bill Sampson met once more before they left the wharf. "Ef they hain't got an overseer, I'm goin' to 'ply fer the job"; said Hank, "never seed sich a booty in my life."

Bill Sampson scratched his head meditatively: "Strikes me, Hank, thet thet ar female's got a black streak in her somewhar."

Hank stared at Bill a moment, as though he thought he had suddenly lost his senses; then he burst into a loud guffaw.

"You git out, Bill Sampson."

"Wall, maybe," said Bill, "maybe so. Thar's too much cream color in the face and too little blud seen under the skin fer a genooine white 'ooman. You can't tell nothin' 'bout these Britishers; they're allers squeamish 'bout thar nigger brats; yas, sah, very squeamish. I've hern tell that they think nuthin of ejcatin' thar black brats, and freein' 'em, an' makin' 'em rich."

"You go to the devil"; returned Hank, as he moved away, "you're wus' nan ol' nigger, allers seein' a possum up a tree; an' 'taint no possum 'tall, — nuthin' but er skunk."

Apologists tell us as an excuse for the barbarous practice of slavery, that it was a godlike institution for the spread of the gospel of the meek and lowly carpenter's son, and that the African savage brought to these shores in chains was a most favored being.

Such may be the thoughts of the careless and superficial mind; but when we survey the flotsam and jetsam left from the wreck of the Civil War, we can deceive ourselves no longer; we must confess that the natural laws which govern individuals and communities never relax in their operation. The fruit of slavery was poisonous and bitter; let us rejoice that it no longer exists.

CHAPTER III.

"COMING EVENTS CAST THEIR SHADOWS BEFORE."

IN sooth I know not why I am so sad:
It wearies me ; you say it wearies you ;
But how I caught it, found it, or came by it,
What stuff 'tis made of, whereof it is born,
I am to learn ;
And such a wantwit sadness makes of me
That I have much ado to know myself.
— *Merchant of Venice.*

THE old Pollock homestead was an exquisite spot. The house was a long, low, rambling structure, consisting of many large, airy rooms inside, and ornamented without by piazzas supported by huge pillars. Immense trees shaded the driveway and embowered the stately white mansion. Gay parterres of flowers ornamented the rolling lawn, which divided the great house from the Negro quarters which were picturesquely visible at a convenient distance from it.

Within the house Mr. Montfort had gathered all the treasures which could possibly add to the comfort and pleasure of his lovely wife. Beautiful rugs covered the floors, fine paintings adorned the walls, gleaming statuary flashed upon one from odd nooks and corners. In the library music had found a home in the most comfortable corner of the room. On a table one might find a volume of Goethe in the original; on the grand piano the score of a then-popular opera; while a magnificent harp, standing near, hinted of musical talents highly cultivated.

Business had prospered with Montfort; his crops flourished; but a nameless trouble seemed to be halting upon the threshold of the home he loved, and to threaten those whom he cherished so fondly.

The first year of residence in Newbern had been very pleasant for the Montforts. Society, such as it was, opened its arms to the family and voted the highly cultured wife and cherub children great additions. The house was a favorite resort for all the young people of the neighborhood. Mrs. Montfort had been educated in England, and had brought with her to the provincial families with whom she now associated all the refinements of the Old World. Having great wealth for the times, she had always been indulged in every whim by the doting bachelor uncle who had made her his heiress, but who had died soon after her marriage to Charles Montfort. As Grace Montfort, she found again the love her uncle had delighted to lavish upon his adopted child.

Possessed of a bright, joyous nature, she liked nothing better than to gather about her the young men and women of the neighborhood and make life pleasant for them; and they in turn learned from her customs and refinements which otherwise might never have come their way. Everyone voted her the dearest and most beautiful woman they had ever known, and all would have gone merry as a marriage-bell, *but* (if it were not for the *buts* and *ifs* of this life, what a pleasant place the world would be) into this paradise of good feelings and admiration came Anson Pollock with his bitter envy and his unlawful love, and finally with his determination to possess the lovely Grace Montfort at all hazards.

Gradually the friendly relations of the neighbors turned to coldness and reserve. It was whispered about that Montfort was about to free his slaves. This in itself was a dangerous doctrine at that time in that part of the world, and a man suspected of entertaining ideas of freedom for slaves must either change his tactics or his residence, or else forfeit life and property. Then again, Bill Sampson's words to Hank Davis had somehow found a voice, and the suspicion of Negro blood in the veins of Mrs. Montfort was a deathblow to a proud spirit and social aspirations. These two serious charges had spread abroad like wildfire.

It was a hot morning, a very hot morning in early summer. There had been no rain for some time. Mrs. Montfort lay in a hammock outside the breakfast-room windows. Lucy, her maid, was mending lace and children's garments a short distance away.

Lucy was Mrs. Montfort's foster sister; both were born on the same day. Their relations had always been those of inseparable friends rather than of mistress and slave.

"No rain today, Lucy. I never used to mind the heat at home (this with a sigh). How fair it must be over the blue waters of the bay; I can almost smell the cedars outside the entrance gates."

"Yas, Miss Grace" (to Lucy her mistress was always "Miss Grace"), "I do feel sort o' squeamish myself sometimes when I tink of the gals all dancin' Sundays in the square; but reckon we'll git used ter these people here arter a-while; leastwise, I hope so."

Mrs. Montfort did not reply, and her maid noticed, as she glanced anxiously at her mistress, that a frown was on her face. Lucy sighed. "Miss Grace" had been noted once for her sunny, cheerful temper. Now all was changed.

Beyond the rolling lawn fields of cotton

could be seen, the leaves twisting in the heat
and the steady glare of the sun. Zigzag fences
separated the cotton from fields of corn; away
in the distance dim aisles of pine trees stretched
their dark arms towards the heavens, their dark
foliage suggestive of cool shadows and quiet
glades. The road wound in and out among
the pines, through a woodland, and terminated
in the highway just visible from the piazza.
Inside the long, open windows little Jesse
played at building houses with the bags of
golden eagles that his father kept in a drawer
of his escritoire.

"Grace, Grace, Lucy," called the child, "my
houses won't stay up; come in and help me."

Just then a group appeared coming around
a corner of an outbuilding. Two men walked
beside a pony, astride whose back sat Master
Charles. As they approached the house the
gentlemen swept off their wide-brimmed hats
in a gallant salute to Mrs. Montfort, which she
returned by rising from her recumbent position
and dropping a low courtesy. The gentlemen
were Mr. Montfort and Mr. Pollock. Jesse,
hearing the pony's feet, came out the window
and ran down the piazza steps to his father, who,
as Charles sprang to the ground, lifted the
excited child to the pony's back. Mrs. Montfort
watched the approach of the little procession

with a pleased smile. She made a fair picture in her elaborately embroidered white morning robe, her beautiful hair arranged in drooping curls at the sides of her head, as was the fashion of the time.

"See me, Mama Grace," cried Jesse, as he clapped his little hands, and dug the heels of his tiny-slippered feet into the pony's side, in imitation of his father on horseback. As Montfort watched him, the picture of his last Sunday in Bermuda arose before him: the little Negro child astride his mother's back, spurring her like a rider his horse; and in his ears rang the pleasant voice of his silver-haired pastor. At the piazza steps he called a servant to take away the pony, and turned to enter the house, followed by Mr. Pollock, with Jesse in his arms and Charles by his side. Jesse kept up an incessant chatter. They passed through the breakfast-room, where Montfort placed the child upon the floor.

"Charles, help me build my houses!" he cried, attracted to his late employment at sight of the golden eagles. "See, papa, all my houses tumble down. Charles' houses don't fall down, but mine always do. Come and help me, Charles."

"You are not patient enough, my son," replied the father, smiling down upon his petu-

POLLOCK STOOD A LITTLE APART, GAZING IN AMAZEMENT
AT THE SCENE BEFORE HIM.

lance. "You must be patient and persevere, and after awhile you will be able to make your houses stand. Isn't that right, Mr. Pollock?"

Pollock stood a little apart, gazing in amazement at the scene before him. *Golden eagles given to a child to play with* was a little beyond him. He made no direct reply to Mr. Montfort's remark, and if the latter had been an observant man, he might have been a bit puzzled at the expression on his face. But Charles Montfort was ingenuousness itself, seeing in no man an enemy. Anson Pollock was his opposite; his ruling passion was covetousness. His eyes were fairly dazzled by the sight of the gold so carelessly strewing the floor. It positively took away his breath.

"Come, Pollock, we will talk over those matters in my study," said Montfort presently. "My son," he added, as he paused at the doorway, "be careful not to lose your ducats. They are your portion to pay your college bills when you cross the ocean to finish your education."

"Going to send him abroad to study?" carelessly inquired Pollock.

"Oh, yes; America's all right for me, but bonny England for my boys."

Anson Pollock, whom Charles Montfort had chosen for his friend, was a man of dashing appearance. He carried his years jauntily, and

had a good opinion of himself where women
were concerned. He was made much of by
the ladies in the vicinity because of his wealth.
It mattered not that his wife had died myste-
riously. Rumor said his ill treatment and infi-
delity had driven her to suicide; it had even
been whispered that he had not hesitated to
whip her by proxy through his overseer, Bill
Sampson, in the same way he did his slaves;
but rumor is a lying jade. Nevertheless, his
fair speech, auburn curls and deep-blue eyes, so
falsely smiling, won his way, and Mr. Pollock
was the popular ladies' man of two counties.

He had showered Mrs. Montfort with as-
siduous attention since her arrival three years
before, but he soon found that he made no
headway. Once he dared to tell her of his passion — that from the first moment he saw her
aboard the " Island Queen " he had been mad-
dened by her beauty.

"Why do you tell me this?" she cried, in
angry amazement at his daring. "Am I so
careless of my husband's honor that his friends
feel at liberty to insult me?"

"Granted that I overstep the bounds of
friendship in speaking thus to you, but it is
from no lack of respect; rather the deed of
one who risks all upon one throw of the dice.
Have mercy, I pray you, and grant me your
friendship — your love."

Then Grace Montfort said, while her eyes blazed with wrath: "Mr. Pollock, we are strangers here, my husband and I. He trusts you, and I have no wish to disturb that trust; but if you ever address such words to me again, I shall let Mr. Montfort know the kind of man you are. I promise you that he will know how to deal with you." This conversation had taken place one night at a grand fête, where Grace had been the belle of the assembly; they were in the conservatory at the time. Anson Pollock was not accustomed to having his advances received in this way by any woman whom he elected to honor with his admiration. As the indignant woman swept back to the ballroom, he stood and watched her with an evil look, which meant no good. After that they met as usual, but Pollock had never ventured to speak to her again of love. Outwardly he was the same suave, genial gentleman, but within his breast was a living fire of hatred. The two men became faster friends than ever. Mrs. Montfort was pleased to have it so; they had so few friends in this alien land; she felt so lonely, so helpless. She dreaded making enemies. It was but the lull before the storm.

When the study door had closed behind the two men, Mr. Montfort dropped his pleasant, careless manner and faced Mr. Pollock with an anxious face.

"Pollock," he began abruptly, "I'm worried."

"What about?" asked Pollock, turning from the window, where he seemed to be viewing the landscape.

"Have you heard the rumors about my wife being of African descent?" Montfort asked, coming very close to Pollock, as though afraid the very air would hear him. "There are threats, too, against my life because of my desire to free my slaves."

"Nonsense!" exclaimed Pollock. "I have heard the rumors about Mrs. Montfort, but that is nothing — nothing but the malice of some malicious, jealous woman. As for the threats against your life, how can you think of such things a second time. You are among the most chivalrous people on the face of the earth, who will protect you in your home."

Montfort stood a moment before his friend, gazing at him earnestly; then he said: "Pollock, if anything happens to me, I want you to promise me to help my wife and babies to get back to Bermuda."

"Why, what can happen, man; you are nervous without a cause."

"In that safe," continued Montfort, not heeding the interruption, "you will find money and deeds; promise me that you will save them for my family."

"I promise; but it is all nonsense."

"I shall hold you to your promise," replied Montfort solemnly.

The committee on public safety generally met once a month. They had a chairman, but no one knew his identity save a chosen few of the committee. Indeed very little was known positively as to the identity of any of the members; certainly no one would ever have suspected the elegant Anson Pollock of being connected with such an organization.

On this particular evening Bill Sampson lounged by the Jefferson house on the lookout for some of his friends. Anson Pollock sat on the broad steps, evidently on the watch for some one, too. "Hi, Bill!" he called, as the latter came in sight.

"Holloa! want me?" returned Bill; and at a nod from his employer, he followed him through the entrance to a small back room, generally used for the meetings of the committee.

"Anything new for the committee to-night?" asked Pollock, as he lounged over the back of a chair. Bill took a seat on the edge of the table and began cutting circles in the air with his rawhide. Bill Sampson was a char-acter in his way. One could not imagine Newbern without Bill, and no one could possibly imagine Bill without his rawhide.

"Wall, mabby, mabby; depends on what you call wurk. Somebody," with a sly glance at Pollock from beneath his bushy eyebrows, "somebody's been circlatin' a r'port about a fren' o' yourn."

"Well," replied Pollock sharply.

"Looks like we'd treed a 'possum, sho."

"Well."

"Somebody says how's Montfort's slaves is wurkin' fur part pay; leastways, every mother's son o' them'll be free inside o' five years."

"Anything else?"

"We kin' o' thought that'd do fer a spell. He's done nuff in that ar to convict him an' buy his halter. Thet'll do fer one pint."

"But that don't cover the case. What luck have you had in spreading the other report?"

"Wall," said Bill, as he shot a copious draught of tobacco juice over the sanded floor, "mos' the fellers think it a pity 'bout Mis' Montfort. Blamed nice 'ooman. She's been mighty good to Jeff Peterson's fam'ly, an' Jeff he feels mighty uncomf'table 'bout hurtin' on her, durned ef he don'."

"You and Jeff want to do your duty," replied Pollock. "No matter about sentiment. Influence is great with certain people, and if niggers are tolerated in any way, it will end in weakening the law, and then good-by to our institutions."

"Course, course; we 'tend ter do our duty; yas, sir, our whol duty; but it beats all nater 'bout Mis' Montfort. I knowed she wuz mixed the minute I seed her, but 'ain't nuff to 'tract 'tention." He paused a moment, and then said with a sigh: "Well, Cap'n, what's yer orders?"

Pollock saw that the man's sympathy was more than half enlisted on the woman's side, and with arch diplomacy changed his tactics. He handed Bill a cigar, saying, "We may as well make ourselves comfortable"; and before the latter had fairly begun to enjoy the fragrant weed, had called for whiskey and was pressing him to help himself. Under its stimulating influence Bill soon lost what slight scruples he had felt, and was as eager for the downfall of the unfortunate family as his patron.

"Well, Bill," continued Pollock, "the first thing to be done is to put Montfort out of the way; then it will be plain sailing. The next question is: Who will do that job?"

"Reckon I know jes' the man — a man o' the right sperrit, who'll be glad to serve his country fer a reasun'ble consideration. An' thet remin's me, how much o' the property is to be resarved fer you?"

"The boys may have what they can get of it; I don't care for any part of the spoils; all I want is the mother and the children."

"Jes' so; wall, now, seein's I understan' the case jes' as you want it, I'll lay low, set the boys on; you keep shady an' stan' ready the minute the mine's fired. I ain't got a cuss agin Montfort myself, but the institootion must be respected. Sure thar's plenty o' whiskey an' stuff in the cellur? 'Twould look kin' o' mean in Montfort not to have a full cellur. It's a big job, an' the boys'll be thirsty." With this, the two worthies arose from their seats and sauntered through the door and up to the bar.

A day or two after the foregoing, Hank Davis, true to his word, formally applied to Mr. Montfort for the position of overseer on his plantation.

"What made you think that I wanted an overseer?" asked Montfort, as he pushed his hat off his face a little farther and eyed the petitioner critically, mentally vowing that he would never place even a horse in the power of such an ill-favored, beastly looking fellow.

"Wall, most Southern gentlemen don't keer ter have a nigger overseer. It spiles 'em; they gives themselves airs, an' git sot up in thar idees. Thought mabby you, bein' a stranger, mightn't know our ways. You see, it's jes' hyar, we have certain rules in this commoonity that we all mus' 'bide by ef we want t'void trouble." As Hank ventured this last remark in a cautious manner, he scraped the gravel of the walk with one foot while he slyly noted the reception of his venture by an upward cast of his eye.

Charles Montfort looked at him a moment with a slumbering wrath before he asked with dangerous coolness: "What do I understand by what you have just said, Mr. Davis? Do you mean to insinuate that a man cannot do as he will with his own property?"

"Wall, no; not eggsactly; but it's jes' hyar, to speak plainly as 'tween fren's," replied Hank, as he shifted his tobacco to the other side of his mouth, "the plain fac' is: I want the job of drivin' yer niggers, an' you'll want me to keep the commoonity fren'ly to yer now it's got out thet yer a-gwine ter set the gang free byme by."

Charles Montfort possessed one character-istic of the West Indian to a marked degree, and that was a bad temper under just provo-cation. Without more ado he seized the offending Hank by the collar, and with his riding whip, which he carried in his hand, he administered a sound flogging to the offender. As he released him, he said: "When you leave my grounds, don't you ever set your foot inside the gates again, or it will be the worse for you."

Hank said nothing as he raised himself from the ground where the irate man had thrown him, but as he turned to leave the place he looked at Mr. Montfort; and even in his wrath at the insolence of such a mongrel cur, as he mentally styled Davis, Charles Montfort felt a shudder of real physical fear pass over him for a moment. Surprised at himself, he turned to enter the house, dismissing the whole incident as a piece of impudence which he had done well to chastise.

Taking it all in all, Mr. Montfort was not feeling very happy on this June morning, as he sat upon the piazza thinking over the late encounter. An hour passed swiftly away; still the master of the house continued his meditations; but now he had changed his seat for a thoughtful promenade up and down the broad piazza. Finally he said softly to himself: "Yes, that is just what I will do; I'll send Gracie and the little fellows home for awhile on a visit, and there they shall stay until I know just what the trouble is here about the slaves, and certain insinuations concerning my family are cleared up." When a man makes up his mind that he has solved a difficult problem that has worried him, he generally has an air of relief which

is the more pathetic, that in nine cases out of
ten he does not believe that his remedy will
prove effective, although he fancies that he so
believes.

When Hank Davis left Mr. Montfort he
moved slowly down the sun-baked road, nursing his wrath and swearing vengeance. Nothing but the life of the man who had inflicted
such an insult upon him could wipe it out. He
had received the same treatment that he had
given hundreds of his associates, until his name
and presence had become a terror in the
county where he resided. Hitherto he had
given his orders and they had been obeyed;
but here was a man, a comparative stranger, for
whom he considered that he had been willing
to do a great kindness, for a consideration,
and not only had he met with a refusal of his
request but at the same time had received
personal violence of a character that was most
galling to the spirit of any free-born Southern man — an ordinary cowhiding, such as he
would mete out to his slave. As he thought
more and more about the matter he grew more
and more filled with a desire for vengeance, —
not the ordinary kind, but something extraordinary. As he gradually turned over in his
mind schemes for the undoing of the Montforts, he was accosted by the voice of Bill

Sampson, calling to him from across the fields.
Bill was overseeing the harvesting of a great
field of cotton, and the voices of the slaves
could be heard droning out their weird and
plaintive notes, as they sought by song movement to lighten the monotony of their heavy
tasks and bring solace to their sad hearts.
Some, in their simple ignorance, may not have
known why they were sad, but, like the captive
bird, their hearts longed for that which was
ever the birthright of man — property in himself. Crushed out of sight for many years, the
seed of desire for all those things which make
a man, and sweeten toil, was struggling ever
toward the light of civilization denied to these
poor, ignorant, enslaved souls.

Hank sat down on a log by the wayside and
beckoned Bill over to him. The latter came
slowly across the field and seated himself astride
one end of the log.

"Howdy, Hank"; "Howdy, Bill," passed in
greeting between the two cronies.

"'Pears like to me, Hank, yer a-lookin' pale,"
remarked Bill, as he trailed his whip backward
and forward in the dust.

Hank could stand it no longer; and with a
terrible imprecation, he unfolded to his friend
his tale of woe and insult. Bill listened with
eager curiosity, and a satisfied, knowing look

might have been seen to settle about the corners of his eyes and mouth.

"Wall, wall," said he, "these ar' great times
when a d—— West Ingy half-white nigger can
raise his hand agin a white man. Be yer hurt
much, Hank?"

"Some in my body, but more in my feelin's."

"What ar' we a-comin' to? I tell you, Hank,
it is 'bout time sumthin' was done."

"That's all well enough to talk," replied Hank,
"but what kin a man do agin the money thet
thet feller's got to back him up? I cayn't see
a handle on him."

"Wall," replied Bill, " I *kin*."

"You *kin!*" exclaimed Hank, while a slow
smile of derision covered his face; "wall, I'd jes'
like to know how."

"Yer kin laugh, Hank Davis, but it's a fac'.
'Taint goin' to be no hard job, nuther, to git all
thet money, all them purty trinkets and fine
furniture, and the seven hundred niggers in our
pockets *ef*"— (and here he paused as though
to give emphasis to his words) "*ef* we wurks
the thing right."

"Damn it all, man, why don't yer let out?"
demanded Hank, as he rose excitedly from his
seat on the log. "I'm the man to help on anythin' agin thet man, an' yer knows it. No need
of yer bein' so infernal aggravatin' 'bout tellin'
me."

Bill laughed at his companion's excitement. "Easy thar, easy, Hank. This ar' a mighty titlish job, but we kin wurk it — we kin wurk it. Fust place, yer see Montfort's brought them slaves o' hisn hyar and don't tend to keep 'em only 'bout ten years, and then every one o' them will have bought hisself, accordin' to the laws thet ar' governin' them over to the West Indies. Now, yer know ther's a bad eggsample to set befo' the niggers roun' this town. Eny way, we's goin' to think so," drawled Bill, with an expressive wink at his friend. "It's a law of the United States that ef eny man is caught creatin' dissatisfacshun among the slaves he desarves death, and death he gits. Now, this ar Montfort has been causin' trouble fer us by his eggsample. Every nigger roun' hyar knows all 'bout his 'rangements fer givin' his slaves thar freedom, and I tell yer, Hank, its causin' dissatisfacshun 'mong all our slaves. An' then the money, honey, the money! sech sights of it all done up in little shammy-skin bags, an' thet boy Jesse settin' on the floor amoosin' hisself buildin' houses with them gold eagles!"

Hank listened to his companion's words with open mouth. As the latter finished he said, with a look of admiration: "Wall, I'll be d——d! Now, look a-hyar, Bill Sampson, yer needn't tell me thet all thet yer have just unfolded to me is

yer own idees, 'cause yer could no more hev
got them thoughts through yer thick head than
I could. Some one's been fixin' yer up. Out
with it now, an' tell me the whole thing. Ef
we's goin' inter this business, we's got to be
square on the deal with our fren's. Who's the
bottom o' this thing?"

Bill produced a plug of tobacco, offered his
friend a chew and took one himself. "What
I'm tellin' yer, Hank, is 'tween fren's," said he,
chewing and crossing his legs.

"Jes' so," replied Hank.

"I wuz tellin' yer the 'riginater o' this plan,
or I wuz about to." Bill paused to spit out
some of his tobacco juice on the ground, so that
it would not overflow the tank, so to speak, and
run out of each corner of his mouth. "Beats
all nater, Hank, how a man'll git dead set onter
a piece o' caliker."

"Meanin' by that, Bill, that Ans Pollock's
got set on some gal."

"Fact!" said Bill, with a wink.

"Who's?" asked Hank.

"It mote be Mis' Montfort herself, Hank."

"Sho, you don' say, re'lly," said Hank, with
a wicked look. "Don' blame him, blamed ef I
do. But thet's all the good it'll do him."

Bill cut the air into imaginary circles with
his whip, and without taking any notice of his

friend, continued: " As I was sayin', Ans Pollock, he says ter me, ' Bill, thet's a dooced purty 'ooman o' Montfort's,' an' I tol' him what I thought 'bout her havin' black blud in her somewhar. ' Mabby,' says he, ' mabby.' An' then he says, kin' o' generous like, ' I'd take the 'ooman an' the two brats, an' the boys might hev the slaves, an' the money, an' the fixin's in the house.' I tol' him I knew the boys 'd stan' by him in enything he might do to rid a peace- ful neighborhood of sech a disturbin' critter as Montfort. I tol' him I thought yer would be 'bout the very match to light on Montfort, so he wouldn't give us eny more trouble. An' so we've been waitin' fer the business ter 'velop itself good an' ripe, an' I jes' think this 'tack o' Montfort's on yer will 'bout do the business fer the whole o' them.

" Bill," said Hank Davis, as he held out his hand to his friend, " we's allers been pardners, an' I reckon we allers will be."

CHAPTER IV.

THE TRAGEDY.

Thus man devotes his brother, and destroys him;
And worse than all, and most to be deplored
Chains him, and tasks him and exacts his sweat
With stripes that Mercy, with a bleeding heart,
Weeps when she sees inflicted on a beast.
— Cowper.

"Kismet," says the Oriental, when unaccountable evils beset his path; "It is fate," says the Anglo-Saxon, under like circumstances: but fate is the will of Providence after all. Nature avenges herself upon us for every law violated in the mad rush for wealth or position or personal comfort where the rights of others of the human family are not respected. If Charles Montfort had been contented to accept the rulings of the English Parliament, and had allowed his human property to come under the new laws just made for its government, although poorer in the end, he would have spared himself and family all the horrors which were to follow his selfish flight to save that property.

The sun rose clear and resplendent a few mornings later. On this particular morning Nature outdid herself. There was a blending together of all the sweet forces — odorous air, golden sunshine, musical sounds from bird and from bush; it was pure happiness to feel the life-blood leaping in one's veins; to feel the marvelous joy of living.

Eight o'clock was the usual breakfast hour for the Montforts. The family had just assembled at the table; Aunt Cindy had brought in the great silver coffee urn and placed it beside Mrs. Montfort. Mr. Montfort had settled himself in his chair with a weekly paper, for in this rural neighborhood a newspaper once in a week was a great luxury, when his attention was caught by the sound of hoofbeats of several horses on the road. Mrs. Montfort, with usual Southern hospitality, looked over her well-appointed board to make sure that all was in order for dispensing those creature comforts so dear to the entertainer and the entertained.

The hoofbeats drew nearer and paused on the graveled walk. Montfort hastened to the door, while Mrs. Montfort turned toward the entrance of the breakfast-room with a pleasant smile of welcome on her lips. She heard a number of voices speaking together in an excited jumble, then a shot, followed by a heavy fall. Little Jesse ran from his station by his mother's side through one of the long windows opening upon the piazza. She heard his scream of "papa, papa!" and then again the jumble of excited voices. With little Charles clinging to her skirts she stumbled blindly to the entrance and faced the crowd of angry men, headed by Anson Pollock. Hank Davis had done his work well, and Charles Montfort lay dead with a bullet in his brain, sped by an unseen hand. Mrs. Montfort's arms were grasped by rude hands, and she was forcibly drawn out upon the veranda, where in the sunlight of the beautiful morning she saw the body of her husband lying face downward. She was dimly conscious of hearing the cries of frightened slaves mingled with the screams of her children. Through it all she realized but two things — that the lifeless object lying there so still was the body of her husband, and that the sensual face of Anson Pollock, whom she had grown to loathe and fear, was gloating over her agony, devilish in its triumph. Then she lost consciousness.

As she lay upon the green sward, oblivious to thought and feeling, supported by her weeping maid, who had been ordered to care for her mistress by Mr. Pollock, Hank Davis came and stood for a moment looking down upon the unconscious woman. Suddenly an evil smile lighted up his countenance. He looked around, but saw nothing of Anson Pollock, who had disappeared within the house, searching for money and papers in the safe. Now was his time. This woman's husband had flogged him — he would have a sweet revenge. Those lily-like limbs, the tender flesh that had never known aught but the touch of love, should *feel the lash as he had.*

He called to Bill Sampson to help lift her; and despite the prayers and tears of the poor slave girl who followed her beloved mistress until Sampson knocked her senseless with the butt end of his rawhide, they bore the hapless lady to the whipping post. She revived as they reached the spot; and when she realized the fate in store for her, the sweet woman's strong soul failed her. She uttered a wild cry of agony as the rough hand of Hank Davis was laid upon her to tear her garments from her shrinking shoulders.

"Charles, my husband, save me!" she cried, and fell fainting upon the ground. There was none to answer the heartrending appeal. He who would have shed his heart's best blood for her, lay cold in death. She was soon restored to consciousness, for Hank's savage instinct for revenge would only be appeased by the victim's full realization of her sufferings.

She was bound to the whipping post as the victim to the stake, and lashed with rawhides alternately by the two strong, savage men. Hank Davis drew first blood by reason of his wrongs at Mr. Montfort's hands. With all his mighty strength he brought the lash down upon the frail and shrinking form. O God! was there none to rescue her! The air whistled as the snaky leather thong curled and writhed in its rapid, vengeful descent. A shriek from the victim — a spurt of blood that spattered the torturer — a long, raw gash across a tender, white back. Hank gazed at the cut with critical satisfaction, as he compared its depth with the skin and blood that encased the long, tapering lash. It was now Bill's turn.

"I'll go you one better," he said, as he sighted the distance and exact place to make his mark with mathematical precision, at the same time shifting his tobacco from the right to the left cheek. Again the rawhide whistled through the air, falling across the other cut squarely in the center. Another shriek, a stifled sob, a long-drawn quivering sigh — then the deep stillness of unconsciousness. Again and again was the outrage repeated. Fainting fit followed fainting fit. The blood stood in a pool about her feet.

When Hank Davis had satiated his vengeful thirst he cut the ropes which bound her, and she sank upon the ground again — unconscious,

bleeding, friendless, alone.   Lucy had hidden
in the smokehouse with the two children, that
they might not witness their mother's agony.

Meantime, the committee on public safety,
instigated by Anson Pollock to put down an
imaginary insurrection (having no existence
but in his own mind, and supposed to have
originated with the slaves of Charles Montfort)
and to legalize the looting of the house, took
possession of the mansion. Soon the crowd
had stripped it of its furniture and all the
articles of value. The house itself was fired,
and Grace Montfort again became conscious
of her misery in time to see the dead body of
her husband flung amid the burning rafters of
his dwelling. Two and two the slaves were
handcuffed together to be driven to the market
place. Mrs. Montfort, secured to her maid,
was placed in a wagon with her two children;
and so the miserable woman was driven away
from her outraged home.

In those old days, if accused of aiding slaves
in a revolt, a white man stood no more chance
than a Negro accused of the same crime. He
forfeited life and property. This power of the
law Anson Pollock had invoked; and to add
to the devilishness of the plot, had used Bill
Sampson's suggestion of black blood in Mrs.
Montfort, to further his scheme for possessing

the beautiful woman. So the two children and
their mother fell to the lot of Anson Pollock
as his portion of the spoils. Shortly after
these events Grace Montfort disappeared and
was never seen again. The waters of Pamlico
Sound tell of sweet oblivion for the broken-
hearted found within their soft embrace.

After the loss of their mother the two lads
clung very closely to each other. So many
changes had come to them, such desperate,
bloody scenes had dazed their brains and ter-
rified them, that even the loss of their mother
seemed but in keeping with the rest. Bewilderment at so much sorrow, the numbness of
black despair was ever with them.

Pollock's rage was terrible when he learned
that Mrs. Montfort had destroyed herself. He
grew morose and unsociable, so that his society
was no longer sought in the county. He
seemed to have a superstitious fear of the children, and for a long time would not tolerate
them in his presence. It was common talk
among the slaves that Mrs. Montfort " walked,"
weeping and wringing her hands, night after
night about the plantation.

But wonder could go no farther when Pollock elected to take Lucy in the place he had
designed for Mrs. Montfort. God's mysteries
are past man's understanding; and thus the

poor black girl became his instrument to temper the wind to the shorn lambs.   Night after
night she stole away to the little attic under the
eaves laden with dainties to tempt the appetite
of the children.   For hours she would sit hush-
ing Jesse's sobs upon her ample breast, and
speaking words of comfort in her poor, blind
way to Charles.

When a year had dragged its slow length
past, a stranger in the town stopped Bill
Sampson on the street one day and asked him
if he knew where he could hire a likely boy to
go with him into the woods for a few days and
help arrange specimens of the quartz in that
locality.   He was looking up the minerals in
that section for speculators, he said.   Bill promised to get him a boy, and asked Pollock's permission for Charles to go with the man.

" I don't care what you do with him, only
keep him away from me.   I'll sell him south
soon," said Pollock.

So it happened that Charles went every day
for a month with the mineralogist.   The lad's
appearance, education and refinement puzzled
the man for a time, until he learned the tragic
story.

" Charles," said he, a few weeks later, " I am
about to leave this part of the country.   I don't
want to leave you here.   Do you think Mr.

Pollock could be induced to part with you?"

"O sir!" cried Charles, throwing himself at the gentleman's feet, "for the love of God buy me and my little brother. If you will only take us to Bermuda, some one there will pay you back. My father had money there; we have friends there. O sir, for the love of God!"

The man looked at the weeping boy as through a mist. He had a tender heart.

"I will tell you something, Charles," said he kindly, as he raised the lad and drew him to a seat beside him on the grass, with his arm tenderly enfolding the child. "I am an Englishman, but it will not do to have that fact known here, for then I would be powerless to help you. Anson Pollock would never sell you to me if he knew that fact. I have been trying to buy you and Jesse, but Pollock wants to keep the boy for a valet. He intends to sell you south; you are too old to forget, and he fears you. Now I propose to buy you; and as soon as possible I shall take you to Bermuda, collect the proofs there concerning your family, and then go to England, invoke the power of the home government, and demand Jesse's freedom and indemnity from the United States government for all the outrages perpetrated against your family. Can you keep this secret, and will you try and be patient until I can accomplish my purpose?"

"I will do anything you say," replied the boy humbly, "but I hate to leave Jesse. O mama, mama, my beautiful mama!" and with a burst of grief he cast himself upon the velvet turf.

The mineralogist lost no time in completing the purchase of Charles, and in a few days they left the town. Then little Jesse, the petted darling of a luxurious home, found himself alone in the power of Anson Pollock. He must wait upon him obsequiously by day, and be ready to answer his call at any hour of the night. Under his enemy's eye by day and night, hopeless, utterly alone upon the wide waste of waters which represented his life. Oh, how black, boundless, trackless, was the unknown future to this unfortunate child! Once, after his brother was sold, he resisted his master — rebelled with all his puny strength. He was severely flogged. That night he slept in the lonely cabin kept as a sort of prison for refractory slaves. Not a sigh disturbed the silence of the night as he lay in pain, gazing up at the stars which shone so peacefully through the dilapidated roof. He thought himself delirious, or was it indeed possible that God had taken compassion on his loneliness and allowed the comfort and help of communion with the dead! He saw his murdered father and mother.

Hand in hand they passed and repassed over the gaping holes in the roof of the hut. His father's noble, loving face smiled upon him; his mother's curls moved in the faint breeze, while her loving glance seemed to say: "Courage, courage, we are ever near you."

"Father, Grace, speak to me!" he shrieked in agony.

Then he seemed to feel their actual presence, tangible though viewless, beside him in the hut. Calmness came to him, and a change grand to see in that slight frame. Unconsciously he asked the question: "How long must I endure before I join you in heaven?"

It seemed to him that he was answered: "Many days, and even years; but fear not, we will never leave thee."

After that night Jesse's childhood appeared to slip from him, and he became a man in thought. He studied his master, and matched low cunning with lofty determination. He rebelled no more, was silent, not provoking Anson Pollock's wrath. The time seemed long and dreary waiting for the freedom he had resolved to have; still he was patient. Sometimes at night, when rolled in his blanket on the hard floor, he would weep over the painful past. Then he would feel the touch of a tiny hand upon his eyelids. It was his mother's hand; he knew it to be so. Then he would lose himself in sweet dreams and awaken in the morning refreshed and comforted. So the years rolled on until he was sixteen. Meantime, nothing was heard from Charles and his supposed friend. Jesse had made up his mind that Charles was either dead or else lost to him forever.

Jesse was now a man in stature, though still slender, with the same haughty bearing and distinguished appearance that had marked his father. Anson Pollock, upon whom age and the memory of dreadful crimes were making fearful inroads, began to look up to the boy and lean upon him for aid in his various plans for making money. He had spoken to him of making him the overseer, in place of Bill Sampson, and had even hinted at his taking a mate. Then Jesse knew that his probation was nearly over. That spring Pollock, as was the common practice among planters, made out passes for Jesse and sent him to New York in charge of a vessel filled with produce, and charged to bring back necessary merchandise for use on the plantation. Pollock thought the boy still too young to venture to leave him. Indeed Jesse had no such idea when he started on his trip to the North. When the vessel reached New York, Jesse performed all the necessary duties

— disposed of the produce, and reloaded the ship for its homeward voyage. The night before they were to sail he sat on the wharf watching the crews of other vessels making ready for departure. His mind was engrossed with thoughts of Charles. He feared some evil had befallen him.

"At any rate," he said to himself, "I shall never see him again. And must I remain in servitude? Can I do nothing to help myself, since all hope is gone in that direction?" Just then a group of men paused in front of him. They did not know he was a slave.

"Will you give passage to two on board your vessel? You are bound for Newbern in the morning, aren't you? We'll pay you what you charge," said one of the group respectfully.

"Speak to the cap'n," called out a man standing near; "that's nuthin' but a nigger you're talkin' to."

"Well," said the one who had first addressed him, "you're a likely boy, anyhow; who do you belong to?"

Jesse arose from his seat, white with passion, and said to the man: "I am no man's property; I belong to Jesus Christ!" The question had answered itself. When the vessel sailed the next morning, Jesse was far on his road to Boston.

Traveling then was done by stage, and was a slow process; but about a week later he stood beside the stone wall that enclosed the historic Boston Common, and as he watched the cows chewing their peaceful cuds and inhaled deep draughts of freedom's air, he vowed to die rather than return to Anson Pollock.

He found work in Boston. It mattered not that it was menial work; he was happy. But fate or Providence was not done with him yet.

One day he received word that Anson Pollock was on his way to Boston in search of him. Again he made a hurried journey. This time to Exeter, N. H. In his character of a fugitive slave, the lad had from the first cast his lot with the colored people of the community, and when he left Boston he was directed to see Mr. Whitfield, a negro in Exeter, who could and would help the fugitive.

Late one afternoon, just before tea time, a comely black woman stood in her long, low-raftered kitchen preparing supper before the open fireplace. There was every indication of plenty in the homely furnishings. As the woman passed rapidly from the cupboard to the table she would touch with her foot the rockers of the little red cradle which stood in the center of the floor. The baby in it was crying in a fretful way. "Oh, hush, Lizzie," said the mother; "don't be so cross." There came a low rap at the open door, and in answer to her "Come in," Jesse stepped into the room.

"Is Mr. Whitfield in?" he asked, as he doffed his hat respectfully.

"No," was the reply, "but I expect him every minute. Sit down, won't you? He'll soon be in to his supper, I guess."

Mrs. Whitfield thought him a white man, come on business with her husband. "A handsome lad," she thought. Jesse seated himself; and then as the child continued to cry, said: "Shall I rock the cradle for you, ma'am? The child seems fretful."

Fifteen years later Jesse married Elizabeth Whitfield, the baby he had rocked to sleep the first night of his arrival in Exeter. By her he had a large family.

Thus he was absorbed into that unfortunate race, of whom it is said that a man had better be born dead than to come into the world as part and parcel of it.

CHAPTER V.

MA SMITH'S LODGING-HOUSE.

LET not Ambition mock their useful toil,
  Their homely joys, and destiny obscure;
Nor Grandeur hear with a disdainful smile
  The short and simple annals of the poor.
                                    — GRAY.

"THANK heaven that is done," said Dora, as she sat down wearily in her mother's large rocker in the cosy kitchen. She had been upstairs the best portion of the day preparing a room for an expected lodger. There had been windows to wash, paint to clean, a carpet to tack down, curtains to hang and furniture to place in position — in short, the thousand and one things to do that are essential to the comfort of the lodger and the good reputation of the house.

"Are you very tired, daughter?" queried her mother, as she glanced with loving pride at the graceful figure before her, at the smooth bands of dark-brown hair, now a little ruffled and disordered, and at the delicate brown face, now somewhat puckered and out of sorts from weariness.

"Well, not very tired, mummy dear; only this continual scrub and dig is not always the cheerful work we would like to think it. Still I don't care as long as the house pays."

The mother sighed as she asked: "Did you give her the front or back square?"

"Oh, I gave her the front square after all. She's too beautiful for that dreary back room. I know that it is not business to let a good-paying room go under our usual price, but she's a 'steady'; she has the best of references. Father Andrew gives her the best of characters, and so I'll chance getting my money back out of the next cross-grained old bachelor who comes along. See how mercenary I am getting to be since I undertook to direct the fortunes of a lodging-house"; and with a gay laugh the daughter jumped from her seat, every trace of fatigue gone, and grasping her mother about the waist, whirled her around the room to the accompaniment of a sweet, shrill whistle of the latest popular waltz. In the midst of the frolic there came a loud ring of the doorbell, and placing her panting and protesting mother in the rocker just vacated, she vanished; and soon her voice was heard above, as she directed the placing of the luggage of the expected lodger.

The Smith family consisted of the mother, daughter and son. A few years before the

opening of our story the father had died, leaving a delicate wife, a young daughter, and a
son just ready to enter college; also a house
in a respectable part of the South End of
Boston, Mass., with a heavy mortgage upon it.
Like many colored men living in large cities,
his life had been a continual struggle with poverty and hard work, combined with a desire for
advancement for his children, and a clean, self-
respecting citizenship for himself.   Smith was a
free-born Southern Negro — a Virginian.   His
father had bought himself and married a free
woman.   After the birth of Henry his mother
died; and when his father married again, his
aunts brought him to the city of New Bedford,
where he had imbibed, along with copious
draughts of salt air, an unwavering desire for
all the blessings of liberty, and strong notions
that a man must depend upon himself in great
measure and carve out his own fortune to the
best of his ability with such tools as God had
furnished him.

Henry Smith's early manhood was spent
upon the sea; and when he at last settled in
Boston, he could converse about foreign ports
and countries with the ease and familiarity of
personal knowledge.   Possessed of very little
education, yet he concealed the fact admirably
under a naturally intelligent manner.   Soon

after he ceased to follow the sea he married a handsome Mulattress from New Hampshire, and with her help saved a small sum of money — enough to make the first payment on a home; then began the struggle of their lives. The masses of the Negro race find for employment only the most laborious work at the scantiest remuneration. A man, though a skilled mechanic, has the door of the shop closed in his face here among the descendants of the liberty-loving Puritans. The foreign element who come to the shores of America soon learn that there is a class which is called its inferior, and will not work in this or that business if "niggers" are hired; and the master or owner, being neither able nor willing to secure enough of the despised class to fill the places of the white laborers, acquiesces in the general demand, and the poor Negro finds himself banned in almost every kind of employment. Henry Smith had his ambitions; but like all of his meek race, he would not or at least had no desire to contend with the force of prejudice, and quietly took up his little business of repairing old clothes in the same patient spirit of the Jew "old clo'" vender or pawnbroker.

Two children were born to this worthy couple — William Jesse Montfort and Dora Grace Montfort. When Willie was seventeen

and Dora twelve their father sickened and died.
Thenceforth the burden of the support of the
little family fell upon the mother. Willie was
preparing to enter college, but he cheerfully
gave up his plans and secured a place as bellboy in one of the fashionable hostelries with
which Boston abounds; and soon by his attention to business, his gentlemanly manners,
and intelligent understanding of all that was
required of him, made himself invaluable to
his employers. Twenty dollars a month with
board and " tips " was a very respectable showing for a lad of seventeen, and Willie felt himself repaid when he saw the great help and
comfort his small earnings gave to his dear
mother. Dora was kept at her studies until
she was graduated from the high school. Meantime Mrs. Smith, or " Ma " Smith, as she was
called by all the young people of her acquaintance, increased their income by letting
furnished rooms. The mother and daughter
shared the same sleeping-room, and Will declared himself in favor of an attic chamber as
being the least desirable for renting purposes.
There he established himself in a very comfortable nest, furnished after the fashion dear
to all young fellows' hearts, with everything
" handy." The only occasions upon which Will
and Dora were known to quarrel were the

weekly cleaning days, when the latter would insist on "tidying up Will's room." Then shoes were moved from the mantel and the blacking brushes from the top of the dressing-case; collars, cuffs and ties were placed in their proper receptacles, and garments hung in the clothespress. Then Will would scold a good deal because he "couldn't find things," but by the next morning he would have them "handy" again. Many lodgers were obtained through Will's acquaintance with young men at the hotel where he worked, and very soon the mother was able to see that the debt upon the home which she hoped to leave her children, was slowly but surely disappearing. Deep in her heart was the cherished hope that when the mortgage was paid Willie would be free to choose a profession; but they never mentioned among themselves the hope which was cherished in each breast.

As the years rolled slowly by the children saw that their mother could not do as much as formerly; and so by degrees, after Dora had finished school, the burden of the care of the house fell upon her strong young shoulders, and 1896 found her taking full charge, and proving herself to be a woman of ability and the best of managers, husbanding their small income to the best advantage.

With about every avenue for business closed against them, it is surprising that so many families of color manage to live as well as they do and to educate their children and give them a few of the refinements of living, — such as cultivating a musical talent, gratifying a penchant for languages, or for carving, or for any of the arts of a higher civilization, so common among the whites, but supposed to be beyond the reach of a race just released from a degrading bondage. Whatever grace or accomplishment may be the order of the hour, it is copied or practiced among some portion of the colored population. We may well ask ourselves how this is done. Among the white Americans who perform domestic or personal service, how rare it is to meet the brilliant genius of a Frederick Douglass; but with this people it is a common occurrence to find a genius in a profession, trade, or invention, evolved from the rude nurturing received at the hands of a poor father and mother engaged in the lowliest of service, who see not the nobility of their sacrifices in the delight afforded them in watching the unfolding of the bud of promise in their offspring. From the bosom of the earth we take the diamond; pearls from the depth of the sea ; from the lowliest walks of life we cull the hope of a future life beyond the perplexing questions of this present existence. Why should we wonder or question, then, when we see the steady advance of a race overriding the barriers set by prejudice and injustice? Man has said that from lack of means and social caste the Negro shall remain in a position of serfdom all his days, but the mighty working of cause and effect, the mighty unexpected results of the law of evolution, seem to point to a different solution of the Negro question than any worked out by the most fertile brain of the highly cultured Caucasian. Then again, we do not allow for the infusion of white blood, which became pretty generally distributed in the inferior black race during the existence of slavery. Some of this blood, too, was the best in the country. Combinations of plants, or trees, or of any productive living thing, sometimes generate rare specimens of the plant or tree ; why not, then, of the genus homo ? Surely the Negro race must be productive of some valuable specimens, if only from the infusion which amalgamation with a superior race must eventually bring. This is a mighty question. Today, with all the heated discussions of tariff reform, the parity of gold and silver, the hoarding of giant sums of money by trusts and combinations, still the Negro question will not "down"; it is the most important, the mightiest in the land, and is quietly assuming greater proportions as it forges its way to the front to take its place shortly as the gravest question in the councils of the nation.

When Dora returned to the kitchen her mother had about finished the preparations for supper. The short winter afternoon had dropped into early twilight. Every alternate night was Will Smith's early night home from the hotel, and the little family always managed to have an inviting tea and to pass a cheerful evening together. Lately another person had attached himself to the Smiths; a fellow-waiter with Will had finally worked himself into the profession of law, and having established himself in business in a down-town office, had put his admiration for Dora into words, and it was understood that in due course of time they would marry.

Dora lighted the lamps, drew the curtains, and looked about the cosy kitchen with a satisfaction which might well be pardoned, for even in palatial homes a more inviting nest could not be found. The table was carefully spread with a nicely ironed cloth of spotless white, red-bordered napkins lay at each plate, a good quality of plated silverware mingled with the plain, inexpensive white ware in which the meal was to be served. Ma Smith, in her neat calico dress and long white apron, busied herself in making the tea and coffee and seeing that the delicate muffins were browned to just the right turn, while Dora busied herself in putting the finishing touches to a house dress for her mother.

"Well, Dora," said her mother, as she bustled about the room, "does the young woman seem pleased with your arrangements? I am sure she ought to after all the labor you spent on that room."

"She says she is greatly pleased with everything. Say, ma, she's got a typewriter, and she says she picks up a good living at home with it. Talk about your beauties! my, but she's the prettiest creature I ever saw! I expect all the men in this house will be crazy over her."

"Yes, dear," replied her mother with a quiet laugh; "you don't want John making eyes at her, do you?"

Dora laughed as she said: "I'd just drop John P. Langley if I thought he admired any woman more than he did me. But really, ma, you won't be able to keep from loving her; she has the sweetest and saddest face I ever saw. I have read of the woman with a story written on her face, but I never believed it anything but a fairy tale. You'll believe me when you see her and talk with her."

"There are the boys," said her mother, as
the sound of voices reached their ears, together
with the closing of the front door and great
stamping of feet to brush away the snow. The
next moment the door opened, and two young
men entered the cheerful room, and with jest
and laugh bade the two women good evening.

Will Smith was tall and finely formed, with
features almost perfectly chiseled, and a complexion the color of an almond shell. His hair
was black and curly, with just a tinge of crisp-
ness to denote the existence of Negro blood.
His eyes were dark and piercing as an eagle's.
Ladies of high position followed his tall form
with admiring glances as he moved about his
duties at the hotel, and wondered that so
much manly beauty should be wasted upon
an inferior race.

John Langley, his companion, was shorter in
stature and very fair in complexion. His hair
was dark and had no indication of Negro blood
in its waves; his features were of the Caucasian
cut. He possessed a gentle refinement of
manner, apt to take well with the opposite sex;
but to a reader of character, the strong manhood and honesty of purpose which existed in
Will Smith were lacking in John Langley. He
was a North Carolinian — a descendant of slaves
and Southern "crackers." We might call this

a bad mixture — the combination of the worst features of a dominant race with an enslaved race; and in some measure John Langley would bear out the unfavorable supposition upon close acquaintance. Many of his young friends did not care for him because he developed a revengeful trait of character. He liked his ease, and enjoyed indulging himself in every luxury that his modest means would allow. He had, moreover, a carefully concealed strain of sensuality in his nature, which as yet had never been aroused to an overindulgence in illegitimate and questionable pleasures; and with it all he had a mercenary streak, which made love of money his great passion. He possessed great political acumen and was strong in debate, which attracted a certain class of politicians around him. These attributes, combined with the practice of his profession, might eventually make or mar his fortunes in the untried future that stretched before him.

Seated at the pleasant tea table, the gay laugh and jolly joke went round, and even Ma Smith forgot her years and contributed her share of mirth to the general good time.

"Talking about funny things happening," said Ma Smith, "your grandfather, Will, was a comical genius. You know that I have told you there were fourteen in our family — all

girls, and very near each other in age. When
your aunts, Fanny and Lottie, began to receive
company there was a great time to keep it from
father for awhile. Mother was heart and hand
with the girls and wanted to see them have a
pleasant time, but father did not like it. Your
grandfather worked hard and at night was very
tired, so the dear old man would go to bed soon
after his supper and pipe. Then was the girls'
time. A fire was made in the parlor, which
was at the front of the house, a good distance
away from father's room, and by the time the
young man arrived to make his call the old
gentleman was generally sound asleep. One
night, however, things did not work so well.
In those days we had large open fireplaces;
stoves did not come in until I was about
five years old. I can see that low-ceiled parlor
now with its brick hearth and brass andirons
holding the glowing logs, the flames crackling
and shooting upward, the firelight dancing and
shining on the little cupboard doors on each
side of the chimney. There was a rag carpet
on the floor — your grandmother made her
own carpets from rags; and our floors were
covered with large handmade rag mats, for no
housekeeper was counted much who did not
have a large supply of such things. There
were china figures on the mantel, and vases

filled with golden-rod gathered the summer
before. The furniture was mahogany, polished
until you could see your face in any part of it.
There was a red cloth on the table which stood
between the two windows, and in the center of
it was a large astral lamp trimmed about the
edges with long crystal pendants, which we
children called diamonds. We thought nothing could be more elegant than that lamp. It
was a wedding present to your grandmother."

" Did you have kerosene in those days, ma ? "
asked Dora.

" Lord bless you, no; we burned whale oil
or sperm oil in that lamp. Poor people used
candles. Your grandmother used to save her
fat and clarify it and mix it with beeswax to
harden it, and we made our candles every week
as regularly as we did the family cooking.
Sometimes there was danger of the supply of
oil giving out in the stores, and then oil cost
ı great deal of money; that never lasted long,
however, and in a few weeks some New Bedford whaler would be in port with a large cargo
of whale oil, and then there would be a big
supply selling cheap."

"I don't see how you got along without
stoves and things," observed Dora ; " baking
day must have been a terror."

" We had tin kitchens and Dutch ovens.
We never had any trouble."

"What's a tin kitchen?" asked John.

"It's an oven made of tin, for roasting meat. It stood on four legs about a foot from the floor, and had a place for a charcoal fire at the back, and a chimney to carry off the smoke. The front fastened by a hasp to the back and could be let down to put the food on the little grate inside. It was a very convenient arrangement, and I wish I had one this minute. A Dutch oven was very much like our iron kettles which we use for boiling; there was a grate inside to hold the food."

"It must have been a great nuisance keeping house under such circumstances."

"Well, what became of the young man that particular evening, ma?" chimed in Will.

"This night father was restless and did not retire with his usual promptness, and we had only just got him out of the way when the expected caller arrived. However, everything went on very well, and you may be sure that there was much peeping and giggling on the part of the half-grown sisters who were denied the great privilege of the parlor and company as yet. Your grandmother sat in the kitchen knitting and trying to keep the younger children in order, when to her consternation the door opened and in walked father. 'Elizabeth,' said he, 'I hear a man's voice in the parlor.

What's the trouble?' Poor mother tried to explain, and murmured something about a gentleman calling on Fanny. 'A man,' roared father, 'calling on my daughter!' and the first thing we knew, he seized the bucket of water from the kitchen dresser — we had wells in those days, and a bucket of water always stood on the dresser — and started for the parlor and flung the door open. Without speaking to the astonished occupants of the room, he stalked to the fireplace and deliberately poured the water upon the blazing wood; then he turned to the caller and said: 'Young man, if you have a home, go to it; this is no half-way house for the accommodation of young squirts. Fanny,' he said, turning to your aunt, 'you go to bed, and don't let this thing occur again.' The young man left as quickly as possible, and poor Fanny retired to her room greatly mortified."

"That's good discipline for girls," said John with a laugh. "If we had more fathers after that stamp, we fellows would get better wives."

"And we girls better husbands," chimed in Dora. "Still, I pity poor Aunt Fanny."

"The fellow wasn't much or he'd have stuck, and not been driven off that way. I'd have made the old gentleman like me in spite of himself if I had meant business," said Will. "Oh, by the by, did your new lodger come, Dora?"

"Yes; and, Will, I never met anyone so beautiful in all my life. You'll be fascinated when you meet her."

"That's you all over, Dora; all your swans generally turn out geese. I'll bet you a new pair of Easter gloves that she's a rank old maid with false teeth, bald head, hair on her upper lip " —

"All right, Will Smith, all right. Just wait until you see her! I'll wager a new pair of embroidered silk suspenders that you're over head and ears in love with her long before that time."

"I'll hold the stakes," cried John.

They rose from the table now, and John said, with a tender glance at Dora: " I thought some one would enjoy seeing the ' Old Homestead.' It's at the Boston Theatre tonight; don't you want to go, Dora?" Dora's eyes sparkled as he held the two tickets before her.

"Get your things on, Dora; you've just time to reach the theatre before the curtain rises," said her brother.

In a little while the house was quiet, and the mother and son settled down to the enjoyment of a quiet evening together.

CHAPTER VI.

MA SMITH'S LODGING-HOUSE.— *Concluded.*

THE gray day darkened into night,
. . . Made hoary with the swarm
And whirl-dance of the blinding storm,
As zigzag wavering to and fro,
Crossed and recrossed the winged snow.
— WHITTIER.

FEBRUARY drew slowly to a close.   Boston had
lain for the past three or four days in the grasp
of the snow king.   At No. 500 D Street each
tenant seemed content to keep within the
bounds of his or her small domain, literally
"frozed up," as Mrs. Ophelia Davis expressed
it.

No one had seen much of the new lodger.
She passed in and out each morning with a
package of work in her hand; and all day long,
from nine in the morning until late at night
sometimes, the click of the typewriter could be
heard coming from the "first front-square,"
which interpreted meant the front room on the
second floor.   Dora had been very neighborly
and had called on Miss Clark frequently.
There was a great fascination for her about the
quiet, self-possessed woman.   She did not, as
a rule, care much for girl friendships, holding

that a close intimacy between two of the same
sex was more than likely to end disastrously
for one or the other.   But Sappho Clark seemed
to fill a long-felt want in her life, and she had
from the first a perfect trust in the beautiful
girl.

Mrs. Smith had furnished her rooms sub-
stantially and well, but there had been no
attempt at decoration. The first time Dora
entered the room after Sappho had settled herself in it, she was struck at the alteration in its
appearance. The iron bedstead and the wash-
ing utensils were completely hidden by drapery
curtains of dark-blue denim, beautifully embroidered in white floss; a cover of the same
material was thrown over the small table between
the windows; plain white muslin draperies hid
the unsightly but serviceable yellow shades
at the windows; her desk and typewriter occupied the center of the room, and a couch had
been improvised from two packing-cases and
a spring, covered with denim and piled high
with cushions; two good steel engravings completed a very inviting interior.

"How pretty you have made it," observed
Dora, looking curiously around the room.

Sappho came and stood beside her, and
the two girls smiled at each other in a glow
of mutual interest, and became fast friends at
once.

"I always carry these things with me in my travels, and I find that I can make myself very comfortable in a short time with their help."

"I wish you would show me how to do this embroidery," said Dora, as she lifted the edge of the denim curtain before the toilet stand and critically examined it. "This is beautifully done. Where did you learn?"

"I will teach you with pleasure," replied Sappho; but Dora noticed that she did not tell her where she had learned.

"Do you like your work — is it hard?" asked Dora, as she idly wandered from one object to another in the pretty room, pausing beside the desk to glance admiringly at a pile of neatly written sheets, just taken from the machine.

"Oh, I like the work very well. Sometimes the dictator is obtuse, or long-winded, or thinks that the writer ought to do his thinking for him as well as the corrections; then it is not pleasant work. But, generally speaking, I prefer it to most anything that I know of. Do sit down," she continued, pushing a chair toward Dora.

"This man receiveth sinners," read Dora from a pamphlet on the desk, as she turned to accept the offered chair. "I see that is your illuminated text for the day. Are you a Christian?" Then she saw an ivory crucifix suspended at the left side of the desk, and stopped in some confusion.

Sappho dropped the dress she was mending, and for a moment her eyes took on the far-away look of one in deep thought. Finally she said: "I saw you glance at the crucifix. I am not a Catholic, but I have received many benefits and kindnesses at their hands. Your question is a hard one to answer. I am afraid I am not a Christian, as we of our race understand the expression; but I try to do the best I can."

> 'And he who does the best he can
> Need never fear the church's ban
> Nor hell's damnation.
> God recks not how man counts his beads,
> For righteousness is not in creeds
> Nor solemn faces ;
> But rather lies in Christian deeds
> And Christian graces ';

quoted Dora softly. "For my part, I am sick of loud professions and constant hypocrisy. My religion is short, and to the point — feed the starving thief and make him an honest man; cover your friend's faults with the mantle of charity and keep her in the path of virtue."

"Then you are not one of those who think that a woman should be condemned to eternal banishment for the sake of one misstep?"

"Not I, indeed; I have always felt a great curiosity to know the reason why each individual woman loses character and standing in the eyes of the world. I believe that we would hang our heads in shame at having the temerity to judge a fallen sister, could we but know the circumstances attending many such cases. And, after all we may do or say," continued the girl softly, "the best of us, who have lived the purest lives on earth that mortal can conceive, find at last that our only hope lies in the words of that text — 'This man receiveth sinners.'"

"You are a dear little preacher," said Sappho gently, as she looked at Dora from two wet eyes; "and if our race ever amounts to anything in this world, it will be because such women as you are raised up to save us."

Dora laughed and said, as she rose from her seat: "I think I am forgetting my errand." And making an elaborate bow, she continued: "If it please your royal highness, I present to you the compliments of the occupants of No. 500 D Street, with the request that you will honor us on Sunday evening, at half after seven, in the parlor of the worthy landlady of said house, where an informal reception will be held to further the better acquaintance of Miss Sappho Clark with her fellow-occupants of said house.

Music during the evening. Refreshments at nine sharp; after which, you are all expected to retire to your rooms like virtuous citizens."

"I herewith most gratefully accept your kind invitation," replied Sappho, with a deep courtesy.

"Ta, ta, then, until Sunday night. I sha'n't see you before that. I shall be lost for the remainder of the week 'getting ready for company'"; and Dora, with a gay laugh, ran lightly down the stairs.

Mrs. Smith, after many trials, found that her house contained respectable though unlettered people, who possessed kindly hearts and honesty of purpose in a greater degree than one generally finds in a lodging-house. Her great desire, then, was to make them as happy together as possible, and to this end she had Dora institute musical evenings or reception nights, that her tenants might have a better opportunity of becoming acquainted with each other. She argued, logically enough, that those who were inclined to stray from right paths would be influenced either in favor of upright conduct or else shamed into an acceptance of the right. It soon became noised about that very pleasant times were enjoyed in that house; and that a sick lodger had been nursed back to health, instead of being hustled into the

hospital ambulance at the first sign of sickness.
It was also whispered that to enjoy these privileges one must be "pretty nice," or as some
expressed it: "You've got to be high-toned to
get in there." The result, however, justified
Mrs. Smith's judgment, and rooms were always
hard to get at No. 500 D Street.

Saturday was a busy day for Dora and her
mother. At these little gatherings Mrs. Smith
always gave her guests plenty of good home-
made cake, sandwiches, hot chocolate, and on
very special occasions, ice cream or sherbet.
Sunday night there was to be ice cream in
honor of the new lodger. "Good things to
eat," said Ma Smith, as she industriously beat
eggs, sugar and butter together in a large
yellow bowl, "good things to eat make a man
respect himself and look up in the world. You
can't feel that you are nobody all the time if
once in a while you eat the same quality of
food that a millionaire does."

Dora lighted the lamps all over the house on
Sunday night as soon as it fell dark. In the
parlor there was a handsome piano lamp, which
was only used on special occasions; it was
lighted, and threw a soft, warm glow over the
neat woolen carpet, the modest furniture and
few ornaments. In a corner stood Dora's
piano, given her on her sixteenth birthday by

her brother. Very soon after seven o'clock the guests began to drop in; and as Dora and her mother were busy still over a few last preparations, Will and John volunteered to act as the reception committee.

The first comers were the two occupants of the basement rooms, — those which would have answered for the dining-room and kitchen of a moderately well-to-do family living in this class of house. Mrs. Ophelia Davis and Mrs. Sarah Ann White were friends of long standing. They were both born in far-away Louisiana, had been raised on neighboring plantations, and together had sought the blessings of liberty in the North at the close of the war. Mrs. Davis had always been a first-class cook, while Mrs. White tempted fortune as a second-girl. As their ideas of life and living enlarged, and they saw the possibilities of enjoying some comfort in a home, they began to think of establishing themselves where they could realize this blessing, and finally hit upon the idea of going into partnership in a laundry. After looking about them for a suitable situation for such a project, their choice finally fell upon Mrs. Smith's house, because of her known respectability, and because they could there come in contact with brighter intellects than their own; for, strange to say, it is a very hopeless case when a colored man or woman does not respect intelligence and good position.

"Yas, Sis'r Smith," said Mrs. Ophelia Davis the day she and Sarah Ann White went to engage the rooms; "yas'm, I'm tired o' livin' in white folkses' kitchens. Yas'm, thar's lots o' talk 'bout servant gals not bein' as good as enybody else, specially cooks. Yas'm, I kin git my five dollars a week with enyone; but ef you puts on a decent dress to go to church with a-Sunday afternoon, the mistis is a-wonderin' how you kin 'ford sech style and you nuthin' but a cook in her kitchen. Yas'm, I've got a silk dress, two of 'em, an' a lace shawl an' a gold watch and chain. People wants ter know how'd I git 'em. I come by 'em hones', I did. Yas'm, when my ol' mistis left her great big house an' all that good stuff — silver an' things — a-layin' thar fer enyone to pick up thet had sense 'nough to know a good thing an' git it ahead of enybody else, I jes' said to myself: ''Phelia, chile, now's yer time!' Yas'm, I feathered my nes', I jes' did. Sarah Ann, you 'member that time, honey, an' how skeered we was fer fear some o' them Union sojers would ketch us. You stuffed yerself with greenbacks, but, honey, I took clo's, too."

"Bless Gawd, Sis'r 'Phelia," replied her friend, with a chuckle and a great shaking of her fat sides; "bless Gawd, I disremember how much I did took in that ar pile; but Lord love yer, honey, I'se got some o' that money yet."

The two women engaged the rooms and prospered in their enterprise. The clothes under their deft fingers seemed to gain an added prettiness. They became the style; and no young bride on the Back Bay felt that she was complete unless "The First-class New Orleans Laundry" placed the finishing polish on the dainty lingerie of her wedding finery.

Tonight Mrs. Davis wore the famous black silk dress and gold watch and chain of ante bellum days, and Mrs. White was gay in a bright blue silk skirt and rose-colored silk shirt-waist. She said that she did not believe in any of your gloomy colors; for her part, she'd be dead soon enough and have a long time enough to stay "moulderin' inter clay, without buryin' herself befo' it was time." The next arrival was the young student preacher from the "first square-back." He was due at a prayer meeting; but when the time came for him to go there, he peeped over the banister and caught sight of Dora flitting back and forth in the entries, and then a whiff of Ma Smith's famous white cake was borne temptingly to his nostrils and banished the last scruple. He satisfied his conscience by hugging to his breast the idea that his presence was necessary to give the festivities the religious air which was needed for Sunday evening. In his Prince Albert coat and high white stock and tie he entered the parlor early, so that proper decorum might be maintained. Two dressmakers from the "second-front and back" now appeared and were made very welcome by the family; and then Sappho entered.

Her dress was plain black, with white chiffon at the neck and wrists, and on her breast a large bunch of "Jack" roses was fastened. With modest self-possession she moved to Mrs. Smith's side, and soon found herself being presented to the occupants of the parlor. For a moment or two there was an unbroken hush in the room. Tall and fair, with hair of a golden cast, aquiline nose, rosebud mouth, soft brown eyes veiled by long, dark lashes which swept her cheek, just now covered with a delicate rose flush, she burst upon them — a combination of "queen rose and lily in one."

"Lord," said Ophelia Davis to her friend Sarah Ann, "I haven't see enything look like thet chile since I lef' home."

"That's the truth, 'Phelia," replied Sarah Ann; "that's somethin' God made, honey; thar ain't nothin' like thet growed outside o' Loosyannie."

"Miss Clark," said Mrs. Davis, during a lull in the conversation, "I presume you're from Loosyannie?"

"My mother was born in New Orleans," replied the girl.

"I knowed it," cried Mrs. White, as she triumphantly glanced around the room. "Ol' New Orleans blood will tell on itself anywhere. These col'-blooded Yankees can't raise nuthin' that looks like thet chile; no, 'ndeed!"

Two or three of the young friends of the family who lived in the neighborhood had now arrived, and the conversation became very animated. Then it was announced that a literary and musical programme had been provided. Dora played an opening piece, which was a medley of Moody and Sankey hymns; Will sang "Palm Branches" in a musical baritone voice; John contributed a poem, and two young friends gave the duet from " Il Trovatore." After a little persuasion Sappho rendered the " Chariot Race " from " Ben Hur " in true dramatic style, and breathing so much of the stage that the Rev. Tommy James, the young theologian, felt that possibly he might have made a mistake in going into such hilarious company on the Sabbath.

"Now," said Mrs. Ophelia Davis, "I'm goin' to sing 'Suwanee River.' None o' yer high-

falutin' things can tech that song." Dora
accompanied her, and soon the air was filled
with Mrs. Davis' ambitious attempts to imi-
tate an operatic artist singing that good old-
time song. With much wheezing and puffing
— for the singer was neither slender nor
young — and many would-be fascinating jumps
and groans, presumed to be trills and runs, she
finished, to the relief of the company. Her
friend, Mrs. White, looked at her with great
approval, and immediately informed them that
'Phelia made a great impression the Sunday
before at Tremont Temple.

"The whole congregation was to sing
'Where's My Wandering Boy.' 'Phelia had
no paper to see the words, — not as thet made
eny matter, 'cause 'Phelia can't read nohow, —
an' the gentleman next us on the other side,
he gave 'Phelia a paper thet *he* had. The
man wanted ter be perlite. Well, 'Phelia was
thet flattered thet she jes' let herself go, an' thet
man never sung another note, he was so '*sprised*.
After the second verse 'Phelia saw the distrac-
tion she was makin', an' she says to me, says
she : '*How's thet, Sarah Ann ?*' an' I says to her :
'*That's out o' sight,* '*Phelia !*' You jes' ought ter
seen them white folks look ! they was paralyzed !
Why, you could hear 'Phelia *clean* above the
orgin !"

Meantime the young people in the room had gathered in a little knot, and were discussing many questions of the day and their effect upon the colored people. During a pause in the music the last remark made by John Langley was distinctly heard: "Yes, I must admit that our people are improving in their dress, in their looks and in their manners."

"What's that, John Langley?" asked Mrs. Davis, as she leaned forward to catch the words of the speaker; "colored people improvin' in ther manners? I should think they was! Don't yer fool yerself 'bout thet, now, will yer? The other night Sarah Ann and me was goin' down to Beacon Street to 'liver some goods, an' the car was crowded with people, an' thar was a pile o' young colored folks on it from the West End. Some o' them was a-standin' up in thet car, an' every onct in a while I noticed thet a passenger'd squirm as ef suthin' had hit him. Finally I got so mad I jes' couldn't see along with sech antics from them critters a-disgracin' theirselves and the whole o' the res' o' the colored population, an' I jes' elbowed myself into thet crowd o' young jades — what's thet (as Will murmured something under his breath), was they gals? yas, they was; young *jades*, every one o' them! Now what do yer think they was a-doin'?" she asked, as she swept her gaze over the company.

"Not being a mind-reader, I wouldn't dare to say," replied John Langley, with a grin of delight.

"*They was a-trampin' onto the feet of every white man an' woman in thet car to show the white folks how free they was!* I jes' took my ambriller an' knocked it into two or three o' them thet I knowed, an' tol' 'em I'd tell ther mothers. Improvin' in ther manners! I should think they was!"

At this moment refreshments were served, and the attention of the company was turned to the wants of the inner man.

Dora had placed a pretty little tea table at one side of the room, and Sappho had promised to pour the tea and chocolate. At a sign from Mrs. Smith she took her place, and soon the steaming beverage was cheering the hearts of the guests. The young men vied with each other in serving her. The tea table became the center of attraction, in fact, for the whole room. Even the divinity student was drawn into the magic circle, and divided his attention between Sappho and Mrs. Ophelia Davis, for whom he seemed to have a very tender regard.

The girl was naturally buoyant and bright, and the influence of the pleasant company in which she found herself seemed to inspire her, and yet no man would have overstepped the bounds of propriety with her in his manner. The pleasant word and jest were free from all coquetry. John was dumb before so much beauty and wit. Will was so blinded by her charms that he was scarcely conscious of what he was doing; but not a word or movement of hers was lost to him.

Dora watched the tea table smilingly. She loved to see her friends enjoy themselves. It never occurred to her to be jealous of the attention given Sappho by her brother and John Langley.

Presently there were many pleasant compliments passed on the enjoyable evening which had so quickly flown, and each gentleman proposed a toast, which was drunk in a cup of hot chocolate; and as the clock struck ten, they all joined hands and united in singing "Auld Lang Syne" and " Praise God, from Whom All Blessings Flow." The evening was over; the lights were out; but up in John's attic chamber the two young men smoked a social cigar before separating for the night.

They were silent for some time, and then Will said: "Miss Clark is a very beautiful woman; don't you think so, John?"

" Well," replied John, " beauty is not the word to describe her. She's a stunner, and no mistake,"

John went to bed; but Will sat by the fire a longer time than usual, thinking thoughts which had never before troubled his young manhood; and. unconsciously, one face — the face of Sappho Clark — formed the background of his thoughts.

CHAPTER VII.

FRIENDSHIP.

WHAT is so great as friendship? The only reward of virtue is virtue: the only way to have a friend is to be one. — EMERSON.

AFTER that evening the two girls were much together. Sappho's beauty appealed strongly to Dora's artistic nature; but hidden beneath the classic outlines of the face, the graceful symmetry of the form, and the dainty coloring of the skin, Dora's shrewd common sense and womanly intuition discovered a character of sterling worth — bold, strong and ennobling; while into Sappho's lonely self-suppressed life the energetic little Yankee girl swept like a healthful, strengthening breeze. Care was forgotten; there was new joy in living. It was the Southern girl's first experience of Northern life. True, the seductive skies of her nativity had a potent hold upon her affections, but truth demanded her to recognize the superiority of the vigorous activity in the life all about her. The Negro, while held in contempt by many, yet reflected the spirit of his surroundings in his upright carriage, his fearlessness in advancing his opinions, his self-reliance, his anxiety to obtain paying employment that would give to his family some few of the advantages enjoyed by the more favored classes of citizens, his love of liberty, which in its intensity recalled the memory of New England men who had counted all worldly gain as nothing if demanding the sacrifice of even one of the great principles of freedom. It was a new view of the possibilities and probabilities which the future might open to her people. Long she struggled with thoughts which represented to her but vaguely a life beyond anything of which she had ever dreamed.

Sappho generally carried her work home in the morning, but ten o'clock would find her seated at her desk and ready to begin her task anew. Some days she was unoccupied; but this did not happen very frequently. These free days were the gala days of her existence, when under Dora's guidance she explored various points of interest, and learned from observation the great plan of life as practiced in an intelligent, liberty-loving community. Here in the free air of New England's freest city, Sappho drank great draughts of freedom's subtle elixir. Dora was interested and amused in watching the changes on the mirror-like face of her friend whenever her attention was arrested by a new phenomenon. It was strange to see this girl, resembling nothing so much as a lily

in its beautiful purity, shrink from entering a
place of public resort for fear of insult. It was
difficult to convince her that she might enter a
restaurant frequented by educated whites and
meet with nothing but the greatest courtesy;
that she might take part in the glorious service
at fashionable Trinity and be received with
punctilious politeness. To this woman, denied
association with the vast sources of information,
which are heirlooms to the lowliest inhabitant
of Boston, the noble piles, which represented
the halls of learning, and the massive grandeur
of the library, free to all, seemed to invite her
to a full participation in their intellectual joys.
She had seen nothing like them. Statuary,
paintings, sculptures, — all appealed to her
beauty-loving nature. The hidden springs of
spirituality were satisfied and at rest, claiming
kinship with the great minds of the past, whose
never-dying works breathed perennial life in
the atmosphere of the quiet halls.

Now was the beginning of the storm season
in New England, and on stormy days the two
girls would sit before the fire in Sappho's room
and talk of the many things dear to women,
while they embroidered or stitched. So they
sat one cold, snowy day. The storm had
started the afternoon before and had raged
with unceasing fury all night, — snow and rain

which the increasing cold quickly turned into cutting sleet. Morning had brought relief from the high winds, and the temperature had moderated somewhat; but the snow still fell steadily, drifting into huge piles, which made the streets impassable. It was the first great storm Sappho had seen. It was impossible for her to leave home, so she begged Dora to pass the day with her and play "company," like the children. Dora was nothing loathe; and as soon as her morning duties were finished, she told her mother that she was going visiting and would not be at home until tea time. By eleven o'clock they had locked the door of Sappho's room to keep out all intruders, had mended the fire until the little stove gave out a delicious warmth, and had drawn the window curtains close to keep out stray currents of air. Sappho's couch was drawn close beside the stove, while Dora's small person was most cosily bestowed in her favorite rocking-chair.

It was a very convenient stove that Sappho had in her room. The ornamental top could be turned back on its movable hinge, and there was a flat stove cover ready to hold any vessel and heat its contents to just the right temperature. Sappho was prouder of that stove than a daughter of Fortune would have been of the most expensive silver chafing-dish. It was very near lunch time, so the top was turned back, and the little copper teakettle was beginning to sing its welcome song. Dora had placed a small, round table between the couch and the rocker. A service for two was set out in dainty china dishes, cream and sugar looking doubly tempting as it gleamed and glistened in the delicate ware. One plate was piled with thinly cut slices of bread and butter, another held slices of pink ham.

Sappho lay back among her cushions, lazily stretching her little slippered feet toward the warm stove, where the fire burned so cheerily and glowed so invitingly as it shone through the isinglass door. She folded her arms above her head and turned an admiring gaze on the brown face of her friend, who swayed gently back and forth in her rocking-chair, her feet on a hassock, and a scarlet afghan wrapped about her knees. Dora was telling Sappho all about her engagement to John Langley and their plans for the future.

" I think you will be happy, Dora, if you love him. All things are possible if love is the foundation stone," said Sappho, after a slight pause, as she nestled among her pillows. Dora was sitting bolt upright with the usual business-like look upon her face.

"I like him well enough to marry him, but I don't believe there's enough sentiment in me to make love a great passion, such as we read of in books. Do you believe marriage is the beautiful state it is painted by writers?"

"Why, yes," laughed Sappho; "I wouldn't believe anything else for your sake, my little brownie."

"No joking, Sappho; this is dead earnest. Don't you ever expect to marry, and don't you speculate about the pros and cons and the maybes and perhapses of the situation?" asked Dora, as she filled the cups with steaming cocoa and passed one to her friend.

"Dora, you little gourmand, what have you got in the refrigerator?" A box ingeniously nailed to the window seat outside, and filled with shelves, and having a substantial door, was the ice-box, or refrigerator, where Sappho kept materials handy for a quick lunch. Dora closed the window and returned quickly to her seat, placing a glass dish on the table as she did so.

"It's only part of a cream pie that ma had left last night. I thought it would help out nicely with our lunch."

"What, again!" said Sappho significantly. "That's the fourth time this week, and here it is but Friday. You'll be as fat as a seal, and

then John P. won't want you at any price.
Take warning, and depart from the error of
your ways before it is too late."

Dora laughed guiltily and said, as she drew
a box from her apron pocket: "Well, here are
John's chocolate bonbons that he brought last
night. I suppose you won't want me to touch
them, for fear of getting fat."

Sappho shook her head in mock despair.
"And your teeth, your beautiful white teeth,
where will they be shortly if you persist in eating a pound of bonbons every day? Think
of your fate, Dora, and pause in your reckless
career — forty inches about the waist and only
scraggy snags to show me when you grin!"

"Thank heaven I'll never come to that while
there's a dentist in the city of Boston! I'll eat
all the bonbons I want in spite of you, Sappho,
and if you don't hurry I'll eat your slice of
cream pie, too." At this dire threat there
ensued a scramble for the pie, mingled with
peals of merry laughter, until all rosy and
sparkling, Sappho emerged from the fray with
the dish containing her share of the dainty
held high in the air.

Presently lunch was over, and they resumed
their old positions, prepared to "take comfort."

"You haven't answered my question yet,
Sappho."

"To tell you the truth, I had forgotten your remark, Dora; what was it?"

"I suspect that is a bit of a fib to keep me from teasing you about getting married. What I want to know is: Do you ever mean to marry, or are you going to pine in single blessedness on my hands and be a bachelor-maid to the end?"

"Well," replied Sappho, with a comical twist to her face, "in the words of Unc' Gulliver, 'I mote, an' then agin I moten't.'"

"What troubles me is having a man bothering around. Now I tell John P. that I'm busy, or something like that, and I'm rid of him; but after you marry a man, he's on your hands for good and all. I'm wondering if my love could stand the test."

"That's queer talk for an engaged girl, with a fine, handsome fellow to court her. Why, Dora, 'I'm s'prised at yer!'" laughed Sappho gaily.

"I'm not ashamed of John P.'s appearance in company; he looks all right; but when one is terribly in love one is supposed to want the dear object always near; but matches, — love matches, — my child, turn out so badly that a girl hesitates to 'git jined to eny man fer betterer or worserer,' as Dr. Peters says. Then I get tired of a man so soon! (This with a doleful sigh.) I dread to think of being tied to John for good and all; I know I'll be sick of him inside of a week. I do despair of ever being like other girls."

Sappho laughed outright at the woe-begone countenance before her.

"It is generally the other way: the men get tired of us first. A woman loves one man, and is true to him through all eternity."

"That's just what makes me feel so *unsexed*, so to speak; I like John's looks. He's the style among all the girls in our set. I like to know that I can claim him before them all. It's fun to see 'em fluttering around him, kindly trying to put my nose out of joint. I must say that I feel real *comfortable* to spoil sport by walking off with him just when they think they've got things running as they wish. Yes, it's real *comfortable* to know that they're all as jealous as can be. But for all that, I know I'll get tired of him."

"Let us hope not, if you have really made up your mind to marry him. Dora, sometimes I am afraid that you mean what you say. I notice that you call him 'John P.' What's the P for?"

"Pollock — John Pollock Langley. His grandfather was his father's master, and Pollock was his name," sang Dora, as she rocked gently to and fro. "Now, there's Arthur Lewis," she continued; "he's jolly fun. He isn't a fascinator, or anything of that sort; he's just good."

"Who is he?" asked Sappho, with languid interest.

"Properly speaking, he's Dr. Arthur Lewis. We were children together, although he is five years older than I. He's a fine scholar and a great business man. He has a large industrial school in Louisiana. He's gone up in the world, I tell you, since we made mud pies on the back doorsteps; but I never think of him except as old Arthur, who used to drag me to school on his sled."

There was a gleam of fun in Sappho's eyes, as she said demurely: "You seem to know all about him. Was he ever a lover of yours?"

"Lover! no, indeed!" Dora flushed vividly under her brown skin. "The idea of Arthur as my lover is too absurd."

"Excuse me, dear, for my mistake," said Sappho mischievously. "I didn't know but that he might be the mysterious link which would join love, marriage and the necessary man in a harmonious whole."

"Well," said Dora, after a slight pause, blushing furiously, "I don't say he wouldn't like the rôle. You'll see him soon; he's coming to Boston on business in a few weeks. Oh, we've had rare times together." She sighed and smiled, lost for the moment in pleasant memories. Sappho smiled, too, in sympathy with her mood.

"Ah, yes; I think I understand. Poor John!"

"John's all right. Don't shed any tears over him," said Dora testily. They sat awhile in silence, listening to the sound of the whirling frozen flakes wind-driven against the window panes. It was scarce three o'clock, but darkness was beginning to envelop the city, and it was already a pleasant twilight in the room.

"Tell me about Dr. Lewis and his work, Dora," said Sappho presently. "Do you know, he interests me exceedingly."

"I don't really understand Arthur's hobbies, but I believe that he is supposed to be doing a great work in the Black Belt. His argument is, as I understand it, that industrial education and the exclusion of politics will cure all our race troubles."

"I doubt it," returned Sappho quickly, with an impatient toss of the head. "That reasoning might be practically illustrated with benefit to us for a few years in the South, but to my mind would not effect a permanent cure for race troubles if we are willing to admit that human nature is the same in us as in others.

The time will come when our men will grow away from the trammels of narrow prejudice, and desire the same treatment that is accorded to other men. Why, one can but see that any degree of education and development will not fail of such a result."

"I am willing to confess that the subject is a little deep for me," replied Dora. "I'm not the least bit of a politician, and I generally accept whatever the men tell me as right; but I know that there is something very wrong in our lives, and nothing seems to remedy the evils under which the colored man labors."

"But you can see, can't you, that if our men are deprived of the franchise, we become aliens in the very land of our birth?"

"Arthur says that would be better for us; the great loss of life would cease, and we should be at peace with the whites."

"Ah, how can he argue so falsely! I have lived beneath the system of oppression in the South. If we lose the franchise, at the same time we shall lose the respect of all other citizens. Temporizing will not benefit us; rather, it will leave us branded as cowards, not worthy a freeman's respect — an alien people, without a country and without a home."

Dora gazed at her friend with admiration, and wished that she had a kodak, so that she might catch just the expression that lighted her eyes and glowed in a bright color upon her cheeks.

"I predict some fun when you and Arthur meet. I'll just start you both out some night, and you'll be spitting at each other like two cats inside of five minutes. Arthur thinks that women should be seen and not heard, where politics is under discussion."

"Insufferable prig!" exclaimed Sappho, with snapping eyes.

"Oh, no, he isn't; Arthur's all right. But you see he is living South; his work is there, and he must keep in with the whites of the section where his work lies, or all he has accomplished will go for naught, and perhaps his life might be forfeited, too."

"I see. The mess of pottage and the birth-right."

"Bless you! not so bad as that; but money makes the mare go," returned Dora, with a wink at her friend, and a shrewd business look on her bright little Yankee face. "I say to you, as Arthur says to me when I tell him what I think of his system: 'If you want honey, you must have money.' I don't know anything about politics, as I said before, but my opinion won't cost you anything: when we can say that lots of our men are as rich as Jews, there'll be no question about the franchise, and my idea is that Arthur 'll be one of the Jews."

"Oh!" exclaimed Sappho disgustedly, as she resumed her lounging position.

"Sappho, how did you come to take up stenography? I should have thought you would have preferred teaching."

"I had to live, my dear; I could not teach school, because my education does not include a college course. I could not do housework, because my constitution is naturally weak."

It was noticeable in these confidential chats that Sappho never spoke of her early life. Dora had confided to her friend every event of importance that had occurred in her young life; and, in harmless gossip, had related the history of all the friends who visited the house intimately; but all this had begot no like unburdening to eager ears of the early history of her friend. Wonderful to relate, however, Dora did not resent this reserve, which she could see was studied. It spoke well for the sincerity of the love that had taken root in her heart for Sappho, that it subdued her inquisitiveness, and she gladly accepted her friendship without asking troublesome questions.

"How did you finally succeed in getting work? I have always heard that it was very difficult for colored girls to find employment in offices where your class of work is required."

"And so it is, my dear. I sometimes think that if I lose the work I am on, I shall not try for another position. I shall never forget the day I started out to find work: the first place that I visited was all right until the man found I was colored; then he said that his wife wanted a nurse girl, and he had no doubt she would be glad to hire me, for I looked good-tempered. At the second place where I ventured to intrude the proprietor said: 'Yes; we want a stenographer, but we've no work for your kind.' However, that was preferable to the insulting familiarity which some men assumed. It was dreadful! I don't like to think about it. Father Andrew induced the man for whom I am working to employ me. I do not interfere with the other help, because I take my work home; many of the other clerks have never seen me, and so the proprietor runs no risk of being bothered with complaints from them. He treats me very well, too."

"I have heard many girls tell much the same tale about other lines of business," said Dora. "It makes me content to do the work of this house, and not complain."

"You ought to thank God every day for such a refuge as you have in your home."

"I cannot understand people. Here in the

North we are allowed every privilege. There seems to be no prejudice until we seek employment; then every door is closed against us. Can you explain this?"

"No, I cannot; to my way of thinking the whole thing is a Chinese puzzle."

"Bless my soul! Just look at that clock!" exclaimed Dora, as she scrambled to her feet and began gathering up her scattered property. "Five o'clock, and tea to get. Sappho, you've been lazy enough for one day. Come downstairs and help me get tea. The boys will be here in no time, as hungry as bears."

Piloted by Dora, Sappho became well acquainted with ancient landmarks of peculiar interest to the colored people. They visited the home for aged women on M—— Street, and read and sang to the occupants. They visited St. Monica's Hospital, and carried clothes, flowers, and a little money saved from the cost of contemplated Easter finery. They scattered brightness along with charitable acts wherever a case of want was brought to their attention.

Dora had accepted the position of organist for a prominent colored church in the city. There was a small salary attached to the place, which she was glad to receive. Sappho usually went with her to choir rehearsals, and sitting in the shadows, well hidden from view, would

think over the romantic history of the fine old
edifice. The building, so the story ran, was the
place of worship of a rich, white Baptist congregation in the years preceding the emancipation. Negroes were allowed in the galleries
only. Believing this color-bar to be a stigma
on the house of God, a few of the members
protested, but finding their warnings unheeded,
withdrew from the church, and finally found a
Sabbath home in an old building long used as
a theatre. These people prospered, and grew
rich and powerful; colored people were always
welcome in the congregation. The society in
the old church, left to itself, had at last been
glad to sell the building to its present occupants. Thus the despised people, who were
not allowed a seat outside of the galleries, now
owned and occupied the scene of their former
humiliation. It was a solemn and wonderful
dispensation of Providence, and filled the girl's
heart with strong emotion.

During these evenings, when she waited for
the close of the rehearsals, she became acquainted with many odd specimens of the race:
men of brain and thought, but of unique expression and filled with quaint humor. One
of these characters was known as Dr. Abraham
Peters. Doctor Peters was a well-read man,
greatly interested in scientific research, but

who had lacked the opportunity to obtain information in his youth. He had been a slave when a boy, a few years before the Civil War. Now he was the church janitor, and to eke out his scanty income kept a little boot-black stand just around the corner from the church, and knowing something of medicine and nursing the sick, had advertised himself as a magnetic physician. He displayed much skill in practice, and had acquired something of a local reputation. Doctor Peters and Sappho were good friends, and he brought out all his store of knowledge, proudly displaying it for her approval.

"You see, Miss Sappho, I've knocked 'bout the worl' some consid'ble," he said one night, in his soft Southern tones and quaint Northern-ized dialect, as they sat in the cosy vestry wait-ing for the close of the rehearsal. "Ben po'rer than eny chuch mouse. But I've saved some-thin', an' I know the worl'. Perhaps you's int'rest'd 'nuff in an ole man to want to hear how I come to 'vertis myself as a magnifyin' doctor, an' where I picked it up, eh?"

"Yes," replied Sappho, "I certainly am inter-ested in your story."

"Well, while they're caterwaulin' on that Easter anthem in ten flats, I reckon I'll have time to tell you all 'bout it. Fust I knowed 'bout magnetics was brought to my 'tention down home. Some people said I had the evil eye, an' some said it was only a *strong* eye, but be that homsomever, it was a bad eye, an' a terror ter watermilyun thieves when it was my watch on the chickun houses. *Magnifyin'* an' *hoodooin'* is 'bout the same thing down thar, tho' sense the 'srender mos' all ol'-time doin's is done 'way. 'Bout the time I realized that I had this power I had 'sperinced ruligeon, an' had been jestified an' concentrated, so that I got the blessin'. Them days, too, I was a-sottin' out to court my Susie (that's my wife), an' all the young fellers 'roun' the county was a-sprucin' up to her jes' like crows 'roun' carr'on. Sunday was the day I had mos' on my mind, 'cause they'd ride up an' hitch thar mules in a line all along the ole man's fence (you see he had right smart prop'ty, an' I spec' that had a mighty drawin' infloonce on some of them shif'less fellers who hadn't nuff skonsh to start thar own mule team up a hill), an' thar they'd sot like so many buzzards, waitin' fer a chance to sly Susie off to chuch under my nose. I had ter wurk lively, I tell you; Susie was kin' o' skittish an' res'less, an' it was fus' come, fus' sarved, with her, bein' she had her choice. Well, jes' at the time I got the blessin' I got the insurance that Susie was gwine ter have me. All the fellers was satisfied but Possum Tooit. Possum an' me was boys together, an' we'd both run each other purty hard strivin' to come through fust at the mourner's bench as well as to git the gal. Possum was beat when he found I had a full hand and had swept the pot."

"Oomhoo!" laughed Brother Jones, who was an interested listener to Doctor Peters' story. "Oomhoo, Brother Peters; done guv yerself 'way. What you know 'bout 'full hands an' pots?'"

"Who give himself 'way, Brother Jones? Ever hear me say Ise better'n enybody else in this chuch? I'm er man, sah, I'm er man! Ise done truspassed on the flesh-pots of Egypt as much as eny other man. Don't yer 'oomhoo' me, Brother Jones, no sah!"

"Tech a sore place, Brother Peters, tech a sore place," laughed the brother as he walked away, his shoulders shaking like great mounds of jelly. It was some minutes before Doctor Peters could recover his equilibrium and go on with his tale.

"Possum Tooit was so mad an' disapinted that he finally challenged me to fight a jewel. I wasn't in no state of mind to be killed by any of his hoodoo tricks, Possum bein' an export at puttin' spells an' sech like on enybody fer from twenty-five cents up to five dollars; neither did I want Susie to think I was 'fraid of Possum Tooit. So thar I was 'tween a hawk an' a buzzard. Well, I accepted the challenge, an' bein' the defendant in the matter, of course, I had the choice of weapins, an' I choose rifles. We kep' mighty secret 'bout the 'rangements, an' met at moonrise on a field jes' back of the graveyard. The seconds measured off ten spaces after we'd shooken hands, an' we each stepped to our places. Tho' it was a solemn 'casion, I wasn't skeered, but Possum was a rollin' up the whites of his eyes, an' you could hear his teeth chatter worse than dried corn shuks. Ike Watkins was head second, an' he stood 'tween us, holdin' his red bandanna in his han' waitin' to say the word. 'Gemplemen, is you ready?' he says. 'Let her go, Ike,' says I. 'Take aim,' says he, an' I pinted the rifle at Possum, an' callin' up all the power in me I threw it along the body of the gun plumb 'tween Possum's eyes jes' above the bridge of his nose. An' that was a fair target, 'cause the bridge of Possum's nose was a miracle fer size. Possum gave a yell when he felt the strength of that eye, that would a splut yer year-pan in two. An' in two seconds he was in the worst alpaca fit you ever seen. The seconds acknowledged me the victor by a reckless invention of Providence, they bein' aware that the adversary

wasn't hit by nary bullet, the rifles bein' loaded
with salt fer fear of mischief. Possum owned
up like a man that I was more powerful than
him, because of the sufernatral strength in my
bad eye.

"Well, I kep' on prayin' fer mo' faith until I
got the power in my hands, an' by layin' em on
a sick pusson I could 'lectrocute 'em instantly,
an' thar bad feelin's would disappear. People
got the notion I could pray a pusson right out
the grave, an' my fame spread abroad until I
began charging fer my services, explainin' to
my patients that the dead might be raised, but
not fer nuthin', after which I seed a fallin' off
in my poperlarity. Business bein' purty brief
jes' then, I took Susie an' moved up Norf, an'
went ter cookin' on a steamboat. I've done
mos' everythin' in this worl', honey, as I tol'
you, to git an hones' livin' without stealin' it.
An' I dunno," added the old man reflectively,
as he stroked the gray, stubby fringe on his
chin, "I dunno as I'm eny too good ef I got
pushed real hard to help myself out; humans
is humans, an' I've seen many a well-'tentioned
feller settin' in the caboose when times was
hard, an' the mule mortgaged for full value to
three men at once to buy meal an' bread, an'
hog an' hominy, an' terbaccer. But mos' in
ginerally, I've got along without silin' my hands

with other people's prop'ty. Well, honey, they gave me fifteen dollars a munf an' found, fer bein' head cook, an' I paid ten dollars a munf house rent out of that. Things was purty brief, purty brief. Times was more an' more spurious, an' it was work yer wits, Abraham Peters, to git a livin'. I jes' didn't know whicher way to turn.

"One day I got a telegraph at the other end of the route that the baby was dead an' no money to pay the undertaker, an' the ole 'ooman sick in the bed from worryin'. The Lord jes' seemed to pour his blessin' down on us in a house full o' chillun. After Susie'd had twenty I used to pray the Lord to stop blessin' us that way, 'cause he could see fer himself that too many blessins was a gittin' to be a nuisance. I cooked the dinner myself that day, bein' the other cook was ashore, an' you believe me, I sung an' I prayed an' I wrastled fer help in that ole steamboat kitchen down behin' my bigges' brass biler where I was kivered from pryin' eyes. All of a suddint I felt the power, an' the Lord spoke to me an' he said : 'Git up, Abraham Peters, an' go out an' hoodoo the fust man you meet.' Bless yo, chile, I riz up in a hurry an' started out, not knowin' no more than nuthin' what was meant by that. Fust man I saw when I got on deck was the cap'n ; I went up to him, an' I smiled. I must have been a purty picture with my face all grease an' tears. I says, not thinkin' what wurds I was goin' ter utter: 'Mornin', Cap'n; how's yer corporosity seem to segashiate?' Cap'n he roared; you could a heard him holler up to Boston. He slapped me on the back, an' says he: 'Abe Peters, that's the gol darndest thing I ever heard.' With that he hauled out a five-dollar bill an' gave me, an' walked off laughin' fit to kill hisself. By night I had twenty dollars in my pocket, an' everybody on the boat was a callin' me 'corporosity segashiate.' I've used that hoodoo ever since, an' I ain't found nary white gempleman can seem to git 'way from it without showing the color of his money.

"One of the owners of the boat took a great liking to me, an' he says to me one day, says he: 'Abe, how'd you like to wurk ashore so you could be nearer your family an' git better pay?' 'Like it?' says I. 'If you don't want to pulverize me, don' make me no sech an offer.' He laughed a bit, an' then he says: 'I've got a big buildin' up Washington Street, an' I want a trusty man to keep it clean an' look after the tenants. I'll give you ten dollars a week.'

"I took off my cap, an' I truly bowed down to that man, an' I says: 'The Lord's been a wurkin' on yer heart, Mr. Pierson.' 'Maybe

he has,' says he; 'anyhow, you can pack up an'
go ashore next trip; your place'll be waitin' fer
yer.' Fust thing I knowed I was a bossin' a
big job of janitorin'. Mos' of the people in the
buildin' was Christian Science. After they'd
got a little bit acquainted with me they found
out the power I had in my hands fer layin' on.
'Twant long before I was a pickin' up right smart
nussin' nights. Don't suppose you know much
'bout this Science business, do you?" Sappho
confessed her ignorance.

"Christian Science is a faith-cure; that is,
it's usin' yer brains an' trainin' 'em to know
that there's nuthin' 'tall the matter with you ef
you only think there ain't. They argify that
all sickness is a mistake, 'cause it's 'maginary.
I don't b'lieve that, though, 'cause I had the
rheumatism while I was there, an' the doctors
started in to cure me by prayin' an' wurkin' on
my body through my spirit, an' it warn't no
more good than nuthin' 'tall. I've got as much
faith as eny livin' man, but rheumatism is one
o' them things that'll convince you agin' your
will; it will draw speech out of a deef mute an'
make a blind man see, when them pains is a
grindin' inter your bones an' jints worse than
a saw cuttin' thro' knots in a cord wood stick.
I'm free to say that curin' my mind didn't have
no effect on my pain, an' I jes' kep' on seein'

blue blazes an' swearin' like mad. I'll 'low that
faith can move mountains, faith, as *leetle* as a
mustard seed, an' that's mighty small. Ef you
b'lieve you'll get what you wants an' asks
fer, that's faith. That's good; that's all right.
Trouble is we *don't b'lieve it 'cordin' to scripter.*
We git mad when our prayers ain't answered,
not thinkin' it's 'cause we ain't got horse sense
nuff to use *discreetion* in puttin' our faith on
subjects that is approvin' to the Lord, an' will
fit in with his own idees 'bout runnin' the business of the universe. An' that's where faith-
cure is weak, 'cause it's comin' in 'junction with
God. Faith-cure won't operate on any man
where it was *pre*ordinated that a *pre*tickler
man was to die with a *pre*tickler complaint.
No'm, we ain't up to comin' in 'junction with
the Lord's business. There's a number of
grand diversions to Christian Science. There's
hypnism an' pessimism an' a number of other
isms, but they all bear the same way — a sort
of applostic healin' of sickness. The doctors
kept after me 'bout my gifts of healin', an' very
kindly showed me wherein I could make an
hones' dollar, an' business bein' business I finally
determined to adop' magnifyin' as a perfeshun.
I've been in the business nigh upon ten years
now, an' I've picked up as good a livin' as any
colored gempleman who has wurked a sight

harder an' had to take piles o' unregenerate sass from his boss."

That night they walked home together after the rehearsal: the four young people — Dora and John, Sappho and Will. Some one of the choir boys walking ahead of them was singing in a sweet, high tenor voice the refrain of an old love song: "Couldst thou but know how much I love thee." It suited Will's mood, and voiced his dream exquisitely. Across the heavens the Northern Lights streamed in radiance. Meteors bright and shooting stars added to the beauty of the night. The moon, at its full, shed the light of day about them. The wind whispered amidst the leafless branches of the huge old trees on the Common and Public Garden as they passed them on their homeward way. Once Will took her hand in his; she let it stay a moment while she made an incoherent little speech about clouds and trees. Will said nothing. It was not time yet, he told himself. He would wait a little longer.

CHAPTER VIII.

THE SEWING-CIRCLE.

WHERE village statesmen talked with looks profound,
Imagination fondly stoops to trace
The parlor splendors of that festive place.

.   .   .   .

Yes! let the rich deride, the proud disdain,
These simple blessings of the lowly train;
To me more dear,
One native charm than all the gloss of art.
— GOLDSMITH.

MA SMITH was a member of the church re-
ferred to in the last chapter, the most prominent one of color in New England. It was
situated in the heart of the West End, and
was a very valuable piece of property. Every
winter this church gave many entertainments
to aid in paying off the mortgage, which at
this time amounted to about eight thousand
dollars. Mrs. Smith, as the chairman of the
board of stewardesses, was inaugurating a fair
— one that should eclipse anything of a similar
nature ever attempted by the colored people,
and numerous sewing-circles were being held
among the members all over the city. Parlor
entertainments where an admission fee of ten
cents was collected from every patron, were

also greatly in vogue, and the money thus obtained was put into a fund to defray the expense of purchasing eatables and decorations, and paying for the printing of tickets, circulars, etc., for the fair. The strongest forces of the colored people in the vicinity were to combine and lend their aid in making a supreme effort to clear this magnificent property.

Boston contains a number of well-to-do families of color whose tax-bills show a most comfortable return each year to the city treasury. Strange as it may seem, these well-to-do people, in goodly numbers, distribute themselves and their children among the various Episcopal churches with which the city abounds, the government of which holds out the welcome hand to the brother in black, who is drawn to unite his fortunes with the members of this particular denomination. It may be true that the beautiful ritual of the church is responsible in some measure for this. Colored people are nothing if not beauty-lovers, and for such a people the grandeur of the service has great attractions. But in justice to this church one must acknowledge that it has been instrumental in doing much toward helping this race to help itself, along the lines of brotherly interest.

These people were well represented within the precincts of Mrs. Smith's pretty parlor one afternoon, all desirous of lending their aid to help along the great project.

As we have said, Mrs. Smith occupied the back parlor of the house as her chamber, and within this room the matrons had assembled to take charge of the cutting out of different garments; and here, too, the sewing machine was placed ready for use. In the parlor proper all the young ladies were seated ready to perform any service which might be required of them in the way of putting garments together.

By two o'clock all the members of the sewing-circle were in their places. The parlor was crowded. Mrs. Willis, the brilliant widow of a bright Negro politician, had charge of the girls, and after the sewing had been given out the first business of the meeting was to go over events of interest to the Negro race which had transpired during the week throughout the country. These facts had been previously tabulated upon a blackboard which was placed upon an easel, and occupied a conspicuous position in the room. Each one was supposed to contribute anything of interest that she had read or heard in that time for the benefit of all. After these points had been gone over, Mrs. Willis gave a talk upon some topic of interest. At six o'clock tea was to be served in the kitchen, the company taking refreshment in squads of five. At eight o'clock all unfinished work would be folded and packed away in the convenient little Boston bag, to be finished at home, and the male friends of the various ladies were expected to put in an appearance. Music and recitations were to be enjoyed for two hours, ice cream and cake being sold for the benefit of the cause.

Mrs. Willis was a good example of a class of women of color that came into existence at the close of the Civil War. She was not a *rara avis*, but one of many possibilities which the future will develop from among the colored women of New England. Every city or town from Maine to New York has its Mrs. Willis. Keen in her analysis of human nature, most people realized, after a short acquaintance, in which they ran the gamut of emotions from strong attraction to repulsion, that she had sifted them thoroughly, while they had gained nothing in return. Shrewd in business matters, many a subtle business man had been worsted by her apparent womanly weakness and charming simplicity. With little money, she yet contrived to live in quiet elegance, even including the little journeys from place to place, so adroitly managed as to increase her influence at home and her fame abroad. Well-read and thoroughly conversant with all

current topics, she impressed one as having
been liberally educated and polished by travel,
whereas a high-school course more than covered all her opportunities.

Even today it is erroneously believed that
all racial development among colored people
has taken place since emancipation. It is impossible of belief for some, that little circles of
educated men and women of color have existed
since the Revolutionary War. Some of these
people were born free, some have lost the
memory of servitude in the dim past; a greater
number by far were recruited from the energetic slaves of the South, who toiled when they
should have slept, for the money that purchased their freedom, or else they boldly took
the rights which man denied. Mrs. Willis was
one from among these classes. The history of
her descent could not be traced, but somewhere,
somehow, a strain of white blood had filtered
through the African stream. At sixty odd she
was vigorous, well-preserved, broad and comfortable in appearance, with an aureole of white
hair crowning a pleasant face.

She had loved her husband with a love ambitious for his advancement. His foot on the
stairs mounting to the two-room tenement
which constituted their home in the early years
of married life, had sent a thrill to her very

heart as she sat sewing baby clothes for the always expected addition to the family. But twenty years make a difference in all our lives. It brought many changes to the colored people of New England — social and business changes. Politics had become the open sesame for the ambitious Negro. A seat in the Legislature then was not a dream to this man, urged by the loving woman behind him. Other offices of trust were quickly offered him when his worth became known. He grasped his opportunity; grew richer, more polished, less social, and the family broadened out and overflowed from old familiar "West End" environments across the River Charles into the aristocratic suburbs of Cambridge. Death comes to us all.

Money, the sinews of living and social standing, she did not possess upon her husband's death. Therefore she was forced to begin a weary pilgrimage — a hunt for the means to help her breast the social tide. The best opening, she decided after looking carefully about her, was in the great cause of the evolution of true womanhood in the work of the "Woman Question" as embodied in marriage and suffrage. She could talk dashingly on many themes, for which she had received much applause in by-gone days, when in private life she had held forth in the drawing-room of some

Back Bay philanthropist who sought to use her talents as an attraction for a worthy charitable object, the discovery of a rare species of versatility in the Negro character being a sure drawing-card. It was her boast that she had made the fortunes of her family and settled her children well in life. The advancement of the colored woman should be the new problem in the woman question that should float her upon its tide into the prosperity she desired. And she succeeded well in her plans: conceived in selfishness, they yet bore glorious fruit in the formation of clubs of colored women banded together for charity, for study, for every reason under God's glorious heavens that can better the condition of mankind.

Trivialities are not to be despised. Inborn love implanted in a woman's heart for a luxurious, esthetic home life, running on well-oiled wheels amid flowers, sunshine, books and priceless pamphlets, easy chairs and French gowns, may be the means of developing a Paderewski or freeing a race from servitude. It was amusing to watch the way in which she governed societies and held her position. In her hands committees were as wax, and loud murmurings against the tyranny of her rule died down to judicious whispers. If a vote went contrary to her desires, it was in her absence. Thus she became the pivot about which all the social and intellectual life of the colored people of her section revolved. No one had yet been found with the temerity to contest her position, which, like a title of nobility, bade fair to descend to her children. It was thought that she might be eclipsed by the younger and more brilliant women students on the strength of their alma mater, but she still held her own by sheer force of will-power and indomitable pluck.

The subject of the talk at this meeting was: "The place which the virtuous woman occupies in upbuilding a race." After a few explanatory remarks, Mrs. Willis said:

"I am particularly anxious that you should think upon this matter seriously, because of its intrinsic value to all of us as race women. . I am not less anxious because you represent the coming factors of our race. Shortly, you must fill the positions now occupied by your mothers, and it will rest with you and your children to refute the charges brought against us as to our moral irresponsibility, and the low moral standard maintained by us in comparison with other races."

"Did I understand you to say that the Negro woman in her native state is truly a virtuous woman?" asked Sappho, who had been very silent during the bustle attending the opening of the meeting.

"Travelers tell us that the native African woman is impregnable in her virtue," replied Mrs. Willis.

"So we have sacrificed that attribute in order to acquire civilization," chimed in Dora.

"No, not 'sacrificed,' but pushed one side by the force of circumstances. Let us thank God that it *is* an essential attribute peculiar to us — a racial characteristic which is slumbering but not lost," replied Mrs. Willis. "But let us not forget the definition of virtue — 'Strength to do the right thing under all temptations.' Our ideas of virtue are too narrow. We confine them to that conduct which is ruled by our animal passions alone. It goes deeper than that — general excellence in every duty of life is what we may call virtue."

"Do you think, then, that Negro women will be held responsible for all the lack of virtue that is being laid to their charge today? I mean, do you think that God will hold us responsible for the *illegitimacy* with which our race has been obliged, as it were, to flood the world?" asked Sappho.

"I believe that we shall not be held responsible for wrongs which we have *unconsciously* committed, or which we have committed under *compulsion*. We are virtuous or non-virtuous only when we have a *choice* under temptation.

We cannot by any means apply the word to a little child who has never been exposed to temptation, nor to the Supreme Being 'who cannot be tempted with evil.' So with the African brought to these shores against his will — the state of morality which implies will-power on his part does not exist, therefore he is not a responsible being. The sin and its punishment lies with the person *consciously* false to his *knowledge* of right. From this we deduce the truism that 'the civility of no race is perfect whilst another race is degraded.'"

"I shall never forget my feelings," chimed in Anna Stevens, a school teacher of a very studious temperament, "at certain remarks made by the Rev. John Thomas at one of his noonday lectures in the Temple. He was speaking on 'Different Races,' and had in his vigorous style been sweeping his audience with him at a high elevation of thought which was dazzling to the faculties, and almost impossible to follow in some points. Suddenly he touched upon the Negro, and with impressive gesture and lowered voice thanked God that the mulatto race was dying out, because it was a mongrel mixture which combined the worst elements of two races. Lo, the poor mulatto! despised by the blacks of his own race, scorned by the whites! Let him go out and hang himself!"

In her indignation Anna forgot the scissors, and bit her thread off viciously with her little white teeth.

Mrs. Willis smiled as she said calmly: "My dear Anna, I would not worry about the fate of the mulatto, for the fate of the mulatto will be the fate of the entire race. Did you never think that today the black race on this continent has developed into a race of mulattoes?"

"Why, Mrs. Willis!" came in a chorus of voices.

"Yes," continued Mrs. Willis, still smiling. "It is an incontrovertible truth that there is no such thing as an unmixed black on the American continent. Just bear in mind that we cannot tell by a person's complexion whether he be dark or light in blood, for by the working of the natural laws the white father and black mother produce the mulatto offspring; the black father and white mother the mulatto offspring also, while the *black father* and *quadroon* mother produce the black child, which to the eye alone is a child of unmixed black blood. I will venture to say that out of a hundred apparently pure black men not one will be able to trace an unmixed flow of African blood since landing upon these shores! What an unhappy example of the frailty of all human intellects, when such a man and scholar as

Doctor Thomas could so far allow his prejudices to dominate his better judgment as to
add one straw to the burden which is popularly
supposed to rest upon the unhappy mulattoes
of a despised race," finished the lady, with a
dangerous flash of her large dark eyes.

"Mrs. Willis," said Dora, with a scornful
little laugh, "I am not unhappy, and I am a
mulatto. I just enjoy my life, and I don't want
to die before my time comes, either. There
are lots of good things left on earth to be enjoyed even by mulattoes, and I want my share."

"Yes, my dear; and I hope you may all live
and take comfort in the proper joys of your
lives. While we are all content to accept life,
and enjoy it along the lines which God has laid
down for us as individuals as well as a race,
we shall be happy and get the best out of life.
Now, let me close this talk by asking you to
remember one maxim written of your race by
a good man: 'Happiness and social position
are not to be gained by pushing.' Let the
world, by its need of us along certain lines,
and our intrinsic fitness for these lines, push
us into the niche which God has prepared for
us. So shall our lives be beautified and our
race raised in the civilization of the future as
we grow away from all these prejudices which
have been the instruments of our advancement

according to the intention of an All-seeing Om-
nipotence, from the beginning. Never mind
our poverty, ignorance, and the slights and
injuries which we bear at the hands of a higher
race. With the thought ever before us of what
the Master suffered to raise all humanity to its
present degree of prosperity and intelligence,
let us cultivate, while we go about our daily
tasks, no matter how inferior they may seem
to us, beauty of the soul and mind, which being
transmitted to our children by the law of heredity, shall improve the race by eliminating *im-
morality* from our midst and raising *morality*
and virtue to their true place. Thirty-five
years of liberty have made us a new people.
The marks of servitude and oppression are
dropping slowly from us; let us hasten the
transformation of the body by the nobility of
the soul."

> For of the soul the body form doth take,
> For soul is form and doth the body make,

quoted Dora.

"Yes," said Mrs. Willis with a smile, "that
is the idea exactly, and well expressed. Now
I hope that through the coming week you will
think of what we have talked about this afternoon, for it is of the very first importance to
all people, but particularly so to young folks."

Sappho, who had been thoughtfully embroidering pansies on white linen, now leaned back in her chair for a moment and said: " Mrs. Willis, there is one thing which puzzles me — how are we to overcome the nature which is given us? I mean how can we eliminate passion from our lives, and emerge into the purity which marked the life of Christ? So many of us desire purity and think to have found it, but in a moment of passion, or under the pressure of circumstances which we cannot control, we commit some horrid sin, and the taint of it sticks and will not leave us, and we grow to loathe ourselves."

" Passion, my dear Miss Clark, is a state in which the will lies dormant, and all other desires become subservient to one. Enthusiasm for any one object or duty may become a passion. I believe that in some degree passion may be beneficial, but we must guard ourselves against a sinful growth of any appetite. All work of whatever character, as I look at it, needs a certain amount of absorbing interest to become successful, and it is here that the Christian life gains its greatest glory in teaching us how to keep ourselves from abusing any of our human attributes. We are not held responsible for compulsory sin, only for the sin that is pleasant to our thoughts and palatable to our appetites. All desires and hopes with which we are endowed are good in the sight of God, only it is left for us to discover their right uses. Do I cover your ground?"

"Yes and no," replied Sappho; "but perhaps at some future time you will be good enough to talk with me personally upon this subject."

"Dear child, sit here by me. It is a blessing to look at you. Beauty like yours is inspiring. You seem to be troubled; what is it? If I can comfort or strengthen, it is all I ask." She pressed the girl's hand in hers and drew her into a secluded corner. For a moment the flood-gates of suppressed feeling flew open in the girl's heart, and she longed to lean her head on that motherly breast and unburden her sorrows there.

"Mrs. Willis, I am troubled greatly," she said at length.

"I am *so* sorry; tell me, my love, what it is all about."

Just as the barriers of Sappho's reserve seemed about to be swept away, there followed, almost instantly, a wave of repulsion toward this woman and her effusiveness, so forced and insincere. Sappho was very impressionable, and yielded readily to the influence which fell like a cold shadow between them. She drew back as from an abyss suddenly beheld stretching before her.

"On second thoughts, I think I ought to correct my remarks. It is not really *trouble*, but more a desire to confirm me in my own ideas."

"Well, if you feel you are right, dear girl, stand for the uplifting of the race and womanhood. Do not shrink from duty."

"It was simply a thought raised by your remarks on morality. I once knew a woman who had sinned. No one in the community in which she lived knew it but herself. She married a man who would have despised her had he known her story; but as it is, she is looked upon as a pattern of virtue for all women."

"And then what?" asked Mrs. Willis, with a searching glance at the fair face beside her.

"Ought she not to have told her husband before marriage? Was it not her duty to have thrown herself upon his clemency?"

"I think not," replied Mrs. Willis dryly. "See here, my dear, I am a practical woman of the world, and I think your young woman builded wiser than she knew. I am of the opinion that most men are like the lower animals in many things — they don't always know what is for their best good. If the husband had been left to himself, he probably would not have married the one woman in the world best fitted to be his wife. I think in her case she did her duty."

"Ah, that word 'duty.' What is our duty?" queried the girl, with a sad droop to the sensitive mouth. "It is so hard to know our duty. We are told that all hidden things shall be revealed. Must repented and atoned-for sin rise at last to be our curse?"

"Here is a point, dear girl. God does not look upon the constitution of sin as we do. His judgment is not ours; ours is finite, his infinite. *Your* duty is not to be morbid, thinking these thoughts that have puzzled older heads than yours. *Your* duty is, also, to be happy and bright for the good of those about you. Just blossom like the flowers, have faith and *trust*." At this point the entrance of the men made an interruption, and Mrs. Willis disappeared in a crowd of other matrons. Sappho was impressed in spite of herself, by the woman's words. She sat buried in deep thought.

There was evidently more in this woman than appeared upon the surface. With all the centuries of civilization and culture that have come to this grand old world, no man has yet been found able to trace the windings of God's inscrutable ways. There are men and women whose seeming uselessness fit perfectly into the warp and woof of Destiny's web. All things work together for good.

Supper being over, the elderly people began to leave. It was understood that after nine o'clock the night belonged to the young people. A committee had been formed from among them to plan for their enjoyment, and they consulted with Ma Smith, in the kitchen, as to the best plan of procedure.

"The case is this," said the chairman, who was also the church chorister: "Ma Smith has bought four gallons of ice cream, to be sold for the benefit of this fair. It's *got* to go, and it rests with us to devise ways and means of getting rid of it."

"Get up a dance," suggested Sam Washington, a young fellow who was the life of all social functions.

"Dance!" exclaimed Ma Smith, "not in this house."

The choir-master surreptitiously kicked Sam on the shins, as he said soothingly: "Under the circumstances I see no other way, as we've *got* to sell the cream, and there's no harm in dancing, anyway."

"You ain't going to object to our dancing, are you, Ma? It's all old fogyism about dancing being a sin," chimed in Sam.

"Oh, but my son, I've been a church member over thirty years, a consistent Christian, and I never was up before the board for behavior unbecoming a professor. Think of the disgrace on me if the church took it up," she expostulated tearfully.

"Look here, Ma, the deacons and ministers are all fooling you. It's the style for church members to go to the theatre and the circus, to balls and everything you can mention. Why, I've seen our own pastor up to see the Black Crook, and laughing like all possessed at the sights. Fact!"

"Why, Samuel!" said Ma Smith, "how can you stand there and tell me such awful stories?"

"Not a bit of a story," declared the brazen-faced Sam, "it's as true as gospel. I'll find out what seat the minister gets next June when the circus comes into town, and I'll get a seat for you right behind him. If you've never been to the circus, Ma, and to see the seven-headed lady and the dancing mokes, you ought to go as soon as possible. Think of the fun you're missing."

"Oh!" groaned the good woman in holy horror, "how you do go on."

"But that ain't nothing to the ice cream," continued Sam, "and them girls in there have got to be warmed up, or the cream will be left, and there won't be a thing doing when the committee calls for the money."

"That's so," replied Ma Smith, beginning to weaken in her opposition.

"Well, mother," said Will, who had been an amused listener to the dialogue, "we'll have the dance, and it shall be *my* dance for *my* company. No one shall trouble you; you will have nothing to do with it."

"Well, if you say so, Willie, it's all right," replied his mother with a fond smile; "you are master in this house."

In the meantime the furniture in the parlors had been moved out by other members of the committee, and in one corner a set of whist-players were enjoying themselves at ten cents a head for a thirty-minute game, which ended at the stroke of a small silver bell, their places being taken by others.

Already it was getting very warm in the crowded rooms. The doors leading into the entry had been thrown open, and couples were finding seats in convenient nooks waiting for dancing to begin. The girls were thinking of ice cream. Rev. Tommy James gravitated toward Mrs. Davis's corner. She had not gone out with the other matrons.

"I enjoy a real good time as much as anybody, children," she said; "and when it comes to dancing, you can't lose your Aunt Hannah."

The Reverend Tommy was always at his ease with Mrs. Davis. She led him along paths which caused him no embarrassment.

He knew that she looked up to him because of his education and his clerical dignity. On his side, he admired her rugged common-sense, which put him at his ease, and banished the last atom of his "ladylike" bashfulness. Early in the winter he had been brought to realize the nature of his feeling for Mrs. Davis, by seeing Brother Silas Hamm, recently left a widower, and having ten children, making a decided stampede in the widow's direction. Reverend Tommy was grieved. To be sure, she was old enough to be his mother, but she had many good points to be considered. She was a good worker, experienced in married life and ways of making a man comfortable. Then her savings must be considered. When Tommy reached this last point he always felt sure that she was the most desirable woman in the world for a young minister. He felt hopeful tonight, because he had seen Brother Hamm and his bride in church the Sunday before. Mrs. Davis opened the conversation by speaking of the bride and groom.

"Hamm and his bride looked mighty comfut'ble in chuch Sunday, didn't they?"

"*He* did. I'm glad he's settled again. It is not good for man to be alone."

"'Deed I'm glad, too."

"*You* — well, well, I'm real glad to hear *you* say it."

"What for?" asked the widow coyly, looking down and playing with her fan.

"I — I didn't know how you and Brother Hamm stood."

"Stood! Well, I never."

"I thought Brother Hamm had been trying to get you," whispered Tommy, sitting closer and putting his arm across the back of her chair.

"Law suz, Mr. Jeems, how nervous you does make me. Do take yer arm away, everybody'll be a-lookin' at yer, honey. I'm 'sprised at yer thinkin' I'd look at Hamm an' all them chillun. Massy knows what the 'ooman he's got's gwine to do with 'em." But she looked so mild and smiling that Tommy went into the seventh heaven of delight, and so lost his head that when he heard the call "Another couple wanted here!" he took Mrs. Davis on his arm and stood up on the floor, forgetful of the fact that he was within a few months of his ordination. A good-natured matron not connected with the church had volunteered to supply the lack of an orchestra. Waltzing was soon in full blast, and the demand on the ice-cream cans was filling Ma Smith's heart with joy, tempered with inward stings of conscience and fear of the Steward's Board. Dora was dancing assiduously and eating ice cream at John's expense, he meantime

saying that if she kept on she would turn into
a frozen dainty, to say nothing of a frost in his
pocketbook.   Dora declared that it was for the
good of the cause, and he'd "just got to stand
it."   She was wildly happy because of the tender
familiarity between her brother and her friend.
A long-stemmed rose that Will wore in his but-
ton-hole had been transferred to Sappho's corsage. Dora smiled as she caught the half-puzzled,
half-wondering expression on her mother's face.

It was approaching twelve o'clock when it
was proposed to wind up the festivities with
the good old "Virginy" reel. Sam Washington was the caller, and did his work with the
fancy touch peculiar to a poetic Southern temperament. He was shrewd and good-natured,
and a bit of a wag. He knew all the secret
sighings of the ladies and their attendant
swains. A lively girl whom everyone called
"Jinny," remarked to Sam, referring to the fact
that Sam was on probation: "Your class-leader
won't recommend you to the Board for membership after tonight."

"Now, Jinny," replied Sam, stopping in his
business of arranging couples, "don't make
yourself obnoxious bringing up unpleasant subjects. I'll take my medicine like a man when
the time comes; but I'd bust, sho, if I didn't git
loose tonight. I'm in good company, too," he

grinned, nodding toward Reverend Tommy and Mrs. Davis, who were just taking their places on the floor. "If this is good for Tommy, it is good enough for me."

All reserve was broken down the instant the familiar strains of the Virginia reel were heard. The dance was soon in full swing — an up-and-down, dead-in-earnest seeking for a good time, and a determination to have it if it was to be got. It was a vehement rhythmic thump, thump, thumpity thump, with a great stamping of the feet and cutting of the pigeon wing. Sam had provided himself with the lively Jinny for a partner, and was cutting grotesque juba figures in the pauses of the music, to the delight of the company. His partner, in wild vivacity, fairly vied with him in his efforts at doing the hoe-down and the heel-and-toe. Not to be out-done, the Rev. Tommy James and Mrs. Davis scored great hits in cutting pigeon wings and in reviving forgotten beauties of the "walk-'round." Tommy "allowed" he hadn't enjoyed himself so much since he came up North.

"Yes," said Sam, "this beats the cake-walk all holler. Now then, one more turn and we're done. Forward on the head; balance yer partner; swing the next gent; swing that lady. Now swing yer rose, yer pretty rose, yer yaller rose of Texas. All promen*ade*."

Everybody declared it had been a wonderful evening. " Thank the Lord it's over," said Ma Smith to Mrs. Sarah Ann White, who was helping her in the kitchen.

" Well," said the latter, pausing in her work with her arms akimbo, " sech sights as I've seen tonight I never would have believed. 'Phelia Davis, what ought ter be a mother in Jerusalem, kickin' up her heels in your parlor like a colt in a corn-field ; and that Tommy Jeems, no more fittin' fer a minister than a suckin' babe, a-traipsin' after her like a bald-headed rooster."

CHAPTER IX.

"LOVE TOOK UP THE HARP OF LIFE."

Love took up the glass of Time, and turn'd it in his glowing hands;
Every moment, lightly shaken, ran itself in golden sands.
Love took up the harp of Life, and smote on all the chords with
    might.   —TENNYSON.

WILL SMITH sat the next evening in his room trying to engage his mind and chain his wandering thoughts upon an important prize thesis. As a brilliant philosophical student destined to shine in the future in the world of science, he had been requested to become a competitor for the prize. Ever and anon his attention wavered, and finally he threw his books and papers to one side with a sigh, and rising to his feet paced the floor impatiently. Two soft eyes looked into his; the low music of a gentle voice seemed all about him.

"Pshaw!" he exclaimed impatiently, " I have laughed at others only to become more of a drivelling idiot than any of the men I have ridiculed. I never thought mere beauty in a woman could move me so." The smile induced by pleasant thoughts lingered on his face as he threw himself upon his couch and tried to bring order out of the chaos of his thoughts.

Smith's hopes were all for a finishing course at college, and then a course in philosophy at some good German university. Philosophy was a mania with him. In vain had bishops and clergymen of all denominations warned him that his mania might become a passion, which would draw him from a right conception of the Word, and dull his appreciation of the beauties of Revelation. Will contended that religion and the natural laws were not antagonistic, and that being convinced and thoroughly grounded in his faith, he but discovered fresh evidence of infinite perfection in the doctrine of his Master when he sought to expand his faculties and illuminate his mind by seeking a clearer perception of the interesting relation which weak humanity bears to the glorious mysteries of life and the grandeurs of creation.

He laughed at the idea of Latin and Greek being above the caliber of the Negro and likely to unfit him for the business of bread-getting in the peculiar position in life to which the Negro, as maintained by some, was destined from the beginning. With him Latin and Greek represented but tools which he used to unlock the storehouse of knowledge. The development of his race was a matter of first importance to his mind. The only way to bring the best faculties of the Negro to their full fruition, he

contended, was by the careful education of the
moral faculties along the lines of the natural
laws.   No Negro college, he argued, ought to
bestow a diploma upon man or woman who had
not been thoroughly grounded in the rudiments
of moral and natural philosophy, physiology,
and political economy.

At twenty-five Smith found himself about to
realize his hopes.   He was fitted to enter Harvard University and graduate after a short
course there.   His articles in local magazines
had attracted the favorable notice of scientific
men, and one wealthy gentleman had offered
him a course at Heidelberg after graduation.
Emerson's words on character were an apt
description of the strong personality of this
man : " A reserved force which acted directly
by its presence, and without (apparent) means."

His sister's friends possessed no attraction
for him ; he treated them as little girls, looking
down upon them from the superior height of
his twenty-five years with a gentle condescen-
sion, tempered always by the natural chivalry
of a generous nature toward the weak and
helpless.   He was a favorite with women, old
and young, in spite of his careless, half-haughty
ways.   Many a sigh was wafted after his handsome, unconscious self, as a pretty maiden who
had fancied that *she* had at length conquered

the unconquerable, saw her chains fall from him
as lightly as a cobweb is brushed away. What
had come to him now at the glance of a soft,
fawn-like eye, the touch of a hand, a caressing
smile, the sound of a sweet voice? Sappho
had been with them two months, but Will felt
that he must have known her for years. Suddenly he passed from youth to manhood, and
realized man's destiny. He had assisted his
mother and sister with happy pride, but now
the desire to shield, to protect, to love one
being supremely above all others, rose and
surged within him with a mighty strength.

Although love had come to Smith like a flood
sweeping all barriers before it, yet the very
strength of his desire for her love but served
to restrain decided action. He approached the
desired end slowly and carefully, not to defeat
his own plans. He was well aware that Sappho's nature was a rare one, dwelling much
upon lonely heights, the home of extraordinary moral sensitiveness and high intellectual
development. Again he saw her advancing
toward him in the mazes of the dance: her
hand lay in his; her soft hair brushed his face;
her sweet breath came to him from smiling
rose-leaf lips, and intoxicated his senses.

"The starlike beauty of immortal eyes,"
fringed by long, curling lashes, flashed at him

from the four corners of his dingy room. What tender thrills of sympathetic feeling had seemed to enfold his senses as he gazed into their limpid depths — what beauty and strength lurked in the mobile, sweetly smiling mouth! The delicately moulded chin on which the God of Love had left his impress, might have served as the model for a sculptor. She and no other should be his wife — God willing.

. . . .

Propinquity is responsible for many matches. It was pleasant for Sappho, when she returned mornings from delivering her work, to find her fire burning briskly and the room well warmed. It was a comfort to her not to have the ugly problem of ashes, wood and coal to solve. Not that she was too proud, or that she thought housework of any kind beneath her; but what woman does not feel it a relief to find the machinery of the home running smoothly without her aid. She thought nothing about ways and means, taking it for granted that there was nothing unusual in finding things pleasant, and she congratulated herself on being so fortunate in having " heat " included in Ma Smith's modest charges for lodging. Upon her return one morning, as she mounted the stairs to her room she saw from the light reflected that her door was open. Someone within the room

was singing in a fine baritone voice a verse of
an old song:

> Of all the days that are in the week,
>   I dearly love but one day.
> That is the day that comes between
>   Saturday and Monday.
> For then I dress all in my best
>   And roam with my dear Sally;
> She's the darling of my heart,
>   And she lives in our alley.

She pushed the door open and entered.   Her
cheeks were glowing from her walk in the brac-
ing morning air, but her face assumed a serious,
questioning look as she discovered Will just
finishing up his self-imposed morning task.
He gave an extra flourish to the brushes to
cover his confusion and annoyance, and kept
right on polishing off the little heater with his
dubious-looking black cloths well filled with
stove polish.

"Well!" she exclaimed.

"Good morning," returned Will, with a busi-
nesslike flourish of his cloth, as, having finished
the stove, he proceeded to touch up the bright
piece of zinc under it.   "How will she take
it?" he asked himself.

"Well!" she repeated.

"Quite well, thank you," said Will, this time
with a quizzical grin on his face.

"I had no idea *you* were the fireman, Mr. Smith."

"No? In the words of Doctor Peters, 'I do mos' anythin' in the wurl, honey, to git an hones' livin' without stealin' it.'"

Will had donned one of his mother's ample kitchen aprons for the protection of his clothing. The bib was pinned well up in front across the broad expanse of shirt bosom; the ample folds of the apron-skirt enveloped his limbs to his ankles; the long strings, crossed in the back, met in front in a huge bow-knot. There was a streak of smut across one eye, and the side of his nose was polished to perfection. The picture was too much for Sappho, and peal after peal of laughter shook her slight frame.

"Oh, Mr. Smith," she said, when she could find breath, "you do look *so* funny!"

"''Twas ever thus from childhood's hour,'" quoted Will, marching up to the mirror to survey his beauty spots; "I do look rather fetching," he continued, with a confidential smile at his laughing companion.

"Do you do this every day?" asked Sappho, suddenly sobering down.

"Do what every day?"

"Why, make my fire?"

"It's not your fire any more than anyone else's fire."

" I'm *very* sorry."

" Sorry! sorry about what? It isn't a crime, is it, for a man to make a fire for his women folks?"

" But I'm not your ' women folks.' "

" Look here," said Will in an aggrieved tone, balancing a hod of ashes in one hand and a pile of stove brushes in the other, " are we going to quarrel?"

" There is no reason why we should if we agree," said Sappho, smiling gravely.

" That means that we shan't quarrel if I agree to whatever you are going to propose. What is it you want to say?" he asked, becoming grave in his turn. " Is it that I have behaved unmanly in visiting your room in your absence? Why cavil about a little thing of that sort? I do this for you as I would for Dora."

" Oh, if you look at it that way "— she began, a trifle confused by his apparent unconsciousness.

" How else ought I to look at it?"

" How horrid you are."

" Horrid! I don't see what I've said that is so very dreadful."

" You speak so — well — so cross."

" I speak like a man talking to a silly girl."

" Now you are rude again; calling me names."

" Children must be kept in their places," he said banteringly.

"You're making fun of me."

"Of course I am. What do you expect?"

"But you mustn't make my fire again."

"I am sorry you found it out; I didn't intend you to know it."

"I can't pay for having the work done, and it is not proper for you to do it; there is no reason why you should do such work for me."

"Suppose we play you are my other sister; that will make it all right, won't it?

"No," came firmly from Sappho's lips; "no more fires."

"See here, I've hit it! Play I'm your *father*."

"Ridiculous!"

"What, neither brother nor father? How'd it do to imagine that you're *my mother?* You can't find fault with that, surely."

"How silly you are."

"No likee me for sonny?" queried Will, with a sad shake of his head.

"If you don't leave this room instantly, William Smith, I'll call your mother," replied Sappho, laughing in spite of herself.

"The best play, though, would be sweethearts," he continued, as though she had not spoken.

"Sweethearts!"

"Yes, sweethearts; and I believe I could win the game, too, in spite of your reserve."

"You must be very sure of your power, young man. You need a lesson in diffidence." He held her gaze for a moment, and there was so much earnestness in the persistent dark eyes that she blushed furiously. He turned and abruptly left the room. No more was said about the fire, but Will continued to perform common everyday duties for her the same as for his sister. She did her part, too. Many an evening he found her helping Dora, darning socks or replacing lost buttons. Will's manner had changed toward her from that day; from easy familiarity it changed to a mixture of timid reserve and marked deference. Sappho noticed it, but somehow she liked it better. It spoke to her silently of tender, sacred thoughts. To-night he thought of the scene just pictured, as he sat there in his room. She and none other should be his wife — God willing.

In another part of the house Ma Smith sat before the fire in her chamber and meditated on many things. The knitting with which the busy hands were always engaged when at leisure, dropped in her lap, and lay there unheeded. She thought of the incident of Sappho and the rose of the night before, and the merry, teasing look that had flashed out at her for one instant from Dora's laughing eyes. Could it be possible that she was about to lose her son? Dora's

engagement to John Langley had been a source
of great satisfaction to her; the old-fashioned
notion was still strong within her that it was
the right destiny for girls to marry, and that
the only cause for a mother to grieve in the
idea of marriage for her daughter was the awful
chance of that daughter's remaining single.
The girl's life should be lost in that of the wife
and mother. Such an end to maidenhood was
a happy achievement for the girl and a glory to
her family. But with her boy it was different.
He was her first-born, and memory was busy
tonight with the past.

Her Will with a wife! herself a grandmother!
To renew at this age the joys which had been
hers when first he lay within her arms a soft
morsel of humanity, with sweet brown face and
melting black eyes that mirrored themselves
within the citadel of her heart. Ma Smith had
known much sorrow in her life. She could tell
you of hard times when it seemed that the
combined efforts of her husband and herself
would not avail to keep the wolf from the door.
She knew what it was to bake and brew, to
mend and make over, to minister to the needs
of childhood with increasing maternal cares
near at hand. With all this, the offered work
which added a few dollars to their little store
was always gladly accepted. But she would

tell you also that she would not have given one
hour of those days, with all their privations,
for the happiness that she enjoyed when in the
privacy of a humble home she counted her
"precious jewels"— an honest husband and two
beautiful children. "Yes," she was wont to
say, "we had a hard time, and sometimes the
waters of affliction seemed about to sweep us
from our foothold, but somehow just when
everything was darkest we could see the light
of prosperity shining through the clouds, and
we would take courage, bless the Lord, and
keep on struggling."

Tonight she lived those struggles over again,
and tried to imagine what it would be to have
another share the love and reverence of the
idolized son. At first it seemed that she could
not endure the thought; but then she remembered how happy she had been in her married
life, and prayed the Lord to deliver her from
selfish desires. Who was she to stand in the
way of her son's happiness — a son whom she
loved? Sappho Clark was beautiful; she believed her to be a girl of exemplary conduct.
Sappho was always deferential to her, giving to
the elder woman the gentle deference which,
coming from youth, is so dear to those advanced
in years. So with a heart overflowing with
love, and filled with kind and tender thoughts,

it was no mystery where the pretty old face had caught its added charm of heavenly brightness. So Dora found her when she returned from spending the evening with some young friends.

"Why, mummy dear, I declare you are growing younger and handsomer every day. We girls must look to our laurels if you keep on growing so pretty."

"Well, my love, I have been thinking of your father tonight, and how happy we were when you and Will were wee tots."

Dora knew well what had set her mother thinking. She appreciated her feelings. She knew that her mother had always felt that no woman could be good enough for Will's wife. She felt instinctively that her mother had faced the difficulty alone that evening and conquered it, effacing herself and her desires for the happiness of her son. With her usual impulsiveness Dora threw herself on her knees beside her mother's chair, and drawing her face down to her, kissed the wrinkled brow and smoothed the soft white hair.

"Mummy, dear," she said, "you have made up your mind to give him up to Sappho if things turn out that way?"

"Yes, my dear," replied her mother, with her hand upon the dark braids beside her. "I will

DORA THREW HERSELF ON HER KNEES BESIDE HER MOTHER'S CHAIR.

not say that it was not a struggle, but mothers
know, if they stop to think, that they must lose
their babies sometime.   Your father and I made
a home for ourselves, so I must look forward
to the time when you young birds will want to
build a nest away from me.   But what is the
matter with you, Dora? you look worried.   Is
anything wrong?"

"Oh, no," replied the girl, as she rose from
her knees by her mother's side and began putting her things away and preparing for the
night. "Isn't it strange what a queer old world
this is? If you are happy I am not, or *vice
versa*. It does seem that one thing or another
is always happening to vex a body. And the
worst of it is that it may happen that we are
impatient and unhappy about things that are
trivial. I don't feel sweet-tempered tonight,
and really, I can't tell why."

Ma Smith glanced at her daughter sharply
but said nothing, as Dora thrust her bare feet
into bedroom slippers and proceeded to undo
the thick masses of curling brown hair, and
brush and arrange it for the night. The mother
knew that her daughter would unburden her
mind presently, and so she waited patiently.
It was not like Dora to be petulant and have
moods. She was a happy, healthy, active girl,
with a kindly disposition.

"Ma," said Dora after a silence, "why is it that Southern colored people seem to be so prejudiced against the Northern colored people? I always fancied that we were all in the same boat, and that mere accidental locality was not to be considered."

"That is true, my dear; but it must be that you *imagine* the prejudice to exist that you mention; surely we have outgrown such ideas, as a race, by this time."

Dora shook her head obstinately. "I fancied that the Wilsons slighted me tonight, and that they would have been better pleased if John had chosen a Southern girl."

"You are over-sensitive, Dora."

Dora did not reply, and after a moment's silence continued: "John said that he had not met a decent-looking woman who was Northern-born, and that when he did see a pretty colored girl on the street he knew without asking that she was a Southerner."

"That was rather thoughtless in John, but I don't think he meant to hurt your feelings, daughter."

"I cannot imagine what has got into him lately; he's not like himself. Oh, I *do* wish I was handsome like Sappho Clark! All the men are wild over her."

"Well, my dear, you don't harbor hard feel-

ings against Sappho on that account, do you?
That would not be like you, Dora, and would
grieve me very much."

"Sappho is the best and dearest girl on earth,
and I only hope that Will may be so lucky as
to marry her. And, mummy, I hope Will will
speak to her right off, so as to get the matter
straightened out; there won't be a blessed man
left to us girls if she remains single long."

Her mother smiled. "Daughter, I want to
say just a word to you about our conversation:
Don't allow jealousy to lurk in your heart;
don't brood over unkind words; cast them
from you. And I would have you remember,
also, that sectional prejudice has always been
fostered by the Southern whites among the
Negroes to stifle natural feelings of brotherly
love among us. Dissension means disunion.
Carry these thoughts always in your mind, and
act accordingly. Do not allow yourself to be
made unhappy."

. . . .

Meanwhile on the floor above them Sappho
turned restlessly on her pillow, thinking of a
noble head and bright dark eyes. She knew
that Will Smith loved her. What woman does
not feel the subtle intertwining of a kindred
spirit linked to her own by the decree of Destiny, long years, perhaps, before either restless

soul has entered upon its earthly pilgrimage. She was not happy in her knowledge. Under cover of the friendly darkness she gave up the long struggle for self-control, and indulged in the grief that she knew was hers for all eternity. Oh, for death, the solitude of the grave and self-forgetfulness.

"What have I done, what have I done to suffer thus? To give up all joy, and have only misery for all my life. I love this man; I know it now! I want his love, his care, his protection. I want him through life and beyond the grave, we two as one — my husband. Oh, my God, help me, help me!" Heavy sobs shook her frame. Broken exclamations fell from her lips. "I cannot! It must not be! So good, so noble! Oh, the happiness of home and love! must I be shut from them forever?"

Far into the night the agony of sobs continued. At last with a murmured prayer for help she fell asleep.

CHAPTER X.

THE FAIR.

" BOISTEROUS jest and humor unrefined,
  That leave, though rough, no painful sting behind;
  Warm social joys surround the Negro's cot.

  No ennui clouds, no coming cares annoy,
  Nor wants nor sorrows check the Negro's joy."

THE days went on apace at No. 500 D Street, but a spirit of restlessness seemed to pervade the atmosphere; expectancy was on tiptoe. Everyone was absorbed in preparations for the fair. Such a time had not been known for years among the colored people. Every available individual was pressed into the service.

Naturally many factions had arisen, and a fierce but friendly rivalry divided the different societies within the church. Some of these were none too cordial to the outsiders who had joined them, and whom they dubbed in derision " the colored 400."

" I'd jes' like to know," said Sister Mary Jane Robinson, with a hand on each hip, " I'd jes' like to know who asked the ' 400 ' fer eny o' thar help ? I've been a member hyar fer more'n thirty years, and this chuch has lived without 'em." This was one morning directly after

service, while the good sisters were waiting for
class to begin. As the fair was the all-absorbing topic at present, conversation naturally
ended in going over all the interesting details
connected with it.

"Lor', Sis' Robberson, what mortal diffur-
unce does it make as long as the chuch gits the
money? The mo' helpers we has the easier it
makes it fer we-uns," replied Sister Scott, as
she endeavored to pour oil on the troubled
waters. Sister Robinson was a veritable fire-
brand; she spoke first and thought afterwards.

"Thar's that Mrs. Willis with her 'High
Chuch' notions," continued Sister Robinson.
"Sister Smith has made her presidunt of the
fine arts and fancy work department. Warn't
eny o' the members o' this chuch good enough,
an' they didn't know enough, did they, to 'tend
to that bisiness! Thar's that pianner an' that
silver set an' that ar gold watch an' chain that's
goin' to be voted fer. Ef that stuff don't be lef'
right hyar in this chuch thar's gwine ter be
trouble. An' as fer that dimon' pin that's to
go to the one who sells the most admission
tickets — well, now, ef the hard wurkin' sisters
o' this chuch what swets over the washtúb
earnin' an'.hones' livin' don't desarve it, then
what's the matter? yas, I wants ter know *what's*
the matter?" Here the irate woman sawed

the air with hand and arm as she laid down the law on the back of the nearest settee. By this time a group of sisters attracted by her loud tones had gathered around, anxious to learn what the trouble could be.

"Well, honey," said one meek-looking woman, "don't le's borry trouble. The way the committee has fixed the bisness I cayn't see how thar can be eny monkeyin' with the votin' or sellin' o' the tickets. I do declar', my dear, I think the right ones will git the prizes."

"I'm a-doin' my level best," said another sister with hands hard and horny with toil, " I'm a-doin' my level best to git that dimon' pin fer my Mandy. I've got William Vanderbilt and Charles Sumner Astor Gould and the twins all out sellin' tickets 'mong my white people. An' I tell you, sisters, you's all goin' to have a hard time to git 'way with yer Aunt Hanner Jackson this time."

The family surname was Jackson, but Mrs. Jackson liked to name her children for all the celebrities that she heard of, and sometimes it made a bewildering combination when one found that William Vanderbilt was represented by a sprightly little Negro boy with crispy hair and beadlike black eyes.

"That silver service is jes' my size," here chimed in another sister, "an' it's goin' hard with anyone what tries to git it 'way from me; I'm sellin' tickets to beat the ban. I've done picked out a sideboard fer it down to Osgood's. I can git it fer a dollar down an' a dollar a week, an' expec' to have it ef it takes me all the summer an' winter ter pay fer it."

"Talkin' 'bout the prizes, ain't yer?" spoke up another sister who had just joined the group, "thet gold watch an' chain is jes' what Jim Anderson wants. 'Jim,' I says to him, 'thar's yer chance fer a good easy way ter git yer a watch.' He's jes' raisin' heaven an' earth a-gittin' votes fer hisself."

"Hope you all won't be disapinted," here Sister Robinson broke in again, "but ef yer listens to me you'll watch them high-toned colored folks you all's been gittin' ter help yer. They never come 'roun' people that they don't hold on a 'quality with theirselves 'thout it means suthin.' These ejecated folks is allers lookin' to make suthin'. Most o' them's too lazy to wurk. They wouldn't tech a flatiron or a washtub with a ten-foot pole, an' they'd ruther live on dried codfish fer a month than to do their own scrubbing. Ef eny o' them white-folksey colored ladies gits them prizes, I'm goin' fer to take out my letter, an' put my wurk into some chuch what will *presheate* it; you hyar me!"

"Now sisters," chimed in the meek one again, "none o' yer ain't said a word 'bout tryin' to git one o' the prizes fer yer pastor. I do think that's a leetle bit selfish in us. S'pose we give him the pianny."

"Hump!" grunted Sister Robinson, "when I jined this chuch I jined the meetin'-house an' not the minister! I reckon he kin jes' look out fer hisself; 'sides he's got a orgin an' don't need a pianny. He gits his cellery, don't he?" she queried, as she glared at the group about her. Taking their silence for consent she continued in a firm voice: "He's too much everythin' to everybody, an' that wife o' hisn is too white fer me. I used ter be takin' fresh eggs an' ham an' chickuns out to that house *all* the time, but resuntly I'se been reasunin' with myself, an' I camed to the conclusion that I won't do it no mo'. Can't tell what *is* the matter with these colored men; a good wholesome-lookin' colored woman with kinkey hair don't stan' no livin' chance ter git a decen'-lookin' man fer a husban', an' I fer one am a-settin' my face agin them men."

"Purty much so, purty much so!" came from various ones in the group.

"Lord knows, Sis' Robberson," said Sister Scott, "may be you *is* right; an' ef thar's eny monkeyin' goin' on we's all goin' ter s'port yer in whatever yer thinks is the bes' course."

"All right," replied Sister Robinson, considerably mollified by this concession. "I'll jes' take good care thet none o' *us* gits imposed on. Phelia Davis an' Sarah Ann White has got charge o' the 'fectionery table an' the salads, but ef I don' knock 'em silly with roast pig, corn dodgers an' biled cabbage, then I'm a sinner!"

Sister Robinson walked away, followed by a number of admiring satellites. Sister Scott and Sister Jackson were left alone.

"Good Lawd!" said Sister Scott to Sister Jackson, "Good Lawd! 'Mandy Jackson, did you hear Mary Jane Robberson talk? Thar ain't nuthin' the matter with her, only she's 'fraid thet somebody's gwine ter hol' the money-draw fastened agin her. I tell yer them '400' folks she's runnin' 'll keep a close watch on her an' how much money she takes in at the 'old Southern dinner-table,' you hyar me!"

"An' I fer one am glad of it," replied Sister Jackson. "Mary Jane Robberson thinks she owns this chuch an' everyone in it sence Mr. Jacobs lef' John Robberson thet five hundred dollars, an' they bo't thet house out o' town."

"Bless yer soul, honey, thet's jes' so. I never see what a little posterity makes some people have a swell head. I tell yer, honey, we'd better all o' us keep our eye on the money-draw.

When folks gits to buyin' houses—um, chile, watch 'em!"

.   .   .   .

On Monday evening the fair opened. At five o'clock in the morning all the women who could get there made their appearance at the church, where the janitor was waiting to receive them. The first floor of the building contained a large lecture-room, three class-rooms, the pastor's study, a dining-room and a kitchen. Each chairman of a committee had a certain space assigned to her by Ma Smith; then that committee took charge and proceeded to beautify the spot and arrange their wares for inspection. Ice cream, oysters, salads and temperance drinks were to be served in a fairy-like grotto formed by grouping evergreen trees together. Among the trees small tables were to be set, making a charming *solitude à deux*. Electricity, cunningly concealed in rose-colored shades, was to furnish the lighting. Pretty girl-waiters, in white dresses and fancy caps, completed a fascinating picture. This section was under the immediate direction of Mrs. Ophelia Davis and Mrs. Sarah Ann White.

"You hear me, Sarah Ann," said Ophelia Davis to her friend, "you hear me, that Mary Jane Robberson means trouble. She's down on the aristocracy; she don't 'tend to give the minister a show over them prizes, an' you an' me's got to keep a whip han' over her some- how. The minister's goin' to git a new suit o' clo's out o' this, an' you an' me's gwine to have thet *pianny!* Lord knows whether there'll be one brick o' this chuch lef' on another when this fair is done, but she ain't gwine ter walk on me, you hyar me. I'm a-studyin' fer her, an' ef she runs up agin me thar'll be trouble."

Meanwhile Mrs. Robinson and her coterie stood around and looked at the unique ideas for a fair which had been developed, and won- dered how it was that the "400" people and their followers always had such a happy knack of getting everything just right. *Her* commit- tee had intended to have nothing but a plain dining-room, but after seeing the gorgeous dis- play made by Mrs. Davis and Mrs. White, a hurried meeting was called to consult about ways and means of defeating the enemy. All the other women stopped their work, too, and came to admire the effects gained by the intro- duction of the lights and the *tête-à-tête* tables.

"A very happy thought," said Mrs. Willis, as she glanced approvingly about her. "Where did you get the idea?"

"I got it up to Mis' Mason's when Molly Mason was merried."

"That's where you lived so long, wasn't it, Mrs. Davis?" asked one of the girls, as she paused a moment in her work of arranging festoons of evergreens, and stood back to note the effect.

"I lived there an' nowhere else the first fifteen years I was up North," replied Mrs. Davis proudly.

"Were they very wealthy? Do you ever see them nowadays?" asked Mrs. Willis.

"Mis' Mason was wurth her *millions*, an' Molly was her only chile," replied Mrs. Davis, now fairly launched on her favorite subject. "The Mason wedding" had passed into a proverb among the young people who were acquainted with Mrs. Davis. "You see, when Molly was married, Mis' Mason took it into her head to have a caterer from Boston do the work of feeding the guests. She was livin' in Worcester then. Even the servants were invited to the weddin'. She had a house that matched her money, you may jes' reckon, and the whole o' her lawn was used fer feeding an' fer dancin'. There were two acres o' lan' nuthin' but lawn, an' all among the trees you could see little tables set out an' plenty o' lanterns, although in the dancin' pavilion they jes' connected a gas-pipe with the main one, an' had the place lit with gas jes' as ef you was in the house."

"You ought to ask them to contribute to the fair, and help you out with your table," remarked Mrs. Willis.

Mrs. Davis cocked her head on one side and said, with a knowing wink at Mrs. Willis: "Now, ain't yer talkin', honey, an' mebe I ain't writ to her an' tol' her all 'bout Mary Jane Robberson! Jes' yer hol' on, chile, tell yer sees me *paralyze* her."

"Did you go to the wedding, Mrs. Davis?" asked Sappho, who, being something of a stranger, did not know all the little points about the wedding.

"*Who, me?*" exclaimed Mrs. Davis; "*yes'm,* I jes' *did!* Lor', chile, but Mis' Mason's a lady borned; she don't know how to be like some o' yer Northern people. Sho! these ladies up here are so 'fraid thet the black 'll rub off. Down South the big white folks has nussed so meny black mammies thet they don' know nuthin' else fer their chillun. It don' matter how black you is ef yer willin' to keep in the mud. Up here it's diffurunt; you can do all right and live all right, but don't put yer han' on a white man or woman, or they 'll have a fit fer fear the black 'll rub off."

"I suppose you went to the wedding dressed to kill," said one of the girls.

"Lor', chile, I had to have a new light silk

fer *that*, I tell yer. An' sech a time as I had
when I went to git me a pair o' paten' leather
shoes. Clorindy, gal," she called to a young
woman who was placing trees in position, "what
kin' o' way do you call that to put them trees?
You ain't got a bit o' eye fer bein' an artis',
your ferpendicler is all crooked. Bring me a
cheer thar, some one o' you gals, and let me fix
thet tree right." Having straightened out the
matter of the trees, she returned panting and
puffing to the refreshment bar. "As I was
sayin', the man said he didn't hev a shoe in the
shop thet would fit me. I tol' him I knowed
better; he jes' said thet 'cause I was a colored
'ooman. Then he went to the show-window
and took out a pair, an' tol' me to set down an'
he'd try 'em on me an' see ef they'd do, an' ef
they would I might have 'em, an' he'd git another
pair thet 'd do fer signs jes' as well as them. I
tol' him I didn't care a bit ef they *was* signs;
why didn't he trot 'em out when I asked him
fer 'em fust? 'Well,' he says, 'they's number
'levens, an' I didn't want ter *insult* yer.' '*Insult
nuthin*',' says I, 'as long as I can git 'em on.'
They fitted me all right, only they kin' o'
cramped me across my bunyon. I always has
a hard time with that dratted bunyon o' mine.
I managed to wear 'em, though I'm free to say
thet I never felt as though I got my muney out

o' the plagy things. As I was sayin', I was cook, an' the second girl was colored, too; we jes' hired an open barush to drive to the chuch in — I b'lieve in doin' things right — an' I tell you the white folks was dumb when we druve up that night to the chuch do' an' stepped out o' the kerrige onto the strip o' carpet under the yawnin', fer all the worl' jes' like quality. We got 'long all right tell we struck the entry, then Sally kin' o' hung back when she saw a big usher lookin' fer all the worl' like a picter-book, standin' ther an' tellin' us to wait our turn to be seated in the fambly pew. Yes, 'ndeed! Bless yer soul, Mis' Mason had done put us into one o' the fambly pews! I'm used to them sort o' things myself, but yer see, Sally she's kin' o' low-down corn-shucker, not used to nothin' 'tall, an' I kep' my eye onto her; I could see it inter her face thet she intended to give me the slip an' bolt an' hide herself. ' Oh, Mis' Davis,' says she, ' has we got to walk all the way up thet aisle with one o' them white gemplemen ?' ' Yes, Sally, we has, an' it won't kill us nuther to be like live gentry fer onct in our lives.' Jes' then one o' them made fer me, an' I only had time to whisper: ' Brace up, Sally, an' be a 'ooman,' when I foun' myself walkin' up the aisle on thet white man's arm, as big as Cuffy, an' a-sweatin' to beat the ban'."

" What became of Sally ? " asked Sappho.

" Bless yer soul, Miss Sappho, when she sawed me go she jes' broke an' run down them steps plum inter the street, an' made tracks fer the house all dressed as she was in white shefong, an' when I got back thar she was a-standin' up in the middle o' the kitchen floor grinnin' like a Chessy cat. ' Mis' Davis,' says she, ' Mis' Davis, I wouldn't a-walked up thet chuch aisle with thet white gempleman fer a thousan' dollars, 'deed'n I wouldn't.' I was so mad with thet fool gal thet I jes' itched ter spank her well. How we to 'vance eny ef we don't 'brace our 'tunities, I'd like ter know? "

All the committees worked willingly, and soon every one of the departments had been provided with appropriate enclosures like quaint pictures set in exquisite frames. The bare walls disappeared, and the whole place burst into beauty bewildering enough to draw the money from the pockets of the spectators who would come with the evening to help a worthy charity. Mrs. Robinson, with her "old-fashioned busy bees," as they called themselves, had hurriedly decorated the dining-room with American flags and Christian Endeavor banners. The long, white-covered tables looked very inviting, and the motherly women in black dresses, white aprons and bandanna handkerchiefs tied into fantastic head-coverings, added another charm which their soft Southern accent completed. Late in the afternoon the tired workers examined the results of their labors with much satisfaction.

CHAPTER XI.

THE FAIR.— *Concluded.*

" IN feasts maturing busy hands appear,
And jest and laugh assail the ready ear."

ON Monday evening at 7 P.M. the doors of
the fair were opened. In the center of the hall
the prize piano was advantageously placed;
and Dora, as the organist of the church, displayed its merits in a few well-chosen numbers.
There were selections given also by a banjo,
guitar and mandolin club of local reputation.
Cozily ensconced behind a bower of tropical
plants and flowers they discoursed popular
selections in a manner which displayed most
favorably the really fine musical ability which
each one of them possessed. In another corner of the hall, under a tent which represented
an Indian lodge, was a great and mysterious
attraction: Madam Frances, spiritualistic sooth-
sayer and marvellous mind-reader, had offered
her services to the committee, and would send
out bulletins, at so much a letter, on subjects
supposed to be unknown to all the world but
the persons themselves. The young people
were in a flutter over this particular feature, the
men no less so than the women. Who could

tell *what* might happen through her agency? Long delayed questions might be asked; unknown feelings might be revealed to anxious hearts. One might buy a lucky charm and present it to his inamorata, and by contact with it her coldness should vanish. Henry might receive a letter whose sweet perfume should banish the thoughts of Susan and turn his wandering heart to its first allegiance. Oh, happy race! which even now, when life is but a bare existence, though torn by howling mobs and scourged by fire, finds pleasure in the simple pastimes of innocence.

Superstition is supposed to be part of the Negro's heritage. They have brought much of it from their native Africa. It gives color, picturesqueness—light and shade we may say — to the darkness of life and complexion which so far has marked the Negro for its own. Claiming kinship with the Egyptians and other black races of the Eastern continent, the Negro is thought to possess wonderful powers of necromancy. Races are like families. The East Indian shows remarkable ability to awaken the superstitious fears of a community in his native country; so with the Egyptian; so with the Negro. But transplant them on a foreign shore and much of their supposed power vanishes. So with the Negro. We hear much of spells and charms being put upon unpleasant neighbors; wonderful stories of lizards being taken from the leg or arm of an enemy, placed there by the arts of the voodoo doctor and cured by the same gifted party. But if we notice, these wonderful and terrorizing acts were never perpetrated against the inhuman master or mistress of the isolated plantation, never upon enemies wearing a white skin, but always upon the humble associate and brother in bondage. Be these things true or false, the Negro no longer holds the distinction of being the only race that believes in the pretensions of those who claim to be able to look into the future with mesmerized sight favored by hidden powers, that have a knowledge of coming events. In these days of palmistry, phrenology, card-reading, mind-reading, lucky pigs, rabbit's feet worn on the watch-chain for luck, and four-leaved clover encased in crystal and silver for the same reason, who shall say that the Negro has not lost his monopoly of one great racial characteristic?

Madam Frances was supposed to be skilled in the occult arts which were once the glory of the freshly imported African. Wonderful tales were told of her ability to foretell the future. Her services were of great value to the managers of the fair, for her fame had been rumored abroad, through the members of the church, and it was popularly reported that some of the richest people in the city would visit the fair, if for nothing but to test the ability of this woman. And as one gazed upon her he might be pardoned for thinking that within that dark house, moulded upon symmetrical lines, and appearing as though cut from purest ebony, albeit somewhat thin and spare, as became one past the meridian of life and now upon the road leading downward into the shadows of the last valley through which we must pass on our outward journey toward the spheres of celestial light, dwelt a rare mind. How did she look?

"I knew a princess; she was old,
    Crisp-haired, flat-featured, with a look
Such as no dainty pen of gold
    Would write of in a fairy book.

.   .   .   .

Her face was like the Sphinx's face, to me,
Touched with vast patience, desert grace,
    And lonesome, brooding mystery.

Nothing of loveliest loveliness
    This strange, sad princess seemed to lack ;
Majestic with her calm distress
    She was, and beautiful, though black."

A quaint conceit which gave great pleasure to the children, big and little, was the pretty great-nephew of the seeress who, dressed in costume, represented Mercury and carried messages to the fortunate ones remembered by the mystic powers of Futurity. Alphonse was a beautiful boy about eight years old, with golden curls and dark blue eyes that looked out on life from beneath their sweeping lashes with a glance all too melancholy for one of his tender years. There are children who seem to have been born with the shadows of life heavy upon them. So it was with little Alphonse. He passed from groups of merry young people and pleasant elders who, attracted by the beauty of the weird child, sought to beguile him with soft caress and loving touch; he would stand quietly waiting until the speaker had finished his question, would answer carefully, and suffer the caresses as though accepting them as a part of his duty, and would return to the tent and his aunt, evincing no desire for the frolic and fun which belongs to the golden days of childhood. Many influential whites were present in order to display their philanthropic interest in the welfare of the colored people. They gazed with surprise upon the child, and could not be convinced when told that he was a Negro, and identified by ties of blood with the blackest men and women in the crowded company. In a distant corner Sappho sat keeping a strict account of the moneys received. Occasionally she would leave her seat and mingle with the crowd. Gowned in a pure white china silk with a bunch of her favorite Jacks in her corsage, she moved "a daughter of the gods divinely fair." And many a thought came into the heart of one learned doctor as he gazed on the child and the beautiful girl, and then upon faces ebony-hued but bright and sparkling with the light of freedom and intelligence. In that moment a cloud passed from before his mental vision, and he beheld in all its hideousness the cankering sore which is eating into the heart of republican principles and stamping the lie upon the Constitution. Expediency and right must go hand in hand. There is no room for compromise.

.   .   .   .

Sappho was tired, and one of the young girls in her Bible class, noticing the weariness of her attitude, insisted upon assuming the duties of cashier for an hour. She gladly availed herself of the girl's offer, and turned with a sigh of relief to find a secluded seat where she could watch unobserved the passing of the gay throng. As she turned a hand was laid gently on her arm, and Will Smith's gay voice sounded in her ear: "Whither away, fair lady?"

Sappho smiled back into the debonair face as she replied: "Just to the fairy grotto to rest a while."

"I will accompany thee, fair queen," hummed Will, as he drew her hand within his arm and moved slowly through the crowd toward the refreshment room. No more was said until they reached the spot; then Will seated her at one of the most secluded tables, placing himself upon the opposite side.

"Lord love yer, Sarah Ann, jes' see that couple!" said Mrs. Davis to Mrs. White. "Ef that ain't a match then no matter! See him look at her! I'se goin' to wait on them myself; an' Sarah Ann, you keep these young squirts busy in some other corner; there ain't nobody goin' ter spile sport ef I can help it."

Mrs. Davis bustled over to the young people and literally beamed upon them. "Good evening; now Mr. Smith, what be you an' Miss Sappho goin' to have? You see I've jes' camed over to wait on yer myself."

"Good evening, Mrs. Davis; you are looking as bright and charming as a rose. How are the refreshments going?"

"Charmin'!" responded Mrs. Davis, secretly delighted at the compliment. "Ain't you 'shamed to talk like that to an ol' 'ooman? You young fellers gits worse every day. Jes' see Miss Sappho lafin' at you! Well, thank God, we's doin' well tonight, took in a pile o' money so fur. Mary Jane Robberson thinks she's goin' to down me in this here refreshment room, but jes' you wait 'tel Friday night!"

"What about Friday night?" asked Sappho.

"Nuthin', only I've got a big s'prise waitin' fer Mary Jane Robberson."

"Friday will be a mighty unlucky day for Sister Robinson, eh?" laughed Will.

"Thar won't be a thing doin' fer her, honey, you'll see. I'se gwine ter paralize her!"

"I'll bet my money on you every time, Mrs. Davis," laughed Will. "I have every confidence in your business sagacity. I feel sorry for Sister Robinson."

"She'll need yer sorrow," replied Mrs. Davis. "Mary Jane Robberson's jealous, an' when people gits jealous they can't do the bes' thing in the bes' place. I ain't jealous o' nobody, an' I'se jes' settin' back here watchin' her kill hersef, as cool as a sittin' hen. I had a letter from Mis' Mason, an' she says as how she's goin' ter stan' by me. You know what that means, don' yer, honey? Oysters, coffee, ice cream and cake fer two," she murmured, repeating Will's order. "My head's level, thar ain't a thing the matter with it," she finished, as she turned to execute the order.

A silence fell between the two as they sat within the shadow of the trees, content to be with each other. Will was happy to have the privilege of feasting his eyes upon the lovely face opposite him, which dimpled and blushed in such a charming manner beneath his glance. Never before had she seemed to abandon herself so completely to the influence of his passion; but tonight she laid aside her coldness and seemed ready to accept the homage which he was longing to lay at her feet. The girl felt it.

"Why," she asked herself, "why should I always walk in the shadow of a crime for which I am in no way to blame? Why deny myself all the pleasures of a home and love with such a man as he who will offer me the noblest heritage of woman?"

The more she thought the stronger became her resolve not to fight against fate, but to accept the goods the gods provided without question. She would rise above maddening fears, penance for involuntary wrongs, the sackcloth and ashes of her life, and be as other women, who loved and were beloved. So she smiled on Will bewitchingly; sallies of wit and fun flashed from her pretty lips in a way which was as fascinating as bewildering. Will knew her to be well educated, but had never supposed that she possessed the exquisite art of repartee. Tonight he caught glimpses of an ideal woman and wife, and the glimpse intoxicated him. Now Love was kind.

They had very nearly finished their lunch when the room was invaded by Dora, followed by Doctor Lewis, who had arrived from New Orleans the last of the previous week.

"Oh, here you are, Sappho, I've been looking for you everywhere. Have you had one of Madam Frances's predictions? She is creating a sensation."

"No," replied Sappho, "I have not. Have you one? Is it good?"

"Yes, I have one. For my part I think it's rubbish. Just listen," and she read from a slip of paper in her hand:

> All that glistens is not gold;
> Often have you heard this told.
> Despise the false; welcome the true,
> So shall you receive your due.

"Now whatever in the world does she mean by all that?"

"Where's John?" asked her brother rather abruptly; "has he had a message, too?"

"Yes; and he's so mad that he won't give anyone a decent word," replied his sister. "I'm sure," she continued, "if I felt as hateful as

John Langley has acted tonight, I'd stay at home."

"Do you remember how his message read?" asked her brother.

"Yes," said Dora, "it was something like this: 'He who expects gain shall lose. Be faithful to the object of your choice, or merit the fate reserved for fickleness and deceit.'"

"Can't blame him for feeling wrathy over such a fortune as that, can you, Lewis?" asked Will, turning to his sister's companion.

"Gad, no!" replied the doctor. "If he *would* only prove unfaithful to 'the object of his choice' how happy some other fellow might be."

Dora looked at her companion with scorn on her countenance. "I just think I hate you sometimes, Arthur Lewis!" she exclaimed, as she turned to leave the room.

"Oh, I say, Dora, do have something before you go," urged the unlucky fellow, as he followed his angry companion toward the door.

"No, I won't have anything. I do believe you just love to see John Langley quarrel with me, but it won't do you a bit of good, Arthur Lewis, not a bit."

As they vanished from sight Will turned to Sappho and said: "Dora and John worry me, Miss Clark; I fear that there is trouble ahead for my little sister if she marries him, and I could find it in my heart to wish that her choice had fallen on Lewis. He is a thoroughly good and capable man, and loves the girl devotedly."

"Let us hope that all things may turn out for the best," replied Sappho.

"I don't know why I should worry you with this, Miss Clark," said Will, as he turned toward her with a light in his eyes which a man gives to but one woman in the world. "Miss Clark — Sappho —"

"Ah, here you are." This time it was John Langley who had broken in upon the lovers. He came up to them smiling, polished, bland. Sappho wondered why she had never noticed how very disagreeable John Langley's smile was. She shuddered a bit as he drew nearer to them. Behind him walked the little Mercury, and in his hand he held a white missive just drawn from the small black velvet bag which hung at his side.

"Mercury wanted to find you, Miss Clark, and as I had a message for you from your mother, Will, I ventured to interrupt your earnest conversation. I hope I don't intrude." He bowed with easy grace to Sappho and bade her good evening, at the same time taking the chair which Will vacated as he rose to go to his mother.

"Thank you, John. No, you do not intrude. Miss Clark, I shall see you again shortly, I hope. I would very much like to finish our conversation."

Sappho bowed and he turned away. She followed the retreating figure with her eyes; John watched her jealously, and the child stood and watched them both. Finally with a sigh she opened the note, but before reading it turned to murmur a gentle apology to Langley.

"Oh, never mind me," he returned pleasantly; "if you get such a mongrel mixture as the one sent to me, I shan't envy you the pleasure you'll get out of it."

"It wasn't pleasant, I remember. Dora told us about it."

"Pleasant! A regular death's head at a feast, I call it. Do read yours, Miss Clark, and see if you haven't something better."

"Let me see: 'The mysterious stars bespeak for you better luck than you have already had. Harassed and perplexed by fickle Fortune, love shall find a way.'"

"Bravo!" cried John. But how could it be otherwise? If the same blood which inaugurated the Trojan wars, of which fair Helen was the object, still runs in the veins of the gods of love and fortune, they could not resist the influence of so much youth and beauty as we are blessed with here tonight."

"And what shall I say in reply to so gallant a speech, Mr. Langley? To my way of thinking, such words should be uttered to one alone. You must have forgotten Dora." Sappho turned to the waiting child and drew him into her lap.

"Because a man is engaged to one girl does that spoil all the pleasure which lies in meeting others? One woman can never tie my wandering fancy; my heart is large enough to appreciate the charms of the fair sex wherever discovered. Dora don't like it, I know, but she'll get used to it after we are married," he said, recklessly.

Sappho kissed the child on her lap, and placing the postage for her letter in his hand, told him to run away. "Truly, Mr. Langley, you appear in a new light. Why do you tell your thoughts to me, who am Dora's friend? I do not wish to hear them."

There was a mocking smile on his face as he turned to her from watching the child. "A pretty boy that. His is beauty of a rare kind. Do you know, I fancy that he resembles you."

"Really, Mr. Langley, you grow very strange in your conversation. I shall have to beg you to excuse me," and with a haughty little bow she left the place.

John watched her departure with a slight

smile on his face. " Oh, beauty is the wine of life, fair woman, for me," he hummed beneath his moustache. The smile was still on his face as he ordered a cup of coffee and proceeded to drink it leisurely.

. . . .

The fair had been very popular, and most successful from a business point of view. The week was now drawing to a close. The community was on the *qui vive* over the rivalry between Mrs. Robinson and Mrs. Davis. Racy developments were looked for on the closing night. Every woman had ranged herself on one side or the other, and not a few of the men had been led by their vigorous wives to declare themselves for a chosen leader.

Friday night was to end the sale of votes on the prizes. Saturday was to be devoted to counting up the votes, so that at nine o'clock that night the successful winners could be announced. The pastor was asked to allow the fair to run another week, but he declined emphatically, saying that so many controversies had grown out of it that another week would seriously deplete his membership and bring disaster upon the cause of religion. So that idea was abandoned. Wednesday Mrs. Robinson was ahead on the piano but behind on the dining-room receipts. Thursday night Mrs.

Davis was ahead on the piano but behind on the receipts in the refreshment room. So luck fluctuated until the rivals found themselves neck and neck, so to speak, at eight o'clock on Friday night. Anyone who had watched Mrs. Robinson would have noticed that her face wore a satisfied smirk which told that she anticipated an easy victory, and the knowing ones of her satellites told each other that "Sis' Robberson was all right."

Mrs. Davis viewed the action of her rival with stolid countenance, from which the envoys of the other side, who stood about trying to catch a word to repeat to their champion, could gain no comfort. To her trusted henchmen she whispered: "Jes' you watch me keep 'em guessin'. I'm a-goin' to show 'em, shortly, that the 'race am not to the swif'er nor the battle to the stron'er, but to her what enjureth untel the end.'"

As half-past seven approached various savory smells could be traced to the "old Southern dining-room," but above all the enticing scents which were ever introduced to aggravate the palate of the lover of good living, the knowing ones could trace the odor of a rare and tempting dainty — the opossum! Yes, Mrs. Robinson had conspired with her Southern friends and received a tempting animal direct from the

"Old Dominion," and on this eventful night she stood in the middle of the dining-room triumphantly directing the placing of the dish upon the main table, which was carefully arranged with covers laid for twenty-five persons. The ordinary patrons of the room were turned from the door, and even the pastor was not allowed to enter, being told that the dining-room had been engaged for an hour by a private party. At eight o'clock a message was brought to her by a lad stationed at the outside entrance to the vestry, and Mrs. Robinson immediately hurried to the door to receive a sleigh-load of young white ladies and gentlemen who had come from among the wealthy people of the city, for whom Mrs. Robinson was a faithful servant, to help her triumph over her enemies. With head thrown back and held very high, and satisfaction beaming from her countenance, the good sister marched in at the head of the company like a successful warrior on his return from victory. The assembled company made way, gazing with awe upon so many representatives of wealth and influence. Then they were lost within the sacred precincts of the dining-room, into which Mrs. Robinson ushered them. The pastor was sent for presently, and attended by the most prominent trustee on the Board, he waited upon the guests who had so honored his flock. During the interview which ensued the door was closed to the gaze of the inquisitive crowd, but after half an hour the good man came forth with the guests and proceeded to show them the points of interest in the fair. A few minutes before nine they took their departure, seemingly well pleased with what they had seen.

"Well, Sis' Davis," said one of the brothers when the door closed upon the visitors and the company felt at liberty to enjoy itself after its own fashion, "well, sister, that ruther gits ahead of you. Sis' Robberson's got you dead sure this time."

He laughed with a good-natured chuckle which was meant to be very aggravating.

"Beats *who? me?*" snorted Mrs. Davis, as she turned upon the questioner with a stony stare. "White folks don't scare Ophelia Davis. I'se seed 'em befo' in my life, an' I've eat at the table wif 'em, that's mo'. Didn't hev to hev the do' shet on me to keep me out the dining-room 'cause they was feered the black'd rub off. I think too much o' my white people to trot 'em up here to this one-cen' 'fair."

"No use, Sis' Davis, we's got yer," laughed another member who had just come up. "Robberson's smart."

"Smart!" cried the irate woman, now thoroughly angry. "You-alls havin' yer hallelujah meetin' too soon. Don' holler 'tell yer knows what yer hollerin' 'bout. I ain't beat tell nine o'clock sharp, when the polls is closed."

"Five minutes is all you's got, anyhow. Can't change much in five minutes," laughed another.

Just at this moment a messenger boy made his way from the door and was conducted to the judges' seat. He handed them an envelope which upon being opened was seen to contain two bits of paper.

"Please step this way, Mrs. Davis, and make your mark for value received," called out one of the judges.

Mrs. Davis was escorted to the table by a curious crowd, anxious to know the meaning of this latest sensation. The judge stood up after she had signed, and said: "Ladies and gentlemen, knowing the interest that you take in all that relates to the two ladies who are rival candidates for the piano, and also for the ten dollars for the largest amount taken at a refreshment table, I beg leave to state that one hundred and fifty dollars have been contributed by Mrs. Mason and Mrs. Molly Mason Farnham, to be used for buying votes in the favor of Mrs. Davis in the contest for the piano, and to swell the receipts at her refreshment tables.

As I hold my watch in my hand it is now one minute of the closing hour of the polls. Any more votes?" He paused and looked around. "No more? then I have the honor of informing you that the polls are closed. No more tickets can be bought, and I may as well say right here that Sister Davis will have the most votes; she'll stand at least five hundred ahead. Now I propose that we give three cheers for Sister Davis."

And they were given with a will, led by the pastor, who stood upon a chair and swung his bandanna handkerchief wildly in the air.

Mrs. Davis was greatly excited. "Sis' Robberson's got me, has she? Beat, am I? How 'bout it, honeys, how 'bout it?"

Sister Mary Jane Robinson was carried home sick, in a herdic.

The next night brought a great crowd to see the distribution of the prizes. The fun waxed warmer and warmer as each name was called. When young 'Mandy Jackson was called to receive the diamond pin, her twin brothers turned handsprings in the aisle, and yelled out: "Hi, 'Mandy, yer a peach! We-uns did the bisness fer yer, yer bet."

Sister Susanna Johnson received the much-coveted silver set, and thought with pride of the handsome sideboard, and made up her mind then and there to give the Stewardess Board such a tea as they had not had for many a day, before another week rolled over her head.

Jim Anderson walked up to the judges' stand feeling very bashful and with a fearful grin on his face, when his name was called for the gold watch and chain.

"Wet it, Jim! wet it!" cried one of his friends.

"Set 'em up, ol' man!" roared another, as Jim returned to his seat. "Don't be 'shamed; do the right thing by the boys."

Jim Anderson was angry. He was a trustee, and was looked up to by all the young members as an exemplary Christian. Jim made up his mind not to stand it, and he paused on the way to his seat and offered to take the speaker and "set him up" by standing him on his head if he'd only come out where he could get at him, "makin' a fool o' him right out in chuch."

This stopped the fun in that direction, for Jim was a beef-lugger at the "big" market, and they had a wholesome regard for his muscle.

But when Mrs. Davis was called for the piano and the ten dollars, the excitement broke out with renewed vigor: "Speech! speech!" resounded from all over the hall.

"You must say a word to your friends, sister," said the pastor. Then she stood up.

"Friends, I'm much oblivigated to yer fer makin' all this noise over me, but bein' a lonesome ol' 'ooman, an' with no ejkation, I cayn't make no speech. I'll jes' say thar's nuthin' mean 'bout me. I don' feel good 'cause some o' us is took sick 'long o' all this. Now, pastor, I want yer to take this ten dollars over to Sis' Robberson an' tell her we's quits, an' I fergive her fer all her mean feelin's to me. Will you do it?"

The pastor promised, and for a while pandemonium reigned. And after that the pastor could not forbear saying a few words about how good it was "to dwell together in brotherly love." Sister Sarah Ann White said "the *brothers* had nuthin' to do with it, it was Ophelia Davis an' nobody else."

Mrs. Davis, true to her word, had not forgotten the pastor; and all the women, mindful of the feeling engendered by Mrs. Robinson against him, had secretly gone about among the "400," and money enough had been contributed to buy him a fine new Sunday suit, made up in the latest clerical fashion. After all the prizes had been presented, the women formed in a body, and headed by Ma Smith, marched up to the judges' seats and presented him with the result of their good feelings. So everybody was made happy.

It was estimated that the proceeds of the fair exceeded the eight thousand dollars hoped for, and no church had more sincere cause to rejoice on the next Easter Sunday than the body of people comprising the church on X Street, who on that memorable day consecrated anew to God their house of worship free from all encumbrances.

CHAPTER XII.

A COLORED POLITICIAN.

O, that estates, degrees and offices
Were not derived corruptly, and that clear honor
Were purchased by the merit of the wearer!
How many then should cover that stand bare!
How many be commanded that command!

— MERCHANT OF VENICE.

JOHN LANGLEY occupied an office in the business portion of the city among the most reliable lawyers in the profession. He held that association with success would in the end bring the desired quality to any one. He had never been moved by a generous heart-impulse in his whole life. Actual need found no pity dwelling in his breast. The comfortable home which the thrift of Smith had founded and the industry of the family had fostered to prosperity, influenced his devotion to Dora to an extent which if realized by her would have led to his instant dismissal by that impetuous young lady. According to his way of thinking, the wife ought to contribute as much to the expenses of the household, by having a comfortable nest-egg before marriage, as the husband. He listened to the romantic story of the Montfort family with eagerness, and while regarding it as a fanciful creation of the mind, yet he felt that he must look it up and be very sure that a dollar could not be gained from it, before he marked it in his mind as valueless. He meditated on the subject constantly, but with the shrewdness characteristic of his nature, carefully concealed his thoughts from every one. He had no idea where he should begin to unravel this great mystery of family connections lost within the fog-banks of life in London, but he intended to try.

Langley's nature was the natural product of such an institution as slavery. Natural instinct for good had been perverted by a mixture of "cracker" blood of the lowest type on his father's side with whatever God-saving quality that might have been loaned the Negro by pitying nature. This blood, while it gave him the pleasant features of the Caucasian race, vitiated his moral nature and left it stranded high and dry on the shore of blind ignorance, and there he seemed content to dwell, supinely self-satisfied with the narrow boundary of the horizon of his mental vision.

He remembered little of his parentage, but what had most impressed him was that somewhere in the dim past a woman, presumably his mother, had boasted that through her he was a direct descendant of the North Carolina

Pollocks.   So he clung to the name, and called himself John Pollock Langley.   Neither the Smiths nor he connected his name in any way with the Montfort story; it was a mere coincidence.

If taken in his first state, fresh from the woods and streams of his nativity, the Negro be subjected to the saving influences of the Christian home where freedom and happiness, education and morality abound, the Anglo-Saxon would lose the main arguments which he uses against the black brother; rather would he bow humbly in recognition of the ebony-hued miniature of God. Subject the Anglo-Saxon to the whip and scourge, grind the iron heel of oppression in his face until all resemblance to the human family is lost in the degradation of the brute, take from wives and mothers the sacredness and protection of home in the time before birth, when moral and intellectual development are most dependent upon pre-natal influences for the advancement of generations to come; join to all this the uncontrolled bestial passions of humanity, and what have you? classic features and a godlike mind? No! rather the lineaments of hideous despair, fearful and hopeless as the angel forms that fell from heaven to the black gulf of impenetrable hell.

Up from the South there came one morning early in March the report of another lynching. The skies were heavy with gray, storm-laden clouds, not darker nor more threatening than the dire and bloody news the daylight ushered in. For a month or two peace had seemingly reigned in southern latitudes, but it was the slumbering of passion, not its subsidence. At table, in the cars, at the office, in the workshop, men read with sick hearts the description of another illegal act of distorted justice, wherein the sufferings of the poor wretches were depicted only too truthfully for the peace of the community:

Jim Jones, a burly black Negro accused of the crime of rape against the person of a beautiful white woman, was taken from his home by a number of our leading citizens, and after being identified by his victim, was carried into the woods, where, before an immense concourse of people, he was bound to a tree, pieces of his flesh were stripped from his body, his eyes were gouged out, his ears cut off, his nose split open, and his legs broken at the knees. After this the young woman stepped forward and poured oil upon the wretch, and the wood being piled about him, she applied the torch to light the fire which was to consume the black monster. Leaving some of the party to watch the funeral pile, a posse went into the city and brought to the scene of vengeance Sam Smith, Bill Sykes and Manuel Jackson, who were accused of hiding the guilty wretch from the justice of the populace. These three men were hanged to the nearest trees in full sight of the burning wretch, who made the day hideous with his cries of agony. We think the Negroes of this section have been taught a salutary lesson.— *Torchlight.*

The American Colored League was made up of leading colored men all over New England. These men were in communication with the colored people in every section of the country, for there is no community of colored people so remote that a branch of the great National League of American Colored Men cannot be found within easy reach of all. To the Boston branch of this society the people of all sections of the country look for aid and comfort, not because of any acknowledged superiority of its members, but solely on account of the advantages which they are supposed to enjoy under the beneficent rulings of the grand old Commonwealth of Massachusetts. We do not claim for Massachusetts, in her policy toward the Negroes within her gates, freedom from prejudice or error. There is prejudice enough, heaven knows, prejudice which is fed every day by fresh arrivals from the South and by intermarriage between Southern women and the sons of Massachusetts. But Massachusetts is noted for being willing to see fair play : she hears the complaints of the Negro, and listens with attention to the accusations of the Southern whites, weighs the one against the other, and, naturally enough, the scales tip in favor of the white brother. From one class the Negro suffers in the state and is contemptu- ously flouted; from another he receives the hearty word of encouragement, backed by the all-powerful dollar which goes to feed such universities as Hampton, Tuskegee, and the like.

News of the latest horrible event had just reached the officers of the American Colored League. A call had been issued through the church and press for a public indignation meet- ing at the church on X Street, and John, as one of the executive committee of the League, was turning over in his mind ways and means of making it a success. With pencil in hand and paper before him he sat thinking. Out- side, the sound of the typewriter clicking away for dear life came to his ears, mingled with the whistle of the office boy as he shuffled in and out, attending to his morning chores. John hired a white office boy and a white stenog- rapher, not because he would not have liked to patronize his own people, but because he thought that it would be pleasanter for his patrons to meet their own race when business compelled them to visit him, and because he wished everyone to realize that *he*, at least, had no prejudice in his heart toward anyone. This was what he told the committee from the League when they waited on him and asked him to give the office work to two worthy representatives of their race, and pointed out to him that it was his duty so to do as a leading man of influence among them. Some of the committee were unkind enough to say that they believed that Langley was as prejudiced toward black people as any Anglo-Saxon; but as he denied it most emphatically, there was nothing more to be said about the matter, though many colored men voted him a "sneak" in private, and had a watchful eye on all his movements.

Usually John had no difficulty in fixing his attention on the humdrum routine of the office, but today his thoughts wandered. Sappho Clark had touched a vein in his nature which was a revelation to himself. Sensuality was prominent in the phrenological development of his head, although no one of his associates would have called him a libertine. Nevertheless, there it lurked ready to assert itself when conditions were ripe to call it into action. Sappho represented the necessary conditions. Her beauty intoxicated him; her friendlessness did not appeal to his manliness, because, as we have intimated, *that* was an unknown quality in the makeup of this man. Her coldness urged him on; and Jealousy, the argus-eyed attendant of Love, and its counterfeit — Infatuation —

warned him that Will's love was returned, and made him impatient to force upon her an acceptance of his own devotion, at whatever cost. He did not contemplate marriage, because he intended to marry Dora for mercenary reasons. But to his mind that was no obstacle to the consummation and lifelong duration of an illicit love. He had detected in Sappho's personality a coldness more in accordance with the disposition of women of the North than with that of one born beneath the smiling skies of the languorous Southland. Where, with such a face and complexion, had she imbibed a moral character so strong and self-reliant as her conduct had shown her to possess? Not by inheritance, if he read the signs aright. Then, he argued, if she had *acquired* that stately, cold, dispassionate bearing by force of habit only, the time would surely come when unexpectedly the true nature would reassert itself. Ah, he could wait! Meantime he could watch for opportunities to coax the unwilling bird within the net.

"Gentleman to see you, sir," announced the office boy, laying a card on the table before him. Langley glanced at the card and then said: "Show the gentleman in, and remember I'm 'engaged' to anyone who calls while he is here." As the boy left the room he thought to himself: " I wonder what brings the Hon. Herbert Clapp here today. Something uncommon, I warrant."

Langley arose to receive his visitor with an easy grace which was a distinguishing point in his personality. Men would tell you privately — keen, far-sighted politicians — that they believed Langley to be " tricky," but that he had such a pleasant way with him that you would give in to him when you knew, within your own mind, that he would " do " you out of a case in court or a hundred dollars with the suavity of a Lord Chesterfield; or, as one politician expressed it: " He has such a d —— oily way with him that a man forgets to ' fire ' him until it is too late." He received his guest with *empressement*, bade him good-morning in a cordial voice, seated him in the easiest chair which the cozy office contained, and, before his hat had fairly reached a resting-place, had produced a box of fine cigars, and made him comfortable.

" Deuced pleasant office you have here, Langley," remarked the visitor as he lit a fragrant Havana and proceeded to enjoy himself man-fashion.

" Oh, it isn't bad," replied Langley, " though if my practice allowed it I would be glad to take more commodious quarters." John had helped himself to a cigar, and was now contemplating

the ceiling through rings of curling smoke.
Apparently he watched a belated fly trail its
body slowly over the white space, but really
his mind was alert and watchful to find a clue
as to the nature of the business which had
caused this man to call upon him. Mr. Clapp
had visited him twice before since he had been
in business, and each time his call had brought
substantial profit, in a political way, to his little
bank account.

"Horrible thing, this latest case of lynching,"
Mr. Clapp remarked after an interval of silent
enjoyment.

"Yes," replied John, "pretty bad. Isn't it
most time for the Administration to take it up?
You can't expect us to stand this sort of thing
always, and not strike back."

"What'd you gain by doing that?" questioned Mr. Clapp.

"I'll tell you," replied John, looking earnestly
at his visitor, "there are thirty-five thousand of
us in this state alone. We can be organized,
if the work is done by the right ones and in the
right way. We can help start a new party, if
nothing more."

"That won't do any good, John, we can down
you. Colored people won't stick together; and
then where'd you be?"

"We'd stick all right if once we got started,"
returned John doggedly.

"No you wouldn't; you're so confoundedly jealous of honors. Each one of you wants all there is for himself, and you never know when to get off, individually. We white men know this, and it is easy to upset your plans."

"I know that there is a great deal of truth in what you say, but that won't always be the case with us; we are growing away from it more and more every day; and with the missionary work that the League is doing, we expect to fight you one of these days, and knock the party clear over the ropes."

"You'll never do it!" declared Mr. Clapp.

"Time will tell. You don't expect to succeed in keeping us out of employment, shoved in a corner to starve and to be burnt alive, without getting square sometime, do you? There would be some satisfaction in throwing you fellows out and putting others in, if a new party is the outcome of the issue, and seeing some of you, who have your pockets filled with the salaries which the Government has heaped upon you, shoved out of a job and your vast schemes for growing richer, at the expense of the lives of just such poor unfortunates as the Negroes you are allowing the South to burn in order to keep in power, blown to the devil. We can at least do that much."

"I didn't expect such talk from you, Langley,"

said Mr. Clapp, his lips tightening in a tense line about the mouth.

"I suppose not. I've always been pliable, like the rest of the race. Things are changing."

"The dollar will fetch you every time, John."

"Not this time, anyhow," was the dogged reply.

"Pshaw! You people are standing in your own light."

"Yes, I think we are. Been doing the same old thing for the last thirty-five years."

"What do you mean?" demanded Mr. Clapp, growing white with suppressed passion. "Is that a reflection?"

"Don't lose your temper, Colonel; the man who gets mad always gets the worst of it," replied John blandly. "I want to ask you a question: Did you ever hear of such a thing as a man being robbed and murdered in the house of his friends?" He looked Mr. Clapp squarely in the eye. The latter shifted uneasily in his seat.

"That's what's been done to my people."

"Well, you can't complain; you've had all you're worth."

"Had all we're worth! Yes, you give us a bootblack stand in the corridor of the State House, and think we are placated."

"You can't expect anything more until you

have earned it. Besides, you're incompetent to fill any higher position. I have had a number of your best men tried in clerical positions, and you always fail to compete favorably with an ordinary white clerk. You can't ask the people to pay for ignorant incompetents."

"Ha, ha, ha!" laughed John, as he lay back in his chair and winked at the Colonel, "that's a good one! What do you think I've been doing since I've been in the law business in this city? Why, the greenest ward-heeler knows that neither a white nor black man is competent to fill an office if the heads of the department where he is employed wish to get rid of him. The civil service is a good thing, but even that can't save a man from becoming incompetent when his resignation is desired by any one in authority. That's no argument at all. And as for our earning our rights — we didn't earn them at Wagner and Fort Fisher and at Fort Pillow; we haven't held the casting vote, and floated you from poverty into afflu-ence."

"But the South, man!" exclaimed the Colonel, pounding the table before him with his fists until the dust sprang from the covers of the volumes lying there, "the South has rights as well as you. They are *white men*, man; you can't expect us to leave them out.

All sections must be satisfied, and if you love your country as you should, you will be willing to sacrifice a little for the good of the whole. It won't hurt you; you can't miss luxuries and positions that you have never been used to!" The Colonel was shouting at the top of his lungs. John sat calmly waiting for the storm to subside.

"Then what I have heard so often is true, that the South is in the saddle."

"Eh?" said the Colonel, subsiding limply into his chair and wiping his heated face on his handkerchief. "Well, I might as well own it, to you; I know it will go no farther. It is so in great measure, Langley. That is the reason we want your people to go slow. This is a great country. Each man is for the good of his own section. Can't blame 'em, can you?"

"No; and neither can you blame *us* for trying to get the best we can for the good of our race. You'll find we mean to do it."

"You mean to do it — yes, but the white man rules in this country every time, John, because he's born for the business, and it's just as well for you to keep the few friends you've got, and not drive them away because you're sore over your disappointments. You know nothing about business, you've no capital, no money, and we've got you every time."

"Threats do not frighten me, Colonel; nearly nineteen hundred years ago Christ sat at supper with his friends, and one of them, with a kiss still warm on his lips, betrayed him to crucifixion. What have we to expect from our friends?"

"Now, look here, Langley, don't say hard things, and don't get mad. I will admit every word that you say. It is all true, d—— it!" he exclaimed as he arose to his feet and began walking up and down the floor with rapid strides. "I imagine I should feel even worse than you do if I were one of your race, but you see things are as they are, and why not make the best of a bad matter? Your people can't help themselves. If you rose in the South and appealed to arms you would soon be exterminated; for of course the South is our brother, and in an uprising of that sort, the National arms would necessarily be directed against the 'rioters,' as they would be termed. Individually, I might feel the justice of your cause; others might feel with me; but expediency would make me fight against you. And that brings me to my errand here today. It is the duty of every one of us to wait for justice, and not to countenance excitement and bloodshed. I assure you upon my honor as a man, that if the colored people are only patient for a while longer, this thing will be settled amicably. We have great plans for pacifying the South, and if we have the help of every good citizen we shall sooner be able to bring about a season of peace and prosperity, not only to the colored people, but to the whole country."

"Talk's cheap. I've heard that old gag so many times that it's grown stale."

"But we intend to do the square thing this time."

"It ain't in you to do the square thing by us. It is as natural for you to cheat us and maltreat us as it is for boys to pull out the wings and legs of flies. You say now you've got no power to stop lynching. If you haven't the power before election, where will you get it after the votes are in? No, sir; it's votes you want, and after you get them, and all the subsidies, corporations, and trusts are riding easily on the front seat of the coach for another year, you won't know us; and robbing and killing the black man can go right on."

"You talk like a fool, John Langley. You're jeopardizing the best chance you ever had since Lincoln issued the Emancipation Proclamation."

"That's all right. Promises are like pie-crust, made to be broken. You may be the best we can do, and the best is d—— poor. Colonel, you just make up your mind to one thing: we're coming high this time. It's going to cost you something; yes, sir, right smart."

"I tell you, Langley, we have a hard fight to give your people even the little that they do get. It's your duty to listen to reason in this matter. What do you want, anyhow?"

"We want our men given something beside boot-blacking in the employment of the state. We want our girls given a chance as clerks; that's what we want. Anything unreasonable in that?"

"No; that isn't unreasonable, but d—— it all, man, other employees would 'kick.'"

"Let 'em 'kick.' Turn 'em out and get others; the civil service lists are always full." John faced the angry man with grim determination on every feature. He thought to himself: "The Colonel wants something done, and he might as well know that it's going to take a good thing to get me on his side."

"All right! I see what's the matter with you; you want to fight!" exclaimed the angry Colonel. "All right! be pig-headed; don't listen to reason; plunge the country into a race war in spite of all we've done for you, especially for your leaders; and when your race is exterminated, put the blame where it belongs. I wash my hands of the whole business!"

"Oh," replied John, with a conciliatory air, "I don't want to see bloodshed any more than you do, and I am just as ready to accept amicable terms for my race as you are to offer them. I only want to convince you that we can do something if conditions are right."

"You're all right, John, my boy," returned Clapp, as he slapped Langley on the back, apparently very ready to grasp the olive-branch of peace; "you stick to the party and the party'll stick to you. We don't want to quarrel, do we?"

"No, that won't pay," said John.

Each man now resumed the seat which he had vacated under the excitement of the moment, helped himself to another cigar, and again contemplated the ceiling through rings of smoke. John noticed that the fly had made the circuit of the ceiling, and was moving toward him from the opposite side of the room. After a moment's silence the Colonel said:

"Your folks are going to have a meeting about this last atrocious affair, aren't they?"

"Yes; I was just looking over the list of speakers as you came in."

"I suppose they're pretty mad?"

"Yes; pretty hot."

"By the way, Langley, your name is up for the place of City Solicitor, to fill the vacancy made by the death of Calvin. I suppose you'll accept it if you pull it off?"

This was the first that John had heard about any such place being offered to him, but he took it as a matter of course, and his eyes sparkled as he replied: "That would suit me to a T."

"That settles it, then; it's a go. Now I tell you what you do," he continued between the puffs of fragrant smoke; "you hold that meeting down among your people to a calm level. Don't let your fire-eaters like Judge Watson raise the devil of a row, and throw dirt on the party. You keep that end down and I'll work the papers."

"Just so," replied John.

"How's the city election going down your way, anyhow?" asked the Colonel, after a few more explicit directions to Langley concerning the work he would have him do.

"Pretty fair. Some of the voters want to take their own heads, but they can be managed."

"Well, here's an order on the committee for money waiting to be used in your district in an emergency. Draw when you need it." Then he arose from his chair to take his leave. "Mighty good cigars you keep, John."

"Help yourself, Colonel, help yourself."

The Hon. Herbert Clapp graciously took a

half-dozen and stored them away in a capacious coat pocket. After a few more commonplace remarks Langley accompanied his visitor to the door, they shook hands, and the interview was ended.

CHAPTER XIII.

THE AMERICAN COLORED LEAGUE.

SHALL tongues be mute when deeds are wrought
    Which well might shame extremest hell?
Shall Pity's bosom cease to swell?
    Shall Honor bleed? — shall Truth succumb?
Shall pen and press and soul be dumb?

No; — by each spot of haunted ground
    Where Freedom weeps her children's fall, —
By Plymouth's rock and Bunker's mound,
    By Griswold's stained and shattered wall,
By Warren's ghost, by Langdon's shade,
    By all the memories of our dead!

By their enlarging souls, which burst
    The bands and fetters round them set,
By the free Pilgrim spirit nursed
    Within our inmost bosoms, yet,
By all above, around, below,
    Be ours the indignant answer, — No!

                                    — WHITTIER.

WHEN Judge Watson, the president of the
League, reached his office on that eventful
March morning, he found his desk deluged
with telegrams from all over the country.
From the South the cry was: " Can nothing be
done?" "Where is Massachusetts? Has our
old friend been turned against us at last?"
"For God's sake help us!" "How long, O

Lord, how long!" "Let the voice of the
League be heard from every city, town and village in the Union. Speak, and let our voices
be heard!"

Such were the messages that compelled the
hoary-haired veteran of a hundred anti-slavery
meetings to crush back the sobs which arose
in his throat as he, too, reiterated the cry of
an afflicted people: "How long, O Lord, how
long!" That day the executive committee of
the League met and asked themselves what
could be done. "Nothing," was the final decision after debating the question, "but to *agitate*." This plan they proceeded to put into
execution. Notices were sent all over New
England of a gigantic public meeting to be
held at the church on X Street, on the Tuesday evening following. The press, with one or
two exceptions, sided either openly or secretly
against the Negroes, North and South. "Ah,
ah!" they cried, "see how the Negro abuses
the great privileges which we have bestowed
upon him." In view of this fact, the League
decided that a conservative white man should
be asked to address the meeting, along with
men imbued with the old abolition spirit, and
in this way each side could have a chance to
represent the subject as seen from its point of
view. "Let us, once and for all, look at the

question dispassionately; if the fault be ours, let us acknowledge it like men, and seek to amend it; if it belongs to others, may God help them to do right."

The excitement among the colored people was intense: prayers were held in all the churches the Sunday preceding. Telegrams were received from the branches of the League all over the state that delegates would represent them. The meeting would be a great expression of public opinion.

Dr. Arthur Lewis was head of a large educational institution in the South devoted to the welfare of the Negroes. Every year he visited the city, and assisted by a quartette of singers, who were also members of the school, collected large sums of money from the best class of philanthropic citizens, who gave to the Negro not only because they believed he was wronged, but also because they believed that in great measure his elevation would remove the stigma under which the Southern white labored. For the loyal white man there would be no greater joy in life than to see his poetic dream of superiority to all other governments realized in the "land of the free and the home of the brave." He knows that this can never be while the Negro question keeps up the line of demarkation which marks the division of the North from the South. True and loyal son of his country, he would sacrifice any race, any principle, to bring about this much-desired consummation; so he contributes his money to build up manufacturing interests at the South to his own material disadvantage in the North: to develop uncultivated land there, and to educate the Negro with the hope that in the general advance the latter question may be buried from public notice, if not obliterated. Delusive hope that grasps at shadows!

That momentous Tuesday evening rolled quickly round. The committee asked that the meeting should open at half-past seven, on account of the time needed by the speakers, and long before the hour appointed the large edifice was filled to overflowing. And what a crowd! They came from towns remote, from the farm, from domestic service in the homes of wealth and from among the lowly ones who earn a scanty living with scrubbing-brush and pail. Doctor, lawyer, politician, mechanic — every class sent its representative there to help protest against the wrongs of down-trodden manhood.

The platform was heavily draped in American flags supplemented by wide bands of mourning. Pictures of the anti-slavery apostles peered out at the audience from the folds of the national colors. Speakers and representative citizens were seated upon the platform, and visiting delegates occupied seats in close proximity. The choir had volunteered its services, and, after a prayer by the pastor, rendered Mrs. Julia Ward Howe's " Battle Hymn of the Republic " in masterly style. In listening to the martial strains the pulse of the vast concourse of people was strained with excitement and expectation. The stillness was intense as the gray-haired president of the League and chairman of the meeting arose in his seat and passing to the desk, rapped for order.

" Fellow-citizens and men and women of my race : The occasion for this meeting is one of great solemnity. Forty years ago, when as a young man I sat at the feet of Sumner, Phillips, Garrison, Pillsbury, Charles Lenox Remond, Nell, Robert Morris, Fred Douglas and all the mighty host of anti-slavery fathers, we thought that with the abolishment of slavery the black man's destiny would be accomplished, and fixed beyond a peradventure. Today a condition of affairs confronts us that they never foresaw : the systematic destruction of the Negro by every device which the fury of enlightened malevolence can invent. In whatever direction we turn, the clouds hang dark and threatening. This new birth of the black race is a mighty agony. God help us in our struggle for liberty and manhood! *Agitation and eternal vigilance in the formation of public opinion* were the weapons which broke the power of the slave-holder and gave us emancipation. I recommend these methods to you today, knowing their value in the past.

> "'Up then and act! Thy courage wake!
> Combat intrigue, injustice, tyranny,
> And in thine efforts God will be with thee.'"

He then called upon the Hon. Herbert Clapp, as a representative of the party and of the sentiment of the best white people of the country, to address the meeting.

The political contingent gave him a hearty welcome as he moved with stately tread to the front of the platform. He said:

"The topic to be discussed is a very serious one, and I feel deeply how incompetent I am to deal with it, how incompetent most of us are to attempt the solution of the question before us. As a white man looking upon the South as my brother, and desiring to see the welfare of that section secured along with the rights of the brother in black, I feel the responsibility which rests upon me tonight to be fair and just, impartial to both sides in what I may say. I ask you tonight as rational people to look at this question from both points of view; to be calm and logical; to be willing, as just men of intelligence and judgment, to see and acknowledge wrong wherever you find it among your own people, and to be willing to consult as to the best method of procedure to rectify mistakes which if corrected may lead to an amicable adjustment of all difficulties in the South. As a friend of both sides, I ask you to do this.

"I am not here to apologize for the South; she has her ills and her sins. What section has not? Let us thank God that sectionalism is dead.

"Now, then, let us try to appreciate the relations of the Negro at the South. All history shows that two races, approaching in any degree equality in numbers, cannot live together unless intermarriage takes place or the one is dependent and in some sense subject to the other. Miscegenation by law will never take place in the South. No matter how much we people of the North may differ with our brothers of the South, this point will always remain fixed. Miscegenation, then, being out of the question, nothing remains for the Negro but to be dominated by the white man there. I hold that the Negro in American civilization is a problem of a vast deal more import than we are inclined to believe. The problem is national, not sectional. The sin of slavery was the sin of the nation, and that sin stands before us today full of menace, full of peril to the whole people. The Southern brother claims, and with some justice I think you will allow, that under the influence of scalawags and carpet-baggers, mostly composed of unprincipled Northern white men, the Negro has opposed, politically, everything that he thinks the white man wants. Upon this subject Prof. H. M. Brown, a Negro and member of the faculty of Hampton Institute, says: 'The greatest enemy to the Negro and the greatest obstacle to his progress is the politician, and the Negro politician is the worst of all.'

"You cannot deny that the well-behaved Negro has the respect of the community in which he lives at the South. Witness the death of a highly respected Negro in Georgia a short time ago. He never dabbled in politics, and his death was deplored by white and black alike. In thirty years forty per cent of the illiteracy at the South among the colored people has disappeared, due no doubt to environment and emulation of the whites. All kinds of employment, trades, professions, etc., are open to the Negro at the South, and you know that counts for a great deal. Here at the North the pressure is so great from the white laborer that we are forced, to some extent, to bar against the colored brother. I am ashamed to say it; but let us state the case truthfully, if at all.

"To come to the case in hand, I wish it to be distinctly understood that I am absolutely opposed to mob law. But there is an unwritten law, not peculiar to any section, which demands the quickest execution, in the quickest way, of the fiend who robs a virtuous woman of her honor to gratify his hellish diabolism. Human nature is the same throughout the civilized world. If in return for all the benefits conferred upon the Negro at the South, which I have enumerated previously, they give us the heinous crime of rape, what shall we say? Where find excuses for such ingratitude? Surely as men we must have sympathy for the pure and virtuous woman who carries with her a living shame, in a living death, in a life all too long for its miseries, if it lasts but for a day."

As he finished and returned to his seat, a sigh like a broken moan seemed to come from the very heart of the multitude, but not a movement broke the stillness. The Hon. Herbert Clapp felt that his part of the exercises was a failure. After a pause, the chairman introduced Doctor Lewis as a leading representative of the race whom they would, doubtless, be glad to hear express his views upon the momentous question under consideration. He was received with liberal applause, and said:

"I agree with our friend the Hon. Herbert Clapp in about all that he has said in relation to the grievous matter before us. I think that he has stated the case as impartially as it is possible so to do. The moment there is a lynching in the South, it is made the pretext for many press comments and public meetings among ourselves, and a general agitation of the question in the wrong way. The result is that you people at the North get a wrong idea of the matter. The published accounts of your meetings here do us at the South, who are working along the best lines that we know of for the elevation of the race, an injury, and often retard us greatly in the accomplishment of our designs. Take the Black Belt, and within its circumference you will find the densest ignorance, as well as bright intelligence of no ordinary quality. Among those people you will find the vicious ones who would rather drink, carouse, and fight than do a day's work to keep themselves from the penitentiary. Such men can be bought, bribed, worked upon for the furtherance of any plan or scheme that may suggest itself to the wily brain of the unscrupulous politician. These men are dangerous to the peace of the community, and it is such men who commit the deeds of violence with which the country is horrified at short intervals. If we cannot reach these men individually, we hope to reach their children. Thus we have planned that with the aid of our universities we shall at length root out evil and ignorance, and in the future give our race a clean, pure citizenship. As our friend has stated — politics is the bane of the Negro's existence. Those of us who eschew that subject, let matters of government take care of themselves, while we look out for our own individual or collective advancement, find no difficulty in living at the South in peace and harmony with our neighbors. If we are patient, docile, harmless, we may expect to see that prosperity for which we long, in the years to come, if not for ourselves then for our children. I am an optimist in regard to the future. I have great hopes of the better class of Southern people themselves.

"Let us remember that the South was more conquered than persuaded. The Confederates did not surrender their convictions with their swords. Immediately after the war Henry W. Grady would have been looked upon as a mon-

strosity. It was a severe blow to the South
when the slave gained his liberty. As the
South gains wealth and resources I think that
the problem will grow less difficult. It is the
idea of the Negro holding political preferment
that is so hard for the North and South to
swallow. But if we give them time and do not
hurry them, they will grow gradually accustomed to the new era. Convince the South
that we do not want social equality, neither do
we wish to rule. We want nothing but our
God-given rights as men.

"I believe in the humanizing influence of
the dollar judiciously expended for educational
advantages, 'holding it better and wiser to tend
the weeds in the garden than to water the exotic
in the window.' We should strive to obtain
the education of the industrial school, seeking
there our level, content to abide there, leaving
to the white man the superiority of brain and
intellect which hundreds of years have developed."

He ceased speaking and sat down amid murmurs of applause, mingled with disapprobation.
Some among the audience began to grow restless. Was this what they came to hear — an
apology, almost an eulogy upon the course pursued by the South toward the Negro? Other
speakers — white and colored — followed; then

the chairman introduced our friend John Langley. He came to the front of the platform with
his usual graceful bearing. He was well known
among the people, especially the younger contingent, and was received with liberal applause.

" My friends," he said, " I shall not detain
you with any lengthy remarks upon the situation, because there are speakers to follow me.
I am glad of the opportunity to say what I
think about lynch law: It is a terrible thing
to contemplate. The crime which provokes it
is still more terrible, to my thinking. I utter
no eulogy upon the position of the South
toward the Negro, neither do I harbor undue
resentment for the grievous wrongs which I
feel they have, in some measure, heaped upon
us. I am willing to leave the punishment of
criminals, the suppression of mob violence,
with the national government, being convinced
that in good time the government so trusted
will acquit itself with equity toward my race.
You have listened to the speeches made by
our friend, the Hon. Herbert Clapp, and our
brother, Dr. Arthur Lewis, upon whose word
we can implicitly rely, because he works, lives,
and moves among the very happenings of which
we know nothing save by reading. It is discretion to act coolly, calmly and deliberately;
to look at all sides of a question before we

jump at conclusions.   I can see nothing to be
gained, if, as we have been advised, we took
up arms in defense of our rights of citizenship.
Extermination would speedily follow.   Let us
not invite destruction.   But we have opportunities of advancement.   Let us seize them.
Let us await the issue of events with patience,
trusting in the fealty of our party leaders, putting faith in their sagacity to push our claims
and redress whatever grievances we may have,
at a seasonable time.   We thoroughly understand the attitude of the whites.   Let us not
offend the class upon whom we depend for
employment and assistance in times of emer-
gencies.   By so doing, if we cannot have amity
we can have peace."

CHAPTER XIV.

LUKE SAWYER SPEAKS TO THE LEAGUE.

MY ear is pained,
My soul is sick with every day's report
Of wrong and outrage with which earth is filled.
There is no flesh in man's obdurate heart;
It does not feel for man: the natural bond
Of brotherhood is severed as the flax
That falls asunder at the touch of fire.
He finds his fellow guilty of a skin
Not colored like his own ; and, having power
To enforce the wrong *for such a worthy cause,*
Dooms and devotes him as a lawful prey.
— COWPER.

SCARCELY had the speaker taken his seat amid suppressed murmurs of discontent, when a tall, gaunt man of very black complexion arose in his seat among the delegates, and in a sonorous bass voice uttered the solemn protest of Patrick Henry, so famous in history : " Gentlemen may cry ' Peace ! peace ! ' but there is no peace ! "

In an instant confusion reigned. Women fluttered their handkerchiefs, and above waves of applause and cheers could be heard cries of " Hear, hear ! " " Platform ! platform ! " The chairman rapped for order, and when he could make himself heard, asked the delegate to come to the platform; another speaker was waiting, but the audience would be glad to hear anything he might have to say. As he passed up the aisle and mounted the steps of the rostrum, the people saw a man of majestic frame, rugged physique and immense muscular development. His face was kindly, but withal bore the marks of superior intelligence, shrewdness and great strength of character. He might have been a Cromwell, a Robespierre, a Lincoln. Men of his physiological development — when white — mould humanity, and leave their own characteristics engraved upon the pages of the history of their times.

"Friends," said he, when he stood before them, " I come from Williamstown, in the western part of this state, to be a delegate at this meeting. Here are my credentials to show that I am in good standing in the League where I belong. (He handed his papers to the chairman.) I want to impress that fact upon the minds of this assembly, because I am going to tell you some awful facts before I get through." He paused, and with his handkerchief wiped the tears and perspiration from his face. " Friends, I am thirty years old and look fifty. I want to tell you why this is so. I want to tell you what brought me *here*. I want to tell the gentlemen who have spoken here tonight that conservatism, lack of brotherly affiliation, lack of energy for the right and the power of the almighty dollar which deadens men's hearts to the sufferings of their brothers, and makes them feel that if only *they* can rise to the top of the ladder may God help the hindmost man, are the forces which are ruining the Negro in this country. It is killing him off by thousands, destroying his self-respect, and degrading him to the level of the brute. *These are the contending forces that are dooming this race to despair!*

"My name is Lycurgus Sawyer; Luke they call me for short. When I was about ten years old my father kept a large store in a little town in the state of Louisany. I had two brothers and a sister. My mother was a fine woman, somewhat better educated than my father. Through her influence he went into this business of trading, and soon had the largest business and as much money as any man in the county. Father didn't care to meddle with politics, for, with the natural shrewdness of many of us, he saw that that might be made an excuse for his destruction. When I was about ten years old, then, a white man in the village, seeing the headway my father was making in accumulating property, opened a store on the same street. Father said nothing, but his customers still continued to trade with him, and it seemed that the other man would be compelled to give up. About this time father received threatening letters ordering him to move, and saying that in case he did not do as ordered he would lose his life. Mother was frightened, and advised father to get out of the place, but he, anxious to save some part of his hard earnings, waited to sell his stock and houses before seeking a home elsewhere. One night a posse of men came to our house and began smoking us out. You don't know anything about that up here, do you? Well, you'll get there if things keep on as they're going. My father had arms. He raised the window of his sleeping-room and fired into the mob of cowardly hounds. Thoroughly enraged, they broke open the doors back and front, seized my father and hung him to the nearest tree, whipped my mother and sister, and otherwise abused them so that they died next day. My brothers were twins, still so small that they were but babes. The mob took them by the heels and dashed their brains out against the walls of the house! Then they burned the house. I saw all this, and frenzied with horror, half-dead with fright, crept into the woods to die. I was found there by a colored planter named Beaubean, who lived in the next township. He pitied me and took me home.

That, gentlemen, was my *first* experience of lynching. Do you think it is possible to preach 'peace' to a man like me?"

The house was filled with the cries and groans of the audience. Sobs shook the women, while the men drank in the words of the speaker with darkening brows and hands which involuntarily clinched themselves in sympathy with his words.

"But that is not the only story I can tell. Here's another. I will tell it to you, and you can digest it at your leisure.

"Monsieur Beaubean was an educated man, descended from a very wealthy family. His father had been his owner. When the father died he left to his son, born of a black mother, an equal share of the estate along with his legitimate heirs. They made no objections, so he got it.

"Monsieur Beaubean had married a quadroon woman of great beauty — Louisany abounds in handsome women of color; they had two children, a boy and a girl. She was three years old when I went to live with them. I remained in the family twelve years. I learned many things there; along with the trade of blacksmithing I learned to esteem myself as a man.

"I cannot describe to you the beauty and loveliness of that child. As a boy I worshipped

BROKE OPEN THE DOORS, SEIZED MY FATHER, AND HUNG HIM
TO THE NEAREST TREE.

her, and as a man I loved her; not with the
hope of ever having a return of the feeling she
had aroused in me, but as a faithful dog that
would lay down his life for those who shelter and care for him, so I felt to Beaubean's
family, and especially to that child.   When
Mabelle, as we called her, was old enough, she
was sent to the Colored Sisters' School in the
city of New Orleans.   It was my pleasant duty
to drive her into the city each day and go for
her at night.

"Monsieur Beaubean had a half-brother — a
white man — who was very wealthy and stood
very high in politics.   In fact, he was in the
State Senate.   He was very warm in his expres-
sions of friendship for the family, and especially
so in his assumption of relationship.   I noticed
that he seemed extremely fond of   Mabelle.
One day, after she had passed her fourteenth
birthday, she had a holiday from school, and
went with some schoolfellows to visit a companion who lived in the city.   They returned
at night without her, saying that she went into
a store with Monsieur Beaubean's brother, and
they had not seen her since.

"Can you imagine what a night was passed by
that family?   No, you cannot, unless you have
been through the same experience.   The father
went in one direction and I in another.   All

night long we searched the city streets; nothing could be heard of her. Finally we went to police headquarters and secured the services of a detective. After *three weeks* of incessant searching we found her a prisoner in a house of the vilest character in the lowest portion of the city of New Orleans — a poor, ruined, half-crazed creature in whom it was almost impossible to trace a resemblance to the beautiful pet of our household. These arms bore her forth from that vile den and restored her to a broken-hearted parent. I think that I must have gone mad. If I had had the man there then that committed the crime (he raised one gaunt arm above his head, and standing in that attitude seemed the embodiment of vengeance) I would have taken him by the throat and shaken him (he hissed the words through clinched teeth), shaken him as a dog would a rat until he was *dead!* DEAD! DEAD! We took her home, but I believe that her father was a madman from the time he placed his eyes upon her until he was murdered. And who do you think had done this foul crime? Why, the father's *half-brother*, *uncle* of the victim!

"Crazed with grief, Monsieur Beaubean faced his brother and accused him of his crime. 'Well,' said he, 'whatever damage I have done I am willing to pay for. But your child is no better than her mother or her grandmother. What does a woman of mixed blood, or any Negress, for that matter, know of virtue? It is my belief that they were a direct creation by God to be the pleasant companions of men of my race. Now, I am willing to give you a thousand dollars and call it square.' He handed Monsieur Beaubean a roll of bills as he spoke. Beaubean seized them and hurled them into the villain's face with these words: 'I leave you to carry my case into the Federal courts and appeal for justice.' Unhappy man! That night his house was mobbed. The crowd surrounded the building after firing it, and as an inmate would show his head at a window in the struggle to escape from the burning building, someone would pick him off. So it went all that night. I seized Mabelle and wrapped her in a blanket. Watching my chance I stole from the house after the fire was well under way, and miraculously reached a place of safety. I took Mabelle to the colored convent at New Orleans, and left her there in the care of the sisters. *There she died when her child was born !*"

As the speaker stood silently contemplating his weeping, grief-convulsed audience, a woman was borne from the auditorium in a fainting condition. John Langley from his seat on the platform leaned over and asked an usher who the lady was. " Miss Sappho Clark," was his reply.

Amid universal silence, the silence which comes from feeling too deep for outward expression, the speaker concluded: "A tax too heavy placed on tea and things like that, made the American Colonies go to war with Great Britain to get their liberty. I ask you what you think the American Colonies would have done if they had suffered as we have suffered and are still suffering?

"Mr. Chairman, gentlemen call for peace, and I reply: 'Peace if possible; justice at any rate.' Where is there peace for men like me? When the grave has closed over me and my memories, I shall have peace.

"Under such conditions as I have described, contentment, amity — call it by what name you will — is impossible; justice alone remains to us."

CHAPTER XV.

WILL SMITH'S DEFENSE OF HIS RACE.

> THANK God for the token!
> Thank God that one man as a free
> Man has spoken!
> — WHITTIER.

SOMEONE at this moment began to sing that grand old hymn, ever new and consoling:

> "Jesus, Lover of my soul,
>   Let me to thy bosom fly,
>   While the nearer waters roll,
>   While the tempest still is nigh."

When quiet once more reigned, amid intense silence the chairman arose and introduced Mr. William Smith as the last speaker of the evening. Tremendous applause greeted him, for he was known to be an able and eloquent debater.

"Friends," he said, "I shall not attempt a lengthy and discursive argument; I shall simply try to answer some of the arguments which have been advanced by other speakers. I have no doubt that they have spoken their honest convictions. Now let us look at the other side of the question.

"We know that the Negro question is the most important issue in the affairs of the

American Republic today. We are told that
there are but two ways of solving the vexed
question of the equality of the two races:
miscegenation by law, which can *never* take
place, or complete domination by the white
race — meaning by that *comparative servitude*.

"Miscegenation, either *lawful* or *unlawful*,
we *do not want*. The Negro dwells less on
such a social cataclysm than any other race
among us. Social equality does not exist; no
man is forced to receive another within the
environments of intimate social life. 'Social
position is not to be gained by pushing.' That
much for miscegenation. The question now
stands: Which race shall dominate within certain parallels of latitude south of Mason and
Dixon's line? The Negro, if given his full
political rights, would carry the balance of
power every time. This power the South has
sworn that he shall never exercise. All sorts
of arguments are brought forward to prove the
inferiority of intellect, hopeless depravity, and
God knows what not, to uphold the white man
in his wanton cruelty toward the American
Ishmael.

"We are told that we can receive education
only along certain elementary lines, and in the
next breath we are taunted with not producing
a genius in science or art. A Southern white

man will tell you that of all politicians the
Negro is the vilest, ignoring the fact that for
corrupt politics no race ever can or ever will
excel the venality of a certain class of whites.
Let us, for the sake of illustration, glance at
the position of the Irish element in politics.
They come to this country poor, unlettered,
despised. Fifty years ago Pat was as little
welcome at the North as the Negro at the
South. What has changed the status of his
citizenship? *Politics.* The Irishman domi-
nates politics at the North, and there is no gift
within the power of the government that does
not feel his influence. I remember a story I
heard once of an Irishman just landed at Castle
Garden. A friend met him, and as they
walked up the street said to him: 'Well, Pat,
you are just in time to vote for the city government election.' 'Begorra,' replied Pat, 'an' is
it a guvimint they have here? Sure, thin, I'll
vote agin it.'

"The Irish vote, then, is massed at certain
strategic points in the North, and its power is
feared and respected. The result has been a
rapid and dazzling advance all along the ave-
nues of education and wealth in this country
for that incisive race. To the Negro alone
politics shall bring no fruit.

"To the defense of slavery in the past, and

the inhuman treatment of the Negro in the present, the South has consecrated her best energies. Literature, politics, theology, history have been ransacked and perverted to prove the hopeless inferiority of the Negro and the design of God that he should serve by right of color and physique. She has convinced no one but herself. Bitterer than double-distilled gall was the Federal success which brought Negro emancipation, domination and supremacy.

" Disfranchisement is what is wanted by the South. Disfranchise the Negro and the South will be content. He, as the weaker race, can soon be crowded out.

"Many solutions of the question of Negro domination have been advanced; among them the deportation of the Negro to Africa has been most warmly advocated by public men all over the country. They argue that in this way the prophecy of the Bible will soonest be fulfilled; that 'Ethiopia shall stretch forth her hand and princes shall come out of Egypt.'

" The late Henry Grady told us 'that in the wise and humane administration, in the lifting the slave to heights of which he had not dreamed in his savage home, and giving him a happiness he has not yet found in freedom — our fathers (Southern men) left their sons a saving and excellent heritage (slavery).' An-

other man, also a Southerner, has told us:
' In education and industrial progress this race
has accomplished more than it could have
achieved in centuries in different environment,
without the aid of the whites. The Negro has
needed the example as well as the aid of the
white man. In sections where the colored
population is massed and removed from contact with the whites, the Negro has retrograded.
Segregate the colored population and you take
away the object-lesson.' Here, then, is the
testimony of two intellectual white men as to
the dependence of the Negro upon his proximity to the whites for a continuance of what
advancement he has made since the abolishment of slavery. Is such a race as this fit at
the present time to carry enlightenment into a
savage and barbarous country? Can the blind
lead the blind? Would not the Negro gradually fall into the same habits of ignorance and
savagery from which the white slave-trader so
humanely rescued him when he transported
him into the blissful lap of American slavery?
The Negro cannot be deported.

" It is being argued that the Negro is receiving education beyond his needs or his capacity.
In short, that a Negro highly educated is a
Negro spoiled. I agree with the gentleman on
the other side that education alone will not

produce a good citizen. But, of those who would curtail his endeavors to reach the highest that may be opened to him, I would ask: Of what use has education been to you in the upbuilding of the social and political structure which you designate the United States of America? What are the uses of education anyhow?

" To those who know the constitution of the brain as the organ of the moral and intellectual powers of man, education is of the highest importance in the formation of the character of the individual, the race, the government, the social life of any community under heaven. The objects presented to the mind by education stimulate in the same manner that the physical elements of nature do the nerves and muscles — they afford the faculties scope for action. Education is knowledge of nature in all its departments. The moment the mind discovers its own constitution and discerns the importance of the natural laws, the great advantage of moral and intellectual cultivation as a means of invigorating the brain and mental faculties, and of directing the conduct in obedience to the laws of God and man, is apparent. It is important that the Negro should not be hampered in his search after knowledge if we would eliminate from his nature any tendency toward vice that he may be thought to possess, and *which has been largely increased by what he has imbibed from the example and the close,* IMMORAL ASSOCIATION *which often existed between the master and the slave.* From my own observation I should say that in this country today the science of man's whole nature — animal, moral and intellectual — was never more required to guide him than at present, when he seems to wield a giant's power, and in the application of it to display the selfish ignorance of an overgrown child.

"We come now to the crime of rape, with which the Negro is accused. For the sake of argument, we will allow that in one case out of a hundred the Negro is guilty of the crime with which he is charged; in the other ninety-nine cases the white man gratifies his lust, either of passion or vengeance. None of us will ever forget the tales told us tonight by Luke Sawyer; the wanton passions he revealed and which it has taken centuries of white civilization to develop, disclosing a dire hell to which the common crime of the untutored Negro is as white as alabaster. And it is from such men as these that the appeal comes for protection for woman's virtue! Do such examples as these render the Negro gentle and pacific? No; he sees himself traveling for years the barren Sahara of poverty, imprisonment, broken hopes and violated home ties; the ignorant, half-savage, irresponsible human animal who forms the rank and file of a race so recently emancipated from servitude, sees only revenge before his short-sighted vision.

" Rape is the outgrowth of a fiendish animus of the whites toward the blacks and of the blacks toward the whites. The Southern white is unable to view the feared domination of the blacks with the dispassionate reasoning of the unprejudiced mind. He exaggerates the nearness of that possibility, which is not desired by the blacks, and, like the physician sick of a mortal disease, is unable to prescribe for himself, and cannot realize that the simple remedy, gently applied, will lift him from his couch of pain. Lynch law prevails as the only sure cure for the ills of the South.

" ' Lynchings are justifiable on two grounds,' says a thoughtful writer: ' First, if they are consonant with the moral dignity and well-being of the people; and secondly, if they stop, and are the only sure means of stopping, the crime they avenge.' Lynching does not stop crime; it is but a subterfuge for killing men. It is a good excuse, to use a rough expression, to ' go a-gunning for niggers.'

" Lynching was instituted to crush the manhood of the enfranchised black. Rape is the crime which appeals most strongly to the heart of the home life. Merciful God! Irony of ironies! *The men who created the mulatto race, who recruit its ranks year after year by the very means which they invoked lynch law to suppress,* bewailing the sorrows of violated womanhood!

"No; it is not rape. If the Negro votes, he is shot; if he marries a white woman, he is shot; if he accumulates property, he is shot or lynched — he is a pariah whom the National Government cannot defend. But if he defends himself and his home, then is heard the tread of marching feet as the Federal troops move southward to quell a 'race riot.'

"The South declares that she is no worse than the North, and that the North would do the same under like provocation. Perhaps so, if the offender were a Negro. Take the case of Christie Warden and Frank Almy, which occurred in New Hampshire only a few years ago. Where could a more atrocious crime be perpetrated? The refinement of intellectual pursuits, the elegancies of social intercourse, were the attributes which went to make up the personnel of the most brutal murderer that ever disgraced the history of crime. Centuries of culture and civilization were combined in his make-up. The community where the girl lived and was respected and beloved did not lynch the brute. The white heat of passion led men to lay aside all pursuits for days in order to hunt the criminal from his hiding-place. New Hampshire justice gave him counsel and every means to defend himself from the penalty of his horrid crime. *That was in the North!*

"Human nature is the same in everything. The characteristic traits of the master will be found in his dog. Black, devilish, brutal as they may picture the Negro to be, he but reflects the nature of his environments. *He is the Hyde who torments the Dr. Jekyll of the white man's refined civilization!*

"My friends, it is going to take time to straighten out this problem; it will only be done by the formation of public opinion. Brute force will not accomplish anything. We must *agitate.* As the anti-slavery apostles went everywhere, preaching the word fifty years before emancipation, *so must we do to-day.* Appeal for the justice of our cause to every civilized nation under the heavens. Lift ourselves upward and forward in this great march of life until 'Ethiopia shall indeed stretch forth her hand, and princes shall come out of Egypt.'"

When he had finished there was not a dry eye in that vast audience. Every heart followed the words of the pastor as with broken utterance he invoked the divine blessing upon the meeting just ended.   Slowly they dispersed to their homes, filled with thoughts that burn but cannot be spoken.

The papers said next day that a very interesting meeting occurred the night before at the church on X Street.

CHAPTER XVI.

JOHN LANGLEY CONSULTS MADAM FRANCES.

MACBETH.— Tell me, thou unknown power,—
FIRST WITCH.— He knows thy thought:
　　　　　　Hear his speech but say thou nought.
MACBETH.— Whate'er thou art, for thy good caution thanks;
　　　　　　But one word more,—
FIRST WITCH.— He will not be commanded: here's another,
　　　　　　More potent than the first.
　　　　　　　　　　　　　　　　　　— MACBETH.

MANY things troubled John Langley. The fact that Dora and he seemed to have lost the close relationship which had distinguished the first period of their engagement, and that she now studiously avoided him and accepted with alacrity all the attention which her childhood's lover so ardently showered upon her, did not disturb him so much as the utter indifference of Sappho Clark. How to bend her to his will was the thought which absorbed his waking hours and haunted him even in sleep. She should not escape him; on that he was determined.

This morning as he walked down town to his office he turned over various plans in his mind, and finally determined to go that very day and consult Madam Frances, who had been

voted such a tremendous success at the fair
which had just closed. John believed that the
seeress could help him, and he was not so
polished and refined as to hesitate to use such
means to accomplish an end.

When he reached the office he noticed that
an invitation to a dinner given that very evening by the Canterbury Club lay upon the desk;
in his absorption in other things he had forgotten the dinner. He pushed his work at the
Court House to a quick finish and retraced his
steps to the office, and telling the boy that he
would not return before three o'clock, hurried
toward the quarter of the city in which the
fortune-teller lived.

J. Street is in the very heart of what is called
the " Negro quarter " of the West End; it is
also popularly known among colored people
as "the Hill." Here Madam Frances lived in
a small ten-foot wooden building which she
hired.

" The Hill " has been the scene of many stir-
ring incidents in the peculiar history of the
colored people. On the J. Street side the old
St. Paul's Baptist Church is situated. This
historic old building was the first church
the colored people owned in Massachusetts.
There were five brothers — black men — bearing the name of Paul, who were educated in

England in the reign of George III. One of them — Thomas — determined to return to England and beg for funds to build a colored church in America. He was well received and his mission was successful. Twenty years ago an old Negress — a centenarian — was living who had herself picked up bricks in the streets of Boston in the early morning, and carried them to the spot where the building was being erected. She did this because although too poor to give money toward furthering the enterprise, she felt that she must contribute in some way to the erection of this first colored house of worship in this part of the country. This same woman remembered seeing Thomas Paul bring into the church a large bandanna handkerchief filled with the English gold he had begged abroad, the first Sunday the building was used for worship.

St. Paul's Church became the sacred edifice where the desire for freedom was fostered in the heart of the Negro. There such men as Garrison and Phillips defied the vengeance of howling mobs that thirsted for the lives of the Negro champions.

O glorious times! who can think of them without a quicker heart-throb and a wildly fluttering pulse? O honored men! O happy dead, gone to receive the reward promised to all who do the work of the Master!

As we read of the deeds of such men the question will obtrude itself: Is it the foreordained destiny of some to achieve greatness? and if not foreordained, would these same great ones remain inert and impotent like the mediocre majority? Many of us strive to do what we can, but our efforts do not seem to amount to much. In the present emergency which confronts us as a race, no leader has yet pressed forward to take command, as in those glorious old days; no Sumner to receive upon his precious body the stripes intended for the poor, downtrodden black man.

> "God rest us all — we know not what we are!
> What nature wills, not what we wish, are we."

Let us press forward and take courage and do the little that we can, leaving the rest to God. The hand of the Divine Architect will fit each life into its own niche, to form an intricate whole of preconceived beauty.

Near the head of G. and P. Streets stands the well-known Twelfth Baptist Church, a split from St. Paul's, and world renowned under its beloved pastor and founder, Leonard Grimes. Just across the way, on P. Street, was the home of the venerable and honored Lewis Hayden. The history of Massachusetts is forever linked with that of the Anti-slavery Movement, and the

Anti-slavery Movement is entwined about the familiar street-corners of the old West End.

John reached the house and rang the bell of the quaint abode. A colored girl, who was evidently a servant, answered the ring, and told him that Madam Frances was now at lunch, and would not be at liberty until an hour later. However, he might come in and wait, if he wished, and she would ask the Madam to see him before her usual time. On second thoughts, she *did* sometimes see people before her hours. (This was after John had discreetly slipped a small piece of silver into her hand.) She waited on him up the narrow stairway and seated him in a small back room adjoining the audience room.

John took a seat a little behind the door, thereby being completely sheltered from observation. Indeed, a person passing the door on entering or leaving the building would not be likely to see him, and would declare the room empty; but from his seat he commanded a full view of the passageway. He had looked the bare and sparsely furnished room over and settled back in his chair for a tedious period of waiting when the door of the next room opened and his attention was attracted by the sound of a voice which he thought he knew: "That money will do what you wish for the boy, Aunt

Sally, and " — then the door was closed. John started to his feet in great excitement. Surely he knew that voice! Again the door must have swung open, for he caught the words of the conversation distinctly: " There is no need for him to know — let him continue to think" — he heard no more. Again the door closed. It must have been fully five minutes that he stood intently listening, but nothing more rewarded him. Suddenly the door opened and shut and then he heard the quick, light footfall of a woman and the frou-frou of silken skirts, together with a delicate perfume that he recognized. He drew back as far as possible behind the shelter of the door, and then as he judged from the sound that she was upon the stairs, he ventured from his hiding place, and finding the entry clear, peered over the banisters just in time to catch a full view of the beautiful face of Sappho Clark. As she passed out she had dropped her handkerchief; John picked it up; there in the corner were her initials: " S. C."

He returned to his seat in the bare little room, holding the delicately scented piece of cambric in his hand with the feeling of a man who is on the verge of discovering something of importance to himself. He was confused and uncertain in his thoughts, but when he could command himself sufficiently to reason, he felt that it was very foolish in him to wonder at Sappho's presence there; all girls were eager to consult those who could unveil for them anything pertaining to the future. How silly for him to make a mystery of a common happening; still he was restless, disquieted; vague suspicions assailed his mind.

Madam Frances's niece! What could be her motive in hiding her relationship to the old fortune-teller? That she had one he was confidant. The child, too! She appeared never to have seen him before the fair. They had acted in concert. Madam Frances and the boy seemed not to know Sappho, and by their manner denied all previous knowledge of her. Here was something to unravel. But he was used to solving mysteries; it was his business. He would constitute himself a committee of investigation, he told himself; he owed it to the community, to himself, to the Smith family, who were so fond of her. So he planned that the sin of another poor human soul, a vague fraud against no one in particular but society in general, doing wrong to no one, should be suddenly stripped of its coverings. He mused here alone, buried in deep thought, forgetful of the hour and his surroundings. Uncanny shadows were filling the corners of the bare little room when an idea came to him which fairly made him shiver. He could feel the blood recede from his face under the excitement of the moment and grow cold in his veins. "Heaven above!" he whispered, "it cannot be possible that what I suspect is true — that child — his resemblance to her — this woman the child's great-aunt and also Sappho's aunt — the secrecy!"

As he sat there engrossed in speculation the maid who had answered his ring came into the room to tell him that the Madam would see him. He still held the handkerchief in his hand, and said as he held it toward the girl: "The lady who just went out dropped it. I think she called Madam Frances 'Aunt Sally.'"

"Oh, yes," replied the girl, as she took it from him. "I will give it to Madam. Miss Clark comes here a great deal. She is Madam Frances's niece."

John's thoughts were in a whirl as he followed the girl to the door of the room Sappho had just quitted. Why had he never heard of this relationship before? He was quite certain that the Smiths knew nothing of it, or he would have heard it spoken of about the house or at the fair. There *was* a mystery, then, about her. Just at this point he awoke to a realization of the fact that he was within a darkened room. It took a moment for his eyes to become accustomed to the semi-twilight of the apartment, and then he seated himself in a chair beside a small table which the girl pointed out to him before she left the room, and which was evidently intended for visitors.

"How do you do?" said a voice, and turning in the direction from whence it came he beheld the wrinkled, black face, and gaudily turbaned head of Madam Frances. As he returned her greeting another voice said:

"How d'y do? Lord love ye, how d'y do?"

Then he saw that a large green parrot was perched on the back of the chair in which Madam Frances was seated. On the table beside him was a silver dish holding two large sea-green stones, in the depths of which one could easily trace the outlines of white coral islands, birds, beasts and reptiles. In one corner of the room was a large screen covered with unbleached cotton. The table beside Madam Frances held a curious instrument which resembled a ship's compass, and on its surface the signs of the zodiac came and went at the will of the seeress. Many curious things were in this darkened room, and no matter how much one might wish to disbelieve the power of this woman to foretell the future, he could not fail to be impressed with the surroundings. And, after all, our surroundings influence our lives and characters as much as fate, destiny or any supernatural agency.

Madam Frances held out her hand for her fee, and as he laid a silver dollar across her palm, she said:

"She will escape you, and you will lose the other one, too. Better stop now, and keep the one you hold."

"Keep the one you hold, fool, fool, fool!" screamed the parrot's shrill voice.

"You come to me for advice about certain property that you would like to get. There is money all about you, piles of it. You will meet one soon who will tell you something of importance concerning a large sum of money. You say you did not come here to find that out. But it is here, and the dial does not lie."

She pointed to the face of the compass-like instrument before her. John felt very uncomfortable as the old woman peered at him from eyes which, while they seemed almost sightless, yet impressed one as being able to pierce the secrets of the soul.

"There are three things you wish to ask about," she continued. "Look on the screen and behold the answer to a question."

John looked toward the screen and saw what appeared to be dim shadows forming there, which gradually took on the shape of a banquet table, and seated around it was a company of men, among whom he recognized himself and his friends William Smith and Doctor Lewis.

"When you are at that table, in the company of those men, you shall have the answer to one of the questions you would ask me. Look again," she said, and John saw to his amazement that the cloth of which the screen was made had resumed its color, and another shadowy outline was beginning to form. As he gazed in wonder the outlines took shape before his astonished eyes, and he saw the altar of a church. Before a priest a man and woman knelt in bridal dress. The man placed a ring upon the woman's finger. As the picture faded the faces of the couple were turned toward him for one moment, and he recognized Sappho Clark and Will Smith.

"Look again," said the voice of the seeress. He did so, and saw before him a noble ship; on her deck stood a man and a woman. The picture faded before he could distinguish the features of either party. "These are all I am permitted to show you now," said Madam Frances. "These pictures contain the answers to your questions."

"Do I understand them to mean that I shall be defeated in my plans? that I shall not enjoy a part of the wealth which you see about me?"

"You will be defeated, and you will not enjoy

HE SAW WHAT APPEARED TO BE A FIELD OF ICE AND SNOW,
VAST AND UNBROKEN.

the wealth that is about you; unless"—she
paused, shook her head, mumbled some unin-
telligible jargon, as if conversing with the unseen, again shook her head.

"If not a sharer of the wealth you see, what
will my fate be, and in what line shall I pros-
per? Surely you can tell me something about
my success in life."

"Enough has been shown to you. Why
persist? But look again, if you will not be
advised."

Again he looked at the screen, and saw dark
outlines resolve themselves into shapes. He
saw what appeared to be a field of ice and snow,
vast and unbroken — terrible in its dreary iso-
lation. It faded, and he turned to the fortune-
teller in desperation :

"What has such a scene to do with me?"

"Remorse, remorse! who can tell the end of
life?" mumbled the crone, as if in self-communion. At length she seemed to come to
herself, and said in clear accents : "If you would
let an old woman advise you, I should say
choose the right path, no matter what the cost.
But men are foolish always, foolish always for
a pretty face."

She touched a bell on the table beside her,
and the boy Alphonse came from behind the
curtain and gravely motioned the visitor to follow him out.

"For a pretty face," croaked the parrot, rousing himself from a nap as John left the room. As he descended the stairs the words of the parrot followed him:

"Fools, fools; all men are fools for a pretty face!"

John cursed his own folly in seeking the fortune-teller's aid as he went slowly back to his office, puzzling over the things he had seen and heard. He was a well-read man, and tried to account for these strange things. He knew from reading, the mediumistic powers of all created things; he knew something of the wonderful agencies of electricity and magnetism. The appliances in the room had suggested magnetism as the medium; "yet," he argued, "the same phenomena might have been produced by the power of hypnotism." He knew enough of the latter to practice it in a way for the amusement of his young friends, but had thought himself impervious to its influence.

But with all his reasoning he could not convince himself that there was not an intelligence — invisible and intangible — that had presented to him those soul-disturbing manifestations.

CHAPTER XVII.

THE CANTERBURY CLUB DINNER.

ILL fares the land to hastening ills a prey,
Where wealth accumulates and men decay.
— GOLDSMITH.

THE Canterbury Club of Boston, which held its annual dinner on this particular evening, was composed of the flower of Boston's literary savans. At the rooms of the club men deep in scientific research touched elbows with the advanced theological scholar and the political economist. Side by side with the vital questions of the hour in the world of progress — wireless telegraphy, the philosophy of trusts, the rise and fall of monarchies, the restoration of Greek art, the philosophy of lynching was beginning to engage the attention of two hemispheres, and information was eagerly sought from every reliable source.

Now it happened that the remarkable ability of Smith in dealing with the acknowledged difficulties of the question had been spoken of to some of the members by the Hon. Herbert Clapp, the president of the club. It had already entertained Doctor Lewis, on account of his great work as an educator among his people.

and John Langley because he was an important factor in his line, doing the work necessary to the life of any organization interested
in active politics with which men of a delicate
moral susceptibility could not be approached.
It was voted to invite young Smith to this dinner as a fresh and interesting specimen of the
Negro. Many fat contributions found their
way annually into the treasury of the African
School of Industrial and Agricultural Development, which was under the able management
of Doctor Lewis, through the influence of this
club. He had accomplished great things; had
made himself the center of this terrible human
tragedy in the heart of the Black Belt, where
the college was situated; but the deadly antag-
onism of the South made even his iron-hearted
stoicism bow to its tyrannical decrees, insomuch
that he had been forced to compromise, and
the educational advantages allowed the pupils
had been curtailed to suit the views of those
who placed a low estimate on the ability of the
Negro, in spite of the many bright examples of
superior intellectual endowments which exist
among them. Such ideas as Doctor Lewis set
forth in his many brilliant speeches in behalf
of his people were logical, and showed a mind
capable of grasping the needs of the moment —
an infinity of powerful thought under a tyrannous self-suppression.

"One man's meat is another man's poison." The colored people north of Mason and Dixon's line are conspicuous for their advancement along all the lines which are distinctive features in the formation of the polished exterior of the good citizen of such a republic as ours. Among the best circles of this community are found the highest types of intellectual, moral, religious and social improvement. What becomes of such a class as this when hampered by rules and laws made to fit the needs of the Black Belt? laws of life and living which cannot be forced, and ought not to be forced, upon the large class of colored citizens who embody within themselves the highest development of American citizenship? We believe that the spirit of fair play is not yet dead in our beloved country. We believe that there still exists beneath the seething cauldron of prejudice with which the South would deluge the advance of the Negro, brave hearts that will answer the cry of distress with patriotic alacrity, and these same brave hearts will demand for every black face, North and South, the fullest opportunity to develop whatever is best within him.

·   ·   ·   ·   ·   ·   ·

The young men had planned to go together. Their entrance created a diversion; the English member of Parliament who was the guest of honor was much surprised, although too well-bred to show it. Certainly they were fine specimens of the genus homo, whose physique demanded more than a passing glance of admiration. Curious thoughts came to Mr. Withington, the English guest; certain truths which, if applicable to England, seemed doubly so to this country, so new and untried, as it were, in the changes and subtle uncertainties of government and revolutions:

> " And a proud yeomanry, its country's pride
> When once destroyed can never be supplied."

Will the Republic learn the value of the black children of her adoption when it is too late?

The presence of these young Negroes was generally received as a pleasant innovation among that company. There was a senator from Alabama present among the invited guests, and for a moment he felt his color rise and all the peculiar feelings of his section protest and clamor to make themselves heard when he found that he must perforce be brought into social contact with the despised ex-slave representatives. But he remembered, in time to save himself from ridicule, that he was in Massachusetts. "What matter?" was his inward thought, "some day we shall change all this."

The first course was about over before Will had a chance to look about him. He did not feel at all overpowered by the grandeur displayed. The great room with its high walls and ceiling of magnificently carved mahogany, the massive brass chandeliers, composed of hundreds of tiny electric lights which threw their sparkling rays upon the exquisitely appointed table, with the priceless ware in which the meal was served, the heavy scent of roses which perfumed the air, the silent waiters gliding in and out among the guests,—all seemed the fantastic creation of a dream.

His neighbor happened to be Mr. Withington; his *vis-a-vis*, a noted editor; farther down the table he recognized a foreign secretary of legation; and so on. Conversation soon became general; flashes of wit, satire, and discussions of rare value to the student — a sumptuous feast of good things. Above the click of glasses he caught snatches of conversation:

"You may search through science and find no evidence of the presence of God in the universe," declared the sharp, decisive voice of a free-thinker, who was plunged in the midst of an argument with a noted theologian of the Episcopal faith. Will listened intently for the answer. It came instantly:

"How could it be otherwise? God has a

subjective existence to man; therefore man must get outside of himself to know God; in fact, man must die to attain God."

"Ah, there you go, with your mythological argument! You cover the clear statement of a fact with a veil of mysticism."

"Very true; but what is the soul, mentality, existence itself, but a living mysticism?" replied the clergyman.

The whole room had become interested by this time, and watched the play of cultured thought and keen argument with great relish.

"It is only when the subjective part of man exists as a distinct entity, then, that you think the presence of God is made clear to him?"

"Yes," replied the clergyman; "for the final end of man is the beginning of spirituality, or the true knowledge of God."

"Ah, but if we let reason speak, we find the flaws in your theory, and your ground becomes untenable. I look forward to the day which coming years shall usher in, when all the discoveries which are being made each year, and the general diffusion of scientific knowledge, shall revolutionize thought, and place God and man on an entirely different plane from that which they now occupy."

"And what is this reason or thought which you feel will do so much? It is but a loan from the Almighty, whose existence you affect to doubt. Man has no title to the property until he has permission to hold it eternally."

" And then ? "

" He must have satisfied the Almighty that he is worthy."

Presently Will plunged into the conversation, impelled thereto by a certain philosophical reference with which he was familiar, and which he had studied with great interest.

" What do you think of reason and religion, Mr. Smith ? " asked the free-thinker, impressed with the intelligence of his comments. " Are you one with the rest of your race in believing all this talk of spirituality ? "

" I believe that reason and religion must act together to discover the perfect power and glory of God," replied Will modestly. (All eyes were for the moment bent upon him.) " There is perfect harmony between them; and it is our own shortsightedness which causes us to doubt."

" Do you not believe that by seeking knowledge, and dedicating life to the welfare of mankind and obedience to God in our several vocations, our best faculties will be gratified? wealth, fame, health, and all other good things will flow in a stream, and our delight remain permanent? " asked Doctor Lewis at this stage of the argument,

"Not necessarily obedience to God," replied the free-thinker. "Certain causes bring certain effects, without reference to a presiding deity."

"That's it!" said the Southerner, *sotto voce*, to his next neighbor. "Negroes are all alike with regard to religion; ignorant, thieving, dirty and lazy, but withal crammed full of religious enthusiasm. You should know them as I do — shouting, screaming, frothing at the mouth with the outpourings of the 'spirit,' and as soon as they are outside of the church door, robbing hen-roosts and watermelon patches. Bah!"

Low as his words were spoken, they caught the ear of Will. His flashing black eyes were turned upon the speaker as he said with a courtly bow:

"Granted that all you say is true, still the Negro does not sin against ages of accumulated knowledge of right and wrong. It is not absolute incapacity in the Negro either, but mere want of information, arising from lack of intelligent exercise of the perceptive faculties. These faults you speak of are but the remnants of an old irresponsible life. The majority of our race has turned aside forever from the old beaten paths of slavery into the undiscovered realms of free thought and free action. Some of the race may abuse the newly acquired liberty by petty pilfering or an overflow of religious enthusiasm, but the Negro has *changed*, whether you realize it or not; *times* have changed, and the Negro with them."

There was a murmur of applause as he finished speaking.

"Well," returned the Southerner, "we will grant that some of you are making progress, but you cannot claim that as a race you are capable of becoming such examples of manhood as you and your friends. To most of you the mystery of government will always remain a mystery; and the hope of assimilating many things which are second nature to the white man, will never become a reality to your race."

"I believe that the same rules which govern all races will be applicable to mine," returned Will. "If men are rude and foolish, down they must go. When at last in any race a new principle appears, an idea, *that* conserves it. Ideas only save races. If the black man is feeble and impotent, unimportant to the existing races — not on a parity with the best races, the black man must serve and be exterminated. *But*, if he carries within his bosom the element of a new and coming civilization, he will survive and play his part."

"Hear, hear!" cried the foreign secretary of legation, applauding vigorously, delighted at the strong, combative style in which the brave young fellow met the ancient enemy of his race. " No race is hopelessly lost to the world of progress that produces such manly specimens within fifty years of emancipation."

"England is troubled over the fact that the two races do not mix, and to all appearances never will," now joined in Mr. Withington. "There seems to be no common ground between them; they cannot live together harmoniously. Can you, gentlemen, explain this to me? I should like to carry back with me, when I return, a clear realization of the facts in the case as viewed by each party to the question. That is part of my mission in this country."

"It is true," said Doctor Lewis, "that our condition is alarming to a degree. Over ten thousand graves made since the war by mob violence, are dotting the South, and of these ninety per cent are the graves of black men."

"You do not get these facts abroad because newspaper reports are doctored by local Southern writers who participate in the lynchings. Free speech and public discussions are not allowed. In the South you must think and speak as the mob dictates," here chimed in John Langley.

"But surely you have constitutional equity

before the law? you can gain redress from the Federal government?"

"Constitutional equity is a political fiction," laughed Will.

"Reconstruction is a failure, then?" asked Mr. Withington.

"Reconstruction is not a failure, although the whole South will tell you so, and the North is being persuaded to so believe; the Negro was the living force which rent asunder the old methods of the slave-holding states and brought them out into the healthful light of decent, God-fearing living. But they are trying to take all the credit for the good we may have done them, from us. The lines are drawn more sharply than before the emancipation. Constitutional amendments are dead letters; the ballot-box is nil," replied Will.

"All of which goes to show that race is stronger than law," broke in the Southerner.

"Rather that barbarism is superior to civilization."

"What about the crime of rape?" asked Mr. Withington.

"In nine cases out of ten," replied Lewis, "you will find that the Negro is guiltless of this awful crime. It is brought forward to alienate the sympathy of all decent men from us. It is a crime that strikes the home ties, and as such is the most deadly weapon that has yet been used against us. We invite investigation in this direction, and you will then find that it is *not* a characteristic of the black man, although *it is* of the white man of the South."

"You cannot prove your assertions!" exclaimed the Southerner, white with passion.

"I can."

"Name a case."

"John Thomas of Georgia."

"He was guilty, and deserved his fate. You, gentlemen, must have heard the story of the atrocities committed by that man. The woman's husband was brutally murdered and she was assaulted. We made the fate of the black devil a terrible example for the rest of his kind in Georgia."

"Do you not know that that story has been proven false all through? It was this way, gentlemen: After the man Thomas was lynched, the colored people were convinced of his innocence. A sum of money was raised by subscription to hire the services of a reputable detective to investigate the matter. He visited the scene of the alleged crime, and it was found that Thomas worked for Cragen on his farm. Thomas heard that his mother was sick, and wished to visit her; having no money, he applied to Cragen for his pay. This enraged the latter, and he drew his revolver to shoot the Negro. Quick as a flash Thomas seized an axe which happened to be lying near, and struck Cragen, killing him instantly. He then fled to the woods. Mrs. Cragen says that Thomas did not assault her; she never saw him."

"And for defending himself they lynched him?" said Mr. Withington, with a look on his face which expressed incredulous astonishment, combined with disgust.

"Yes; that was the detective's report, given under oath. What the man suffered at the hands of the lynchers could only be equalled by the sufferings of the martyrs of Nero's time. If every case of Negro lynching could be investigated, we should discover fearful discrepancies between the story of the mob and the real truth."

"That does not prove that white men are ravishers," said the Southerner, returning to the charge.

"Oh," replied Will, with a significant shrug of the shoulders, "take the representatives of my race who are with you tonight. How did we get our complexions, soft curls and regular features? Our ancestors were black, flat-featured, and had many other racial marks. Your race does not intermarry with Negroes, does it? That being the case, the answer is self-evident."

"Do you not think, then, that under the circumstances the Government ought to assist the Negro to leave the country?" asked Mr. Withington.

"Never!" cried Will, with glowing countenance, "Never! Here where we have been so outrageously maligned, let us refute the charge like men!"

"That sounds well," said the Southerner with a sneer, "but how will you do it?"

"By using the methods of the South," replied Will quickly; "create sentiment *for* the race and *against* its detractors."

"And if you get nothing else out of it, the agitators will do a good business and fill their pockets with money."

"Agitation will do much," said Will calmly, unruffled by the other's display of anger. "It gave us freedom; it will give us manhood. The peace, dignity and honor of this nation rises or falls with the Negro. Frederic Douglas once said: 'Ultimately this nation will be composite. There is a strong demand — a growing demand — for a government capable of protecting all its citizens — rich and poor, white and black — alike.' The causes for such a government still exist. It remains to be seen if the prophecy will be fulfilled."

One of the founders of the American Academy at Rome was present, and conversation now turned upon the development of American talent in art. The political aspect of Great Britain in South Africa and the complications likely to arise therefrom was another interesting topic, but under it all the sentiment expressed and the words spoken by the representatives of an humble race that night lingered in the heart of each scholar and thinker who had heard them.

Will had a pressing engagement, and was obliged to excuse himself to the president of the club. He withdrew as quietly as possible. Those nearest him shook him warmly by the hand, and told him that they hoped to hear from him again, and soon, on the same interesting topic.

Mr. Withington now attached himself to John Langley for the remainder of the evening, seeming well pleased to find himself in such company. As they bade each other good-night at the close of the festivities he said to John, as he placed his card in his hand:

"I leave tomorrow for Canada, on business connected with the Home Office. I may never return to this country, but I want you to believe that I am deeply interested in the welfare of your people. Write to me whatever comes up of importance to the race, and I will do what I can to make sentiment in my own country for you, and as far as money will go, you shall have the benefit of the help it will give."

John bade him good-by, and even his conservative heart was warmed by contact with so good a man. After he had reached his room he took the card from his pocket, and before putting it in a place of safety read the address:

CHARLES MONTFORT–WITHINGTON, M. P.

BLANKSHIRE,

ENGLAND.

For a long time he sat there staring at the card in his hand. Where had he heard that name before? "Charles Montfort!" Why, it was the family name of Mrs. Smith! Instantly the words of Madam Frances came to his mind, and a great light seemed to illumine his thoughts: "When you are at that table in the company of those men, you shall have the answer to one of the questions you would ask me."

How often he had listened to the story told by Ma Smith with an incredulous smile. It had seemed to him the idle boasting of a mind entering its dotage. Charles Montfort!—and from England! Heavens! if there should be truth in this fairy tale!

CHAPTER XVIII.

WHAT EASTER SUNDAY BROUGHT.

'TWAS Easter Sunday. The full-blossomed trees
Filled all the air with fragrance and with joy.
— LONGFELLOW.

THE days passed very quietly at No. 500 D Street. The excitement occasioned by the fair, and the extraordinary agitation which had attended the meeting of the American Colored League, had somewhat abated. Softer thoughts and feelings had taken possession of the public mind, for it was very near to the celebration of Easter. The two girls, Dora and Sappho, felt restrained in their intercourse because, although by tacit consent nothing was said of John's treacherous conduct toward Dora, each knew that the other had discovered it. Dora felt aggrieved and ill-treated; and who could blame her? Doctor Lewis was drawn into the trouble through his attachment to Dora. He pitied her injured feelings; he knew that if she were free and he offered her his love, it would be accepted, and he was not too proud to have done this if it had been an honorable act. He knew that it would not be an honorable act to ask her to break her promise to Langley at this stage of the drama, but within his heart hope grew stronger each day. He saw that John was hopelessly infatuated with Sappho; he saw Dora knew this and resented the wrong done herself, although as yet she could hardly put her thoughts into words. Day-dreams began to break in upon the dull monotony of his methodical existence; he watched the signs of growing discontent with all a lover's impatience to grasp the happiness which he felt would, after a time, be his. He was willing to work, to wait, to serve, if only he might claim her love at last. Oh, the nobleness of a good man's love! If women would but prize it, how many more happy homes we should see, and how much brighter the world and life would be. Toward Langley he was savage; and then, too, he was puzzled.

One night they were all invited to attend a reception given at the house of a friend. He was with Dora and John. Dora addressed a remark to John, and receiving no answer, turned to look in his face for the reason. His gaze was fixed upon Sappho, who was surrounded by every eligible man in the house. And such a look! love — hatred — tenderness — the gamut of passion was disclosed by the look bent upon the unconscious girl before

them.   Dora shuddered as if a chill had struck
her, and turning to Lewis held a cold and
trembling little hand appealingly toward him.
He took it gladly into his firm and loving
clasp, and tenderly asked her if she would like
to go home.   She grasped the offer instantly
with evident relief.   She left John's side to
seek the ladies' dressing-room for her wraps;
he, absorbed in thoughts of Sappho, did not
miss her presence.   Lewis sent word to Will
that he was taking Dora home because she was
feeling very tired.   He apologized to the host-
ess, engineered all the delicate details of social
life with neatness and dispatch, and met the
harassed girl at the foot of the staircase, ready
to lead her home without arousing disagreeable
comment.

"What does the beggar mean?" he asked
himself more than once that night.   "He does
not seem inclined to give Dora up, and yet he
is completely 'gone' over the other one."   But,
like a prudent man, he said nothing; he kept
his own counsel and watched.

Since the meeting at which Sappho had
fainted, the girl had grown more silent and
depressed.   People said: "Yes, she is beautiful, but so cold and silent."

She and Will had scarcely spoken since the
night of the fair, but each felt and knew that

it would be but a short time before the story
of their love must be settled for good and all.
So the days crept by and brought the crisis
of these lives, so strangely interwoven.

.   .   .   .

Easter Sunday fell early in April that year.
The city had donned its gayest attire to welcome the return of the celebration of Christ's
triumphal resurrection. The morning service
was ended. The exultant organ peals, the glorious strains of hymns of victory poured forth
by highly trained voices in hundreds of aug-
mented church choirs all over the city, still
seemed to vibrate upon the listening air even
after the churches had given up their crowds
of worshippers. Sappho had been to the mission church of St. Augustine, on P. Street, at
the West End. Here the good Fathers of the
Mission of St. John had reared a church, and
elected to bend their efforts particularly to the
salvation and upraising of the poorest of God's
children. This church, with its beautiful silver
chimes, given by a wealthy Boston woman in
commemoration of the life and services of the
lamented Bishop Brooks, is destined to stand
for ages as a memorial of the deeds of philan-
thropy which have always been a distinguishing feature of the true spirit of Massachusetts.
The sound of the bells lingered with her like

a benediction. For the first time in weeks a
tranquil mind was hers. The spirit of the day
was upon her in full measure; to her the risen
Christ was a reality, and his triumph over sin
and death was to her bruised spirit a promise
and a blessing. Stepping lightly along she
gained the Public Garden and crossed the
rustic bridge, skirting the lake as she walked
toward the Arlington-street entrance. Many
admiring glances followed the graceful figure,
clad in its fresh, jaunty, tailor-made suit of
gray. The strong wind kissed the pure face
and gently lifted the clustering curls from the
white brow, where Cupid lurked in every curve
and delicate thread of gold. The Garden was
very beautiful this year; it had blossomed with
more than its usual luxuriance for the annual
festival. Beds of crocuses, gaudy tulips and
hyacinths dotted the landscape side by side
with the modest violet and exquisite pansy.
God's smile was everywhere. April's sun and
showers had blessed the earth, and

> " Cold Nature, by his amorous kiss
>   Stung sweetly, stirred his limbs and felt
>   A thrill of immemorial bliss."

Someone sat upon a garden seat awaiting
her coming. Far down the mall he espied the
solitary figure. 'Twas she herself! As he gazed

upon the advancing figure of the girl he loved
he felt his heart swell within him, and tender
thrills of joy filled his soul, too full for utterance.   He noticed that she wore a bunch of
violets today, instead of her favorite Jacks.
They were more in keeping with the sentiment
of the day.   There they rested in a splendid
cluster upon her breast — modest and beautifully fragrant.   " As sweet as a violet herself,"
he thought, as he murmured to himself:

> "The breeze runs riot with thy charms,
>   O faint, delicious, springtime violet!"

As a man Will Smith was not ashamed of
the passion which consumed him.   An honorable love has its own subtle charm.   Now was
his opportunity!   The almost deserted paths
were secure from intrusion.   She was not indifferent to him; today should end suspense.
He would have her answer.

Sappho caught sight of him directly she
entered the path.   She hesitated — turned —
then stood still, as if conscious of his resolution.   He saw her hesitation, and read her
thoughts by virtue of that harmony which is
love's perfection.   He arose and stood before
her, hat in hand.   His apparent coolness and
self-possession did what he intended it should:
restored her calmness; and when she placed

her hand in his and responded to his cheery greeting, she was herself again.

"Do not hurry away," he said, as she turned as if to resume her walk. "Let us sit a moment and enjoy this charming view of beautiful Boston."

She stood a moment gazing at the fair prospect spread out before them.

"How peaceful, beautiful and calm the landscape seems. If earth be so fair, what must be the beauty of heaven?" she said, after a slight pause.

"Indeed, yes," replied Will, as he glanced at the fair face beside him with something like awe. For a moment he felt that he stood in the presence of a saint; earthly passion seemed out of place.

After a moment's silence she seated herself, mechanically protesting that she had promised Dora to help her with her Sunday-school class at half-past one.

"Never mind," said Will, "it is real Sunday-school work for you to look after me a bit. I'm sure I need Bible lessons." At this they both laughed, and then Sappho asked:

"Where ought the lesson to be?"

She saw instantly by the change in his expression that she had given him his opening, and immediately lost the self-possession she had just gained.

"'And Jacob loved Rachel; and said, I will serve thee seven years for thy younger daughter,'" quoted Will softly, as he looked at the gentle face and downcast eyes beside him. Sappho said nothing, but gazed intently at the landscape with unseeing eyes, as she nervously clasped and unclasped her delicately gloved hands. Suddenly she felt one small hand drawn within a strong, warm clasp.

"There are shadows on your face; why are they there? You think all kinds of sad thoughts. Tell them to me, Sappho."

"Nay," she said at length, "why should I? they are not clear even to myself. You would not understand my vagaries. Why should you be bothered with them?"

"Because, Sappho, my beautiful one, my darling, I love you — surely you know it — I have loved you from the first moment that I saw you. Be my wife, my blessing."

She did not answer; her face had grown very white.

"Have I frightened you? Do not think me cruel, Sappho; you do not know how much I love you."

She was still silent, but another look satisfied him that she was not angry. The gloved hand stopped fluttering, and lay quietly within his clasp.

"You do not think me presumptuous? You are not angry? Tell me that you love me."

"Wait one moment," she said; and then he saw that she was trembling violently.

"Don't you care for me a little?" he asked anxiously, "or have I been living in a fool's paradise the past two months?"

"I do care for you," she whispered, in a voice so low that only a lover could have heard it.

"Ah!" he cried impetuously; "then I will never let you go!"

"Ah, Will, I wonder if it is right for me to love you, or to allow you to love me?"

"Most decidedly it is right. Why do you doubt?"

"You have known me such a short time," she protested.

"I know that you are the dearest girl in all the world to me," he replied, holding her hand still more tightly clasped. "You are mine now, and nothing shall part us. I shall always remember this day as the happiest of my life. You do not know how dearly I love you."

"I shall know if you persist in telling me so often," she said, smiling at his impetuosity.

"Heaven bless you, Sappho, my dearest. I shall never tire of ringing the changes on love."

"Why should you care so much for me?" she asked wistfully. "I have no family — no friends — no money" —

"I have family enough for both of us," he returned quickly. "My mother loves you, my sister adores you; what more is there to be desired?"

"But there are things which you ought to know — things connected with the past" —

"I do not care for the past," he broke in; "all I ask is that you love me above all other men, as I adore you above all other women."

She was carried away by the vehemence of his wooing. All obstacles seemed, indeed, but trifles before this all-absorbing, passionate, eager warmth of youth's first love. Poor soul! poor starved and storm-beaten heart! Something of life that was dead leaped again into existence and loosened the icy hand that had for years locked up the fountain of youthful joy. She felt drawn out of herself as she looked into the eyes of love and met the luminous light which transfigured the face of her lover.

> "Ask me no more; thy fate and mine are sealed:
>   I strove against the stream and all in vain;
>   Let the great river take me in the main:
>   No more, dear love, for at a touch I yield;
>   Ask me no more."

Silently she turned to him and placed the other hand within his clasp, and burst into a tempest of weeping.

"Sappho!" he cried, in a transport of delight, as he tried to dry her tears; "my darling, my wife!"

O happy Easter Day!

They sat there a long time in heart communion, reviewing the history of their short acquaintance, and the wonderful thing that had happened to them. They planned that Sappho should stay with Will's mother while he went abroad, and then when his course was finished they would be married immediately upon his return. They would keep their sweet secret a little while. They could not share this hallowed day with others. It was consecrated and holy to them because of its dear association with the hidden stream of their united lives.

. . . .

John Langley was returning from an errand down town, and attracted by the beauty of the morning, determined to cross the Garden on his way to the South End. Suddenly, beneath the trees he espied the lovers. He paused a moment. They were so much absorbed in each other that they had not seen him. He turned aside into a path which ran very near to them on one side, and paused beneath the shadow of some friendly trees where he was secure from observation and could watch their movements unseen.

The happy light on Will's expressive countenance did not escape him; he noted, too, the shy happiness and deep, tender love which shone in Sappho's eyes. His heart was on fire with hot, jealous rage, and he resolved that their marriage should never take place. He was not sure of Sappho's past, but he would try a bold manœuvre and trust to luck. He would accuse her as though certain of the facts. If that did not work, he would try some other game. He who had laughed at love without money, found himself even contemplating the sacrifice of one for the other, if dishonest means should not succeed in winning her. He watched them for a time, and then, judging by their movements that they were about to leave the spot, turned reluctantly away, planning ways and means of bringing his schemes to a successful issue.

.   .   .   .

Sappho had been taking her meals with the family lately, but tonight she excused herself from dinner on the plea of a headache. Will had gone back to the hotel.

"Headache must be a great cosmetic," said Dora slyly. She had seen that Will and Sappho returned from morning church together and from certain signs had drawn her own conclusions about how matters stood between them. "I never remember seeing you look better or more beautiful than you do tonight." Sappho laughed joyously as she ran lightly up the stairs to her room. Tomorrow they would know her secret.

She glanced at her mirror as she passed it. Where was the usually pale, sad face that it reflected? They called her cold and proud. What would the world say if it could see that brilliant, vivid, flashing beauty that the mirror gave back to her astonished gaze? Truly love was a wonderful cosmetic. She sank into the inviting willow rocker, and for a while gave herself up to the happiness which was so intense as to be almost painful. There was no thought of evil mingled with the joy that wrapped her round about. No forebodings assailed her; the intoxication of the moment was complete. She was lost in dreamland as she sat there thinking of her lover. Will had said to her: "I am not a man to hold love lightly; it is no jest with me. My love is the one woman in the whole world to me above all others. I shall love you living and dying, and be true to you in life and death." The words rang in her ears like sweetest music.

There were extra services at all the colored churches that night, because owing to the fact that most of the worshippers were employed as domestic servants, evening was the only time convenient for their employers to spare their services. She heard the outer door close upon one after another until the house settled down to the perfect quiet of solitude.

She then arose from her seat and proceeded to change her street attire for a pale blue cashmere house dress with delicate ecru lace at the throat and wrists. She hummed strains of the *Gloria* heard that morning in church as she stood before the glass and took the pins from her hair. The shining coil of burnished gold fell almost to her feet. So she stood with the brushes poised in air as the door opened softly and John Langley came quickly into her room. Thus they stood for a brief second of time: she colorless with amazement and fear; he overwhelmed with the exquisiteness of the picture before him. The brushes falling from her hands broke the silence. Anger flamed in her eyes.

"I did not hear you knock, Mr. Langley; what can I do for you?"

His face was pale, his eyes wavering and bloodshot; his whole expression indicated a terrible determination. The almost insulting coldness of her tone exasperated him.

"I did not knock," he replied, as he stepped into the room. "You do not offer me a seat," he sneered, as he sat down on the couch.

" This is hardly the time or place for parlor civilities," she replied significantly. " Do you not know that the house is empty ? "

" I do; and as I wish to speak with you privately, and as this is my only chance, I will not let it slip me," said John.

" Really! I cannot understand what private business you can have with me," returned Sappho haughtily; " but if it be so, pray state the nature of it as quickly as possible."

" I will," he replied. He paused a moment, as if collecting his forces. " You and Will seem to have come to an understanding, judging by what I saw on the Public Garden this morning," he said finally.

Sappho flushed warmly as she replied : " And in what way does that concern you ? "

The girl looked so beautiful and spirited that he longed to crush her with the weight of his surmises.

" Will Smith is a very proud man as well as a very just man. His pride of family is his besetting sin. Do you think that it will be for his best interest to marry you ? " he asked significantly.

" And why should it not be ? " questioned the girl haughtily, although a hand of ice seemed closing about her heart.

" *You* can best answer that question," was the guarded reply.

" Mr. Langley, your intrusion into my private apartment is unpardonable; your innuendoes are still more so. If you have anything to say, please say it; if not, let us close this remarkable interview." She moved toward the door as if to open it. In an instant he seized her arm and stopped her.

" Do not be rash. It is better for you to listen to me and not arouse my enmity. *I have seen Luke Sawyer, and I know your secret —* MABELLE BEAUBEAN !

The attack was so sudden she did not think of defending herself. He had never in his life seen emotion so terrible depicted upon the human countenance as her face presented at that moment. She shrank from him with shivering dread, beating the air with both hands, as though in her agony she warded off the approach of some gruesome apparition.

" Not that name — not that name !" she gasped, as she turned her beautiful, ghastly face from side to side, as though seeking air. She seemed about to faint. Then she sank upon the floor and literally grovelled there, her face hidden by the long hair which enveloped her like a veil.

John was nonplussed at the perfect success of his plot; he was exultant. The terror of the girl was awful to behold. Surely he had her now. She must turn to him for help.

"Sappho," he said in feigned pity, "I feel for you. God knows I am sorry for this, and that I should have been the one to bring it upon you. But think of your story, and its effect upon Will if he should learn it after marriage!"

"I was a victim! an innocent child!" moaned the figure on the floor.

"I know," said John, "but girls of fourteen are frequently wives in our Southern climes, where women mature early. A man as supercilious as Will in his pride of Northern birth would take no excuse, and would never forgive."

"Ah! what can I do?" cried the unhappy woman, as she rose to her feet and began to pace the floor. "Have I not suffered enough?" Now was the time for which he had waited and planned.

"Sappho, do not think that I forget how abominable I must appear to you. I know what you will say — that I betray my friend, and worse than that, the girl who holds my promise; but my excuse is that my passion is stronger than honor, stronger than reason. There are men in the world who would not forsake you, and who would always befriend you. *Give up Will, and trust yourself to me.* I am making money in my profession. I can and will do well by you. Your story need never be known."

"Doubtless you mean it in kindness," replied the girl wearily, "and I thank you, but I can never marry anyone but Will."

"Marriage!" exclaimed John, "who spoke of marriage? Ambitious men do not marry women with stories like yours!"

At last the murder was out — his meaning clear!

For one moment Sappho was speechless with disgust.

"Infamous villain!" she said at length, "you abuse my forlorn condition. Leave me! Never till this moment have I realized the depths of my degradation!"

"I go at your command," said John. "I give you one week to think over what I have said. At the end of that time"—

"Go! go! will you go?" interrupted Sappho, pointing to the door with queenly dignity.

With a low bow John Langley passed out and closed the door behind him.

Sappho turned the key in the lock and sank upon the couch overcome with the horror of her situation. Nervous spasms shook her frame as she mentally measured the abyss of social ostracism and disgrace which confronted her. A thunderbolt from a clear sky had shattered her hopes and dashed the cup of happiness from her lips. Heartrending sobs of anguish

"GO! GO! WILL YOU GO?" INTERRUPTED SAPPHO.

mingled with passionate appeals to heaven for
mercy, tore her frame as she contemplated this
sudden overthrow of her dreams of a bright
future. The quiet which had attended her life
since she had settled in Boston was rudely interrupted, and the ruin which threatened her was
the more stupendous because unlooked for in
the direction from which it came.

She got up at length, and going to the dress-
ing-table, began mechanically to collect her
jewelry. She caught sight of her face in the
glass. What a change from the glowing beauty
of one short hour ago! She looked at the pale,
drawn countenance with scorn. "Men call me
beautiful," she murmured bitterly; "what has
beauty been to me but a curse?"

She heard the closing of doors and the voices
of the returned church-goers. Could it be possible that she was the same happy girl whose
smiling face had been given back from the mirror so radiantly a short hour ago? She heard
the front door close again. It was Will's step
upon the stair. He paused at her door a moment,
and then passed on to the floor above. How
often she had listened for that familiar tread.
Her heart kept repeating: "Never again —
never again."

Two hours later deep silence had fallen upon
the house. A form attired in black, closely

veiled, and carrying a traveling bag, passed from
No. 500 D Street into the night, boarded an
electric car, and was swallowed up in the heart
of the metropolis.

Will in his room had fallen into his first sleep
when he thought he heard the sound of noiseless footsteps in the hall. He listened a
moment, and then concluded that he was mistaken. Who could be moving through the
house at that hour? No, he was mistaken.
His thoughts were all with Sappho. He lived
over again the words and scenes of the morning. He heard the clocks strike twelve, one,
two; then he fell into a deep, dreamless sleep.

CHAPTER XIX.

THE BITTER ARROW.

O, BREAKING heart that will not break,
    Oriana!
O, pale, pale face so sweet and meek,
    Oriana!
        —TENNYSON.

THE next morning found the household early astir. It is a rule in hotels that a "late watch," as it is called, exempts the employee from an early appearance for duty the next morning. On these mornings Will breakfasted with his mother and sister. Since Sappho had boarded with them this humble meal had become a feast to him.

He arose very early on this eventful Monday morning and hurried down the stairs, bursting to impart his good news to the sympathetic ears of his loved ones. He entered the kitchen just as Dora was laying the cloth for breakfast.

"What in the world brings you down so early?" she asked in a surprised tone as he entered the room.

"Oh, I couldn't stay in bed this morning of all others," he said, as he kissed her lightly on the cheek; "I am too happy."

"What under the sun is the cause of so much joy, that it brings so lazy a boy out of bed an hour before his time?"

"How did you feel when you were first engaged to John? weren't you light-headed and silly?"

"Oh, I dare say I was silly enough," replied Dora with a sigh. At the mention of John a cloud seemed to settle down upon the brightness of her usually sunny face. "But what has that to do with your early rising? I don't see the analogy between the two."

"Congratulate me, Dora, Sappho has promised to marry me."

"Oh, Will! Why did I not think of that? I declare I suspected something of the sort yesterday, but other things put it out of my mind. I am so glad!" cried Dora. "Where — when — how did it occur?"

"Yesterday on the Public Garden. I met her coming from church," he replied proudly. "Do you see the analogy now between your engagement and my early rising?" he added, laughing.

"I should say so! How selfish of you to keep it to yourself all this time; you might have told us. Mother! mother! come quickly, I have something to tell you!" she called, moving toward the next room.

"Yes, Dora, dear," replied the voice of Ma Smith, "just a minute!"

"Oh, hurry, hurry, mummie; it won't keep."

"Yes, yes, you excitable child; what is it?" Nothing wrong with your brother"— she stopped as she caught sight of his smiling face. He went up to her and took her in his strong young arms — he was an affectionate son.

"Nothing wrong, mummie dear, but your boy is very happy. Will you have Sappho for a second daughter?"

"Gladly, my son," replied his mother; and then she sank upon a chair, overcome as she comprehended the full meaning of his words.

"Why do you cry, mother dear, if the idea is not unpleasant to you?" asked Will, somewhat alarmed by her tears.

"Oh, Will, my boy, you will not let this new love cause you to forget the love of your old mother?"

"Never!" cried Will, as he pressed his lips to the sweet old face. "I would not be worthy of happiness could I be so ungrateful."

"Don't mind mother, Will; she cries on principle, because it is the proper thing for weddings and funerals. Isn't that so, mummie mine?" laughed Dora, as she wiped a suspicious moisture from her own eyes.

"But what keeps Sappho so late? she's generally down by this time," she continued, with a glance at the little Swiss clock on the mantel.

"I'm going up stairs after the laggard, and have it out with her for keeping such news to herself. I know she's bashful."

Dora sprang up the stairs with a bound, and paused outside the door to rap. Receiving no answer she rapped again, and then tried the handle of the door. It yielded to her touch, and then she noticed that the key was on the outside. She threw the door open with a vague sense of something unusual in such a proceeding. The room was empty. She paused a moment in bewilderment as she glanced about her, and then saw the bed undisturbed in its snowy smoothness. Thoroughly alarmed now, she ran to the head of the stairs and called her brother.

Wondering what could be the trouble, Will hurried from the kitchen, closely followed by his mother. Upstairs they found Dora standing in the middle of the room with a frightened face.

"I found the key on the outside, the door unlocked. She is not here ; and see, the bed has not been slept in ; the closet door is open; some of her clothing is gone, and all her jewelry."

Will stood beside her, gazing about the cozy nest with troubled eyes.

"When did you see her last?" he asked finally.

"At dinner yesterday; she complained of a headache, and went to her room to lie down."

"She was here at half-past eleven, when I came in, for I saw a light in her window as I came down the street."

"Well, children, there is nothing to worry about," said Mrs. Smith; "she has probably gone out and will return shortly. There can't be any great mystery about her absence."

Just then the door-bell rang.

"There she is now," said Will, as he bounded down the stairs in answer to the summons. The two women stood expectant, waiting for the sound of her voice. They heard nothing but the closing of the door and Will's steps returning. Presently he stood before them with a letter in his hand.

"It is for me," he said, in answer to their looks of inquiry. "I think it is from Sappho."

His face was ashen; his hands trembled. He turned the square package over once — again — then mechanically, as in a dream, he tore the envelope open. The anxious women watched him as he ran his eyes rapidly over the written page, and then with a groan sank into a chair.

"What is it, Will? what has happened?"

cried his mother and sister with one voice. Great drops of perspiration stood upon his forehead.

"O my God!" was his reply to the agonized entreaties of the two women. He threw his arms upon the desk beside him and dropped his head upon them. The letter fell upon the floor.

Mrs. Smith was a great sufferer from nervous weakness. Seeing her son's unhappiness, she began to tremble and sob hysterically. Dora was badly frightened; but knowing that she must be calm for all their sakes, said:

"Mother, calm yourself. Do you not see that Will needs help?" She closed the open door to keep out curious intruders who might possibly be about, and then she picked up the letter.

"Read it!" groaned Will; "I can never tell you."

Dora read it aloud:

WILL:

When you receive this I shall be far away. What I am writing to you I ought to have told your family long ago. It must forever stand between us and marriage.

You remember the story told the night of the public meeting of the League by Luke Sawyer — the night I fainted? *I am the unfortunate Mabelle Beaubean!*

I did not die. The good Sisters gave out that story

in order to destroy my identity. Madam Frances is my grand-aunt. The boy Alphonse is my child! O my God! how can I live and write these words?

John Langley came to my room tonight, after everyone was at church. He has found out my story, and has offered me the greatest insult that a man can give a woman. He has made me realize how much such a marriage with me would injure you. Disgrace shall never touch you or yours through me.

Forgive me for deceiving you — for loving you ; it is all the wrong that I have done you.

O love — my love — how can I give you up? You will never know the bitterness of the step I am taking!

SAPPHO.

Mrs. Smith shuddered as she listened to the words being read. Could it be possible that this strange, unexpected confession had come from the beautiful girl they knew so well?

Dora was weeping bitterly when she finished; so was her mother. They sat there stunned into silence. Every pulse beat at fever-heat in Will's body. His nerves were strained almost beyond endurance; they were a thousand needle-points of pain. How could he bear this terrible news that had come to him! Luke Sawyer's story was written before his eyes in letters of fire. He saw with acute clairvoyant sight the beautiful child — the brutal captor — the horrid surroundings of the vile den to which he had consigned her — her struggles within

the brutal grasp — all the sickening details of
that horrible violation of chastity were mir
rored within his brain. Time could never
eradicate them. God of heaven! how could
he bear to think that his beautiful Sappho —
his pure girl-love, had been subjected to such
brutality! And then the child! Agony of
agonies! He could not suffer more and live!

There was something awe-inspiring in his
great affliction to the women who loved him.
Dismal silence had seized upon them all.
Then a sob — dreadful to hear — broke from
Will. He staggered across the room and fell
on his knees by his mother's side and buried
his face in the folds of her dress. It was a way
he had in early childhood when anything distressed him. Then his mother comforted him
as in childhood days — his head upon her tender breast — her dear wrinkled hands, as if in
blessing, resting upon his grief-stricken brow.

At length Dora broke the silence.

" Oh, that poor, miserable girl! think of her
sufferings — of the weight of the secret she
carried with her. What a crucifixion for a
proud spirit like hers! This terrible curse of
slavery! shall we never lose the sting of degradation? Think of John, too! How did he
find it out? what a heartless scamp he must
be! I confess the whole thing is an enigma to
me."

"To think she should believe us capable of feeling anything for her but sympathy! You must find her, Will, and bring her back home," said Ma Smith.

"Yes, mother; but any girl would act as she has. Think of her humiliation to be obliged to own such a story to her lover! I do not wonder that she turned a coward and fled. But Will will find her, never fear."

Will had regained something of self-control. But what a change had come to that debonair countenance! Dora's heart ached as she looked at him. He arose from his knees by his mother's side and stood a moment as if bewildered.

"I am going to hire the best detective in the city to find her. But first I will settle with John Langley," he said at last.

"Give him this!" cried Dora, snatching her engagement ring from her finger. "Tell him I hope never to see his face again."

"Poor little sister. Must you suffer, too?"

"Don't pity me, Will!" she exclaimed with flashing eyes. "I am well rid of such a man."

Will kissed them both solemnly and went out.

The two women, left alone, went softly about the pretty room folding away the scattered articles of wearing apparel, which they watered with many bitter tears, and finally closing the blinds and drawing down the curtains. She will return, they told each other, hoping against hope. We will leave things as they are. And then went out and locked the door.

.   .   .   .

Such incidents as we have pictured above are not uncommon in any community where slavery has cast its baleful shadow. Emancipation has done much, but time and moral training among the white men of the South are the only cures for concubinage.

We may right a wrong, but we cannot restore our victim to his primeval state of happiness. Something is lost that can never be regained. The wages of sin is death. Innocent or guilty, the laws of nature are immutable. So with shoulders bent and misshapen with heavy burdens, the Negro plods along bearing his cross — carrying *the sins of others*.

Time was no more. I stood there gazing at the approaching forms of matchless beauty advancing toward the judgment seat of God. And I asked a question: "Who are these arrayed in white?" And one of the elders answered: "These are they who come out of great tribulation!"

Fortunately it happened that it was an hour when the inmates of No. 500 D Street were busy attending to their various vocations. No one need know more of Sappho's disappearance than the family felt to tell. They made one exception to this resolve. It was about ten o'clock when Doctor Lewis called. The mother and daughter were just sitting down to the meal so sadly interrupted. In answer to questions asked in friendly solicitude because of their troubled looks, the whole miserable story came out.

"It is fortunate that I happened in," he said, when he had heard all they could tell him.

"I will go right down to Langley's office. It is useless to allow more trouble to grow out of this unhappy affair. Those men must not meet alone."

Amazed, startled, dumbfounded at this romance in real life, he hurried away toward the business portion of the city. But under his anxiety to serve his friends, who could blame him if thoughts of the broken engagement and all that it meant to him would intrude upon him? His heart kept singing: "Free to be won — free to be won."

.   .   .   .   .   .

John had risen early and left the house before any one was astir. He could not sleep.

Up and down the deserted streets he paced, gazing at the silent stars and baring his head to the cold, refreshing breeze of the April morning. Haunted — tormented — conscience not yet sufficiently seared to commit so mean an act without regret, would be heard. What if the girl should defy him — expose him! He cursed his own folly, her beauty, his own infatuation. Turn as he would, he could not shut out the beautiful, despairing face.

> "And there rises ever a passionate cry
> From underneath in the darkened land" —

There is something magical in the mystery of night and the shadows of early dawn. Then the mystery of creation and our own hidden nature seem to be revealed faintly to our dull sensibilities. The soul beholds itself all unadorned as it must stand before Almighty God. He raised his eyes to heaven and there beheld the beauty of myriad stars and undiscovered worlds bespangling the firmament. Never before had he noticed their sublimity. By the tremulous half-light of the early dawn his deed of the night before appeared despicable — devilish. For a time his head dropped in shame before the accusations of his soul. There came dimly to his beclouded faculties a realization of the possibilities of a life which might have been his under opposite conditions

from those in which he was born. Events of
his childhood in the South came to him
through the mist of years. He saw himself
a half-starved beggar in the city streets, a
deserted child claiming kindred with none,
allowed a shelter in a poor Negro cabin for
charity's sake, begging his bread from the
generous passer-by. Somehow he had learned
his letters. Then he became ambitious to
learn more. He heard talk of a country to the
north which seemed to his childish imagination a fairyland. He determined to go there;
so he started on his wearisome journey at an
age when the loving mother trembles to have
her darling exposed to the perils of the busy
streets without a strong hand to guide him
through its dangers. All his capital was in his
nimble baby feet. He charmed coin from the
people wherever he went by his expert dancing. He could do the breakdown and many
intricate shuffles in a way that delighted his
audiences. When he reached the North he
managed to buy a bootblack's outfit; then he
worked his way into a hotel kitchen. He went
on from one thing to another, always keeping
the one end in view — to acquire an education.

He had prospered. He had accomplished
the acquisition of knowledge at the expense of
the non-development of every moral faculty.

He did not realize that he was a responsible being, or that morality was obligatory upon him. With him, might was right. This man was what he was through the faults of others. If there be truth in the assertion that we create ourselves in the life we live on earth, the sphere that makes our heaven or hell within the illimitable realms of futurity, then it may be that the pitying eye of Heaven sees the struggles of these irresponsible ones of earth who are monuments of man's inhumanity to man, and sends a warning, pleading voice along the dim, resounding aisles of self-communion. It is a law of the All-wise that Nemesis shall walk beside us in every wrong that we commit. For joy we pay, for sorrow, too, and also for the ill we do. We call the recoil which comes from evil-doing, retribution, which being the fruit of evil, is coexistent with it. John had given no thought to the needs of his soul in his pursuit of wealth and position. Tonight he had the feeling that he had given all for nothing; that in his blind, egotistical seeking for his own gratification he had overstepped the bounds, and that retribution would put a check upon his desires.

That night his better angel triumphed, and he resolved that he would apologize to Sappho, make up with Dora, and tell Will all his surmises about Mr. Withington. But when daylight flooded the city he had resolved to let matters remain as they were. Love, honors and a competency were his for the taking, but he had risked all — for what? He would soon know.

. . . .

Ten o'clock found him sitting listlessly before his desk. It happened that he had no cases in court that morning. He pushed his work one side; he could not think; ever before his eyes was a vision in pale blue, with floating golden hair and appealing eyes. His hand shook as if with the palsy as he raised his pen to dip it in the ink-well. With an oath he dashed it from him. He did not indulge in liquor as a rule, but he made up his mind to have a glass of whiskey when he went to lunch. Presently he heard the door open. He looked up at the sound, and met the eyes of the friend he had betrayed — Will Smith stood before him! John sprang to his feet. His eyes dropped before the steady regard of the other. Thus they stood a moment. At last Will broke the painful silence.

"What have I ever done to you, John, that you should treat me as you have?"

"What do you mean?" stammered John.

"Do you ask me that?"

"I do," came faintly from John's lips.

"I will reply by asking you another question.

Has your love for Dora turned to hate, that
you can deliberately humiliate the girl you
have wished to make your wife, as you have
her?"

John's courage seemed to have deserted him.
He stood before Smith like the culprit that he
was.

"Of what do you accuse me?" he cried at
length, in desperation.

"Does not your conscience answer? If not,
read that," and Will handed him Sappho's
letter.

John took it, and even as his hand grasped
the sheet of paper he began to turn over in his
mind a way out of this dilemma. As he finished reading it his mind was made up. He
returned it to Will with a shrug of his shoulders
and a smile more significant than words. The
ashen face of his friend should have warned
him.

"I did not intend to humiliate Dora, for men
do many like things which never come to the
ears of the woman they call wife. Accidentally
I learned Miss Clark's story. I also learned by
observation that there were other stories just
as piquante. You will thank me when you
know all. She is beautiful. What would
you have? Am I different from other men
who have made like proposals to a *fille de
joie?*"

Scarcely had the words passed his lips when Will was upon him.

"You miserable, lying hound!" he shouted, beside himself with rage and grief. He grasped John by the throat. Again the door opened, and Doctor Lewis ran toward the struggling figures.

"Will! John! are you both mad? Do you want to create a public scandal?" He succeeded in separating them, and then threw himself between them. So they stood panting and glaring at each other like angry beasts.

"Take me out of this, then!" cried Will, "or I won't answer for myself! Here is your ring!" He took the ring Dora had given him, and threw it at Langley. "I will give you until tonight to get your luggage out of my house. If you are there tomorrow morning, I will shoot you like the cur you are."

Doctor Lewis drew him from the room. The door closed. Thus they who had been friends for years parted.

John stood there alone in his silent office, looking out on the dreary vista of brick walls and the network of wires, in awful solitude with his thoughts of the past and his blank future. The sun of prosperity had set on him forever — he felt it — knew it. His own hand had wrought this ruin to himself, said his heart and conscience.

CHAPTER XX.

MOTHER-LOVE.

WHAT is it to die?
To leave all disappointment, care and sorrow,
To leave all falsehood, treachery and unkindness,
All ignominy, suffering and despair,
And be at rest forever! O dull heart,
Be of good cheer! When thou shalt cease to beat,
Then shalt thou cease to suffer and complain!

— LONGFELLOW.

MEANTIME Sappho had descended from the car at the corner of Arlington and Boylston Streets on that eventful Easter night; she entered the Garden, and impelled by an uncontrollable impulse, walked again through the paths where a few hours before she had known so much happiness. She knew no fear; the darkness concealed her. Again she sat upon the seat where she had passed the brightest moments of her life. A neighboring clock struck one. It was then the first hour of a new day — the dawn for her of fresh misery. A cold, sharp wind struck her with chilling force; she shivered, but still sat there buried in hopeless despair.

Fearful indeed is the plan of existence which

rules our mortality. Innocent or guilty, our
deeds done in the flesh pursue us with relent-
less vigor unto the end of life. Sometimes
the rough winds of adversity are tempered to
the shorn lamb who is not responsible for acts
which are forced upon him; God in infinite wisdom and justice remits the severity of our sufferings; but the tracings still remain upon the
sands of life — we bind up the wounds — they
heal, but the scars remain.

Sappho possessed a brilliant mind and reso-
lute character. If she had been a religious
devotee she would have been as devout and
as fervid as a disciple of old. If a sinner, the
queen of them all. She had strength of will
enough for a dozen women, which, if ever
started on the wrong road, would be difficult to
redirect into the paths of right. She had suffered much in meekness, but now dumb rage
awoke her passions. For a time the spirit of
revenge held full sway in the outraged heart.
Revenge was all she craved; she shivered at
the dark thoughts which came to her. "Revenge" whispered the swaying branches of the
trees above her head —"revenge" seemed
whispered in the chilling winds about her —
revenge upon her seducer and upon the man
who had dashed the cup of happiness from
her lips and most wantonly insulted her in her

weakness. Then came the blessed relief of
tears — like a flood — they relieved the over-
charged brain and saved her reason. She
fancied, as she sat there trying to account for
the evil that pursued her, that Conscience
spoke in condemnation of her neglect of her
child. She had felt nothing for the poor waif
but repugnance. Her delicate nervous organization was naturally tinged with superstition,
and she felt that God had sat in judgment
on her willingness to forget her child. "Dost
thou question the providences of God? Know
that my ways are not the ways of men. A
tender soul will be demanded at thy hands
in the vast eternity. Who art thou, to question
the ways of Infinity? Jesus Christ came into
the world under the law. Who art thou, to question the wisdom of the Most High? Lo, there
is the field — the life of a child — work for a
bounteous harvest." At length she rose from
that seat resolved that come what would she
would claim the child and do her duty as his
mother in love and training. She would de-
vote her life to him. They would nevermore
be separated.

She met no one in her lonely walk through
the now-deserted city streets. She was so be-
numbed by the shock she had received that
she would hardly have noticed any insult that

might have been directed to her. At length she reached the door of Madam Frances's house. All was dark. No light, no welcome. So was her life made dark and desolate by the curse of slavery. She rang the bell twice with a strong hand; presently she saw the faint gleam from a lamp through the sidelights, and then her aunt's familiar voice asked: " Who is there ? "

"It is I, Sappho; open the door, Aunt Sally."

She heard the click of the key as it turned in the lock, and in another moment she stood within the entry facing her aunt's curious, frightened face. In another moment she dropped her weary frame in a chair in the reception room. Sappho told her aunt the whole story. The elder woman was nonplussed and startled; she had not counted that any one would be able to identify her niece with poor, unfortunate Mabelle Beaubean. They sat there for a long time going over the situation, and consulting about what was best to be done. Sappho told her aunt that she was determined to take the boy with her in future. Madam Frances said nothing, for she saw that her niece was determined.

"I must leave Boston; that is clear," said Sappho.

"Certainly, that will be best for a while," replied her aunt. " But you must remember that it is always darkest just before the dawn."

"I shall return to New Orleans and lose myself in that city. I shall get work there, and
my case will not be noticed, because it is not
uncommon. In time I shall forget."

"As soon as you are settled there I will join
you with the boy. I will continue to tell fortunes, and we shall live very happily, no doubt.
I shall not be here long; my sands are almost
run, but I should like to see you safe and happy
before I go. But remember what I say to you
now, Sappho child: in doing your duty, happiness will come to you, the greater and more
abiding for the trouble which has preceded it."

"Perhaps so," replied Sappho; "but, Aunt
Sally, I shall take the boy with me tomorrow
when I leave for the South. I will never part
with him again on earth."

"Well, my dear child, I see no necessity for
you to become a martyr in order to do your
duty. However, do as you think best. Now
go and try to get a little rest."

"Here is one of my mother's diamond rings;
take it, Aunt Sally, and sell it for me. I have
no money."

The old woman took the ring, and Sappho
went into the small side-room where Alphonse
slept. She undressed and lay down beside the
boy, but not to sleep. She gazed on the inno-

cent face with mingled feelings of sorrow and
regret as she thought of the lonely, loveless life
of the child. She had been so wicked to put
him from her. It was her duty to guide and
care for him. She would do her duty without
shrinking. Her head ached and her eyes
burned and were hot and dry; they refused to
close. So the moments flew by as she tormented herself with fancies of Will's horror of
her when he should learn her story on the morrow, and remembrances of John Langley's
coarse insults, which even now made her cheeks
burn with shame. She wept bitter tears over
her cherished love dream. But under it all
there was a feeling of relief now that she had
made up her mind to a future which the child
should share. Her shipwrecked life seemed
about to find peace. There was a new light in
her eyes as she gazed on the sleeping child.
Impulsively she folded him in her arms, and
Alphonse awoke. The awakening of childhood
is beautiful. She gazed with new-found ecstacy
at the rosy face, the dimpled limbs, and thought
that he was hers. Her feeling of degradation
had made her ashamed of the joys of mother-
hood, of pride of possession in her child. But
all that feeling was swept away. Alphonse
looked at her first in wonder and then in alarm.
Again she kissed him passionately — the frail

little child, whose delicate frame seemed cut from alabaster. She had only this tender creature to cling to in all the world; the only plank between her and desperation.

"I am your mother, Alphonse," she said in answer to his looks of inquiry.

"My mamma is gone away to heaven," replied the child solemnly, as he watched her earnestly with great dark eyes of wonder.

"No, dear, I am your mamma, come back to keep you with me always. Won't you love your poor unhappy mamma?"

The child put up one slender hand and smoothed her cheek.

"You're the pretty lady I saw at the fair. I didn't know you were my mamma."

"Mamma couldn't claim you then, darling, but now she's going to take you away, and you will always live with her. Won't you like that?"

The boy nodded his sleepy little head, put up his dewy red mouth and pressed a sweet, wet kiss on her face, then he nestled confidingly in her arms and fell fast asleep again. She held him closely folded against her throbbing heart, and something holy passed from the sweet contact of the soft, warm body into the cold chilliness of her broken heart. The mother-love chased out all the anguish that she had felt over his birth. She wondered how she had lived without him — how she could have remained separated from him. In this new and holy love that had taken possession of her soul was the compensation for all she had suffered. She could not see it then, but in the long intervals of time it would be revealed to her understanding. Now she felt that her losses could not be paid, but in the years which followed she learned to value the strong, chastening influence of her present sorrow, and the force of character it developed, fitting her perfectly for the place she was to occupy in carrying comfort and hope to the women of her race.

The next evening Sappho left Boston. As the train rolled out from the station on its southward journey her heart sank; tears were in her eyes; she felt that now, indeed, all links were severed between her and Will. She had borne up bravely, and now she told herself that she must not give way. She clasped the tender fingers of the boy closer still. He was her anchor. The lady passengers on the train regarded her curiously, she was too beautiful for pity; the men with equal curiosity, but compassion for her youth and beauty mingled with it. When she reached Washington fatigue began to tell upon her — fatigue and hopeless misery. She longed for the journey's end. Mentally and physically she was overtaxed, and but for the child she would have broken down.

She did not mind anything now. As she moved farther south the brutality of the conductor who ordered her out of the comfortable day-coach into the dirt and discomfort of the "Jim crow" car, with the remark that "white niggers couldn't impose on him; he reckoned he knew 'em," failed to arouse her.

The Sisters of the Holy Family always have representatives at the various railroad stations in New Orleans. These Sisters not only solicit alms, but look out for friendless or unfortunate colored women. As Sappho stepped from the train, holding the child by one hand and her baggage check in the other, a Sister, impelled by something in the white, worn face, stepped up to her and spoke a kindly word of interest. Sappho looked at her and tried to answer, as she placed the check and her purse in the Sister's hand. The nun put out her arms just in time to receive Sappho's form as she was sinking insensible upon the platform, her strength at last succumbing to the terrible strain upon mind and body. The nun obtained a carriage and took the two travelers to the convent— the child to the orphanage, the mother to the hospital. So once again Sappho found a refuge in the convent in her time of dire necessity. No one recognized her, for a complete change had been made in the Sisterhood.

A long spell of low fever ensued, but to Sappho in her weakness the rest and comfort that came to her harassed mind was like sun and shade in a grassy glade of perfect peace. The nuns were greatly interested in her, and concluded that she was as good as pretty.

"She is like the angels in the picture of the Crucifixion, so sweet and sad. She has more tears in her heart than in her eyes."

"She is not of our faith," said another, "but we will do our best for her, as the Mother says: *le bon Dieu* knows best."

.   .   .   .

It was evening in New Orleans. The streets, the great arteries of a crowded metropolis, were lighted by the glare of myriad gas-lamps, thus dispelling the darkness like artificial suns. The roll of vehicles blended with the other sounds, the hum of millions rising in a confused roar above the housetops and mingling with the clouds of evening.

In a small, bare room Sappho lay, at the end of a long corridor. The rays from a lamp outside the room came faintly in, dispelling the semi-darkness. The light from the soft Southern moon gleamed faintly through the windows, making the room like the cloisters of heavenly mansions. To that quiet haven of rest the turmoil and bustle of life did not reach. There the dying, the sick, the convalescent lay undisturbed by the hurrying march of humanity.

She had just sent Alphonse away. Evêry day he had been allowed to go to her since she had been getting better. It was a rare sight to see the two together — the lovely girl who held the child in such a passionate embrace, and the delight of the child in his "beautiful mamma."

No questions had been asked her concerning her life or history, but she felt it her duty to make a confidante of the Mother Superior. Tonight she had sent for her, and presently the Mother glided in, with her noiseless step and gentle, assuring manner. The holy woman sat there a long time in silence after listening to Sappho's story. Such confidences were not new to her. At length she placed a toil-worn brown hand upon the girl's head with a murmured "Benedicite."

"What shall I do, Mother?" asked the girl, as she reverently kissed the gentle hand.

"Ah, we must think and pray. You do not wish to become a Sister?"

"No; I must accept the desire of God in the child. I will take a mother's place and do my duty."

"It is hard for one so young and beautiful to resist the world and its temptations," replied the Mother regretfully; "but we will help you, and the convent will be a home for you always."

Sappho thanked her tearfully.

"My child, I will think over all you have said; I will pray to be shown what it is best to do. Now, go to sleep; rest, and pray to the Holy Mother of Sorrow, and Christ will comfort you."

She glided noiselessly from the room. Sappho, already comforted by her benign influence, fell asleep.

.   .   .   .

A month later Sappho had very nearly recovered from the effects of her illness. She moved — a quiet and subdued figure — about the convent corridors, helping in every way. She had written to her aunt, and received an answer saying that she would soon be in the city. The old fortune-teller returned to her home only in time, however, to die at the convent. So Sappho found herself doubly alone in the world.

One day soon after the death of her aunt the Mother Superior sent for her to come to her in her private room — the parlor of the convent.

"My child," she said, "I have been thinking much about you, and I have tried to benefit you. Are you still determined to pass as the boy's mother?"

"Yes, Mother, I am."

"Well, then, you must be Madame Clark."

"No," replied Sappho hastily; "no more deception."

"I am glad to see that you are ready to bear all things in meekness for His sake. But you are not called upon to make too many sacrifices. God sees your heart and will reward you in his own good time. I have a place for you that I think will just suit you. Monsieur Louis of Opelausas is in want of a governess for his two granddaughters. He is a man of color, and has lost all of his family but these two children. He is an old man with a competency, and he will pay you well for your services. Alphonse can stay with us; you can pay a stipulated sum for his board and be able to see him every week. What do you think of it, my daughter?"

"I will do as you advise, Mother; you are only too kind. When shall I go?"

"Monsieur Louis will be here tomorrow to see you. If everything is satisfactory, you can go next week."

The morrow came, and with it Monsieur Louis. He was a tall, aristocratic-looking man of dignified bearing, though one soon perceived that age had bent his once firm shoulders. His hair, now entirely white, added to his venerable appearance. His face was gentle and

kindly, and immediately won Sappho's heart.
He, in his turn, was much impressed by her
youth and beauty. He thought of the days of
his own youth, when such a face as hers would
have robbed him of his sleep. He thought,
too, of the wife and daughter who had been
taken from him, leaving his life but a succession of lonely days. "Let the past die," he
murmured impatiently to himself; "I feel this
beautiful girl-widow will bring peace and joy to
my poor motherless girls."

In another week Sappho had accepted the
liberal terms Monsieur Louis offered her, had
taken a tearful farewell of Alphonse and the
Sisters, and was ensconced in her new home.

The house was pleasant; it stood in its own
grounds; an old-fashioned, typical Southern
residence, with wide gardens and a carriage-
drive winding around a smoothly cut lawn.
The interior was well furnished, comfortable,
and every want abundantly supplied. She
combined the duties of housekeeping with
those of teaching, and soon became the moving
spirit of the home, warmly loved by her little
charges, and enthusiastically admired by the
servants. It was a happy, restful life; it suited
her. Its retirement, its quiet interior, recalled
her childhood's happy home. Monsieur Louis,
although much older, reminded her of her

father, and attracted her by his gentleness.
Traveling in a desert, as it were, she had come
suddenly and unexpectedly upon an oasis of
grass, cool shadows and running streams. Here,
indeed, was peace. Had her lot been always
cast in these pleasant, peaceful shades, how different her life might have been. But the iron
of suffering had seared her heart. Her life
now bade fair to be tranquil and monotonous
enough. Why could she not be happy? she
asked herself. She tried not to allow herself
to think upon the past; but when night came
she lay awake hungering for the sight of a
face, the touch of a hand, the glance of an eye.
Sometimes the craving grew almost too powerful to be resisted, and once she started to dress,
resolved to return to Boston, find Will, and
trust all to his love. But she remembered.
"His scorn I could not bear. I should die at
his feet." She told herself that life was done
and nothing remained but patience. So she
sat dumb and submissive beneath her martyr-
dom.

Monsieur Louis was puzzled by the beautiful
girl-widow, but he asked no inconvenient questions. He was content to accept the goods
which the gods had provided him in the person
of his governess, deeming himself very fortunate to have a woman of her refinement to

take charge of the education of his granddaughters. He did not believe her to be a
widow. He had strange thoughts when he
looked at the pretty child Alphonse, who came
so frequently to the house to visit his mother.
The child was always made welcome for his
own sake as well as for his mother's. He shook
his head and sighed as he watched the two together. Such cases were only too common in
the South. Like a wise man he accepted the
inevitable, and tried to do the best with it that
he could. "Let me bring as much good as
possible out of evil," was his thought in self-
communion. So he smiled on the two forlorn
ones; encouraged the mother and respected
her secret. One year glided slowly by; another
followed. Sappho had grown accustomed to
her new duties and resigned to her life.

Monsieur Louis's great hobby was his rose-
garden. There he worked, assisted by the
children. Alphonse spent a great part of his
time with his mother, sharing the instruction
of the two girls. No one would have recognized in the gay lad the quiet, melancholy child
of three years before. Sappho would often sit
on a garden seat watching the three children.
For a time she would forget her troubles in the
joy of gazing upon the animated, happy face
of her child. Yes, there lay consolation for all

her sufferings. Alphonse was expanding like a flower beneath the influence of his mother's love and devotion. He was her consolation.

Late one afternoon she sat on the terrace, a book in her lap, her thoughts far away. Alphonse brought her a bunch of roses. The child looked at her earnestly a moment, and then said:

"Mamma, why are you always so sad when you sit on the terrace alone?"

"I am not sad, Alphonse," she replied, kissing him on his forehead.

"Oh, yes, you are. When I am a big man I shall find the tall, handsome gentleman who gave you flowers at the fair."

"Why, Alphonse!"

"Have I said anything wrong, mamma?" he asked anxiously.

"Not wrong, my child, but mamma prefers that you never speak of the past to anyone."

"I will do just as you say, Mamma Sappho!" he cried, impetuously throwing his arms about her neck in a bearlike hug.

Somewhat startled by the child's precociousness, she sat there after he left her, watching the red sun slowly dropping out of sight in the west. The peaceful stillness of approaching darkness rested on the landscape. She heard a step and turned to perceive Monsieur Louis, who seated himself beside her on the rustic settee.

"We shall have a thunder shower before morning; see how heavy the clouds are hanging."

"I have been watching them," replied Sappho.

"Miss Clark, how long have you been with us?" he asked abruptly.

"A few months more than two years. Why, Monsieur Louis?"

"You have been happy?" he asked, ignoring her question.

"Happier than I can say."

"Do not let what I am about to say distress you; but I want you to make me your confidant and tell me all your sad story, not from idle curiosity, but because I have grown to love you and the boy."

"Oh, monsieur!" was all Sappho could say.

Then he spoke again. She had only a confused idea of his words, but his meaning was clearly written in her heart.

"My child," he said gravely, taking her hand, "I am an old man, experienced in the ways of the world. I have seen and understood more of your story than I have seemed to. My heart yearns for you and the child. I am old and selfish, perhaps, but I offer you a home for yourself and the boy, an honorable name, and ample means to protect you when I am gone. In short, will you consent to marry an old man and make his few remaining years peaceful? Take time to reflect," he said, as she started to interrupt him; "and my child, while you reflect, think of me. You have grown about my heart-strings. I could not rest in my grave if I left you alone and friendless."

About Sappho's heart there was a strange feeling of suffocation, a feeling such as a martyr might have experienced at the stake.

"I cannot answer now," she said at length; "this is a strange idea to me."

"Take time," he replied; "but weigh my proposition well. There is plenty here; there is no one in the wide world to mar your peace, only an old man and two little girls. You shall be happy and honored."

"I will give you my answer in a week," she said, as she arose trembling from her seat.

"It is two weeks to Easter. Let me know your answer then." And turning, he left her as abruptly as he had come.

CHAPTER XXI.

AFTER MANY DAYS.

"THE Lord blessed the latter end of Job more than his beginning."

THE days dragged their weary length along. May passed; June and its roses faded into the languid heat of July. Still no trace was found of Sappho. Madam Frances had gone from the little house on J. Street, and she, together with the child, had vanished and left no trace. There had been a nine-days' wonder over the departure of Miss Clark, but outside of the few who were in the secret, no one knew the facts.

Will had received his degree from Harvard and was now looking forward to going abroad. But the eager zest and joy of pursuit and accomplishment were gone; duty alone remained.

It was rumored that John Langley had attached himself to the family of a well-to-do colored man of prominence in the city, and that he was very busily engaged in ingratiating himself into the good graces of the daughter of the house. People gossiped and speculated as to the cause of the broken engagement between him and Dora Smith, but from lack of information this sensation died out also.

. . . .

Three months after Dora had broken with Langley the situation between her and Doctor Lewis was unchanged. The intimacy of early childhood was resumed, but she was shy and reserved beyond a certain point. Finally Doctor Lewis had been obliged to return to his charge in the South, but before he went he had obtained a promise from Dora to enter into correspondence with him. He had not dared to express the real interest and meaning which lay behind his request. The poor girl felt humiliated; her womanhood shamed; although to her surprise the happiness of life which had seemed quenched behind this flood of sorrow that had overtaken her was beginning to shine upon her again as buoyant youth regained its wonted sway. She respected Doctor Lewis, and appreciated the value of the position he had made for himself, but she did not intend to enter into another engagement immediately; she had almost determined to remain single for life until she heard of Langley's conduct. After that came the fear that he might think that she regretted the past. No; she could not remain single; she would marry one whose manliness she could respect, if she did not love him. Love was another thing, with which, she told herself, she was done.

Dora possessed the rare talent of being an interesting correspondent; indeed, her literary talents would have been valuable if cultivated. Doctor Lewis soon found this out. She gave him fascinating glimpses of the possibilities of an inner nature which perfect love and trust might develop. These short views thrilled his being with the hope of winning so rare a prize for his life companion. He pursued her unceasingly. Flowers of rare beauty and fragrance, fruit and books, found their way to her home each week. John had been rather an indifferent lover; but who could resist the impetuous onslaught of a generous nature that truly loved?

Now, when the heat of July had brought with it his annual vacation, he had returned to the North. Upon their first meeting he said to her:

"Dora, I will take no denial. No; do not speak. I know what you would say. I am willing to wait for love, because I feel sure that it will come in time."

And she, nothing loth, yielded to the stronger nature with a feeling of peace and contentment to which she had long been a stranger. So October was set for the wedding; and as the days passed, Dora felt that this time she had made no mistake.

.   .   .   .

It was toward the end of July Ma Smith sat in her pretty parlor talking with Mrs. Ophelia Davis. Mrs. Davis had just heard the news of Dora's prospective marriage to Doctor Lewis.

"I'm jes' as glad as I can be. Dear, dear; it don't seem possible that so many things have happened to change the prospectus since last winter when we sat in this very room having such a good time, an' Miss Clark had jes' ben interduced, an' was so hansum, an' sech a way with her an' so forth. You know, I thought your Will was goin' to git completely smashed on her. It's funny how mistook a body can git 'bout fellers and gals. You think they're goin' crazy over each other when all of a sud-dint — Lordy! they've up an' married some po' plain critter that you never thought they'd give a second look to. They'd heve made a hansum couple, too. Jes' borned fer each other. Then there's the smashup 'twixt Dora and Langley. Mercy knows, I don't blame her. I allers thought he had a downish sort o' look. Drat them sickly, peeky lookin' men! *Me! no ma'm!* I wouldn't look at one o' them! No ma'm! Dear, dear! it do seem strange. But that wasn't what I wanted to say tickler to you."

She smoothed down her long white apron as she murmured to herself: "'Phelia, whar is you?" She was evidently embarrassed. After thinking a moment she continued:

"Now, 'bout this house. What are you goin' to do with it?"

"We haven't concluded yet what we will do with it. I'm going South with Dora until Will finishes at Heidelberg; then, after he has settled upon his future field of work, I am to live with him."

"Exactly so. Then I s'pose you'll be willin' to rent the house ef you git a good tenant?"

"Yes; I suppose so."

"Now, Sis' Smith, I want to ask you ef you've eny ejections to my takin' it?"

"Certainly no objections; but isn't it a great responsibility for a woman alone in the world?" asked Mrs. Smith, greatly surprised.

Mrs. Davis smoothed the folds of her ample white apron nervously — coughed — stammered — blushed.

"Well, truth is, Sis' Smith, you know people make changes in this life; fac' truth, indeed, ma'm, we's always changin', an' I'm thinkin' o' changin' to double harness fer a while."

"I want to know!" exclaimed Ma Smith, now properly astonished and interested. "And who is the happy man?"

Mrs. Davis wiped the perspiration from her face with the back of her hand as she replied with a nervous laugh:

"Oh, you know him well! It's Mr. Jeemes."

"What! Mr. James! why, he's nothing but a boy!" exclaimed Ma Smith.

"Course I know he's young, but I'm not so old myself."

"Why, how old are you, Sister Davis?"

"I don't know that I mind tellin' you, 'cause you're safe. I'm all of thirty-five. Ginerally speakin', I never tell nobody my exac' age, 'cause it's none o' thar bisiness."

"*Thirty-five years!* Impossible! Why, it's thirty-five years *since* the war. You were a widow at that time, weren't you?"

"That's my age, anyhow," was the sullen answer.

"But, Sister Davis, you must be fifty years old at the very least," said Ma Smith, persisting that she was right in her calculations.

"Fifty nuthin'!" replied Mrs. Davis, somewhat offended at Mrs. Smith's pertinacity. "I'm thirty-five years old, an' I reckon thet I'm the one what knows best when I was borned."

"I'm sure I hope you will be happy with Mr. James," Ma Smith hastened to reply, seeing that Mrs. Davis was really offended.

"Is he going to leave college?" she continued, retiring with graceful discretion from the contest.

"No; he's goin' to graduate. The society he's been preaching fer Sundays is goin' to give him their church, and I'll keep the laundry a-goin' an' rent rooms."

"I'm sure I'll be very glad to let you have the house. I don't know anyone I'd rather let it to."

"Then that's settled," said Mrs. Davis, with a sigh of relief. "I thought you'd say that. Now, you see, all yer ol' lodgers can keep their rooms, an' it will seem jes' like home to them. Mr. Jeemes is that fond o' me tell Sarah Ann calls me an ol' fool, an' says all he wants is my money, and a right smert 'ooman to work fer him. I telled Sarah Ann, 'go git a man fer yourself an' quit bein' jealous.' She says to me, 'I will, an' it won't be a boy jes' turned twenty-one.' Sarah Ann an' me'll have to part after I'm married, she's that jealous." Mrs. Davis had regained all her good humor, and was very complacent over Ma Smith's evident interest in her story.

"Now that would be a pity, after you've been together so long," remarked the latter.

"She's got to drop sayin' ticklish things to me. A 'ooman's got a right to git merried, ain't she?" Mrs. Davis was now fairly started on a congenial subject, and her words flowed in a torrent.

"Mr. Jeemes says he knows the Lord sent me fer to be a helpmeet to him, an' I dassay he's right. Sarah Ann says my money's the 'helpmeet' he's after, an' somebody to cook good vittals to suit his pellet. But I know better; he's a godly man ef he ain't much to look at."

"How did you happen to take a fancy to each other?"

"Lord, he's sech a good critter! The first I noticed was the night you had that swaree here last winter. Some o' the men got to talkin' 'bout 'ooman bein' the weaker vessel, an' subjugatin' theirself to be led by men an' not go prespirin' after work an' sech likes which belongs to men. Mr. Jeemes he held to it thet 'ooman's all right to ejecate herself even to be a minister, fer no man could be suferior to 'ooman, 'cause she was his *rib*. An' ever sence that I kin' o' thought what a shame it was fer a man to be minus one o' his ribs all along o' 'ooman, untell I made up my mind thet ef Jeemes wanted me he *could have back his lost rib*. All this spring he's been a-ridin' me on his bike down in the kitchen every day after we got through washin' an' had cleaned up, so I could go ridin' with him in the Fens an' all

"EVERYBODY WAS A-LOOKIN' AN' A-GAPPIN' AT US."

out o' town this summer. After I'd learnt, one day he came in with a beautiful bike an' saddle. The nex' day we was ter ride ter the Park. I hed on my new pale blue bicycle suit with a pink shirtwaist an' a white sailer hat an' tan-colored shoes an' gloves. I tell you I looked some! Mr. Jeemes had on a black suit with a gray linen duster, an' he did look extinguished in his beaver hat an' that white choker an' tie o' hisn which I must say I do admire. We got along purty well. Everybody was a-lookin' an' a-gappin' at us. Sarah Ann says it was 'cause we looked like a couple o' jay birds stuffed.

"We got along all right untell we was a-comin' down a hill. Mr. Jeemes was a-coastin', an' the tail o' that linen duster o' hisn was a-sailin' out behin' like a flag floppin' in an east wind. The fust thing I knowed he was a-stickin' fast head fust into a pile o' sand where they was makin' mortar to build a cellar, an' me on top o' him! Wasn't it a mercy thet we wasn't stuck in the mortar? Jeemes is purty black, but he was a white man when he got out o' thet san' heap. As fer me, I tore my gloves, los' my hat, an' busted a new pair o' corsets right off me. Besides thet, I nearly swallered my upper teeth, an' I lost my bangs. They picked me up an' carried me into a house they was a-buildin', an' give me a chance to fix myself up a bit.

But I 'clar to you them corsets was no good never after thet; an' it cost me ten dollars to fix thet upper set o' teeth so I could wear 'em agin; I never have seen them bangs sence.

"We was thet done up that Jeemes sent fer a kerridge to bring us home; an' fifty dollars won't excuse the damages to them bikes. Comin' home an' settin' so close together, beside the trouble we'd had makin' us feel kin' o' tender o' each other, Jeemes put his arm 'roun' me — an' I don' see how ever in time he did it, bein' the corsets warn't no good, an' me 'bout as small as a bag o' taters — he put his arm 'roun' me, he did, an' he says, says he: 'Le's git married, 'Phelia!' I was thet stonished an' set back you could heve knocked me down with a feather, an' was thet weak from bein' overcamed by my feelin' thet all I remember was thet I fell on his neck like the patrihawks did in the Bible where they tell 'bout Abraham, Isaac an' Jacob, Shem, Ham, Meshack an' 'Bednego — you 'member how the minister tol' us all 'bout that in the Skripter lesson las' Sunday night, don't you? I ain't got no 'bility fer readin', but I's got a mem'ry, thank Gawd. As I was a-sayin', I jes' fell onto his neck, an' I says to him: 'Mr. Jeemes, *ef you want yer rib, I'm her.*' Thet's the way it camed 'bout, an' we's goin' ter be married purty soon, 'though Sarah

Ann says I'm a mortalized ol' ijit, an' a insane mannyack, an' Jeemes knows what he's a-fishin' fer. She's insultin', mos' insultin'."

Mrs. Smith sympathized with her, and after more talk about the rent of the building and other matters dear to the heart of the house-wife, they separated.

For a long time Ma Smith sat there in the quiet, shaded room, buried in deep thought. She made a charming picture. White was her favorite color for summer wear, with a tiny crimson cashmere shawl thrown about her shoulders, to keep off the chill which comes so naturally to old age. She had been a handsome woman, and still retained traces of former beauty. Thick bands of snowy hair, falling in natural waves, were coiled closely at the back of a well-shaped head. Her clear olive com-plexion contrasted pleasantly with eyes large, soft, and black, heavy black eyebrows and long curling lashes. An aquiline nose, thin lips and delicately shaped ears gave her a very pleasing countenance.

As she sat there her whole life passed in review. She thought of her children, and how much she had to be thankful for in them. But more than all, the story told her so often by her father of his early life and that of his father and mother, was fresh within her mind as she

sat there dreaming.   Months afterward she
looked back upon that day, and remembered
with wonder her own tranquility.

> " The supreme hours unnoted come.''

She heard the door-bell ring, but it did not
disturb her reverie.   There was a knock at the
door of the room where she was sitting.   Then
the door opened, and Mrs. Davis ushered in
a tall, elegant white man of distinguished address, and about her own age.   Mrs. Davis
closed the door behind him and vanished.

"Mrs. Smith, I presume?" he said in a pleasant voice as he advanced toward her.   It was
a voice of rare carrying power — deep, rich,
musical, and had moved the House of Commons to enthusiasm on more than one memorable occasion in the politics of Great Britain.

" Yes," she replied, rising from her seat.

" I called to see Mr. William Smith, and I
dislike to be disappointed.   Will he be at home
soon?"   He handed her his card as he finished
speaking, and she read the inscription:

CHARLES MONTFORT–WITHINGTON,

BLANKSHIRE,

ENGLAND.

" Pray be seated, Mr. Withington," she said,
as she placed a chair for her visitor.   " I am
William's mother; he will be in very soon."

Mr. Withington thanked her, and having seated himself, glided easily into conversation; at the same time his keen eye noted his surroundings. Nothing in the quiet, unpretentious, shaded room escaped him. The large glass bowl of flowers — sweet peas and nasturtiums predominating — filled the room with fragrance; there were three or four water-color paintings set in simple frames — pictures of rural scenes. The few choice pieces of china and bric-a-brac which adorned the mantel, the open piano, the general good taste, even elegance of the apartment, appealed strongly to the artistic sense of the cultured gentleman who had been reared in the luxury of ample wealth. Mrs. Smith herself was a revelation to him. By what art of necromancy had such a distinguished woman been evolved from among the brutalized aftermath of slavery?

"I had the pleasure of meeting your son and conversing with him at the annual dinner of the Canterbury Club in February last. I was much impressed with his views on the condition of the Negroes in this country. Being interested in every phase of racial development which bears upon the science of political economy, I felt that after my Canadian business was settled I would try and meet him again. I intended to write and ask him to meet me at the Vendome, but on second thoughts I concluded to try and see him in his own home."

"He will feel greatly flattered at your kind remembrance," Mrs. Smith replied.

"Are you aware, madam, that your son possesses rare intellectual gifts?" he continued, after a slight pause. "I must confess to a feeling of curiosity to learn how such characters are nourished among a people like yours."

Mrs. Smith looked at him thoughtfully a moment, and then said:

"Sir, it would afford me great pleasure to give you a sketch of his life so far, if you would care to listen."

"It is what I desire most to hear."

The great man listened to her humble story with marked attention, as she related the history of early struggles which her husband and she had braved for the maintenance and education of their children. It was a story common enough among Negroes ambitious to avail themselves of the privileges which were now open to them — a story of faithful fathers bearing insult and injury to keep the meanly paid employment; of mothers "spending weary days and nights over the washtub and ironing-board in order to get money to educate their children." It seemed marvelous to the listener. As she closed, he said impressively:

"Your story is a revelation to me, madam. Are there many histories like yours among your people? In what a different light you would appear as a race, if the statements made by your detractors could be stripped of calumny and deception. Believe me, you have my heart-felt sympathy, and I shall do all that I can to promote kindly feelings in England for our unfortunate black brother in America. And it is against such spirits of nobility and self-sacrifice that many would close the entrance door to the higher education of the century! Blind and foolish prejudice! Monstrous injustice!" He paused a moment to collect himself and overcome his indignation.

"Madam, how is it that you maintain so excellent an address and manner? and from whom, may I ask, without being considered impertinent, did you inherit your superior intelligence?"

"Ah, sir; that is a sad story connected with the lives of those long since passed away."

"But you seem perfectly happy."

"Yes; but it is the happiness chastened by wrongs endured and grief subdued." She paused as though forgetful of her visitor, and then resumed in a low tone:

"Yes; there are strangely tangled threads in the lives of many colored families — I use the word 'colored' because these stories occur mostly among those of mixed blood. But few have a stranger or more romantic history than my father's,— Will's grandfather; I never speak of it for fear of ridicule. I was attracted by the name of Montfort on your card. It is uncommon; I was a Montfort before marriage."

Mr. Withington uttered an exclamation which was unheeded by the woman before him, who was lost in the clouds of the past. His face wore an expression of intense interest. Presently she continued:

"It is a homely subject to introduce to one familiar with the sorrows of the wealthy and prosperous alone; but it teaches that misfortune is the common lot of all mankind."

"I await your story with anxiety." And truly it seemed so, for Mr. Withington had left his seat and was pacing slowly up and down the room. Mrs. Smith began her tale like one who describes a vision passing before her eyes. She told it in almost the exact words of the story which we have given as the first part of this narrative. In the midst of the recital Will entered the room from another door, and paused in astonishment at the scene before him. Mr. Withington shook hands with him noiselessly, and signed him to keep silence and not disturb the speaker. His own emotion was intense;

tears trembled in his eyes; his bosom heaved; his countenance was pale and distressed. When she had finished he said:

"And have you no proofs of this story — no letters?"

"Alas, nothing! Poor father destroyed all in a fit of despondency when his brother's letters ceased to come. Then he lost his little property, and after that he removed to Boston. I believe my father died of a broken heart. God did not intend that his wrongs should be righted." As she finished, the tears were streaming from her eyes.

Mr. Withington ceased his nervous promenade, and taking both her hands in his, replied solemnly:

"Not so, dear cousin, for such I believe you to be; never doubt God's goodness or justice. I believe that I hold the key to solve this riddle! I believe that I am your relative, descended directly from your father's brother; your grandfather's brother," he said, turning to Will, who stood an amazed spectator of this extraordinary scene.

"Impossible!" exclaimed mother and son with one breath.

"Nothing is impossible with God. How often have I heard *my* father tell very much the same tale I have just listened to. *Let me assure you that the letters of Jesse Montfort to his brother Charles are still in existence !* They are preserved as a sacred legacy, together with a sworn statement of the main facts as we know them, in this remarkable case. Your uncle Charles married his rescuer's daughter, and as is the custom among old English families where the name would become extinct upon the marriage of the only child — a daughter — he assumed the name of Withington in conjunction with his own. The United States Government was sued by Withington, Sr., and he recovered one hundred thousand dollars damages for Charles, but no trace of Jesse could be found. The money is held for him or his heirs by the Government. I can furnish you the necessary proof upon my return to England. Tell me not that the time of miracles has departed! Is not this a direct intervention of the hand of Providence that we, so widely separated, should at last become known to each other?"

He paused, overcome by emotion. Mrs. Smith wept quietly. Broken words of praise to God — of joy — of sorrow for the dead — of hope for the future — passed her lips from time to time. Ah! who can paint such a scene? Finally Mr. Withington embraced them both — his kinswoman and Will, his kinsman.

"Be assured that I shall bend every effort to

prove this story, and spare no money to establish you in your rights."

Then, unable longer to control his feelings,
telling Will to join him in an hour at his hotel,
he hastily left them.

Alone together the mother and son fell upon
their knees to give thanks to God for his unspeakable goodness.

.   .   .   .

When Mr. Withington had thought over the
story which had come to him so strangely, he
was profoundly impressed with the inscrutable
ways of God.   How wonderful was the knowledge that he had been led by devious paths to
find these humble relatives.   By accident alone
had it been accomplished.   " No, not by accident," he told himself, " but by the direct intervention of All-wise Justice."   So noble was the
nature of this man that he never once thought
of the possible ridicule that might come to him
through his new kinspeople.   He thought only
of the tie of blood.   When it was placed before
him in this light by Will, his reply was characteristic of the man:

" At home it will not be noticed ; the opinion
of narrow-minded, prejudiced people *here* does
not matter."

Mr. Withington now spent long days with
the Smiths.   There was much to learn of the

past history of each family. These were days
of happiness to the newly found relatives —
days fraught with wise lessons to himself. He
was the best of friends with Dora; indeed, he
was a man who inspired confidence and love.
Very soon he was the recipient of the story of
all her recent trials with John, and poor Will's
unhappy love episode. He approved Dora's
choice in Doctor Lewis, and had the latter's
promise to take her across to Europe at the
earliest opportunity. For Will he had a strong
man's sympathy, and encouraged him to hope
that all might yet be well. So potent was his
hopefulness that Will brightened perceptibly
and became more like his old ambitious self, to
the great delight of his mother and sister.

He in his turn told them the story of Charles
Montfort: How his benefactor had returned to
America in the hope of finding and rescuing
Jesse, after establishing the boys' claim to the
estate of their murdered father. He found that
the child had disappeared, leaving no trace behind him. How Charles had rejoiced over the
later discovery of his brother, and how he had
grieved over the final estrangement. Then on
the eve of his departure for America to personally search Jesse out, he was stricken with
paralysis, and remained a helpless invalid until
his death. Meantime the business of establish-

ing the identity of the Smiths was going forward as swiftly as possible.

Mr. Withington communicated with his family lawyer, who came from England, bringing with him certain valuable papers bearing upon the case, engaged a leading firm of American lawyers to act in conjunction with the English lawyer, interviewed the authorities at Washington, and secured the services of one of the best detectives in the country to ferret out evidence to prove Jesse's identity. Money flowed from his lavish hand, and all the legal machinery that was essential to prompt action was soon set in motion. One day Mr. Withington received a letter from the detective asking him to go to Bermuda and see an important witness. He started immediately upon receiving it, accompanied by Will Smith and his lawyer. A letter from Will to his mother after they had reached the island was filled with fresh surprises. What follows is an extract:

We have come across a wonderful coincidence. In hunting for evidence in Bermuda, the detective heard of an old woman — a centenarian — who was formerly a slave in North Carolina. We found her living with her daughter and granddaughter (both old women ; the granddaughter is sixty); all of them were once slaves. The old woman's mind is clouded on all subjects but one — the Montfort murder ! She was an eye-witness of the

atrocious crime. She lived for years as the mistress of
Anson Pollock, and knew that he tracked Jesse to Boston,
where he lost all trace of him. The day we visited her
it was pathetic to hear her grieve over the children; one
would have thought them still helpless little ones. My
dear mother, this woman is but another evidence of the
all-powerful hand of the Almighty — this poor, decrepit,
half-blind centenarian is *Lucy, Grace Montfort's foster-
sister and maid!*

The granddaughter is married, and her husband and
children are here. When the Civil War ended they determined to settle in Bermuda, and here they have lived ever
since in a cottage which is almost a hut, supporting themselves by selling sugar-cane in small sticks — the same as
our candy-shops sell sticks of candy to the children —
and other products of their garden, in the market-place.
Prepare yourself for another surprise.

The youngest woman had a child while in slavery, by
Anson Pollock, Jr., a grandnephew of old Anson Pollock,
whom we all have so much reason to remember. The
poor woman seems much distressed over this boy, who, it
appears, was taken from her when he was but six months
old, and sold with many others to a man who farmed
Negro babies for the market. She asked me if I had
ever in my distant home met a young man called John
Pollock Langley. *He is her son!* I gave her an evasive
answer, and told her I would inquire about such a person,
and let her know the result. I shall write John these
facts. He can use his own pleasure then about claiming
his relatives. How fortunate the estrangement which
resulted in breaking the engagement between John and

Dora. I never could have tolerated the idea of a descendant of the Montforts being united in the close relation of marriage with one of the villainous and unscrupulous Pollocks. Let us thank God for another mercy. Mr. Withington feels as I do. He has invested some money in a small annuity for our humble friends, — enough to keep them from want. The nobility of this man is something remarkable. We sail from here for home by the next steamer, so we shall be in time for the wedding.   Your loving son,

WILL.

P. S. — I reopen this letter to tell you of the death of Lucy ; old age the cause. After she learned that I was Jesse's grandson, and heard the story of his life, with the renewed intelligence often vouchsafed to those just upon the border of the happy land, her prayer was : " Now let Thy servant depart in peace." How soon her prayer was answered.   WILL.

.   .   .   .

In the last beautiful days of October Dora became the wife of Doctor Lewis, and went with him to his far-off Southern home to assist him in the upbuilding of their race.

And what a wedding it was ! The skies were fair and bright. The romantic story of the Smith family had become noised about, and as it was a church wedding the sacred edifice was crowded to suffocation. Doctor Lewis was well and favorably known, and that was of additional interest to the spectators. The small girls who formed Dora's class in Sunday-school, dressed in white, preceded the pretty bride, strewing flowers in her path. Then the bride followed on the arm of her brother, Doctor Lewis meeting them at the altar, where he had been accompanied by the ushers. Dora would have no bridesmaids. Gowned in the simplest white muslin frock she stood and solemnly plighted her vows to the man of her choice.

They were a striking couple: she serious, he so grave and steadfast. So it should be, taking up a new life, with its endless need of forbearance, trust, and mutual affection. Each knew that with one all was not yet given with the abandonment of perfect love. Each felt, too, the deep waters that surrounded Will — the shadow of a tragedy that lay about his life. What wonder that an unusual solemnity enfolded this couple as they took their vows upon them. But it was a solemnity that quiets, soothes and strengthens.

As the bride came down the aisle on her husband's arm at the conclusion of the ceremony, she caught for one instant the full gaze of John Langley. She never forgot that look; so full of despair and unhappiness. She said nothing about it to husband or brother, but it haunted her for many an hour.

Well, well, it was over, and they passed out to the carriage, and thence to the house.

There was a great reception after the ceremony; but just before Dora left her room to take her place with the receiving party, a package was placed in her hand. She opened it, and found it a jewel-box containing a heavy gold bracelet set with pearls, which outlined a delicate vine of pansies traced about the golden band. No note or card was attached — nothing but her name and the date of the marriage. Dora locked it away with her many gifts, amid painful thoughts; she knew instinctively that John was the giver. A week later the happy couple left Boston, accompanied by Mrs. Smith, followed by the heartfelt good wishes of all who knew them, for their future prosperity. So with fair skies and favorable winds they entered upon the untried sea of matrimony.

. . . .

The case of Smith *vs.* the United States did not come to a public trial; it was heard privately before a court composed of the judges of the Supreme Court of the United States. The English heirs had received their portion years before; the Government only awaited the production of the necessary proofs to establish the identity of Mrs. Smith beyond a peradventure. Detectives went over the ground carefully. The records of real estate transfers, chattels, etc., were all found intact among the files of the courthouse at Newberne, North Carolina. Jesse was traced from the time he fled from Anson Pollock until he settled in Exeter, New Hampshire, and married Elizabeth Whitfield.

By this woman he raised a family of twelve children, five of whom, including Mrs. Smith, were born in Exeter. Up to the time of her birth he had prospered, and had accumulated a good property, but in an evil hour he went upon the bond of his employer, who, failing to meet his liabilities, involved Montfort in his ruin. Unmanned by recurring misfortunes, Jesse Montfort removed to Boston, and never again seemed to have the ambition to try to retrieve his losses. Born in an evil hour, under an unlucky planet, this man's life was but a path of sorrow to the grave, which he welcomed as a refuge from all vicissitudes.

As Mr. Withington had said, the letters in his possession from Jesse to Charles Montfort, yellow and time-stained, completed a perfect chain of evidence. The sum of one hundred and fifty thousand dollars was awarded to Mrs. Smith as the last representative of the heirs of Jesse Montfort. Justice was appeased.

The case was a nine-days' wonder; startled society and all the world — a life drama whose power touched the deep wells of human feeling.

CHAPTER XXII.

"SO HE BRINGETH THEM INTO THEIR DESIRED HAVEN."

ALL is ended now, the hope and the fear and the sorrow;
All the aching of heart, the restless, unsatisfied longing,
All the dull, deep pain, and constant anguish of patience !

Even as rivulets twain, from distant and separate sources,
Seeing each other afar, as they leap from the rocks, and pursuing
Each one its devious path, but drawing nearer and nearer,
Rush together at last, at their trysting-place in the forest;
So these lives
Rushed together at last, and one was lost in the other.

— LONGFELLOW.

THREE years rolled slowly away and were numbered with the past. Will Smith had finished his course at Heidelberg, and for nine months had traveled in foreign capitals. He was much changed. Honors were thick upon him ; *honores mutant mores*. His bearing was that of a man accustomed to the respectful attention of his equals, sure of himself, his position, his attainments — a wealthy cosmopolitan. He had been a handsome young fellow ; he added now to mere good looks, grace, ease, elegance, and an imposing, well-developed intellectuality which marked him as a thinker and an originator. His eyes alone were unchanged, and had the same kindly expression, although there lurked within their hazel depths a sadness which in repose became absolute mournfulness.

The ambition of his life was the establishment of a school which should embrace every known department of science, where the Negro youth of ability and genius could enter without money and without price. This was his pet scheme for the future. No wife or child would ever be his, he told himself; but he would be a father to the youth of his race. Thus he mused and planned until one day there came a letter from his sister saying that his mother's health was very much broken, and that she longed for the presence of her boy. Will packed up, and April found him in the United States once more, at the home of his sister in New Orleans.

Thoughts of Sappho were seldom far from him; he thought of her as one gone to the land of delight — purified by her sufferings here. The first night that he passed on board ship he had dreamed of her. He dreamed that he stood in a grand cathedral, and listened to strains of delicious melody chanted by an invisible choir. *Christe eleison, Kyrie eleison*, floated to his ears, and the glad strains of the *Gloria*. Presently upon the altar before him appeared a vision of the Virgin and Child, but the face of the mother was Sappho's, the child by her side was the little Alphonse. He tried to reach her in vain. She smiled and beckoned him on as she receded at his approach; then he awoke. His dream haunted him. He interpreted it as a promise that they should be united in heaven. The meeting with his mother and sister and the renewal of old ties somewhat deadened painful memories, until reawakened when he heard them call his sister's beautiful child "Sappho."

The home to which Doctor Lewis had taken his bride was very beautiful. One passed from the highway down a long avenue framed by majestic palms, and so upon the college campus which was surrounded by dormitories built of substantial brick. Doctor Lewis's house was a fine brick cottage, plentifully supplied with porches and piazzas. Its framework was a succession of terraces planted with gorgeous beds of flowers indigenous to the Southern clime. The long French windows stood open to catch the soft breezes of April. This house and the numerous dormitories, museums, the chapel, and buildings which held lecture-rooms and class-rooms, were all built by the pupils of the school. The students made the brick which entered into the composition of the various buildings; the carpenter shop, carriage and blacksmith shops afforded fine facilities for imparting practical knowledge of these useful industries.

Beyond the college grounds — to the right — extended the market gardens, which not only supplied the school with vegetables, but also added a goodly sum to the college fund. There, too, were the grazing pastures for horses and cows. The dairy was a long, low, shedlike brick building, beautifully clean and sweet; its brick floors were spotless, the walls adorned with shining utensils for setting milk for cream, and for churning this same cream into butter. Hundreds of hens and chickens roved in small family bands about the immense poultry yards; from all of which came some revenue to help defray the expenses of this human hive of industry. "Many institutions do not spend one cent for domestic labor during the whole school term. The time usually given to football and other games in white colleges is utilized by the colored student in useful toil." Doctor Lewis's school was of this class. The tuition, board, lodging, laundry work and incidentals were not over twelve dollars per month. "People with such a love for knowledge that they are willing to toil for it, may be relied on to use that knowledge properly."

Will threw himself into the work of visiting

Doctor Lewis's pupils and the neighboring schools with eagerness. He acquainted himself thoroughly for future reference, with the curriculum of academical life as conducted along the lines pertaining to Negro education. After gaining a clear insight into it all, he said to Doctor Lewis:

"I hold that a man to gain true self-respect and independence must not be hampered in any way by prejudice. I would remove my school far from such influences."

"Where would your choice fall for the establishment of such a paradise?" asked Doctor Lewis with a smile.

"There are places enough in the world. One could easily find such an environment abroad. There across the water, associated on equal terms with men of the highest culture, the Negro shall give physical utterance to the splendid possibilities which are within him."

"Chimerical and quixotic," returned Doctor Lewis with a shake of the head. "It can't be done."

"I shall try it, nevertheless, and leave the results I hope for to the leveling hand of Time."

.   .   .   .

If ever a doubt of Dora's happiness had troubled Will's thoughts, it was dispelled now that he saw her a contented young matron, her own individuality swallowed up in love for her husband and child. She had apparently forgotten that any other love had ever disturbed the peaceful current of her life. She was pained, however, to find, in their first private interview, that Will still clung to a hopeless memory, as it seemed to her.

"You say that you never expect to see her again, that you think her dead. Why not, then, seek to solace yourself for her loss by marrying some good girl who will make you happy?"

"Sappho is the kind of woman to occupy a man's thoughts. Beside her all others are uninteresting and tame."

"I know it, Will; but it would please me, and mother would die happy if she knew that you were at peace in your mind."

"Do not talk of it!" he cried impatiently; "I cannot please you in that way. I shall never marry."

After that Dora said no more, but tried to make his visit pleasant in every possible way. Will wished to establish a home with his mother in the North, but she was feeble, and he did not care to separate her from Dora. So he drifted with the tide, waiting for circumstances to direct his wandering feet.

"Have you visited the Sisters of the Holy Family yet?" asked Dora on Good Friday morning as they sat at breakfast.

"No," replied Will. "Arthur has promised to accompany me there, but something always intervenes."

"Don't miss it on Sunday morning. The Easter service is divine."

. . . .

The convent of the Holy Family was founded in 1842 by three good women, in the very heart of the stronghold of slavery, and under the most depressing influences. There is but one other mother-house and novitiate for colored women in the United States, and that is in the city of Baltimore. The service held in the chapel by the Sisterhood of the Holy Family on Easter morning is famous throughout the South. Easter is Easter the world over, and the earth seems to take on an added beauty in honor of the day. But Easter in New Orleans is something to dream of, and defies description.

Will's thoughts were solemn ones, and mingled with pain, for was not this the anniversary of his greatest joy and his most bitter sorrow. He walked toward the chapel through silent streets filled with earnest worshippers on the way to early Mass. It was a familiar sight to Will, who had passed so many months in Catholic countries. Morn was breaking in the east; the air was filled with the faint sounds

of returning life; the sweet odor of the mag-
nolia, mingled with a thousand other subtle
perfumes, intoxicated the senses. The sun had
not yet risen as he glided quietly into the
church and took a seat in a secluded corner, to
watch the entry of the congregation.

Until Easter morning the pictures of Christ,
Mary and Joseph were veiled, but now the
statues had emerged from their concealment
in indication of the spiritual change in us which
was wrought by the coming forth of Christ from
the tomb. Tapers glowed and flowers bloomed
everywhere. The Sisters stood with their dark
faces uplifted in the full light which fell from
the stained glass windows, making a picture
long to be remembered. The stillness, the
coolness, the swiftly moving, silent figures, the
slanting rays of sunlight growing higher and
higher, seemed to calm the troubled spirit of
the man, and to impress his very soul with
the greatness and glory of pure religious devotion. Involuntarily his thoughts were wafted
upward in solemn supplication to the Father
of all good.

He saw the entrance of the convent boarders,
the orphan girls, the orphan boys and the nov-
ices, still in an exalted state of religious enthusiasm. All in the crowded edifice were on
their knees now, listening to the intonations

of the gold-robed priest.   The sun burst forth
in full glory and poured its rays in dazzling
hues through the rose-stained windows.   Simultaneously, the choir of female voices filled the
air with the heavenly strains of the *Kyrie
eleison*, gliding swiftly into the grandeur of the
Gloria in Excelsis.   It filled every corner of
the building, stole into the heart and overflowed into space.   Then the whole congregation, led by the Sisters, moved toward the Holy
Communion — backward and then toward the
right.   As the children passed him Will started
to his feet and almost cried out, for there before his eyes was the figure of little Alphonse,
clad in the regulation garb of the Orphanage !
He restrained himself by a mighty effort, and
fell back in his seat overcome.   Tumultuous
thoughts overwhelmed him.   The mother must
be near !   Could it be possible that she lived ?
and if she lived, was she indeed dead to him in
her refuge behind convent walls ?   He heard no
more of the service, but waited impatiently for
the end.   It came at last.

It was some time before he could reach the
street on account of the dense crowd, but finally
he found himself upon the sidewalk, and asked
a passer-by to direct him to the Orphanage.
The stranger politely piloted him to the door
of the house on St. Peter Street.   He rang the

bell, and sent his card to the Mother Superior by a novice in the regulation black dress and white bonnet. She bade him enter, and left him in a bare room overlooking a paved court, where groups of children could be seen at play. He stood there with his back to the door, buried in deep thought and filled with misgivings. Suddenly a door opened behind him and a voice said: "I will bring him back tomorrow, Sister."

Surely he knew that voice! He turned, and there before his blinded vision stood the realization of his dream, holding the boy by the hand! One swift glance showed him that she was in street attire; that she was not a member of the Order. She saw and recognized him at the same instant. With a mighty cry of joy and thanksgiving he clasped her in his arms.

> " O, that 'twere possible,
> After long grief and pain,
> To find the arms of my true love
> Round me once again ! "

. . . .

Sappho was welcomed right royally by Doctor Lewis, Dora and her mother, as one risen from the dead; tears, smiles, kisses greeted her. It seemed that they would never be able to control their emotion. Then she told them

THERE BEFORE HIS BLINDED VISION STOOD THE REALIZATION
OF HIS DREAMS.

of her flight to New Orleans with the child, of the death of the old fortune-teller, and her own employment as a governess in the family of the wealthy colored planter in Opelausus, and the placing of the boy with the Sisters. She in her turn listened with wonder to the fairylike tale of the wealth that had come to her lover's family.

Late that afternoon she sat once again in close heart communion with her lover. Each had much to tell.

Seated beside her on the sofa, Will folded her closely to his heart again with one deep, heavy sob which attested the man's suppressed anguish.

"Oh," he said, at last, "it has been like a hideous nightmare since I read that letter which you sent me. I can scarcely believe in the blessed reality that I hold you safe in my arms once more."

She put back the clustering curls from his brow, noting with pain the many white hairs which threaded those raven locks. She laid her cheek against his as she said:

"I know only too well all you have gone through."

"Why did you leave me, Sappho? Had you no confidence in my love for you? How meanly you must have judged me if you thought me capable of holding you responsible for the monstrous wrong committed against you."

"Ah, Will; I had suffered so much at the hands of selfish men! Can you wonder that I mistrusted you, and felt that you would only despise me when you knew all?"

Then he told her of his interview with John Langley, holding back nothing but the insulting insinuations.

"But, dearest, the detectives were at the convent; they even interviewed Luke Sawyer. Poor fellow, he was completely overcome when he found that you were alive, and he dropped his work and devoted months to tracing your whereabouts in this very city. How you have managed to hide yourself, and Dora living right here in New Orleans with you, is the mystery."

"Yes; but it is an easy matter to become lost in a great city like this. You must remember that I kept away from every familiar spot; even the Sisters in the convent had been changed, so that there was no one to remember me, the former Mother Superior having died. When I was strong enough to go about, you had ceased searching for me."

"And all this secrecy was for what?" asked Will reproachfully

"I thought it was for the best."

"I loved you, Sappho; could you not trust that love?"

"Ah, Will, forgive me for all the suffering I have caused you."

Will laid his cheek to hers. "What is there I would not forgive, if anything there were to forgive, for the sweet comfort of holding you once again to my desolate heart."

Then she wept a few delicious tears within the shelter of his arms, and he told her of his plans for her and the boy. They would go abroad; but first they would seek out Luke Sawyer and reward him for his faithfulness; every one who had ever been kind to her or the boy should be rewarded.

That evening Will accompanied Sappho home. Alphonse was left with Dora. Monsieur Louis was astonished to see a handsome stranger assisting Sappho from the carriage. Her joyous face told its own story, and the kind old man knew instinctively that she had found her lover and he had lost the joy of his old age. Will was delighted with all he saw and heard in the peaceful, happy home, the refuge of his love. In the soft twilight of the fragrant terrace Sappho told Monsieur Louis her story, her hand tightly clasped in Will's. "Ah!" cried Monsieur Louis, "I thought it; I

thought it!" Then Will supplemented it with
the romantic history of his family, and his life
since Sappho's flight. The old gentleman listened entranced. "It is indeed a fairy tale of
love and chivalry such as we read of only in
books," he said at last with a long-drawn breath.
Then he told them many interesting tales of
slave life and its complications as he had known
them. It was nearly midnight when Will left,
promising to return the next day and complete
arrangements for a wedding which was to take
place immediately. Monsieur Louis insisted
that he should furnish the wedding dress and
breakfast, and be allowed to give the bride
away. So a second Easter Day closed on happy
love — a love sanctified and purified by suffering.

.   .   .   .

John Langley, soon after Dora's marriage
and the acquisition of fortune to the Smith
family, suddenly gave up his business, and
started off with the first daring adventurers
who were allured from home by the dazzling
promise of immense fortunes to be dug out of
the earth in the new Eldorado — the Klondike
gold-fields.

John was unhappy. He was willing to admit
that he had viewed things in a false light, and
consequently had made a mess of his own

happiness. He still retained an ardent enthusiasm for his profession, but he needed a change. He would divert his mind from his recent disappointments by travel in strange lands, and after he had acquired a large fortune he would settle down to the practice of law and do good among his fellows as a sort of atonement for his early mistakes. He placed his business in the hands of his partner, first making a will, in which he bequeathed to his mother's family in Bermuda the savings he would leave in the bank, in case he did not return.

"I only make this will for form's sake," said he to his partner, as he gave it into the latter's keeping. "I'll be back here inside of two years and dazzle you with my wealth."

He joined a party made up of hardy Eastern men, and they started on their journey with bright anticipations of a golden future. After many adventures and much suffering they reached the goal, only to find gaunt famine awaiting them with gruesome countenance. Day by day the cold increased; day by day the stock of provisions dwindled. Each morning they counted up the dead. One morning it was five; the next, fifteen. Ten only remained alive out of a party of thirty, and these so weak as to be unable to remove the bodies from the common cabin. John learned to pray then: "May the Lord, in His infinite mercy, come to our rescue."

One morning seven more bodies lay close together in the bunks. It was plain then that a few hours would end the sufferings of the remainder. The last spark of fire had gone out. Two biscuits and a quart of water was all the sustenance left. Delirium seized upon all but John. He felt sick at heart. He prayed "God's will be done!" All that night a heavy gale blew, and before morning two more poor souls went out into space. John was then alone, the last survivor of thirty gallant men. He dragged his body outside the door and away from the charnel-house. "Let me die under the open sky, with the moon and stars for company." He told himself that the old fortune-teller had been right in her prediction: the field of ice and snow which had been shown to him stretched before him in dreary, unbroken silence. Overhead unknown constellations looked down upon his misery; the moon, cold, large, and spectral, poured an intense yet dreary light upon the scene.

He recalled the deep wisdom of lessons he had recently learned — the philosophy of life and death, assurance of the soul's individuality, and the worthlessness of this earthly clay tenement. He thought of his newly found mother, whom he had been ashamed to acknowledge. His sight failed, his limbs lost their feeling, his heart was nearly pulseless — it was death. " O God! receive my soul. Dear, dear mother " — The child of sunny climes folded himself more closely in his blankets for the last time, and slept to wake no more on earth. So the dawn of Easter Sunday found him. That undisciplined soul went forth to wander in celestial spheres, there to continue the salutary lessons begun on earth, under the guidance of God's angels, who minister to the needs of the immortal soul.

. . . .

Not many months after a merry party might have been seen upon the deck of a Cunarder bound for Europe. It consisted of Doctor Lewis, Dora, little Sappho, Ma Smith, Will, Sappho — now Will's wife — and little Alphonse. They were all going to make the long-promised visit to Mr. Withington.

Sappho was happy in contemplating the life of promise which was before her. Will was the noblest of men. Alphonse was to him as his own child. United by love, chastened by sorrow and self-sacrifice, he and she planned to work together to bring joy to hearts crushed by despair.

They stood upon the deck that night long

after the others had retired to their staterooms,
watching the receding shores with hearts filled
with emotion too deep for words.

> " My wife, my life.   O, we will walk this world
>   Yoked in all exercise of noble end,
>   And so through those dark gates across the wild
>   That no man knows.
>
>   .   .   .   .
>
>   Lay thy sweet hands in mine and trust to me."